Covenant in Blood

ARIEL TACHNA

Volume 2 of the
Partnership in Blood Series

Dreamspinner Press

Published by
Dreamspinner Press
4760 Preston Road
Suite 244-149
Frisco, TX 75034
http://www.dreamspinnerpress.com/

Covenant in Blood

Cover Art by Dan Skinner/Cerberus Inc.   cerberusinc@hotmail.com
Cover Design by Mara McKennen

ISBN: 978-1-935192-27-5

Printed in the United States of America
First Edition
October, 2008

eBook edition available
eBook ISBN: 978-1-935192-28-2

To my adopted sisters, Nancy, Holly, Connie, Cat, Carol, Madeleine, Gwen, and Julianne, who read and reread and edit and encourage. Without you, this dream would never have come to pass.

Chapter 1

THE sun would rise today on a new era, Marcel Chavinier, general of the Milice de Sorcellerie and commander-in-chief of the war effort against Pascal Serrier and his rebel wizards, thought with grim satisfaction as he surveyed the scene in the waiting room off the main tracks of the Gare de Lyon. He and his wizards no longer faced the two-year-old threat alone. Around the room, each of his twenty operatives still present was joined now by a vampire attuned to his or her magic, fruit of the alliance he had worked to forge with Jean Bellaiche, chef de la Cour of Parisian vampires, these past six days. They had just faced the first test of the new bonds, their maiden battle against Serrier's forces as a single force, vampires and wizards working side by side: twenty pairs of Milice operatives against twenty of Serrier's rebels. They had captured fifteen and killed the other five with no losses of their own. He counted that as quite a success, especially given how quickly they had defeated their foes.

The functional details of the alliance still had to be smoothed out, but as his eyes settled on Alain Magnier, one of his two top captains, and his partner, Orlando St. Clair, he knew that the partnerships could work. He had been a little stunned at how quickly and deeply the two men had bonded, Alain offering Orlando the deepest commitment a mortal could offer a vampire within days of their first meeting. Alain seemed happy, though, a fact that comforted the old patriarch still residing beneath the façade of military man Marcel was obliged to project. So many of those he was now ordering to fight, possibly to die, were the children he had never had. Marcel's pet project, Raymond Payet, a defector from Serrier's ranks, had formed his partnership at almost the same time, with the chef de la Cour himself, but Marcel had his doubts about how well that union would work. Raymond was distrustful in the best of circumstances, and being all but forced to share his blood with a vampire on a regular basis did not qualify as anywhere near the best circumstances. He had promised Raymond and the others that they only needed to give enough blood to protect their partners from sunlight while they were on patrol, a promise he would do his damnedest to fulfill. He could not help marveling at that twist in this saga. Who would have thought that the right wizard's blood could allow a vampire to feel the sun and survive? He certainly would not have believed it if anyone other than Alain and his other captain, Thierry Dumont, had told him.

He glanced to Thierry where he stood with his partner, Sebastien Noyer, the apparent black sheep of the Parisian Cour, if Bellaiche's shocked, almost angry reaction to his arrival was any indication. He thought that match rather fitting given Thierry's own habit of bending the rules when it suited him. He only hoped Bellaiche – Jean – would be able to set aside whatever animosity lay between the two vampires. For the sake of the alliance, if nothing else.

Seventeen other sets of newly-discovered partners stood scattered around the room, wizards and vampires flanking the dark wizards they had just defeated, one on each side, ensuring that they did not escape. Marcel surveyed the prisoners, noting the restless movement as the less experienced ones sought solace in the expressions of the older ones. He recognized some of them. Others he had never seen before. It worried him a little that Serrier was recruiting wizards from somewhere, but they could do nothing about that at the moment, certainly not without more information. He wondered if they would be able to learn anything pertinent from the prisoners.

A wave of his hand wrapped the fifteen prisoners in spells that left them blind and dumb to all around them. "Now we can talk without worrying about them overhearing," the general declared. "I don't know how long it will be before Serrier comes looking for them, but we certainly don't want to be here when he does. We need to get them back to base where we can interrogate them properly."

As he spoke, a distinct shudder ran through the room and the vampires began backing toward the far wall. "What...?" Thierry began, unsure why his partner and the others suddenly pulled away. Realization dawned. The sun was rising and none of the vampires, except perhaps Orlando, had fed deeply enough to survive the light of day. He looked around the waiting room. In its current state, there was no private place for the pairs to go to feed, and Thierry suspected, from Bellaiche's earlier comments, that none of the vampires would want to feed in the open room.

Orlando felt the unease that daylight always brought, but he rejected the impulse to cower against the far wall. The large windows faced north, so the sunlight would not come in for hours, if ever, but even if it did, Orlando knew he had nothing to fear from it. He could still feel Alain's magic singing through his body, surrounding and protecting him. He turned to the other vampires. "Watch," he said, starting for the door, his confidence in Alain's magic complete.

Alain fought the urge to pull Orlando away from the door. It had been hours since he had fed and they had no idea how long the protection would last. He knew better than to stop Orlando, though. His lover had an independent streak a mile wide and Alain recognized he had to trust that Orlando knew what he was doing. If he felt protected still, Alain would have to accept that it was so, no matter how much he feared otherwise. He watched with apprehension knotting his stomach as Orlando walked out the door and onto the platform, right into a patch of sunlight. He stood there grinning broadly for several minutes, the early winter sun warm on his face there out of the breeze. He tipped his head back, rejoicing in being out in daylight. He had spent the day before outside as well, but the experience was still new enough to savor. Finally, though, he went back inside. The point was to show the others that there was nothing to fear once they had fed.

Alain met him at the door, eyes flying over Orlando's face and hands, searching for signs of the ashy grey color that had indicated his overexposure the last time. He wanted to pull Orlando against him and order his lover to cease such recklessness, but that was not the image that either group needed of how the alliance would function. Nor was it the dynamic he wanted between Orlando and himself. Orlando had been abused, controlled, dominated for far too long in the past. Alain would not do that to him, however much he wanted to protect his vampire.

The vampires, even Jean who had stood in the sun the day before, examined Orlando just as closely as Alain did, though for a different reason. "Will this really work for all of us?" Jude asked. "It's not just because of the Aveu de Sang?"

"It worked for me," Jean replied, "and I have no Avoué." As he spoke, his gaze clashed with Sebastien's. Sebastien looked back impassively, refusing to acknowledge Jean's silent accusation, but likewise refusing to look away.

Thierry was aware of the interaction between the two vampires, but had no idea what caused the tension between them. He would ask Sebastien about it later. They could not afford conflict within the alliance. They needed to be able to rely on each other, within pairings and between pairings.

Once he had assured himself that Orlando was unharmed by his time in the sun, Alain turned back to look at the waiting room. With memories of his own experience fresh on his mind, he saw immediately the problem the open room would pose.

Crossing to Marcel, he murmured, "We can't do this here. It's too personal, and the room is too open."

"And yet they can't leave," Marcel replied just as softly. A simple wave of his wand could have sent the vampires anywhere they wanted to go, but that would not set the tone of cooperation between partners he wanted to establish, nor demonstrate the advantages of the alliance to the vampires. He looked around the room. Chairs could be transformed to create a physical barrier and magic could silence any sounds, creating at least a modicum of privacy.

"I'll take care of it," Marcel said. "You and Thierry figure out who we can get some information from, and quickly. I don't know how long the feeding will take, but Serrier isn't going to give us all day."

Alain nodded and crossed back to where Thierry still stood. "Marcel wants us to start the interrogation while the vampires feed. It won't do any good to start with Pacotte. He's undoubtedly the leader, but he won't tell us anything."

Sebastien coughed uncomfortably when he heard Alain speak so casually of feeding. He looked around the large room. It did not offer even the illusion of privacy. Even as he opened his mouth to protest, some of the chairs began to change, metamorphosing into walls the height of a man.

Thierry looked up and followed Sebastien's gaze. "Privacy," he said with a smile. "It's not what we might have hoped for, but we aren't completely uncouth."

Sebastien chuckled. "Not everyone is aware of our sensibilities, and given the way we met...."

"We're learning," Alain assured him. "As quickly as we can. Don't hesitate, though, to tell us if there's something we still need to know. As Thierry said, it's hardly perfect, but with Marcel's magic added to the screens, it will be as private as a completely different room. It won't stop everyone from knowing what's happening, but it will mean that no one sees or hears what transpires." He risked a glance at Orlando and saw the hunger in his eyes, a hunger he felt reflected in the pit of his own stomach. Orlando did not need to feed, but the memory was bright in his eyes and heart. Alain knew it would be a long and busy day, but he hoped he could steal a few minutes alone with Orlando, even if just for a kiss and a cuddle.

Jean, too, saw what Marcel had done and appreciated the gesture, one more example of Marcel's respect for the ways of the vampires and one more reason to respect him. Three cubicles stood in separate parts of the room, providing the vampires with a place to feed away from prying eyes. Now it fell to him to make sure they were used. After Orlando's demonstration, Jean knew he would not need to feed, so he could not rely on Orlando to provide the example. He would have to be the one to go first. He grimaced at the thought of tasting Raymond's fear again, but he really had no other choice. The sun had risen and he could not stay in this room all day. Serrier had found out about the meeting somehow and would be expecting his people to return. When they did not, he would undoubtedly come looking. Leaving was the only safe option, and that meant Raymond. He walked over to where Raymond stood guard still on the dark wizards. "Come," he ordered, heading toward one of the cubicles.

Raymond glared at Jean's retreating back, but he followed grudgingly. It was not as if he had a choice. Any resistance would be turned into treason, the one threat the vampire could use against him to make Raymond do just about anything.

"Shall we do this?" Sebastien asked, glancing at Thierry.

"Yeah," Thierry replied. "I'll be back in a few minutes, Alain, and we'll figure out who to question then." Alain agreed and watched the pair walk toward the second cubicle.

"I'm nervous," Thierry admitted as they reached the entrance. "I don't really know what to expect."

"I'll go easy on you," Sebastien quipped. Then his face grew serious. "I trusted you to protect me out on that platform. Trust me to take care of you now."

"I can do that," Thierry replied and knew that he was telling the truth. He and Sebastien had worked together beautifully, anticipating each other's moves. He would trust Sebastien to help him through this new experience as well.

They stepped behind the screen and as the rest of the world fell away in the silence of Marcel's magical vacuum, Thierry understood the vampires' preference for privacy. Raising his wrist, offering his arm to Sebastien was as fraught with tension and emotion as his first kiss with Aleth, his estranged and now-deceased wife. His mind shied away from the comparison. He had made his peace with the exigencies of the alliance as he dealt with her death two days before, and he could not have been more pleased with his partner. The way he and Sebastien had worked together rivaled the way he worked with Alain. It was not the partnership he feared. It was not the pain of being bitten. He had already been bitten enough times that night as he searched for a partner among the gathered vampires to get beyond that issue. It was the intimacy he could not wrap his mind around. He had seen the almost instantaneous connection between Alain and Orlando, and it scared him. He had lost his wife two days ago, damn it! He could not just forget her and jump into a new relationship with the first person to come along. No matter how tattered their marriage had been, its ending, particularly as it had, was still a cause of grief, and Thierry would not dishonor Aleth's memory by moving on so quickly.

Sebastien took the hand Thierry offered and turned it over, examining the wrist. "It's going to hurt if I bite you here," Sebastien said, gesturing to the puncture-riddled skin.

"It's only pain," Thierry replied, his hand steady in Sebastien's. Sebastien thought again how well matched they were in temperament. He would have found it very difficult to work with someone who complained at the slightest problem.

"Maybe so," Sebastien agreed, "but there's no reason to make it worse. May I?" He gestured to Thierry's sleeve.

Rather than replying, Thierry pulled up the sleeve of his sweater himself. He did not think he could handle having Sebastien do it. He closed his eyes when he felt Sebastien's gentle lips and tongue on his arm. The vampire was not doing anything to intensify the sensation, to make the act overtly erotic, but nothing could change the fact that Sebastien's lips and fangs were moving over his skin in a way none but a lover's ever had.

Sebastien could feel the tension gripping the wizard and knew instinctively that waiting to bite him would not help, so he let his fangs move onto and into Thierry's skin, feeling the hot blood fill his mouth. He had gotten a taste of Thierry before, but this was his first chance to really enjoy the flavor that revealed so much about the man.

Once again, Thierry's strength and determination flooded Sebastien's senses, showing the vampire Thierry's depth of commitment. Beyond that, there was grief, so strong that it overwhelmed everything else. Sebastien fed deeply, letting the blood strengthen his body and the magic surround him, layer upon layer until the feeling of insulation was complete. And with every swallow, Sebastien's own determination grew. Jean might not want him here. Jean might prefer that he roast in the fires of hell, but Sebastien would fight at Thierry's side as long as there were enemies to fight. For a brief moment, he knew a perfect communion with another soul, a feeling he had thought lost to him when his Avoué died four hundred years ago.

Finally, he raised his head and offered his own hand for Thierry to take. When Thierry gripped it firmly, Sebastien shook to seal their unspoken bargain. "Thank you, my friend," Sebastien said.

Friend. Thierry could live with that. "Anytime," he replied, starting to leave so the next pair could use the cubicle.

"Wait," Sebastien said. "Who did you lose that your grief is so strong?"

"My wife was killed in battle two days ago," Thierry replied dully.

Sebastien flinched. No wonder the emotion was so powerful. "I'm so sorry. I know how hard it is to lose someone you love."

Thierry simply nodded, hearing some echo of his own grief in Sebastien's voice but not yet ready to talk about it, and left the cubicle. Sebastien followed behind, resolving to respect Thierry's loss. He would offer Thierry his friendship if the wizard would accept it, but nothing more. It would not be fair to offer something he knew the other man could not accept.

Alain watched the cubicles as the first pairs came back out. Raymond and Jean were the first, and Raymond looked pale and wan. He left Jean's side immediately, finding a chair in the corner and collapsing into it. Alain frowned. That was not at all the reaction he had to Orlando's feeding. He wondered why Raymond had reacted that way and wondered if that, too, was an effect of their Aveu de Sang, the bond that tied them together for the rest of his life. When Thierry came out a moment later, his face set but strong, Alain decided Raymond was the problem, not the process. Adèle's face glowed when she reappeared, much the way Alain imagined his had done by the time Orlando had finished with him the morning before. He relaxed. As long as Raymond was the only one showing ill effects from the vampires' bites, Alain would not worry about it. Thierry led Sebastien back to where Alain and Orlando still stood, surveying the captives.

Alain gestured to the young man he and Orlando had captured. "That one, I think," he told Thierry. "He's young, and clearly didn't know what he was doing. If any of them will break, it's him. It's sad, really, to see one so young so full of hate. If we knew what had drawn him to join Serrier in the first place, perhaps we could persuade him back."

"It would depend on how firmly he believes in what he's doing," Thierry replied. "If he has doubts, we can prey on them, perhaps, and use them to our advantage."

"And if he doesn't, we've exposed our hand too soon," Alain countered. "I wish there were a way to be sure."

Jean arrived in time to hear the end of their conversation. "But there is a way to tell, or have you forgotten who your allies are?"

Chapter 2

"IF one of us bites him, we can tell if he has any doubts," Jean reminded them.

"I hadn't forgotten," Alain said, "but after the mistake I made last time, I certainly wasn't going to ask." He shuddered still at the thought of how badly he had insulted Orlando by insisting he taste Payet's blood as a way to prove that the other wizard was not trying to undermine the alliance. His hand lifted to the brand on his neck, the badge of the Aveu de Sang he had accepted as a way to make amends and to ensure that no such misunderstanding occurred in the future.

"You didn't ask. I offered," Jean reminded him. "That's the difference."

"Shall we release him before you bite him?" Thierry asked.

"Not yet," Jean replied. "What have you done to them?"

"They can't hear us or see us," Alain explained. "They're awake, but they have no awareness outside of themselves."

"Will he feel the bite?" Jean asked.

"I don't know," Alain said with a shrug. "I've never been held in that particular spell. It seems wrong, though, not to give him a chance to speak for himself first."

"But if he's aware of what I'm doing, his feelings toward me will be in his blood as well. That could mask what we're trying to learn. If he doesn't know what I'm doing, then everything I taste will be what he feels more generally," Jean explained.

"Then we need to know if he can feel what you're doing. The more accurately you can tell us what he feels, the better we'll be able to question him," Thierry agreed.

"That's easy enough to find out," Alain said. "Put me under, just like Marcel did them, and then Orlando can bite me. When you bring me out, I'll tell you what I felt." He did not even hesitate to make the offer. He had trusted Thierry with his life so many times that he had lost count. This harmless little spell was nothing in comparison to what they had faced together in the past.

Orlando listened to the exchange between the two wizards and bristled as soon as he heard Alain talking about being under a spell. Not because he did not want to bite his lover again, but because the thought of someone, anyone, pointing a wand at Alain and casting a spell on him made Orlando nervous. What if something went wrong? What if Thierry could not reverse the spell? Orlando thought that not being able to look in Alain's blue eyes and see the desire and tenderness that flickered there whenever their eyes met would destroy him as surely as walking in the sunlight unprotected by Alain's magic.

Before he could protest, though, Alain and Thierry were walking toward the cubicles that Marcel had erected. Orlando caught up quickly, and when they reached the entrance, he turned to Thierry. "Give us a minute?" he asked, tilting his head toward the private area.

Thierry agreed and watched them walk behind the magic screen. Just before they disappeared from sight, he saw Orlando reach out and take Alain's hand. It was such a simple gesture, that bridging of the distance between them, and yet it resonated in Thierry's soul, reminding him of what he had felt when Sebastien fed from him. That, too, had bridged the distance between two distinct areas. He wondered what Sebastien had tasted in his blood, besides the grief he had asked about. He looked up to find the object of his thoughts walking toward them.

"Did you cast the spell already?" Sebastien asked.

"Not yet," Thierry replied. "They wanted a minute alone first."

"It's quite a show of trust on Orlando's part to let you do this, you know," Sebastien pointed out.

"What do you mean?" Thierry asked.

"When a vampire makes an Aveu de Sang like Orlando did, his protectiveness and possessiveness know no bounds. That he would let you do anything to Alain, no matter how seemingly innocuous, is a huge leap of faith. And we vampires are not known for our faith."

Thierry stared at the cubicle in silence. He wondered if the Aveu de Sang was something that all vampires were familiar with or if Sebastien was speaking from experience. The pang of jealousy that he felt at that thought shocked him. He had no business feeling that way. His claim on Sebastien's attentions now was little enough. He certainly had no claim on Sebastien's past. He did not know how long Sebastien had been a vampire, but to think that he had come to this moment without anyone touching his life was naïve. Thierry was many things, but he liked to think that was not one of them. He glanced sideways at the dark-haired vampire, really taking in his appearance for the first time. His dark hair fell to his shoulders, accentuating the strong line of his jaw and chin. Thierry knew stubborn when he saw it. He had been accused of that trait often enough to recognize it in others. It did not bother him. In fact, he respected it, respected the self-assurance and determination it took to be stubborn, to stand your ground regardless of who or what came against you. Sebastien was a handsome man, Thierry acknowledged, a compelling one. Then a pang of guilt nearly bent him double. Aleth had only been dead for two days. He had no right to be thinking of someone else so soon, regardless of how strained their relationship had been before her death. They had separated, at her insistence, but in Thierry's eyes and heart, they had still been married. He had not stopped loving her just because their relationship was going through a difficult time. He had only just lost her and yet he was looking at someone else. He did not like what that said about his character.

As soon as they were inside the cubicle, Orlando pulled Alain into his arms. "Is this safe?" he asked softly.

Alain cradled Orlando's face between his hands, staring deeply into the coffee brown eyes that revealed so much of the vampire's soul. "Of course it's safe," he reassured his lover. "I've cast the spell more times than I can count, and I've released it without there ever being any side effects on the person bound. All it does is mute the senses temporarily and keep them in place. It would be like putting on a blindfold and earplugs and then tying someone to a chair. This is just faster because it's a simple spell."

"But anything could happen while you're under," Orlando protested.

"What could happen?" Alain asked. "You're here with me, and I know I'm safe with you, and Thierry is right outside to keep anyone else from disturbing us."

"You really trust me that much?" Orlando asked, amazed.

Alain bent his head and kissed Orlando tenderly. "Yes, I really trust you that much. Now, can Thierry come in and cast the spell?"

Orlando took a moment to reply, stunned into silence by the magnitude of Alain's trust and the effect that realization had on him. Orlando had always been the young one, the innocent one, the inexperienced one, in all of his relationships, such as they were. He only bore the rank of private when his maker whisked him away from the army. That relationship had been one of total submission on Orlando's part, though he had not wanted it that way. Jean saw him as a younger brother. The other vampires simply saw him as young.

No one had ever trusted him, relied on him, looked to him for anything. Alain, though, was different. He was younger than Orlando, for one thing, despite their appearances, but more importantly than that, he respected Orlando. Alain did not want a younger brother or a submissive slave. He wanted an equal. He expected an equal, which was even better. "Yes, let him in."

Alain stepped outside the cubicle, leaving Orlando alone for a moment in the magical silence Marcel had created. He knew the rest of the world was still there, just outside, and he knew that all he had to do was step through the barrier and it would be there again, but the sense of isolation was intense nonetheless. He wondered if that was what Alain would feel when Thierry cast the spell. If it was, it made Alain's trust all the more meaningful because Alain would not be able to simply step through a barrier if he wanted out. He would have to wait for Thierry to undo the spell, and in the meantime, Orlando could do whatever he wanted to him. It humbled Orlando to realize Alain believed that he would not do anything to abuse that trust.

He watched silently as Alain and Thierry came back into the cubicle, tensing when Thierry drew his wand and cast the spell. "Is he under?" Orlando asked when Thierry lowered the wand.

"Yes," Thierry replied.

"Then I can say this. I know you would never do anything to hurt Alain intentionally, but if something goes wrong with your spell, if he doesn't come out of it, you would do well not to cross my path."

Thierry tensed at the threat, about to be offended that Orlando could even suggest it, when Sebastien's words echoed in his ears. Orlando was not making idle threats; he was protecting the most important person in his life. Thierry knew the feeling. He had been thinking the same thing just six days before when he first realized that Alain had been bitten by a vampire. How far they had come since then!

"He's as important to me as he is to you, though in a very different way," Thierry replied. "You have nothing to fear from me." He stepped back outside, leaving the lovers alone.

Thierry was a better man than he to leave him alone with Alain in this state, Orlando decided as he stared at his lover's unmoving form. This was different from watching Alain sleep. Then, his face was relaxed, his eyes closed, his body at rest, but not completely motionless. Now, though, his face was tense, his eyes open but unseeing when Orlando moved his hand in front of them, his body still but so clearly not at rest. A sense of power surged through Orlando as he looked at Alain. The wizard was helpless. Orlando could do whatever he wanted. What he wanted was to finish this test so that Thierry could release Alain and give Orlando his lover back. When Orlando had first marked him, Alain thought he wanted a thrall, a slave to his desires. Orlando had denied that desire automatically then. Looking at Alain now, seeing what it would be like to have total control, he knew he had spoken the truth. He did not want a thrall. He wanted Alain, with his own mind and his own control and the ability to help decide what happened between them. He lifted Alain's wrist to his lips and bit gently, just enough to draw a taste of blood. What he tasted reaffirmed everything he already knew about Alain: the strength, the integrity, the desire. Those flavors were already so familiar, so vital, but this time Orlando tasted something new, or heretofore unrecognized: the flavor of Alain's trust in him underlay all the rest.

Closing the wounds, he returned Alain's wrist to his side and went to get Thierry. "Release him," he pleaded.

Thierry heard the urgency in Orlando's voice and undid the spell as quickly as he could. As soon as awareness came back into Alain's eyes, Orlando threw himself into his lover's arms. Embarrassed at seeing such an intimate moment, Thierry stepped back outside, giving them their privacy again. He could wait to ask Alain what he had felt while under the spell.

"Are you all right?" Orlando asked Alain, running his hands over the wizard's body as if checking for injuries.

"I'm fine," Alain assured Orlando, catching his hands and raising them to his lips. "I'm fine," he repeated, just to be sure.

"Don't do that to me again," Orlando ordered vehemently. "Don't go away and leave me alone like that. You were there and yet you weren't."

"Orlando, it was just a spell. It's over now, and I'm right here with you." He tightened his arms around his lover's quivering body to provide another layer of reassurance.

Orlando heard Alain's words, but they had not sunk in yet. He tilted his head and kissed Alain fervently, as deep and passionate a kiss as any they had shared. Alain returned the kiss ardently, parting his lips willingly to allow the invasion of Orlando's tongue. It had not even occurred to him that the spell might affect his lover so. If he had known, he would never have suggested it.

Finally, he lifted his head. "We should go back out to the others," Alain said softly. "They'll want to know if I could feel your fangs and we need to question that wizard if we're going to do it this way. We don't have all day."

Still hand in hand, they stepped out of the enclosure. Alain knew they were opening themselves up to more comments and perhaps even censure, but he found he did not care. The vampires had surely guessed given the mark of

Avoué on his neck, and the wizards would figure it out quickly enough. Orlando needed the comfort of his touch, and that overrode any other concerns.

"Well?" Thierry asked impatiently. "What did you feel?"

"Nothing," Alain said, "until I came out of it. Then I could feel where Orlando had bitten me, but even though I knew it had to be happening, I couldn't feel it."

Orlando knew that was good news. It meant Jean could bite the wizard in question and find out what he was feeling, but it was still a blow to Orlando's heart. He had shared the most intimate act he knew with Alain and Alain had not felt it.

"It will work then," Jean said with a grin. "Good. Let's get started."

Alain was a little unsettled by Jean's enthusiasm, but he did not question it as he, Orlando, Thierry, and Sebastien trailed behind the chef de la Cour. Alain spared a glance for Raymond as they headed back to the wizard they planned to interrogate, wondering how the other wizard felt about Jean volunteering for this task. It was no longer an option for Orlando, but Alain knew that had it been, he would have protested if Orlando had made the offer. It had been bad enough watching Orlando bite Thierry before they promised their fidelity. To watch him bite a dark wizard would have been more than he could stand. Raymond, though, seemed oblivious to the proceedings. Alain shrugged. At least he was not interfering.

Raymond was indeed lost in his own bleak thoughts, but he was not as oblivious as Alain believed. He had seen the group standing near the dark wizards, and he watched as Jean reached for the hand of the one wizard Raymond did not know. He dared not utter the protest that rose irrationally from within him for fear that Jean would use it against him. It would not matter that he had fought with them today and for most of the past two years, if Jean suddenly declared him a traitor. They would believe the vampire if he told them he had tasted a lie in Raymond's blood. They would take the word of a vampire over the word of one of their own for the sake of their precious alliance. He had not needed a vampire's help to subdue his target. He had brought his opponent down just fine on his own. It was not his fault if the others could not do the same. He forced himself to watch as Jean bit the wizard so that he would have that image to remind him why he could not trust the vampires. The chef de la Cour would use him for what he needed, but he offered nothing in return. The others did not see it, but they would. Maybe not before it was too late, but they would see it eventually. Raymond did join the others, though. Perhaps an opportunity would arise for him to express his concerns in a way that could not be used against him.

Jean looked up at Raymond over the dark wizard's wrist when he joined them, but he continued defiantly with the planned course of action. Raymond had kept him from participating in the battle, but he would not keep him from participating in its aftermath. He bit down juicily on the boy's wrist, for he was little more than a boy, letting the blood flow into his mouth and out of it as well so that when he raised his head, his lips and teeth were covered with blood. He watched Raymond flinch slightly, but when he did not speak, Jean turned his attention to the flavors on his tongue. He could taste the taint of dark magic immediately, much stronger than the residual traces in Raymond's blood. It was enough to make him want to gag, but he quelled the impulse, trying to see what else he could learn. He could taste anger and even hatred, but as he concentrated more deeply, he also tasted doubt and fear. Spitting the rest of the blood out of his mouth, he looked at his allies. "There is fear and doubt beneath the anger. If you can find out what has caused it, you might succeed in swaying him. He has done evil things, but I don't think he is altogether evil."

"How do we want to do this?" Alain asked Thierry.

"Same as always," Thierry replied, "but this time, I have a little extra backup if I need it. If our new allies don't mind looking threatening, that is." He grinned at Sebastien, Jean, and Orlando.

Jean and Sebastien grinned back at him, their fangs showing clearly, though both of their smiles turned into scowls when they saw the each other's reaction.

Orlando looked confused. "It's simple," Alain said. "I talk nice to the boy and Thierry makes threats. Eventually, we convince him to talk to me as a way to avoid Thierry. Thierry will just add the threat of letting one of you bite him. It won't come to that. If he breaks, he'll do so before we carry out the threats, and if he doesn't break, I'll intervene and we'll just send him to prison with the others."

"If it will help, I'd be glad to bite him this time," Sebastien offered. "If we make good on that threat, he'll be more likely to believe that we'll make good on any others."

"That won't be necessary," Jean said. "I'll do it. I already know what he tastes like. I'll be able to tell if we're reaching him."

Seeing a conflict brewing, Thierry intervened. "We'll worry about that if it becomes necessary. For now, let's see what he has to say for himself." With a wave of his hand, Thierry undid a portion of the spell, releasing the dark wizard's senses, but not his hands and feet, or his magic. As soon as he felt Marcel's magic dissipate, his hand flew out to strike the boy's face. Alain's hand caught his right before it connected.

"Give him a chance to speak first," Alain said soothingly. "Perhaps he'll be willing to cooperate." He turned to the young man. "What shall we call you?" he asked.

"What business of it is yours?" the wizard spat back.

Thierry moved forward again, and again Alain restrained him. "It's my business because you were caught in the act of using dark magic to attack others," Alain explained. "If you cooperate, I might be able to help you. If you don't, I can't help you, and you'll be at the mercy of these fine gentlemen, none of whom are as patient as I am."

Alain watched as the boy's eyes darted around, taking in Thierry's scowl, Jean's hungry grin, Raymond's impassive face, Sebastien's glower, and Orlando's smirk. They were not a sympathetic audience.

"Who are you to tell me what kind of magic I can do? No one should have that right!"

Alain had expected it, the propaganda Serrier used to try to sway others to his side, but it always bothered him to hear it. "Do you really believe that?" he asked. "Do you really think that magic is the answer to everything and that wizards should be able to use it in whatever way they please without considering how it affects others?"

"Wizards shouldn't have to answer to non-wizards for their use of magic. What do the non-magical know of what we do?" the boy challenged.

"He's not listening," Thierry growled. "Give me five minutes and he'll be more receptive."

Alain looked at the young wizard. "Shall I give him what he wants, or are you going to talk to me?"

"He can't do any worse to me than Serrier would do if he found out I talked," the wizard replied.

"Then why stay with him?" Orlando asked, breaking into the conversation. The wizard's head swiveled around to land on the youngest of the three vampires. "If you fear him so, why not leave?"

"And go where?" the young man asked, his face showing his consternation. "If I leave, he'll kill me unless I can hide from him or find some other protection. And if I turn myself in to get away from him, I'll go to prison for what I've done."

Alain met Thierry's eyes. Thierry nodded, almost imperceptibly. "If you could convince us that you were serious about changing sides and provide us with useful information, we might be able to work something out," Alain suggested.

"What... What do you mean?" the other wizard asked.

"Let's start at the beginning. Why don't you tell us your name?"

"Dominique Cornet," he replied.

"All right, Dominique," Alain said. "How long have you been with Serrier?"

"About three months is all," the boy answered.

"And what were you supposed to do here today?"

"Serrier wanted to know why the vampires were meeting. He said it wasn't like them to gather together, especially in so public a place. He sent us to spy on them, but the room was warded, and we couldn't hear anything. Then you attacked us. That's all I know," Dominique said.

"Does Pacotte have any way of communicating with Serrier while in the field, or does he report only after the fact?" Thierry interrupted.

Dominique jerked his head around to look at the blond wizard with the menacing gaze. "I don't know," he babbled. "He never let me in on the planning stuff. He'd just tell me where to go and when. Please, you have to believe me." The glimmer of hope for escape made Dominique almost frantic to convince his saviors.

"How did you get mixed up with Serrier?" Raymond asked, speaking for the first time since he had joined the others. "You don't seem the type."

"What would you know about the type?" Dominique challenged, a little of his old bravado coming back.

"I got out," Raymond replied simply. "Now answer my question."

Dominique dropped his eyes, trying to take in that revelation. One of the wizards questioning him had escaped Serrier's clutches. That meant that the others protected him from anyone Serrier sent after him. He began to really hope they would do that for him as well. "I was born in a small town," he said, trying to explain. "But more than that, I grew up surrounded by people who distrusted and rejected anything magical. When my abilities started to manifest, I was punished. They said they would drive the devil out of me. I had no training. I couldn't control it so I kept doing magic inadvertently. Each time I did, it was another beating. Six months ago, Hector found me and stopped the mob that would probably have killed me. He explained about my magic and started teaching me to control it. He also started talking about a group of wizards who were fighting the kind of injustice I had faced, who were fighting to give wizards the choice of when and where to do magic. What was I supposed to think? To me, it sounded like paradise. And so when I had learned enough, he took me to meet Serrier. He was so apologetic when he heard what had happened, saying he was so sorry they had not found me sooner. It took me some time to realize that while I wanted to be able to do magic, I didn't like Serrier's methods or his... cruelty. But by then, I didn't see a way out."

"All wizards have those kinds of outbursts as they're first learning to use their magic," Alain explained gently.   "And even some older wizards occasionally lose control when their emotions get the better of them. As for the rest, yes, there are limits on the ways we use magic, even outside your small town, but magic, in and of itself, is not poorly thought of. We don't kill with magic, except in self-defense. We don't use magic to deprive others of their freedom or their property, but that doesn't stop us from using it to ease our everyday lives. Serrier would create an oligarchy where wizards made all the decisions for everyone else. Anyone who isn't a wizard would have no say in the government, in the running of their lives. Despite what Serrier would have you believe, that doesn't make us anti-magic. It doesn't make us fascists who would steal individual rights from the wizards. If anything, the opposite is true. In giving more power to the wizards, Serrier would steal it from everyone else."

"You have two choices at this point," Thierry informed Dominique. "You can run and hide and hope that we stop him. Or you can help us bring him down."

"I'm not much of a wizard," Dominique said. "I don't know what help I could be."

"There's more to winning a war than fighting," Alain said. "Information is the key. Serrier trusts you right now, at least as much as he trusts anyone. If you go back there, you could send us information that would help us win this war faster."

"You want me to spy for you?" Dominique asked, incredulous.

"That would be one way of putting it," Thierry replied drolly.

"Why should you trust me? I mean, how do you know I'm not just telling you all of this to get loose and take word back to Serrier?"

"We don't know yet," Thierry replied, "but we will shortly. I'm quite sure Serrier never told you that others besides wizards have magical abilities."

"What? Who?" Dominique wanted to know.

"Vampires, for one," Alain replied. "A vampire can read your heart in your blood. So you're going to offer your wrist to one of these good vampires and let him tell us if you're telling the truth."

"I can choose which one?"

"Either of those two," Orlando said, indicating Jean and Sebastien. "I'm bound to another by a promise I will not break."

Dominique looked back and forth between the two vampires. He could see little to choose between them. "Who would you pick?" he asked Orlando, feeling an affinity with the vampire's apparent youth.

"Jean has been my friend for a long time. I trust him completely. Sebastien, I have only just met," Orlando replied.

"Jean," Dominique decided, taking Orlando's advice. Jean shot Sebastien a triumphant grin as he reached for the wizard's magically bound wrist.

"Will you be able to heal these marks?" Jean asked suddenly. "Because if Serrier sees them, he's going to ask questions that could be difficult to answer."

"That's an easy enough spell," Thierry assured him. "Find out what we need to know."

Raymond could not make himself watch the second time. He turned his head away bitterly. Jean noticed, but he could not stop and deal with Raymond's reaction. He wondered if it was time for the two of them to have a little talk. First, though, he had to wade through the morass of Dominique's emotions. He bit down, letting the blood fill his mouth. The dark magic was still there, of course, and the anger, but the hatred had lessened, and a new resolve had replaced the doubt and fear. "He intends to do as he said," Jean said, raising his head. He could not predict what Dominique's future actions would be, of course, but the wizard's heart was on their side.

Dominique sighed in relief when he heard the vampire's pronouncement. The others seemed to place great faith in his words so he hoped they would release him.

"Marcel," Thierry called, catching the older wizard's attention.

That was a name Dominique knew. He had heard it reviled often enough. Maybe it was not the same Marcel, but Dominique hoped it would be Chavinier. He was curious to see the head of the force that was successfully opposing Serrier. He knew how powerful and ruthless Serrier could be. That Chavinier was strong enough to oppose him made Dominique think that perhaps Marcel was strong enough to protect him, too. The man who joined them was easily old enough to be Dominique's grandfather, a shock of strikingly white hair topping a gently lined, genteel face, the smile on his face kind as he approached. The rebel leader wore a habitual sneer, his expression as cold as his attitude toward those who failed him. Serrier was much younger as well, closer in age to the wizards who surrounded him during his interrogation than to the Milice general approaching now. Dark and light. The contrast struck him firmly as he found himself returning the old wizard's smile, a completely different reaction than he had to any wizard serving in Serrier's ranks. With this man, he truly felt he could relax.

"Who do you have there?" Marcel asked.

"This is Dominique," Alain said, introducing the young wizard, "and he's come to the conclusion that he's been deluded. He's offered to gather information for us. The more we know, the better we can plan our battles."

Well Marcel knew that. He had his own sources of information, but another one was always an asset. "And how do you propose to make this work? I assume you have a plan."

"Something like," Thierry replied. "Here's what we need to do…"

Chapter 3

MARCEL looked down at his new spy, unconscious on the floor at his feet. If Serrier searched for traces of magic, he would detect Marcel's last spell. His magical signature was strong enough that it should mask Alain's residue and lend credence to the story they had made up to explain Dominique's "escape." He hoped it would work because otherwise, he was sending the young man to his death.

"Let's go, Marcel," Alain said. "We've done all we can for him. The rest is up to him. Let's get these others some place more secure before Serrier comes looking for them."

Marcel nodded. A quick spell sent the remaining prisoners to secure holding cells deep within Milice headquarters, leaving only the Milice wizards and their partners in the waiting room. "I need to go deal with them. Can you help our new allies make their way back to base?"

"Of course," Alain agreed. As he headed toward the door, he paused at Jean's side. "We'll go through the subway and stay underground as much as possible, but we'll eventually have to go outside. It'll be up to you and Orlando to help the vampires through their first walk in the sun. We've got wounded who can't go magically because of their injuries. They'll need to get to headquarters as quickly as possible. As soon as they're inside, I'll come back and show you the way."

"That's fine," Jean said. "We'll wait for you inside the subway and join you outside when you come back."

Alain nodded. "Okay, let's go," he ordered. He waited by the door for Orlando. They would go first as point. Thierry would take the rear guard as always. The other pairs formed a protective circle around the wounded, Caroline and Mathieu. Alain was pleased to see their vampires hovering protectively.

Alain led the group swiftly down into the subway, his drawn wand and strange following clearing the path easily. They boarded one of the trains, and Alain watched in amusement as the other passengers quickly debarked, leaving them alone in the car.

The ride passed uneventfully, much to Alain's relief. They arrived at their stop and Alain took the lead again, heading up the stairs and outside. One by one, the vampires stopped, all except Orlando. He stayed boldly at Alain's side as they walked into the sunlight. "I'll go back with you to encourage them," Orlando murmured, "but my confidence will do as much to convince them as anything else."

"You know how you feel," Alain replied. "Just be aware of it. I don't want to lose you."

"I'll be careful, I promise, but I want to enjoy my newfound freedom."

"And so you should. Let's get the wounded inside."

Alain worked his way through alleys and courtyards, moving from building to building without ever reappearing on the street.

"I'll never find this again," Orlando said with a laugh.

"There's a front door which we use if we're alone or in pairs, but we're a little obvious right now. This just helps protect the location of the base."

When they reached the entrance to Milice headquarters, Alain waited only until Thierry reached his side. "I'm going back for the others," he said.

"I'll get the injured settled and help Marcel," Thierry replied.

Alain led Orlando out by a much simpler route, directly to the street not a block from the subway.

"That really is quite a maze!"

"It is, but anyone who sees us go in will be nowhere near the actual base. If they follow us inside, they'll trip the alarms we have set up. It's pretty secure."

"It seems that way," Orlando agreed, impressed. This was not just a ragtag group of wizards. They had organized themselves as well as any army. They rounded the corner to the subway stop to find all the vampires waiting for them outside. "I guess they didn't need my help after all," Orlando smiled.

Alain grinned at him. "Let's go back to the base. There's a courtyard where they can go outside if they want, but we'll attract attention standing here."

"Jean, Sebastien, Mireille," Orlando called, naming the vampires he knew well. "Let's go."

As one, they moved down the street toward the pair. Alain took the short route this time. The street was deserted so no one would see them entering. Angelique Bouaddi, owner of Sang Froid, an establishment that provided vampires with willing prey, knew she was gawking as she followed the others, but she could not seem to help herself. All the experience and sophistication she projected in her usual milieu fled before the wonder of seeing the world bathed in sunlight. With the advent of electricity, she no longer lived in darkness, and movies and TV had shown her images of the changing city in the daylight, but she had never believed she would see it with her own eyes. She knew from what she had tasted that David saw only her brash exterior and imagined her a flighty woman with loose morals because of her profession and appearance. She would bring him around. In the meantime, she was grateful to him for the opportunity his blood was affording her.

Sebastien did a better job of masking his delight, though he felt it as strongly as the others. He was the outsider here, and he knew it. The others, relatively secure in their positions, were willing to let their emotions show. For Sebastien, that sign of vulnerability could be deadly, his status as a relative outsider subjecting him to even more scrutiny in the Jeu des Cours than most vampires. He would not take that risk with Jean around. He had been the first to follow Jean out into the sun after Orlando and the others left for just that reason. Jean had challenged them all, reminding them that they considered Orlando to be little more than a boy and that if he could walk in the sun, surely they could, too. They might have protested, mentioned the Aveu de Sang again, except that Jean, too, was bathed in daylight and his wizard sported no such claim. Sebastien did not know Orlando, and all he had seen, especially the Aveu de Sang, had only earned his respect, but the challenge in Jean's voice was as clear as a bell, regardless of what reason he was using for it. It was the challenge Sebastien could not let pass, not the comparison to Orlando. The others had followed suit more or less quickly. Sebastien was impressed. Jean was a capable leader. Sebastien just wished things could be different between them, could be like they were before…. He could not even think it. It hurt too much still, even after all the years that had passed. He forced himself to focus instead on where they were going so he would be able to find his way again.

Though she was as amazed as the others at being in the sunlight, Mireille's mind was taken up with other concerns. Caroline was injured. Mireille had no idea how serious the injury was, but that did not seem to matter. Her wizard was injured and every instinct she possessed was driving her to check on Caroline as quickly as possible. She kept telling herself it could not be too serious since Caroline was walking, but Caroline had been concerned enough about it to mention it to Mireille.

They had been behind the screen at the time. Out of habit, Mireille had reached for Caroline's right hand, but the wizard had stopped her. "Don't," she had said. "A dark spell hit that shoulder. I don't know if it can infect you through my blood, but we shouldn't take that chance."

That said, Caroline had offered her other arm instead. Mireille had not tasted any difference in Caroline's blood, but that did not necessarily mean anything. If the magic could spread through her blood, it meant only that it had not spread that far yet. As soon as they crossed the threshold into Marcel's base, Mireille turned to Alain. "Where's Caroline?" she asked, struggling to keep the desperation out of her voice.

"In the infirmary, I'm sure," he assured her. "Hold on just a second. I'll get someone to take you there." He motioned another wizard over and asked her to take Mireille to the infirmary. Then he turned back to Mireille. "Go with Catherine. She'll show you where Caroline is."

"Thank you," Mireille said as she started after the other wizard. The short trip to the infirmary was passed in silence.

"Here it is," Catherine said, indicating a door. "Just ask for Caroline. They'll take you to her."

Mireille nodded but did not reply. Her entire focus was on the next room. A small, still rational part of her mind questioned her reaction, but the rest of her could not be bothered with making sense of it. She needed to see that Caroline was all right. The rest could wait for later.

Oblivious to the events in the infirmary, Marcel convoked his lieutenants and their partners. "I doubt we'll get anything out of the other prisoners, but we owe them the chance to show remorse or agree to cooperate before we send them to prison. Your strategy worked with the last one. I suggest you try it again."

"Fine by me," Thierry said, looking at Alain who also nodded.

"I'm willing to help again," Jean offered.

Hearing Jean's offer to taste the dark wizards again, Raymond could not silence his sound of displeasure. From what little he understood of the vampires' ethics, if such creatures could be said to have ethics, biting another was supposed to be a private action. Did Jean not even have enough respect for him to offer him the courtesy of not making him watch? What did he have to do to prove himself worthy of the same consideration everyone else merited?

Marcel had more consideration for the vampires' feelings, in providing them screens, than for Raymond's!

Jean turned and glared at him, upset that Raymond was interfering. They needed this information if they were going to fight this war successfully. Raymond frowned but did not look away.

"Don't steal the spotlight, Jean. It's unbecoming," Sebastien interrupted. "There are other vampires here besides you, and we all have the same talents."

Jean scowled again, but ignored Sebastien for the moment. He had other things to deal with, namely a recalcitrant wizard.

"Excuse us a minute," Jean said coldly. "Raymond and I need to talk."

Jean rose and stood expectantly at the door. Raymond was tempted to challenge him right there, but he thought better of it. If he could placate Jean, hopefully he would be able to retain his position in Marcel's ranks. He rose and walked out into the corridor.

"Where can we talk in private?" Jean asked him.

"Down the hall," Raymond replied with a shrug, leading Jean into a little room.

Locking the door behind them, Jean turned to Raymond who stood awkwardly in the middle of the small space. "What the hell is your problem?"

"My problem?" Raymond demanded disbelievingly. "MY problem?" His voice grew louder. "What's yours?"

"Your attitude," Jean snapped. "You have done nothing to make this partnership successful. Not one damn thing."

"And what have you done?" Raymond asked. "At least I let you feed from me. All you've done is threaten me."

"Threat…" Jean sputtered. "All I want is for this to work, and for that, I need your blood. When you didn't offer to share it willingly, what choice did I have?"

"Did you even ask me to share it?" Raymond retorted. "No, you just demanded. How was I supposed to feel?"

"Would you have agreed if I had asked?" Jean countered.

"Maybe," Raymond replied, looking down, though he knew he would have refused. "Now we'll never know. I'm giving you what you want. The least you can do is show some gratitude."

"And how would you suggest I do that?" Jean asked angrily, beginning to pace.

"You could start by not making me watch you bite someone else," Raymond said. "I thought you were supposed to be biting just me."

Jean was speechless. Of all the answers he had considered, that one had not occurred to him. "Why should it bother you?" he asked finally, turning back to Raymond. "You don't want me to bite you. Why should you care if I bite anyone else?"

"Whether I wanted it or not, you're my partner. You said yourself that vampires equate feeding with sex. So wouldn't it be common courtesy not to make your partner watch you with another?"

"I haven't fed from anyone but you since the alliance formed," Jean pointed out. "I didn't even swallow Dominique's blood. I just tasted it to see what he was feeling."

"And put on quite a show while doing it," Raymond shouted.

"So what?" Jean challenged. "You don't want my attention so why does it bother you so much when I pay attention to someone else?"

"Because it makes our partnership meaningless," Raymond said slowly as if explaining something to a small child.

"What partnership?" Jean asked. "You haven't acted like I'm your partner yet. You didn't wait for me to help in the battle. I had to come find you to feed. You don't walk beside me the way the other wizards do with their partners."

"What about you? Ordering me around, treating me like your lackey instead of your equal. Yes, I made a mistake when I joined Serrier at the beginning of this war. I believed his propaganda. Then I saw his cruelty and I got out, with no promises from anyone. I watched my own back until Marcel took me in. What do I have to do to convince everyone that I am honest in my convictions now?!" This last was a wailed shout as all of Raymond's pent-up frustrations came to the fore.

"You could start by acting like you want this to work," Jean suggested.

"Is that a suggestion or an order, O Lord and Master?" Raymond asked sarcastically.

"A suggestion," Jean replied, finally understanding the problem. "I don't want a slave, Raymond. I want a partner. Did you see the others fighting on the quai? Did you see them working together? That's what I want. I want you watching my back while I watch yours."

"You certainly haven't been acting like it," Raymond groused. "You can barely stand to look at me."

"That's not true," Jean retorted. "You're no hardship on the eyes."

Raymond looked up, surprised. "You were flirting with Adèle."

"Have you looked at Adèle? I'd have to be a whole lot more dead than I am not to flirt with her."

"That's not funny," Raymond said, even as he chuckled.

"Yes, it is," Jean said. He took a deep breath. "Can we start over? Pretend we've never met and create our partnership anew?"

Raymond smiled shyly, the first genuine smile Jean had seen on his face. "I'd like that."

"Hi, I'm Jean," he said, holding out his hand. "What's your name?"

"Raymond," he replied, tentatively taking the offered hand.

"Nice to meet you, Raymond. You want to try a spell, see if we're partnered? It'll be less painful than if I bite you."

"Okay, if you don't mind."

"Something simple," Jean warned, "in case it works."

"A levitation spell," Raymond suggested. "That's what the others used."

"That will work," Jean agreed.

Raymond drew his wand and cast the simple spell. Jean could feel the brush of the magic, feel it wrapping around him, but his feet remained firmly planted on the ground.

"I guess we're partners," Jean said with a smile.

"I guess we are," Raymond replied. "So what does that mean?"

"It means you give me the blood I need to face the sunlight. And it means that if I go somewhere else for sustenance, when we aren't fighting, I'll do it where you can't see me. Within the bounds of the alliance, I will bite no one else. And when we go into battle, we go as equals, helping each other. Is that all agreeable?"

Raymond considered the question. "And when there are decisions to make, we will make them together," he added.

Jean nodded.

"Nice to meet you, partner."

"If I forget," Jean said, "remind me rather than just glaring at me silently. I'm not a mind reader."

"Do the same for me."

"I will," Jean said. "Can I ask why you were so afraid of me? I know you didn't want a vampire for a partner, but that's not fear."

Raymond swallowed nervously. "I knew someone who took up with a vampire," he said slowly. "At first, he fairly glowed with health and energy. Then, less than five weeks later, he was dead. We never found out what happened."

"Five weeks?" Jean echoed. "That's strange. Unless the vampire was careless, it shouldn't have mattered how long they were together. Either that, or your friend got caught in a struggle between two vampires. Not all vampires are honorable, any more than all wizards are."

"And you?" Raymond asked. "Are you honorable?"

Jean flinched as he thought about another young man caught between two vampires. "Yes," he replied bitterly, remembering how that had ended, with him alone and the young man happily in the arms of the other. "Now, let's go tell Marcel that he needs to find an unpaired vampire to use in his interrogation."

"Sebastien offered," Raymond pointed out.

"I know he did, but I don't see any reason for any other pairing to have the same problems we did. I know a vampire who would be perfect for the job. Big, brawny, full of bad attitude. No one would ever know he's all bark and no bite."

Raymond laughed. "Sounds a little like you."

Jean grinned. If Raymond could tease him, they really were on better footing than before. "Let's get back. I want to know what else Marcel has planned."

Chapter 4

"WHERE'S Caroline?" Mireille asked, her concern getting the better of her manners.

"The medic is tending to her," an orderly replied. "Have a seat."

"I need to see Caroline," Mireille repeated, more urgently.

"You can't go back there right now," the orderly repeated. "I'll let you know when you can."

He started to turn away, but Mireille grabbed his arm. "Let. Me. See. Caroline," she ordered, her grip tightening.

When he shook his head as if to refuse, she threw him aside, pushing deeper into the infirmary.

"Caroline!" she yelled, pulling aside the first curtain. The body on the bed was unfamiliar.

"Caroline!" Her panic escalated as she moved on to the next, and then the next. Another set of hands reached for her, but she shrugged them off, growing more and more frantic as each cubicle revealed an unknown wizard.

She burst into the final drape-shrouded area to see Caroline on the bed, eyes closed. "What have you done to her?" Mireille shouted.

"She's fine," the medic replied placatingly. "I put a sleeping spell on her so I could tend her injury. She should wake up any minute."

"But she's all right?" Mireille asked, the rage leaving her as suddenly as it had come.

"She's fine. I had to do a little repair on her shoulder, but she'll be as good as new in a day or two as long as she rests."

"She'll rest," Mireille declared. "I'll see to it."

"I'm sure you will," the medic replied. "I'll leave you two alone. Call me when she wakes up and don't let her get up until I've checked her one more time."

"I'll do that," Mireille agreed.

As soon as the drapes fell closed behind the medic, Mireille reached for Caroline's good hand, clinging to it like a lifeline. Emotions settling with the reassurance that contact brought, she had a moment, finally, to think about all that had transpired since that morning. She knew she was fairly sheltered for a vampire. Working for Monsieur Lombard as she did, she had little contact with the outside world, except for finding sustenance, and only marginally more with other vampires. Monsieur did not encourage visitors. Nothing in that sheltered existence had prepared her for the whirlwind her world had become.

She had never before experienced an affinity like the one she felt for Caroline. She wondered if it was because she usually hunted for Monsieur and his taste rather than her own. She had never before intentionally done violence to another being, though it had been easy once Caroline was threatened. She had never known the degree of possessiveness she was feeling nor flown into a rage like she had when they would not let her see Caroline. She looked down at the peaceful face in front of her. Gently, she brushed the strands of dark blonde hair back from Caroline's forehead, a sense of wonderment filling her.

Caroline's eyes fluttered open at her touch. Mireille stared into the blue eyes in front of her as confusion gave way to recognition. Creases appeared along with a sparkle that could only have come from a smile. "Hello," Caroline said softly, her voice cracking as she spoke.

The catch in Caroline's voice drew Mireille's attention away from Caroline's eyes. "Don't talk," she ordered, looking around for some water to give the wizard. She found a pitcher and poured a little into a cup, supporting Caroline's head so that she could drink.

"I'm not an invalid," Caroline teased when Mireille lowered her head to the pillow again, Mireille's hand finding hers again as soon as Caroline was comfortable.

"Maybe not, but the doctor said you had to rest."

"Lifting my head is not work. I am resting," Caroline replied.

"We'll let the doctor be the judge of that," Mireille insisted tartly. She let go of Caroline's hand long enough to pull aside the curtain and call for the doctor she had spoken to earlier. "She's awake."

The doctor came inside the cubicle and smiled at Caroline. "Now, Miss Breaux, how are you feeling?" he asked.

"I'm all right," she replied immediately.

"In that case, move your right arm for me."

Caroline started to lift her arm as the doctor instructed, but the pain had her dropping her hand back to the bed almost immediately.

"That's what I thought," the doctor observed. "I've countered the spell, but your body has to recuperate on its own; a day or two should be enough. You'll need to keep your arm immobilized until then, though. I'll give you a sling. Can I trust you to do this?"

"Yes," Caroline replied. "I want it healed so I can get back to my unit. I'm not going to do anything to slow that down."

The doctor pulled a sling from a drawer of a nearby supply rack and bound Caroline's shoulder. "Pay attention," he told Mireille. "You'll have to do this for her. She won't be able to put it on herself."

Caroline started to protest that Mireille would not be around to help her, but the vampire squeezed her hand. "Show me what to do," she told the doctor. He explained it again and left the two women alone.

"Why did he assume you'd be going with me?" Caroline asked.

"I... Well, I... sort of made a scene when they wouldn't let me see you," Mireille explained, a rosy blush staining her cheeks. "I didn't mean to, but I felt this compulsion to see you. I've never felt anything like it. And when they wouldn't let me back here, I forced my way in."

"So I guess we get to leave here together," Caroline said.

"I guess so," Mireille agreed slowly. "I have to make one stop. I have a job, and I have to go explain what's going on to my employer."

"Will he understand?"

"I think so," Mireille said. "He encouraged me to go to the gathering even though he wouldn't. He says he's too old to meddle in the affairs of wizards. Why don't you come with me?"

"To meet your employer? Won't he think that odd?"

"He's also my friend. And the oldest living vampire in Paris. He'd like to meet you, and you can help me explain all that's happened. He'll certainly have questions I can't answer."

"And you think I'll be able to answer them?" Caroline asked.

"You can at least give him one wizard's perspective on all that's occurred. Say you'll come with me."

"I'll come with you," Caroline agreed. "Let's get my clearance and we'll go now. Is the magic still strong enough for you to go outside?"

"Absolutely," Mireille asked, wondering if that had something to do with the unexplained shifts in her emotions. She would have to ask Monsieur.

MIREILLE rang the bell, not because she expected anyone to answer, but because she wanted to let monsieur Lombard know to avoid the hallway. Even then, she opened the door only enough for Caroline and herself to slip through. It took Caroline's eyes a minute to adjust to the somber interior.

"We have electricity," Mireille said, "but Monsieur says even the artificial light makes him nervous. Candles and firelight are all that he can tolerate."

"It's fine," Caroline said nervously. She could not imagine that Mireille had brought her here with any foul intent, but she could not help but be apprehensive when she thought about meeting the most senior of all vampires. She followed Mireille into a library filled with old books. Caroline could not help herself. She went to the shelves and skimmed the titles. She had no doubt most of them were first editions.

"So, you have brought me a lover of books this time," a voice boomed from the darkness.

"Only to talk," Mireille said swiftly, interposing herself between monsieur Lombard and Caroline. "Caroline is my partner in the alliance."

Monsieur Lombard stepped into the light. Caroline had the impression of great age and great wisdom. Despite the power in his voice, she also saw the fondness in his eyes as he looked at Mireille. Perhaps they would be all right after all. "You have still brought me a lover of books. It's all right, young lady. You may touch."

Reverently, Caroline raised a hand to the leather bindings. "I have never seen so many first editions," she said.

"I have a collection many would envy," monsieur Lombard agreed, "though most would not be willing to pay the price that allowed me to have it."

"I think you're probably right," Caroline replied.

"So tell me about this meeting," monsieur Lombard directed, towering over the two women until he took a seat, gracefully gesturing for the other two to do the same.

Mireille sat on the loveseat and patted the space beside her in invitation. Caroline took the offered seat with a sigh of relief. Mireille was much less intimidating than the other vampire.

Slowly, haltingly, Mireille began to describe the meeting, explaining what Marcel and Jean had said and the process by which the pairings had been made. She smiled at Caroline as she described their meeting.

Monsieur Lombard interrupted at that point. "Caroline approached you?" he clarified.

Mireille nodded.

"Why?" he asked, turning to Caroline.

Caroline squirmed uncomfortably under his penetrating stare. "She looked as nervous as I felt. It seemed like a way to start a conversation, to make the process a little less anonymous."

"And that mattered to you?" the vampire elder asked.

"Of course it did," Caroline replied. "I knew she'd be my partner if it worked. I wanted someone I could work with, and having something in common seemed like a good place to start."

Monsieur Lombard nodded. "Go on," he said. "What happened next?"

Mireille picked back up the threads of the story, telling him about Sebastien's arrival and the discovery that magic did not work between partners.

"Good," Lombard murmured. "I hoped he would come."

"What do you mean?" Mireille asked.

"Sebastien and Jean have been at odds for too long. It is time they made their peace with one another. This alliance needs everyone if it is going to work. I simply made sure Sebastien got the message," he explained. "Now, tell me more about this resistance to magic."

"Right before Sebastien came in, one of the other wizards lost his temper," Caroline explained. "Alain channeled the magic that exploded as a result into the door, thinking it was safe. Right as the magic hit, Sebastien came through the door. It wasn't a spell, just unfocused magic, but it was strong enough that it should have knocked him off his feet at the very least. He just stood there, like nothing had happened. When it became clear that he and Thierry, the other wizard, were paired, we decided to test and see if it was just Sebastien who was immune to magic or if it had something to do with the pairing. A few simple spells revealed that a wizard's magic won't work on his or her counterpart. I could cast spells on Mireille all day and nothing would happen."

"Interesting," Lombard mused. "Go on."

Together, they described the battle with the dark wizards and its aftermath. "When we got back to Marcel's base," Mireille finished, "I went to the infirmary to check on Caroline. I felt as if I had no choice. It's like something was driving me to get to her. I was able to control it at first, but when they wouldn't let me see her, I lost control. I threw a man across the room, Monsieur. I don't act that way. You know I don't, but I had to find Caroline. I tore through the infirmary, looking for her. When I finally found her and touched her hand, all the rage, all the anger was gone, and I was myself again."

"Were any other vampires similarly affected?" Lombard asked, wondering at the cause of Mireille's odd behavior.

"Not that I could tell," Mireille replied, "although I noticed many of them staying very close to their wizard."

"Especially Orlando," Caroline commented. "I don't think he let Alain out of arm's reach almost the entire time."

"Not very often," Mireille agreed.

"That could be the effects of the Aveu de Sang, though," Lombard said. "Did Alain seem like he wanted to get away?"

"Not at all," Caroline chuckled. "He was constantly looking around to make sure Orlando was there. I've never seen him like that before."

"What about you?" he asked. "How did you feel when you and Mireille were apart?"

"I was in so much pain from the spell that hit me that all I wanted was to get to the infirmary. Once I got there, they had me unconscious. I woke with Mireille's hand in mine. There wasn't time to react to her absence," Caroline replied, not seeing the surprised look on Mireille's face. The vampire had known her partner was injured, but she had not realized until much later how seriously. She would have to have a word with Caroline about being more frank about her physical state.

"Interesting," Christophe said.

"You keep saying that," Mireille blurted out. "What does it all mean?"

"I don't know. I need more information. I need to talk to Jean."

ERIC SIMONET and Vincent Jonnet came slowly out of the subway, looking around the train station carefully. They had debated how to get here after Serrier ordered them to find out what was keeping Robert and the others. If foul play was involved and any of Chavinier's wizards still lingered, arriving magically would open them to instant attack. They had decided to take the subway despite the greater time involved. It would be worth it to arrive unnoticed.

The signs of battle were immediately obvious. "Chavinier's been here," Vincent said.

"So I see. Let's see if anyone can tell us what happened," Eric replied. He moved deeper into the station, searching for survivors or witnesses. A moan drew his attention. He turned and saw Dominique lying on the ground near a pillar. He rushed to the wizard's side. "Wake up, Dominique," he urged. "Come on. Wake up."

The young man's eyes flickered open slowly. "What happened?" he asked Eric.

"I was going to ask you the same thing."

Dominique closed his eyes in concentration. "I... We were watching the room," he said slowly, as if trying to remember. "We couldn't hear anything so Robert crept closer. I remember hearing a shout and then the fighting started. I guess I got hit because the next thing I remember is waking up."

Eric frowned. Dominique was relatively new, but the rest of the contingent were experienced fighters. Chavinier had not just stumbled upon them by accident. He must have brought an overwhelming number of wizards to have taken out all the others. "Let's get you back," Eric said. "Pascal will want to talk to you."

"I don't know anything else," Dominique said. "I told you all I remember." He really did not want to face Serrier if he could get out of it.

"I'm sure you did, but Pascal will want to hear it himself. He might have questions you can answer. Tell the truth and you'll be fine," Eric said soothingly.

That was what Dominique was worried about. Spying had seemed like a good idea when surrounded by Marcel and his allies, but now, faced with the prospect of explaining himself to Serrier, and deceiving him in the process, Dominique wondered at the wisdom of his choice. Eric was not bad as far as Serrier's minions went, but Eric would not be the one extracting information from him if Serrier decided he was lying. Escaping from the dark wizards had sounded so possible when faced with Marcel's kindness, but with Eric and Vincent staring at him suspiciously, Dominique began to have doubts. Then he remembered the vampire's threats. Blanchet could torture him; Serrier could kill him; Bellaiche, though, could condemn him to living death. He would take his chances with Serrier.

Eric looked at Vincent. "Take Dominique back. Let one of the medics check him over. Chavinier's wizards don't usually use dangerous spells, but you never know. I'll meet you there in a bit."

"What are you going to do?" Vincent asked.

"Look around a little more, see what a few seeking spells can tell me," Eric replied.

Dominique felt the panic rising again. If Eric searched very hard, he would surely find evidence of Marcel's spells in the waiting room. He forced himself to relax. He would claim ignorance. He was unconscious. He had no idea what Chavinier did with the others. Perhaps they had used that room as a holding area if they took prisoners or an infirmary if they had wounded.

"Do you see my wand?" Dominique asked. "It was a gift, and I'd really hate to lose it."

"I'll keep an eye out for it," Eric promised, "although Chavinier's people usually do a pretty thorough job of cleaning up after themselves. I have no idea how they missed you."

"Me either," Dominique lied, "but I'm not complaining. I don't want to go to jail."

"If that's what they really do," Vincent growled. "I've heard stories about wizards having spells cast on them and…"

"That's a load of bullshit and you know it, Vincent," Eric interrupted. "I don't like the guy and I don't agree with his politics, but he's not one to engage in torture."

"Things could have changed in two years," Vincent defended himself.

"Not that much," Eric said, shaking his head. "Take Dominique to the infirmary. I'll meet you there." Without another word, he stalked off, beginning a series of complicated seeking spells.

"Let's go, pup," Vincent said, cuffing Dominique's shoulder. "Eric wants you checked out."

"I feel fine," Dominique protested.

"Uh huh. That's what they all say. I'll believe it when I hear it from a medic. Let's get out of here. This place makes me nervous. What if Chavinier comes back?"

Dominique shivered involuntarily as Vincent cast the spell. He arrived right outside Serrier's lair. He had offered Marcel the location, and while the wizard had accepted the information, he had also warned Dominique not to expect an attack any time soon, explaining they did not have the numbers for a straight assault. The casualties would be too high. They preferred to weaken Serrier little by little until they could take him out completely.

Almost immediately, Vincent appeared beside him. He followed the older man inside and straight to the infirmary. Vincent told the medic what had happened. The medic ordered Dominique up on a table so he could examine him.

The medic's spell wrapped around Dominique, revealing Marcel's spell immediately. Dominique held his breath, hoping the earlier spells, Alain's that had taken him down and Marcel's that had bound him, would not be visible. He let out a sigh of relief when the medic found nothing else. "It's a standard incapacitation spell," the medic informed Dominique and Vincent. "It leaves you unconscious for an hour or two, and then wears off. There are rarely any side effects, and I didn't detect any. You may be a little tired for the rest of the day, but you'll be fit for duty tomorrow."

"Thanks, doc," Vincent said. "We'll just wait for…"

"No need," Eric interrupted, walking into the infirmary. "I'm back. Is he clear?" he asked the medic.

"He should rest today, but he can go back on duty tomorrow."

Eric nodded. "Let's go tell Pascal what we found."

Dominique could not quite decide if he was a prisoner or not as Eric and Vincent escorted him to Serrier, one on each side of him. They did not touch him or in any way restrain him, but their hulking presence made sure he did not balk either. Just before they entered the room where Serrier waited, Eric stopped and pulled Dominique's wand from his pocket. "Here," he said softly. "I thought you might want this back."

Dominique looked at him in surprise and some bit of reverence as he pocketed the magical memento. "Thank you."

"Well?" Pascal demanded from inside, drawing their attention back to their mission.

"We found young Dominique here, unconscious at the train station. The others were long gone, though to where, I don't know," Eric reported.

"Well, boy, what happened?" Pascal demanded.

Dominique stuttered out the same story he had told Eric.

"So you have no idea why the vampires met?" Pascal asked.

"No, sir. Robert went to try to listen in right before the attack occurred. Maybe he heard something, but he didn't make it back to us to share if he did," Dominique replied.

"How many vampires would you guess there were?"

"I didn't count, but at least two hundred," Dominique replied.

"Two hundred," Pascal echoed. "I didn't know there were that many vampires in Paris. Did you see any of the attackers before you lost consciousness?"

"There was an older man, short white hair. He seemed to be giving orders."

"Chavinier," Eric interrupted.

"Probably," Pascal agreed. "Anyone else?"

"Um, I think a saw a tall, blond wizard, but I didn't get a good look at him. He was fighting with a young guy, curly brown hair," Dominique added.

Eric frowned. "It could be Magnier or Dumont," he said, "but I can't be sure. I detected Chavinier's magic, and Rougier's, but I couldn't identify any of the other markers. They were too mixed up."

"What about the other one, the one with curly hair?"

Eric concentrated, trying to remember any wizard from Chavinier's camp that fit Dominique's description. "I don't know," he said finally. "It doesn't sound at all familiar. Could he be recruiting wizards from further afield?"

"It certainly seems possible," Pascal said. "There's also the question of how he found out about our little mission. If he took out nineteen wizards, he didn't just stumble across them by mistake."

"I thought the same thing," Eric replied coolly. "I have no idea how he found out, but it certainly didn't feel like an accident. There was too much magic for it to have been coincidence. What time did the attack start, Dominique?"

"About six, I think," Dominique said. "Robert went closer because he was surprised the vampires hadn't come out yet. It was getting close to sunrise."

"Chavinier might have set alarms in the station," Eric suggested. "He's done that before. Something Robert or the others did could have triggered the alarm and he showed up to attack. His magic was all over the place. Some of that could have been wards. If Robert and the others were there for two hours, Chavinier had plenty of time to plan an attack."

Pascal considered Eric's thought. "Possible, I suppose. What do you think, Vincent?"

"It seems a little too neat for me," Vincent said, "but then, Chavinier's always had the devil's own luck."

"Too true," Pascal sighed. He turned to Dominique. "Have you been to the infirmary yet?"

"Yes, I went there first," Dominique replied. "The medic said to rest today, but that I could go back to duty tomorrow."

"Good. Get some rest and report here in the morning. I'll have your new assignment."

Dominique thanked Serrier and left, relieved to have survived unscathed.

When the young wizard was gone, Pascal turned to the other two. "Nineteen experienced fighters captured or killed and one inexperienced boy escapes. Does it seem a little odd?"

"The way he was lying behind the pillar, he wouldn't have been easily visible," Vincent said. "We didn't see him until he started moaning."

"I found his wand," Eric added. "It wasn't anywhere near him, so even if they did find it, they might not have found him. I checked, and he hadn't done any spells with it at the station, so they wouldn't have been looking for him. It's odd, but not implausible."

Pascal shrugged. "If he's lying, I'll find out about it soon enough. Right now, though, I want to know why the vampires met. Maybe it was nothing, but I still want to know what could bring out two hundred of them and keep them talking until close to dawn. Gentlemen, I think we need to find a vampire."

Vincent's grin was almost as evil as Pascal's.

"Just to talk," Pascal added. "We'll decide what else to do after that."

Chapter 5

THIERRY rose from his seat. The meeting had been long, a lot longer than Marcel's meetings usually were, but it had been productive. Much to Thierry's surprise and eventual delight, Jean had returned to the room after leaving abruptly with Raymond to declare that, for the good of the individual partnerships, he thought only unpaired vampires should actually bite any captured dark wizards. Several other wizards had seconded that suggestion so Marcel had accepted it, much to Thierry's relief. He had not looked forward to seeing Sebastien bite someone else, even though he knew he had no claim on the vampire's attention. His was not a logical reaction, but it was there anyway.

"It won't hurt them to stew a little longer," Marcel decided. "Jean, can you find a vampire for us tonight?"

Jean nodded. "I already have somebody in mind. I'll contact him and have him meet us here tonight after sundown."

They had talked a while longer, making plans, discussing options, but Marcel could see exhaustion creeping over them after another sleepless night. That was the price, apparently, of consorting with vampires. Marcel had finally dismissed them, telling them to get some rest and to be back at nightfall.

Thierry met Sebastien's eyes awkwardly. He had no doubt that Alain and Orlando would go home together, and he was not sure how much rest they would get, but he was not ready, did not know if he would ever be ready, to extend the same invitation to Sebastien. "I'll see you tonight then," Thierry said, trying to figure out how to make this less awkward.

"Yeah, tonight," Sebastien replied, turning to leave.

Thierry wanted to call after him, to tell him to wait, but he was not ready to take that step. He made himself turn and look for Alain. His friend was talking with Marcel, Orlando all but glued to his side. Thierry joined them as Marcel said goodbye.

"I was going to get some lunch. Are you hungry?" Thierry asked Alain.

"Lunch sounds great," Alain replied. "Maybe that little café down the street. They usually have a good menu at lunch."

Listening to the two wizards, Orlando decided to give them a little time alone. He had been monopolizing Alain's attention, and he imagined Thierry would like a chance to talk to Alain. "I'll just go see Jean," he said.

"You don't have to go," Thierry insisted.

"I know that," Orlando replied, "but I really do need to talk to Jean. I'll meet you back at the apartment, Alain. Can you let yourself in without a key if you get there first? I only have one."

"Not a problem," Alain assured him, pulling Orlando to him for a light kiss. "I'll see you at home. Enjoy your talk with Jean."

"I will. Have a good lunch."

The two wizards watched Orlando cross the room to Jean and speak to him softly. Jean nodded. Orlando turned back and waved goodbye to the wizards. "He is pretty amazing," Thierry murmured.

Alain chuckled. "He is indeed. Come on, let's get some food. Then you can tell me what's on your mind."

"How do you know I have something on my mind?"

"I can tell," Alain replied. "After thirty years, I'd better be able to tell."

They left Marcel's base and made their way down the street to the café. The owner was happy to give them a table in the back, far away from the other patrons who were watching the world go by through the plate-glass windows. People-watching was every Parisian's favorite pastime.

They ordered quickly and waited while the waiter brought their wine. Once he left them in peace, Alain looked at Thierry expectantly.

"What do you feel when Orlando bites you?" Thierry said, finally breaking the silence.

"His fangs," Alain replied facetiously.

"Imbécile! That's not what I meant," Thierry protested.

"I know," Alain teased, "but it was too good to pass up." He paused for a minute to consider the question more seriously. "I feel connected to him," Alain began, "like I'm giving myself to him. In a way, I suppose I am since he can read my heart when he feeds."

"Does that bother you?" Thierry asked.

"That he can read my heart or that I feel connected to him?" Alain replied.

"Either. Both." It made Thierry more than a little uncomfortable that Alain had so quickly identified the source of his unease so quickly.

"No," Alain said after a moment's consideration. "I was attracted to him from the moment I laid eyes on him. I was nervous the first time he bit me, but only because I'd heard stories. Marcel set me straight, pointing out that if they could control people by biting them, they wouldn't be in the position they're in. I want the connection. I want the intimacy. I want everything Orlando will give me and probably more."

"More?" Thierry asked.

"He's 251 years old, Thierry, and he's never had a lover. He was abused when he first became a vampire and he's avoided intimate contact since then."

"But I thought…," Thierry trailed off.

"That we were lovers?" Alain asked. "We are," he replied when Thierry nodded, "but very much on his terms. I take what he gives me and give what he will accept."

"And that mark on your neck?"

"Came from what we were, or at least what I was, already feeling. I wouldn't have done anything differently had the mark not been there. It's a sign of what I feel for him. Nothing more."

"The other vampires seemed to think it was more," Thierry pointed out.

"I caught that, and maybe when it comes to magic, it is more, but I would still have stayed with him last night and the night before. I would still have given myself to him. I would still have let him feed. Not that I mind telling you, but why are you asking?"

"I felt… something when Sebastien bit me. I don't quite know how to describe it or what it means. I can't do this, Alain. I just lost Aleth!" Thierry's torment was clear in his voice. Alain knew exactly how he felt. The fact that he and Edwige were divorced had not softened the blow when she was killed. The estrangement with Aleth changed nothing for Thierry either.

"I know, and it feels terribly disloyal to have a connection to anyone now that she's gone," Alain agreed. He remembered how he had felt after Edwige and Henri died. He had hated himself and everyone else. It had taken him weeks to forgive himself and months before he could look at anyone with interest. "I do know how you feel. I also know that life goes on, whether you want it to or not. Denying yourself won't bring Aleth back, and doing what it takes to make the alliance work isn't betraying her memory."

"It's not the alliance," Thierry said. "It's wanting more. I can't. Not yet." Alain understood, but he could not help hoping that Thierry would eventually reach the point of accepting more, whether from Sebastien or from someone else. His best friend deserved to be happy again, but Alain was afraid seeing his own happiness with Orlando only made Thierry more aware of what he had lost.

"Did Sebastien pressure you for more?"

"No! If anything, he seemed concerned about not pressing me. He asked about Aleth. He said he could taste my grief."

"And when you told him about her?" Alain prompted.

"He said how sorry he was and that he knew how hard it was to lose a loved one," Thierry replied.

"Then what's the problem?" Alain asked. "He's not asking for more than you're willing to give."

"He's not," Thierry agreed, "but my heart is."

ALAIN'S lips left Orlando's. "I'll see you at home. Enjoy your talk with Jean."

"I will. Have a good lunch."

Home. It was such a wonderful word when it fell from Alain's lips. It warmed Orlando's heart to know that Alain was referring not to his own apartment but to Orlando's when he said it. It was the first time they had been apart since they made their Aveu de Sang, and while Orlando would miss his wizard's presence at his side, he knew Alain and Thierry needed time to talk. Thierry had offered to let Orlando go with them, and Orlando was sure the offer was sincere, but he also knew that Thierry would be much more likely to talk to Alain without Orlando's constraining presence. They were on better terms than before, but they could hardly be called friends yet. They would get there, but from the bemused look on Thierry's face, he needed a friend now. That meant Alain. Besides, Orlando really did want to talk to Jean. He had some questions for his big brother.

"Let's take advantage of the magic and go for a walk," Orlando suggested, reaching Jean's side.

Jean looked at him, surprised.

"I want to talk to you," he added when Jean did not immediately reply.

"All right," Jean agreed. "Where do you want to walk?"

"The Buttes Chaumont are just a few blocks down," Orlando suggested, thinking of the old trees and quiet pathways that ran through the park. In October, it would not be very crowded and he and Jean would be able to talk in peace. "We can walk there. I've never seen them in the daylight."

"Nor have I," Jean replied. When he was made, Paris barely extended beyond the Ile de la Cité and the Ile St-Louis. The Buttes Chaumont were practically wilderness at the time. "It's as good a place as any."

"And better than most. Let's go."

"Just a second," Jean said, conscious of his new pledge to treat Raymond as an equal. "Let me tell Raymond I'm leaving."

Orlando waited while Jean got Raymond's attention. "I'm going to check in with Orlando. I'll see you tonight, all right?"

"That's fine. Have a good afternoon," Raymond replied with a smile, pleased that Jean was keeping his promise.

"You, too," Jean said, heading back to Orlando, amazed still at the change their argument had wrought in their relationship. "Okay, now we can go."

The two vampires left Milice headquarters and headed down the street in the direction of the park. The day was clear and sunny but cool as they passed through the quiet streets. Eventually, they reached the major boulevards. More than one passerby stopped to look at the two handsome men, but no one approached them. "They don't even realize," Orlando murmured. "To them, we're as normal as they are."

"Just one more reason to be grateful for this alliance," Jean replied. "For a time, at least, we can live almost like normal men."

They fell silent again until they reached the park. Walking down into the man-made grotto, Orlando finally worked up the nerve to ask, "What is there between you and Sebastien? I've never known you to react this way to another vampire."

"It's nothing," Jean said.

"Then why are you acting the way you are?" Orlando pushed.

"Leave it," Jean ordered.

"No. Tell me what happened."

"Fine," Jean spat. "He stole the one I loved, and bound him with an Aveu de Sang before I ever had a chance to protest."

"When?" Orlando asked, shocked at Jean's revelation. This was the first he had heard of the matter, and he had thought that he knew Jean fairly well.

"Centuries ago, before you were ever made, but it doesn't matter. Sebastien betrayed me, and that's something I will not forgive."

"He's not going away," Orlando pointed out. "He's Thierry's partner, and that means he'll be involved in most everything we do."

"I'll tolerate him," Jean said. "I'll even work with him, but I don't have to be nice to him, and I certainly don't have to like him."

Orlando paused in front of the lake and sat down on one of the benches. Jean joined him after a moment. "Enough about Sebastien; how are you?" Jean asked.

"I'm well," Orlando said.

"Truly?" Jean pressed. He had known Orlando for over a century, and in all that time, he had never seen the other vampire take a lover. He could not help but wonder why it had happened so quickly. "He didn't pressure you?"

"He has been the perfect picture of patience," Orlando assured Jean, smiling as he remembered all that had occurred between Alain and him since they bound themselves to one another. "I've never felt so safe, except with you."

Jean smiled. "I'm glad. You deserve to be happy."

"I am happy," Orlando said slowly. "Alain makes me happy."

"Good. I can see a difference already."

"A difference?"

"A week ago, you would never have spoken out the way you have these past two days. You would never have participated in something like the interrogation. You would've hung back, convinced that no one would listen to you," Jean explained, thinking about the timid young vampire he had rescued. He had been trying all that time to restore some self-confidence in Orlando, without success. Alain had done in two days what Jean had failed to do in a hundred years.

"That's just it," Orlando said. "I know he'll listen to me. I don't have to worry what his reaction will be. He might not agree with me, but he'll listen. He'll consider my point of view. No one else but you has ever done that."

"And the rest?" Jean asked.

"He stayed at my side until we left Milice headquarters."

"And that didn't bother you?"

"Bother me? It would have bothered me if he left. Do you know what he said to me before we separated just now?"

Jean shook his head.

"He said he'd see me at home. I asked him if he could let himself into my apartment, and he said yes and that he'd see me at home. Not at my apartment, Jean. At home."

Jean stared at Orlando, stupefied. He had known that Orlando was taken with Alain. He had known it since he saw them together in the cemetery two nights ago, but he had not realized quite how taken Alain was with Orlando. "He's moving in with you?" Jean's voice was incredulous. If asked, he would have guessed that Alain would expect Orlando to move in with him.

"Yes. He said my place is bigger than his and that his apartment doesn't have a room with no windows. He's not pretending I'm something I'm not, yet he sees me as so much more than just a vampire, Jean. From the moment I was turned, everyone outside our kind has looked down on me for what I am and everyone inside our community has looked down on me for not being strong enough to escape on my own. Alain doesn't look down on me at all. He doesn't see a worthless vampire. He sees me."

Jean raised his hands in surrender. "You've convinced me. Does he know what happened to you?"

"Some of it," Orlando said. "The worst of it. He knows the bastard raped me repeatedly and held me prisoner. And he knows that I ended the salaud's existence." Orlando's words were cold with the anger that still dwelled within him. For over a hundred years, he had lived at his maker's mercy, but even escaping and destroying the bastard had not freed Orlando from the prison the other vampire had created. Orlando knew his limitations, knew how his past kept him from experiencing all the pleasure to be found in the bedroom. And now he had a new fear to lay at his maker's feet: the fear of Alain's reaction to his continuing hesitation. So far Alain had been patient, but Orlando could not help wondering if Alain would some day get tired of abiding by Orlando's limitations. He could not lose Alain. It would kill him.

"And he was careful with you?" Jean asked, still concerned that Orlando had been pushed into a more intimate relationship than he was ready to deal with.

"No, I was careful with him. He gave me complete control, accepting the limits I set. He didn't even try to take anything I wasn't willing to give. Do you know how incredible that felt? I can trust him, Jean. Even at the height of passion, he didn't try to trespass where I had asked him not to."

"It looks like you chose well," Jean said, finally understanding that Alain really had done what was best for Orlando.

"I chose very well," Orlando amended.

"Then trust yourself also," Jean insisted.

"What do you mean?"

"You said you could trust him not to cross your boundaries. Trust yourself not to cross them either. What did he feel when you fed from him?"

"That's personal," Orlando replied, blushing as he remembered the climaxes his feeding had provoked.

"All right then. Consider this. Consider how intimate feeding was and how intimate making love was. Now imagine how much more powerful they both would be if you put them together."

"I'd be afraid to lose control," Orlando admitted. "I can't hurt him, Jean. I won't drive him away!"

"That's right," Jean said. "You won't. You'll only bring him closer."

"But what if I hurt him?" Orlando worried. He knew all too well the pain a vampire's fangs could inflict during sex. His maker had reveled in biting him as he raped him.

"Have you ever tasted fear in his blood?" Jean asked.

"Only once," Orlando replied. "When Raymond first arrived and cast a spell at me."

"And what was your reaction?" Jean pressed.

"I stopped." Orlando did not say it, but Jean heard the rest of that sentence. *What else would I have done?* Orlando's tone asked.

"Then why would it be any different if you tasted fear again, or pain? His fear stopped you once. If you hurt him accidentally, his fear will stop you again," Jean said. "You are not Thurloe. He cared about nothing of what you felt, only of his own pleasure. You would never treat anyone with such disregard, especially not your Avoué."

"Don't say that name," Orlando ground out. "He doesn't deserve to be called by name."

"No, he doesn't," Jean agreed, "but my point remains the same. You are a different vampire. You will cherish Alain the way you want to be cherished and he will treat you the same way. Don't hold back. Don't limit your relationship with imaginary fears."

"I don't know," Orlando said, still hesitant.

"There's no rush," Jean assured him. "You don't have to go home and try to experience everything before we meet back up tonight. I just don't want you to reject an experience if it comes up. Talk to Alain. See what he wants, too. If he wants to keep the two separate, then that's fine, but don't make that decision for both of you. Let him help you make it."

Orlando nodded. "I'll think about it."

"That's all I ask," Jean said. He smiled at Orlando who was getting increasingly twitchy beside him. "Are you ready to go? You look eager to be home."

"I am," admitted Orlando. "I need to see him again, touch him again, just to remind myself that it's real."

"Look around you," Jean said, gesturing to the sunlit trees and the tumbling waterfall. "It's real."

"Thanks, Jean," he said, leaning over to kiss the older vampire's cheek impulsively. "Thanks for everything."

"You're welcome," Jean said to Orlando's retreating back, amusement coloring his voice. He looked around the park and wondered how he should spend the rest of his day.

Chapter 6

ORLANDO considered walking home from the Buttes Chaumont since the park was on the same side of town as his apartment. Two days ago, he would have been returning to an empty apartment, and so he would have walked, simply to delay the isolation. He did not know how long it would take Alain to eat and talk with Thierry. He knew it was possible that he would arrive before Alain, but the thought of his lover waiting for him was enough to drive Orlando out of the sunlight and into the subway. Regardless of which one of them arrived first, the apartment no longer signified isolation in Orlando's mind. Alain and memories of him were already a part of that space now, and even in the wizard's absence, it would not be empty as long as Alain lived. If Orlando did arrive first, he would not be alone for long. His heart pounded ever harder in his chest as he thought about being with Alain again.

The quick ride, the change, and the remaining couple of stops passed in a haze of growing desire as Orlando imagined various ways he and Alain might spend what remained of their time off. They all involved the two of them naked and in bed. He almost missed his stop, so lost was he in anticipation. He jumped off the train right as the doors closed and headed home, walking down familiar streets. Familiar beneath the moon, anyway. He did not know if would ever get used to seeing them in the daytime. He took the stairs two at a time, eagerness to be with Alain speeding his steps.

Images of Alain lying naked in their bed, body writhing as Orlando made love to him, swirled in his brain and made his hands fumble as he tried to insert the key in the lock. He only had to turn it once, a sure sign that Alain had already come home. "Alain?" Orlando called as he walked in.

"In here," Alain's voice replied from the kitchen.

Surprised that Alain would be in what Orlando had always considered the least comfortable room in the apartment, the vampire walked into the tiny room to see his lover putting away the contents of several bags. "I hope you don't mind," Alain said, "but you didn't have anything, and I'd rather not always eat out."

Orlando took the package out of Alain's hands without even looking to see what it was and cradled Alain's cheeks with his palms, kissing the wizard. The kiss started slowly, belying Orlando's newfound confidence. Alain's hips rested against the counter, his arms drawing Orlando to lean against him. The increased contact of their bodies and Alain's obvious willingness bolstered Orlando's self-assurance and he deepened the kiss, his tongue flicking out to tease the seam of Alain's lips. They parted eagerly, inviting Orlando inside. He accepted the invitation, pouring all his delight and desire into the touching of their lips. Alain relaxed into Orlando's hold and gave the vampire control of his mouth, enjoying the increasing power of their kiss. Orlando's tongue surged between Alain's lips, making love to his mouth. It made Alain hope that more than their mouths would soon be engaged.

When breathing became necessary again, their lips separated, but their foreheads remained pressed together. "What brought that on?" Alain asked.

Orlando struggled to find the words to describe what he had felt upon seeing Alain making himself at home. He gestured to the bags on the counter. "What do you see when you look around?" he asked.

"My groceries," Alain replied, not sure what Orlando expected him to say. He saw nothing special in what he had done.

"Exactly," Orlando replied as if Alain had stated something incredibly profound. "Your groceries. You bought groceries and brought them here." It was such an ordinary gesture, an everyday act, and yet, in Orlando's world, it was extraordinary. "You didn't think twice about doing it."

"Why would I?" Alain asked, still not understanding why such a simple errand had such an effect on Orlando. "We already talked about me living here. If I'm going to be here, I need some basics."

"That's just it," Orlando said. "You've started moving in, without any fuss or drama. Do you have any idea how good that makes me feel?"

A radiant smile beamed from Alain's face as he rested his hands on Orlando's hips. "No, I don't. Tell me how it makes you feel," he requested, appreciating Orlando's joy in the development of their relationship. It was a reminder to him that each step along their journey would be new to Orlando and thus should be given the appropriate significance.

"It's so simple for you," Orlando struggled to explain. "Or maybe simple isn't the right word, but it's natural to you. You're going to be living here, you need stuff, you bring it here. To you, that's the normal progression of events. I haven't had anything even approaching normality for over two hundred years. Every time you treat me like I'm normal, you give me a gift."

"If treating you decently is a gift, then it's one I'll gladly give you for the rest of my life," Alain vowed earnestly. He had taken his welcome in Orlando's apartment for granted, though he would never take Orlando for granted. Seeing the happiness his unconscious gesture brought his lover, Alain would make an effort to do the little things that were an everyday part of life as a couple. If this was Orlando's reaction to a simple gesture, Alain could not help but wonder how he would react to a grander one. "I hope you'll occasionally accept other gifts as well, ones that are as special as you are."

"Maybe," Orlando said, not sure how to react. It had been centuries since anyone had offered him a gift. The last time, it had been his maker, tempting an innocent boy away from the safety of his regiment with the ring that was supposed to symbolize a life of ease.

Alain smiled and brought Orlando's hands to the buttons on his shirt. "Why don't you unwrap this gift?" he asked with a grin.

Orlando grinned back. This was more familiar ground than the awe that had come when he realized Alain had brought groceries. It was still new and exciting, but at least Orlando knew what to do in this situation. His fingers set to work on the buttons. "Definitely," he said in answer to Alain's question. He made swift work of Alain's shirt, opening it all the way and pulling it from the waistband of his pants. He ran his hands over the solid planes of his lover's chest. Alain was a man in his prime, and Orlando had every intention of appreciating him.

Alain's hands went automatically to the hem of Orlando's shirt to free it from his pants. The shiver that went through Orlando could well have been desire, but it was enough to remind Alain of his lover's terrible past and the fear that haunted him still. Alain's hands froze, wondering if he had found an invisible scar. "Tell me what the limits are," he said softly, "so I don't cross them accidentally."

Orlando's heart melted hearing those words. He had told Jean that Alain had not pressured him, and it was the truth, but having it happen again, having Alain not only respect his limits but have enough respect for him to ask for them, proved to Orlando once again how truly lucky he was to have Alain as a lover. There was no impatience in Alain's words, only concern, and it touched Orlando profoundly. "Above my waist," he said, "and don't bite me."

"Can I kiss you?" Alain asked, threading his fingers through Orlando's belt loops. "Can I taste you?"

"No teeth," Orlando specified. His maker had tortured him that way too many times, using his fangs to rend Orlando's flesh as a prelude to rape. It was one of the nightmares that haunted him when he slid into what passed for sleep among the vampires. Though he knew that Alain's teeth could not do the same damage, he feared feeling them on his skin, lest the nightmares overwhelm him and force him to retreat from what little intimacy he dared to allow. Having set that caress out of bounds, he was confident that Alain would not trespass.

"No teeth," Alain promised, realizing he had just found one of those invisible scars. "Shall we move this some place more comfortable?"

"What?" Orlando teased, pressing his hips against the wizard's. "You don't want me to take you against the countertop?"

"I'd much rather you take me in bed," Alain said, "so we'll be comfortable enough to make love. You can have me in here some other time."

"Promise?"

"Absolutely."

Orlando's nerves tingled at the thought. He imagined how it would feel to turn Alain in his arms, to push their pants down around their ankles, and push into his lover with all his strength. It would be so easy, so enjoyable, so erotic. He was tempted to press, but it was not what Alain wanted. As patient as Alain was being with him, it seemed fitting to accede to his wishes in this one respect. They would do this right, with all the tenderness and care that had grown between them, the passion and power that bound them. He took Alain's hand and led him across the little hall into the bedroom.

Orlando wondered if he would ever get less nervous about making love with Alain. He had spent half his existence at the hands of a monster and the other half alone. He had no idea what it really meant to be part of a couple. He was beginning to trust that he would not hurt Alain, but Orlando still did not know if he was giving or receiving appropriately. The nerves were not such a bad thing, he decided. They reminded him how precious a gift Alain was giving him by allowing their intimacy, and he never wanted to take that for granted.

When they reached the edge of the bed, Alain drew Orlando into his arms. "Relax," he urged, sensing Orlando's unease. "Nothing you don't want," he reminded Orlando. "Whatever you do will please me."

Orlando knew what he wanted to do first. He seized Alain's lips with his own, kissing his lover with all the desire that had been growing since he had left Jean in the park. His hands slid beneath Alain's shirt, pushing it off the wizard's shoulders, leaving him bare to the waist. He latched immediately onto one hardened nipple, shivers running through him at the thought that Alain was already aroused from their two kisses and their conversation. He ran his tongue over the taut peak, savoring the scent and flavor of Alain's skin.

Alain threaded his fingers into Orlando's hair, cradling his head, encouraging the kiss, hoping Orlando would do more. He did not ask, though. He would let their relationship develop at its own speed. He sucked in a sharp breath when Orlando pulled hard on his nipple with his lips. No teeth, Alain noted. He would have to ask, at some point, why Orlando feared using his teeth except to feed. That could wait, though. For the moment, Alain was more interested in divesting Orlando of his shirt so he could start seducing his lover within the boundaries Orlando had set. He urged Orlando to raise his head so he could kiss the vampire again. When their lips engaged, he reached for the buttons on Orlando's shirt, freeing them from their holes one at a time. Orlando's hands settled at his waist, the mirror image of their pose in the kitchen. As the sides of Orlando's shirt separated, Alain caressed the revealed skin, light touches intended to enflame his lover's senses with their absence as much as their presence.

Orlando's eyes drifted shut as Alain stroked his flesh. His lover touched him like he was a gift beyond measure. When they had made love the last time, Orlando had been nervous about accepting Alain's caresses. He had tensed every time the wizard's hands had neared his waist, ready to stop Alain if he crossed the line. As much as he had enjoyed the caresses, a part of him had been waiting for Alain to trespass. This time, he had no such fear. He could relax and enjoy his lover's careful, devoted ministrations. And so he left his hands idly at Alain's waist and reveled in the sense of freedom he felt as the wizard unbuttoned his shirt and touched his skin. The nerves remained, even now, but his burgeoning confidence allowed him to ignore them, to subsume them in the pleasure of Alain's touch.

Alain sensed the difference, though he could not have said what caused it. The reason did not matter. It was enough that Orlando seemed accepting of his touch instead of hesitant. He bent his head and kissed Orlando again, then let his lips wander over the vampire's face. They trailed across the wide forehead, along the arched eyebrows and down over Orlando's nose. "Beautiful," Alain whispered. "My angel."

Orlando pulled away. "I'm no angel," he said.

"You are to me," Alain insisted. "You've brought light back into my life."

Orlando shook his head. "I'm a creature of darkness. How could I possibly bring you light?"

"You might live in the darkness," Alain said, kissing Orlando tenderly, "but you are not a dark creature. If you were, my magic would do nothing for you."

Orlando laid his head on Alain's shoulder for a moment. "I still don't know how it could be possible, but if you say it, then I'll believe you. You've brought me light as well."

Alain nodded toward the bed. "Show me. Share with me the beauty we create together."

That plea, that request, was all it took. Orlando bore Alain down to the bed, coming up over his lover, letting their bare chests rub together as he sought Alain's mouth.

Alain relaxed onto the bed, his arms encircling Orlando's shoulders, holding his lover gently in encouragement, not restraint. He wanted to whisper words of love in Orlando's ear, to explain in no uncertain terms exactly what Orlando had restored. He did not think the vampire was ready for such declarations, though, not if his reaction to the one Alain had just made was any indication. The time would come. He just had to keep telling himself that. The time would come when he would offer Orlando his heart, sure in the reception he would get from his beautiful lover. Until then, he would show Orlando the depths of his feelings in every way he could devise.

Orlando's lips sliding down his neck distracted Alain from his thoughts. *Bite me*, his heart begged. He arched his neck, baring the tender flesh that bore Orlando's mark to his lover's fangs. Orlando's lips lingered, his tongue teasing the brand that signified their promise, but his fangs remained safely out of the way. He hungered, but not for blood. He hungered for intimacy, for the joining of Alain's body and his, for the rest of what their bond implied. His hands roamed lower, reaching the waistband of Alain's pants. The thought of that fabric, of anything, separating them was unacceptable. He tugged at the belt, undoing the buckle and the button, sliding down the zipper, urging Alain's hips up so he could pull the wizard's pants and boxers down and off. His hands and lips flew over Alain's skin, rediscovering, relearning what was already familiar, well-loved territory. It would have been so easy, as he traced the back of Alain's knee, the inside of his thigh, to sink his fangs in deep and taste his lover. He could understand the appeal, but caution held him back. Another time.

Naked on the bed, desire pulsing through him, Alain itched to reach for what remained of Orlando's clothes, to bare his lover to his gaze as he was bared to Orlando's. The jeans the vampire wore, though, rode low on his hips, and even if the button was not that far below Orlando's waist, the zipper would be by the time it was lowered, and pulling them off would definitely require Alain's hands in places that were outside the limits Orlando had set. Orlando would have to take his own pants off.

Orlando could not figure out why Alain did not undress him. Finally, tired of waiting, he pulled his own clothes off, leaving them both unclad. Alain reached for him immediately, aligning their bodies, pressing against Orlando eagerly. His lips went to Orlando's chest, tongue flicking out to taste the vampire's honeyed skin. He licked and sucked on the patch of skin right below Orlando's collarbone.

Orlando tensed when he first felt Alain's mouth on his skin. It was a reflexive reaction, learned from years of that sensation leading to bites which led to violation. He relaxed consciously. His maker was destroyed and it was Alain in his bed, gentle, caring Alain who respected him, who had bound himself to a vampire, to Orlando, for life, who would not trespass, who would not hurt him. The lips that teased his skin slid lower, languorously making their way toward his nipple. Orlando's breath hissed out between his teeth when they closed over his hard bud of flesh. The touch itself sent sparks down his spine, but the tenderness, the care that Alain took not to let his teeth touch, even when he sucked Orlando's flesh into this mouth, soothed one more scar on his battered soul.

Orlando's hands resumed their wandering as Alain kissed and licked at his torso. He could not get enough of touching the wizard and, he was discovering, of being touched by him. His erection throbbed, demanding attention. His hips rocked unconsciously against Alain's.

Alain recognized the signs Orlando's body was sending out. If it had been another lying next to him, he would have reached down and encircled the erection that prodded his hip so eagerly. He was quite sure, though, that Orlando was not even aware of the signals he was giving off. And even if the signals were intentional, they were beyond the limits Orlando had laid out. Alain was not about to cross those lines, not now that Orlando finally trusted him enough to let him participate at some level. He contented himself with running his hands over Orlando's back, kneading at the muscles there as he continued to suckle on Orlando's chest.

"Please," Orlando begged, his arousal growing even more demanding.

Alain intensified his caresses, but he did not change them. To do more would be to cross Orlando's boundaries.

Orlando clutched at Alain's forearm, pulling the wizard's hand around from his back and guiding it to his straining erection. "Touch me," he pleaded, closing Alain's fingers around his shaft, thinking only of how good the touch felt. His limits and concerns were forgotten in his enjoyment of Alain's touch.

Alain kept his touch light, stroking Orlando's cock, but nothing more. He was in uncharted territory with nothing to guide him. Now was not the time, but they were going to have to find a better system than what they had been doing.

Even with Alain holding back, the increased intimacy overwhelmed Orlando's senses. With trembling hands, he reached for the lube by the bed, slicking his fingers and beginning to prepare Alain.

The hand that had remained on Orlando's back dropped to the sheets, clutching at them frantically to provide some outlet for his desire so he could keep his touch on Orlando's cock gentle. Orlando's fingers were driving Alain to distraction, stealing his thoughts and his breath. He moaned against Orlando's skin, his hips bucking up, trying to draw Orlando's digits deeper inside him. He cried out in ecstasy when Orlando's fingers brushed his prostate, not just once, but repeatedly. Feeling his climax fast approaching, Alain reached for Orlando's hip, urging his lover to move over him and into him. Orlando gave in to this silent plea, settling between Alain's legs and thrusting deep inside. Alain's hips rose to meet his invasion, slamming their bodies together.

Orlando tried to slow down, to retrieve the tenderness that he so wanted to give Alain, but it had fled in the wake of their passion. Alain's legs had come around his waist, and his heels were pressing against Orlando's arse, spurring him to greater lengths. It only took a few thrusts before Alain lost his fight to stave off his release. He came with a hoarse shout, his seed coating their stomachs.

Orlando felt Alain's climax in the tight passage that surrounded him. The muscles contracted firmly, repetitively, massaging Orlando's cock, sending him over the edge as well. He thrust erratically as he spilled into Alain's sheath. Panting heavily, he collapsed next to Alain and pulled his lover into his arms.

It took several minutes before Alain regained enough logical thought to speak. "I didn't mean to cross the line," he said softly, thinking about his hand on Orlando's erection.

"I wanted you to touch me," Orlando replied, remembering how good it had felt when Alain caressed him. "Couldn't you tell?"

"That's not the point," Alain replied, pulling Orlando into an embrace and tucking the vampire's head into the crook of his shoulder. "If you tell me ahead of time where you expect me to stop, I have to respect that. I can't just think,

'Oh, Orlando's rubbing against me like he wants me to touch him. Let me ignore what he said and give him what I think he wants.' How will you ever be able to trust me if I do that?"

"I don't know what else to suggest," Orlando replied. He was not sure what the solution was, but the fact that Alain had brought it up, that Alain wanted to find a solution, was one more proof of how much the wizard respected him, fears and all.

Alain considered the problem for a moment. "What about a safe word?" he asked.

Orlando squirmed uncomfortably. "Aren't those for... dom/sub relationships?" Just the thought was enough to make him withdraw. He knew what abusive relationships felt like. He could not even begin to count the number of times he wished he had a way to make his maker stop what he was doing. He knew this was completely different, but it was still enough to bring back bad memories, and he did not want those tainting his time with Alain.

"Usually," Alain replied, "but we could use it rather than having pre-set limits. If I do something that makes you uncomfortable, you just say the word and I'll know not to do that anymore. That way, I can react to your signals while we're making love without worrying about whether I'm crossing some line. And if I do, you have a way to tell me so I don't go there again."

Orlando thought about it for a few moments. It was unconventional, but then again, so was their relationship. "I guess we could try it," he agreed. "What could we use?"

Alain considered the question. "Why not the name of Madame Marceline's bistro? That's a safe place for you, so if you say St. Vincent, I'll know you need to feel safe and I'll stop."

Orlando smiled. Alain had turned the situation around. With just those few words, he had eased Orlando's fears. Their relationship was not changing, or only for the better. Once again, Alain was proving, in subtle ways, how important Orlando was to him. He kissed his lover. "You should get some sleep before we have to go back tonight," Orlando told Alain.

"Guard my dreams?" Alain asked, yawning a little with the thought of sleeping.

"Always," Orlando promised.

Chapter 7

JEAN roused himself from his contemplation of Orlando's retreating back. The other vampire was long gone, leaving Jean alone in the quiet park. He knew it was a popular place in the summer, but despite the sun, mortals would find it unpleasantly cool at the end of October. He had not seen anyone since Orlando left, but he was in no hurry. He had always enjoyed being surrounded by growing things. It came, perhaps, from living so close to the land before he became a vampire. He could still remember the little town that Paris had been that summer in the tenth century when the Norsemen attacked. They came up the Seine in their longboats, pillaging and plundering. Jean pushed those memories aside, focusing instead on the days before that fateful attack. His life had not been easy as the son of a peasant, but Père Emmanuel, the local curate, had befriended the inquisitive lad he had been and had taught Jean far more than most of his peers would ever know. At fifteen, he had known how to read almost as well as the curate. He had even contemplated the priesthood himself as a way to escape the drudgery of his life. Priests took vows of poverty, but they never had to worry about starving either. Père Emmanuel always had enough on his table to share with his oft-hungry student.

The curate had taught Jean other things besides reading, too. He had walked with the young man in the woods and shown his young pupil plants that could heal and plants that could kill. He had explained the cycles of nature to the best of his understanding. The memories made Jean smile, as much at the inaccuracies of Père Emmanuel's statements as at the happiness of those days. The Vikings had come the summer before Jean would have taken his vows. It did not matter to them that they attacked an abbey along with everything else. Jean was badly wounded in the attack and left for dead. Père Emmanuel found him, but had no hope of curing him in that state. Jean had resigned himself to death, praying for mercy and salvation. He had gotten a vampire.

Grégoire Casile had been, along with Christophe Lombard, one of the oldest vampires in Paris. He had watched Jean from childhood, always hoping that a moment would come when he could approach the boy, then the young man, but seeing him enter the abbey had convinced the vampire not to try. Until he had seen Jean wounded beyond hope. Then he had dared, giving Jean the choice to live, albeit in a very different manner, rather than to die. Jean had considered his options and had realized that he was not ready to leave this earth, not ready to go to his eternal reward. He still had experiences to savor, mysteries to explore. He had resigned himself to dying, but Grégoire had offered him another path, and he seized it with alacrity.

The transformation had been abrupt. One moment he had been lying in bed, in great pain. The next moment, he was healed. Once he got over that shock, he had discovered the other changes in his body as well. The candlelight, which had been barely enough to light Grégoire's face, suddenly illuminated the entire room. When he rose and opened the door with his customary force, he almost pulled it off its hinges. When he stepped out into the hall, he could hear the beating of each heart in the abbey, could count exactly how many priests and monks remained. And with the sound of their heartbeats, he could smell them, smell the blood that flowed in their veins.

"Not here," Grégoire had said. "They will not understand."

But Jean had refused to leave without saying goodbye to Père Emmanuel. He had crossed the sill of the priest's cell, only to be met with prayers and incantations, as the man of the cloth tried to ward him off as one would a devil. Jean had protested, had sworn that he felt no different than before the attack, that if anything, he felt better. Père Emmanuel had refused to listen, chanting Ave Marias and Pater Nostrums until Jean left, wanting to cry. Only to discover that he had lost that ability when he lost his mortality.

Grégoire had led the grieving young man out into the town and helped him find his first victim. He had not known her name, but she had been willing, and her blood had been sweet. He tasted fear later and decided that he did not like the flavor. That experience had kept him searching for willing victims ever since. Except whenever anyone threatened his abbey; despite the curate's rejection of him, Jean watched over the abbey as long as Père Emmanuel lived, using his new abilities to stop anyone who came in the night with ill intent. When the old priest finally died, Jean stood at his gravesite and said goodbye to the life he had known. The peasant's son, the seminarian, was gone. Only the vampire remained.

He had not regretted it. For over one thousand years, he had lived as a vampire, content with the society of his kind and the occasional company of mortals. Usually, he remained with them only as long as it took to feed, but from time to time, he found one whose company he desired for longer. Thibaut had been first, until Sebastien had come along and stolen Thibaut's interest. Since then, he had only returned to one other mortal for more than just blood.

For ten years, he had visited Karine, sometimes frequently, sometimes with months between visits. Though he had seen her only a few days ago and did not need to feed, Jean could not think of anyone he would rather share the sunlight with than her. He wondered if she would be at home. He realized with embarrassment that he had no idea how she spent the daylight hours or what she did for a living. It had never mattered before because he could have no part of those areas of her life. Now, though, he had a freedom he had not had in a millennium. He could join her for lunch, see her before sunset or after sunrise. Perhaps not every day, but from time to time. He could finally offer her something.

With a smile on his face, he left the Buttes Chaumont for Karine's apartment. As Orlando had done on their way into the park, he marveled that none who passed him noticed anything unusual about him. Certainly, he was fair-skinned, but not that much more so than anyone else. If he moved with an animal grace that few others possessed, they watched him admiringly, thinking only that he was more attractive, more coordinated than most. It did not occur to any of them to associate his grace with a vampire, not during the day. He descended into the subway, heading up to Jaurès and then south toward the Mairie d'Ivry. He got off at the Opéra and walked down the rue du 4 septembre toward Karine's apartment on the rue de la Michodière. He remembered when the Opéra had gone up, when the façade that now spoke of a bygone age had been at the height of modernity. He remembered as well the controversy that had stopped construction for a time. The nineteenth century engineers had been stymied for a time by the underground lake and stream that still hid beneath the venerable old building's foundations.

RAYMOND let out a sigh of exhaustion as he left Milice headquarters. He wanted to go home and sleep. He wanted to forget about the alliance, about vampires, about everything but relaxing for a few hours. That was what he wanted to do, but he knew he would not. So much was happening, with the alliance, with the odd connection that seemed to be developing between the vampires and the wizards. He had nothing in his library that addressed his concerns, which meant a visit to the bouquinistes. Surely, among the stalls of rare books, he could find something that would answer his questions. Jean-Paul had as great an interest in the old lore as Raymond did himself. If anyone along the river had an idea where he might find the answers to his questions, it would be Jean-Paul.

JEAN knocked on the door to Karine's apartment, eager to see the look on her face when she saw him, but, for the first time in their association, she did not open the door. He let his senses stretch, but he could not detect her heartbeat. Wherever she was, she was not at home.

With a resigned sigh, Jean retraced his steps, trying to decide what to do since Karine was unavailable. He could go home, or he could go to Christophe's. A part of him knew he should check in with the older vampire and update him on the situation, but Jean really hoped Mireille had done that. He could always wander down by the Seine, see in the daylight how the city had changed since last he walked those shores. The bouquinistes would be out, even in the chill weather, selling their books and postcards to anyone with an eye for the antique, the unique, or the gently used. He saw their stalls at night when he walked, but he had never seen them open, never seen the men and women who made a living from their love of the ancient and rare. Or he could go to the Ile de la Cité, to the Marché aux Fleurs. The flower market was renowned the world over, and Jean had haunted its streets many times, but always at night, when the flowers were gone. He could buy some roses for Karine to put in the vase she kept filled with fresh flowers even in the winter and leave them on her doorstep before he went to find the other vampire to help with the interrogations. He could leave her a note, tell her some of what had happened, beg her to meet him for lunch tomorrow. Except that he did not know if he would be free the next day for lunch. Or dinner. Or even in the night. He sighed. He would get the flowers and leave them for her, telling her he had missed seeing her. At least she would know he had thought of her.

With that thought in mind, he headed down the Avenue de l'Opéra to the rue de Rivoli, through the place du Carousel and on to the banks of the Seine. He crossed the river so he could walk past the bouquinistes on his way to the Marché aux Fleurs.

AS Raymond had expected, Jean-Paul was fascinated by the question of a magical connection between wizards and vampires. He had willingly searched his stall, looking for any arcane text that might provide some reference, however vague, to the effects of magic on vampires. It was a new topic for Raymond, so there were many tomes to peruse as they examined indices and tables of contents. Jean-Paul was not convinced that any of the books would contain the answers Raymond sought and promised to consult his never-disclosed sources for more books.

"Discreetly," Raymond warned. "We don't want Serrier and his minions to get wind of what we're doing. Already, they attacked us this morning, trying to keep the alliance from forming. We caught or killed them all, so Serrier should still be in the dark. We want to keep it that way as long as possible."

"Bien sûr," Jean-Paul assured him. "You know I'm the soul of discretion."

Raymond laughed and paid Jean-Paul for the books they had found that might serve the wizard's purposes. He thanked the bookseller and turned toward the subway. He had taken two steps when he felt a prickling along his nerves. Instantly on alert, he slid a hand in his pocket for his wand. He did not draw it yet; that would attract too much attention. He simply kept it at the ready. Looking around, searching for the cause of his sharpened awareness, he saw the last person he would have expected to encounter. Jean was walking down the quai toward him.

Raymond stayed where he was, letting Jean come to him rather than the reverse. When the vampire finally saw him, he looked surprised.

"What are you doing here?" Jean asked.

"Looking at books," Raymond replied with a gesture toward the bag he carried.

"Some light afternoon reading?" Jean wanted to know.

"No," Raymond said seriously. "It's quite heavy." He handed Jean the bag to prove his point.

Jean laughed at Raymond's play on words. "Seriously," he said when his laughter died, "you must be exhausted. What was so important that you couldn't wait?"

Raymond's first reaction was to declare that Jean was not his keeper, but then he realized that there was only curiosity and concern in Jean's voice, not reprimand.

"I like to understand why things work," Raymond explained. "I've always enjoyed studying the arcane, the archaic, the fantastic, to try to find the grain of truth beneath it all. What passes for truth is often not the whole story. There is so much knowledge out there that's suppressed. We don't learn certain spells because they're deemed evil, but that means that we don't learn to counter them either. Knowledge is never evil, despite what some would have us believe."

"I've tasted your blood; I know you're not evil. Was the search for knowledge what led you to Serrier in the first place? His position on the freedom that wizards should be allowed to exercise?"

"Yes," Raymond admitted. "And while there's some question about the politics, there is no question about his methods. When I saw beyond the propaganda, I left. It's possible to seek knowledge, even the kind that fascinates me, without the cruelty that Serrier so often employs. Right now, I'm wondering how the partnerships work so I came looking for books that might contain the answers I seek."

"Here?" Jean asked, surprised.

"You'd be surprised what you can find in these stalls if you know where to look," Raymond replied, "or who to ask."

"I take it you know," Jean continued.

"Very well," Raymond said. "I've been buying books here for almost twenty years, usually from the same bouquiniste. Jean-Paul keeps an eye out for rare books that might catch my interest. Texts on alchemy, on sorcery, on anything related to the magical. I try to come by once a week to see if he's found anything for me."

"I had no idea," Jean said with a shake of his head, amazed at this freshly discovered facet of his partner. He could not help but wonder what kind of discussion Raymond could have with Christophe. The old vampire, too, was fascinated by the esoteric. "So did you find what you were looking for?" he asked.

"Not really," Raymond admitted. "I've never collected information on vampires before so Jean-Paul doesn't keep those books for me. He had a couple that might have something relevant. I have to read them and figure out how what they tell me fits in to what I already know."

"What if I could save you the time spent reading them?" Jean asked. "I think I know where you can find all you'd ever want to know about vampires."

"Where?" Raymond asked eagerly.

"The only vampire in Paris older than me. Christophe Lombard is, by right, the chef de la Cour, but he retired from society years ago. Now he lives surrounded by books, immersed in the lore of our kind. He was the one who suggested that a wizard's blood might protect us. If anyone knows more about the effect of magic on vampires or of a vampire's feeding on wizards, it would be him. We should go talk to him," Jean said, excitement coloring his voice.

"Where?" Raymond asked again, more hesitantly this time.

"He has a house not too far from here," Jean said. "We can go there now. He obviously can't come out during the day, but I know he'd love to talk to you."

Raymond was torn between trying to please his partner and protecting himself. He wanted to talk to the old vampire; he wanted to show Jean that he had accepted their new partnership; he wanted to make that gesture of good faith. The ingrained fear of vampires, though, was too strong. He had let Jean feed from him, but it had always been when others had been around. He and Jean were talking now, but on a public street. "I can't," he said finally. "I want to, but I just can't. If we waited for dark, would he come out, to a café or somewhere, to meet me?"

"Don't you trust me?" Jean asked, hurt that Raymond was not willing to go with him.

"I trust you," Raymond replied, "at least more than I trust any other vampire, but it will take me time to overcome the fear I've lived with for all my life. I'm not there yet."

Jean nodded. He could understand Raymond's fear, having believed for more than a thousand years that wizard's blood was poison. Experience had shown him now that what he had believed was false. Raymond's fear could not be dispelled so rationally. One vampire's trustworthiness was no guarantee that others possessed the same trait. "I'll talk to him and see if he'll meet us late tonight. You should get some rest," Jean said. "You can't go without sleep indefinitely."

Raymond nodded even as he yawned. "I think you're right," he agreed. "I'll meet you back at Milice headquarters tonight after dark and see what your friend said. We'll decide then what to do next, if that's all right."

"That's fine," Jean said. He looked up at the sky, trying to judge the time until sunset by the location of the sun in the sky. "I have a couple of stops to make after nightfall before I come back to base. Antonio can't move in daylight."

Chapter 8

MARCEL took a calming breath and stepped into the room full of the members of the Fourth Estate. He saw reporters from Le Monde, TF1, France 2, France 3, Canal +, Libération, and Le Figaro. He did not see the usual faces from M6 or TV5, but there were several unfamiliar faces as well. Perhaps they were replacements. "Thank you for coming, ladies and gentlemen," he said with a smile. "I am sure you are all aware of the incident that took place this morning at 6 AM at the Gare de Lyon. If you will be patient with me, I will explain what happened. Then, if there is time, I will answer any questions you may have."

A murmur of agreement went around the room. "I received an anonymous tip yesterday," Marcel began, "that a group of rogue wizards planned to attack a meeting of vampires that was scheduled for this morning. Seeing no reason why the vampires should not exercise their constitutional right to gather peacefully, I ordered Capitaines Magnier and Dumont to head a company from the Milice de Sorcellerie to intervene. At precisely 6 AM, they successfully completed their mission. Fourteen wizards were captured and five were killed. There were no casualties among our forces, among the vampires, or among civilian bystanders. Nor was there any disruption of commuter traffic because of this engagement. It is our expectation that the fourteen prisoners will be indicted on charges of misuse of magic since they were caught in the act of using illegal spells. Are there any questions?"

The hand of the reporter for Le Figaro went up immediately. "Why were the vampires assembling?"

"You would have to ask a vampire that question," Marcel replied. "I don't mean to sound flippant, but the reason for their meeting was irrelevant as far as we were concerned. *Toute personne a droit à la liberté de réunion et d'association pacifique.* That is the guarantee of our constitution, the right to assemble as long as it does not disturb the peace. The only people disturbing the peace this morning were terrorists, not vampires."

"Disturbing the peace?" the reporter from Libération challenged.

"Yes," Marcel replied firmly. "The rebel wizards started the exchange of spells. Milice operatives simply responded in such ways as to ensure the safety of innocent bystanders and the security of the infrastructure, as has been our policy since we were commissioned two years ago. We attack when attacked or, when possible, to prevent attacks based on credible evidence. How many times do we need to have this conversation, monsieur?"

"At least once more, apparently," the Libération reporter replied. Marcel wanted to roll his eyes, but he refrained. To do so would undermine his credibility with the other reporters.

"How many Milice operatives were sent?" the representative from France 2 asked. "We heard rumors of overwhelming numbers."

"Forty operatives were sent," Marcel replied, careful to use that word rather than saying forty wizards. He and Jean had agreed to keep quiet about the vampires' involvement for as long as possible in order to protect their advantage. As far as Marcel was concerned, the vampires were now members of the Milice de Sorcellerie just as the wizards were and so were operatives as well. "Under the command of my two top commanders."

"Why so many?" she pressed.

"Because my tip did not include the number of terrorists and we wanted to make sure we could end any hostilities as quickly as possible and with minimal loss of life or property. That strategy paid off," Marcel explained.

Before he could entertain more questions, Mathieu opened the door to the press room. "Excuse me for disturbing you, General, but you're needed in the command room."

Marcel nodded and turned back to the press corps. "That concludes this morning's session, ladies and gentlemen. I've been called away. You will be notified of the next conference when it's been scheduled."

The calls and questions followed Marcel out of the room, but he ignored them, shutting the door firmly behind him. "Thank you, Mathieu," Marcel said as he walked toward his office. "You always know exactly when to intervene."

"It's a gift," Mathieu smirked. "I don't know why you put up with them."

"Because this is as much a fight for people's minds and hearts as it is for anything else. The public needs to see the Milice de Sorcellerie in charge and in control so they continue to believe that we're fighting for their best interests, not just for our own interests. So far, we're winning on that front, even if we're not making much progress on the military front. It's popular opinion that will eventually allow us to change the laws that discriminate against our new allies. If we lose the battle for public opinion, we will never fulfill our promises, even if we win the war," Marcel reminded the young wizard.

"I know you're right. It just seems like you shouldn't have to be the one to deal with them."

"Who better?" Marcel asked. "I am such a foil to Serrier; an elderly gentlemen, soft spoken and reserved. I come across as everyone's favorite grandfather, and who better to assure them that everything is under control and that we are protecting them and their rights?"

JUDE knocked on the door to Colin's apartment. Like Jude, Colin had found a partner at the gathering, but he and his partner had not stayed to fight. That was not what was bothering Jude. Many more vampires had left than had stayed. No, Jude's problem was his partner. "Colin, unlock the door and then go back in your room. I'll wait before I open the door," Jude called when he heard movement inside the apartment. The last thing Jude wanted was to endanger Colin by exposing him to the sunlight if he had not fed properly from his partner. His sensitive hearing detected the snick of the lock and the retreating footsteps on the other side. When the footsteps stopped, Jude judged it safe to open the door and slip inside.

"It's safe," he called when he shut the door behind him.

Colin came out from his room with a smile for his friend. "To what do I owe this honor?" he asked Jude.

"I needed to talk to someone who would understand," Jude replied with a frown. "Did you see the brazen hussy that I paired with?"

"She's quite beautiful," Colin commented.

"If you like overstated, obnoxious, forward women," Jude agreed sarcastically. "She has no concept of her place."

"As much as I miss the demure, reserved women of our time, you know as well as I do that times have changed," Colin reminded him. Life had indeed changed since he and his friend were turned at the advent of Elizabethan era. They had emigrated to France when George IV got wind of one vampire's excesses and declared England closed to all vampires.

"That's why I avoid their company whenever possible," Jude retorted. "Women should be seen, not heard. There is no place for them in war. They're what we fight to protect. They shouldn't be the ones fighting."

As fervently as he believed this, he had not found a way to stop Adèle from fighting at his side that morning, and that failure bothered him to no end. Nor had he been able to discourage her unseemly participation in the war council that followed.

"I agree," Colin replied. "You know I do. We were raised the same way. I also know that our beliefs aren't as commonly held as they once were."

"So what do you propose?" Jude asked. "Do we ignore all we were taught and let them risk their lives at our side?"

"What choice do we have?" Colin asked. "Your partner didn't seem biddable in the least. Mine wasn't quite so forward, but she clearly intends to participate in this war. Either we find a way to work with them or we abandon our part in this alliance. I have no particular loyalty to the wizards, but I don't like the idea of letting our fellow vampires fight without us. That goes just as much against my beliefs as seeing women fighting."

Jude sighed. "What choice, indeed? This won't be easy. She won't make it easy." She had already not made it easy, with her insistence on putting herself forward and on participating in every aspect of the discussion, even matters better left to men.

"Probably not," Colin agreed, "not from what I saw of her. She seemed one to want to take charge."

"Yes, and Chavinier encourages her, apparently. I don't know how to make this work."

ANGELIQUE looked around her office. It was a new experience, seeing it in the daylight. That was why she had a manager. François Roche had run the daytime part of the business for almost twenty years. She stared down at the designs that covered her hands and spiraled up her arms. They had been inked onto her skin in the harem before she was turned, and they had followed her ever since, a mark of her past that she could not erase and that would never fade. Most days, she did not even notice them, but every once in a while, something would happen to draw her attention back to them. This time, it was David's reaction. He saw the patterns, saw the way she looked, and judged based only on that. Once, just once, she would like to meet a man who waited to know her before judging her. With a sigh, she pushed those thoughts aside and called for François to join her.

"Angelique! What are you doing here?" François exclaimed when he walked into her office. "How did you get here? I know you weren't here when I arrived this morning. I checked."

"Shut the door," Angelique instructed, "and I'll explain." When he was settled, she went on. "First of all, what I'm about to tell you cannot leave this room," she warned him as she summarized the events of the morning, from the initial gathering and the formation of the alliance to the battle and the meeting that followed. "The end result," she added, "is that the blood of my partner protects me from the sunlight."

She neglected to mention that her partner made the same mistakes in judging her that far too many men had made. She knew what François's reaction would be. He would fly to her defense and insist on setting David straight. While Angelique appreciated the thought, she knew that would in no way help her cause. She needed David to see her as capable in her own right, and François's words, no matter how fervent or true, would only add to David's misconception that she needed a man to defend her. He would learn. She only hoped she did not kill him before he did.

"So what happens now?" François asked.

"Now we fight," she replied. "We already knew that if Serrier wins the war, life will be difficult for the non-wizards, but life is already difficult for vampires most of the time. Chavinier has offered us a chance to change that, to prove our value once and for all. He intends to push for laws that would guarantee us the same protection and the same opportunities as you now enjoy. That's too good to pass up. This means, though, that there will be times I won't be here, even at night. If I fight during the day, I'll have to rest some at night. If not, I'll fight at night. It might not be every day or every night, but I have to be available. My responsibilities here will have to fall on you."

"That's not a problem," François said. "I can oversee whatever needs to be done, but what about you? Are you sure it's safe? What if you're wounded, or even killed?"

Angelique was touched by François's concern. "We vampires are not so easy to kill as that," she reminded him. "And we fight in pairs, with a wizard and a vampire together. The wizard's job is to deal with the spells. The vampire's job is to disarm the dark wizard. You've seen more than once that I'm quicker and stronger than any mortal man. Once I get my hands on the wizard, it won't take me long to relieve him of his wand."

François nodded. Despite Angelique's policy of only selling blood, mortals occasionally came into the building, thinking to find more than she was willing to sell. He had seen burly men laugh at her insistence that they leave because she had nothing to offer them. He had also seen her throw them bodily out the door. No one ever underestimated her twice.

"You'll do what you believe is best," François said. "You always do. What do you want me to do?"

They spent the next two hours going over the details of Angelique's business, discussing which aspects would need François's personal attention and which ones could be handed over to people already in place, with François's oversight. When they were done, Angelique left the office, confident that her business was in the best possible hands beside her own. Glancing down once more at her tattooed limbs, she closed and locked the office door and went upstairs to her rooms to prepare for whatever the night would bring.

DAVID was not much of a scholar of history, not like some of his colleagues, but he was not completely ignorant either. He had recognized the marks on his partner's hands and arms. He knew what she was. A concubine, some sultan's bed warmer, a bit of fluff with no purpose other than to look pretty and please her master. He rolled his eyes. He did not mind being paired with a woman. He knew lots of women who were perfectly capable individuals. And, he thought darkly, he knew a few men who were not. He minded being paired with a courtesan. And not merely a courtesan, but a procuress as well if the comments he had heard were to be believed. He dreaded having to go back to work and deal with someone who would probably not even be able to make decisions for herself. He would have to tell her everything: what to do, when to do it, and even how. Unless, of course, it involved seducing some hapless fellow. She could probably manage that on her own. Giving her direction was all right if everything went according to plan, but how often did that happen? Not often enough to reassure David, that much was certain.

Trying to forget his woes for a few moments, David switched the television on to see what had happened while he slept. The news coverage on France 2 caught his attention immediately. The anchor was introducing a story on the battle that morning and Marcel's response. Settling down with a cup of coffee, David prepared to listen to the company line. It was, to David's mind, fairly standard coverage. The reporter explained what had happened, outlining the facts and then mentioning the press conference. As she spoke, two pictures appeared on the screen, Marcel's and Serrier's. David smiled at the contrast as Marcel's voice spoke over the images. "Seeing no reason why the vampires should not exercise their constitutional right to gather peacefully, I ordered

Capitaines Magnier and Dumont to head a company from the Milice de Sorcellerie to intervene."

David's scowl returned. It was always those two, he thought bitterly. No matter who else participated in a mission, Marcel's golden boys always got the credit. David did not have a problem with Thierry. The man came in, did his job, and that was that. Magnier, on the other hand, got on David's last nerve. It had been bad enough when they were studying together, learning to use their magic, but after the Milice was formed, it had gotten progressively worse. Alain was a good wizard, but David did not think he was that much better than any of the others, yet he continued to get promotion after promotion despite having killed Eric's wife and kids. David understood that it had been during a battle, but there had not even been an investigation. If it had been anyone else, the wizard would have been suspended pending the investigation and probable court martial. But not Alain. Oh no, Marcel's pet had escaped all of that. And it was that lapse that David could not forgive. If Alain had stood trial and the deaths had been judged accidental, David would have accepted it, despite losing Eric to the dark wizards. He would not have been happy, but he would have accepted it. What bothered him was that Alain was never held accountable for the spells that killed three innocent bystanders. Deciding that listening to any more would only upset him, David switched off the TV and went to get ready for the evening.

Chapter 9

ADÈLE stared at the contents of her closet. She never had any problem choosing something to wear. She had three kinds of clothes: work clothes, exercise clothes, and formal clothes. All she had to do was reach in and pull something out. Cursing under her breath, she grabbed the first thing she could reach and got dressed without looking at it. It would not matter what she wore. Nothing she owned would meet his approval, especially nothing she wore to work. They were all pants. She did not know what era Jude was from, but she could guess from his attitude that women had not been wearing pants when he was made. Without even looking in the mirror, she left the apartment and headed into the night toward the subway. She would deal with his attitude later.

The door to the subway closed behind the last passenger and the train began its trajectory toward the next station. Even as Adèle's eyes scanned the car reflexively, her mind wandered over all that had transpired in the last twenty-four hours. Meeting at Orlando's apartment, planning and executing the beginning of the alliance, the gathering itself. Jude. That was where her mind lingered, where she stumbled in her thoughts. The waves of disapproval rolling off of him from the moment he saw the bite marks on her arm had been tangible. He was obviously a throwback to another century, judging by his remarks and the unspoken criticism every time she made a comment or suggestion at the meeting after the battle. He clearly expected her to sit quietly and look pretty. He was in for a rude awakening. She could certainly look pretty, but that had nothing to do with the Milice and her role in it. Marcel had not recruited her because she was pretty. He had recruited her because she was a smart, savvy, capable wizard with talents that could serve in the fight against Serrier's bid to overthrow the government. Jude would simply have to accept that or their partnership would be short-lived, alliance or not.

She understood the advantages of the alliance. She had seen it at work in the battle that morning. She could not have overpowered the dark wizard the way Jude had. The duel between them would have gone on much longer without his help, and that could have resulted in damage or even casualties, two things she definitely wanted to avoid. Her knack for avoiding collateral damage was one of the abilities Marcel depended on in her. If Jude continued with his patronizing ways, though, she would return to fighting alone. There were other ways to minimize collateral damage, ways that did not force her to deal with Neanderthal attitudes like her current partner's.

She had hoped for an attractive partner, wanting the full sensual experience that Alain seemed to be relishing, and she had gotten that. She might have done better to wish for someone she could work with, she admitted to herself ruefully. Being bitten by Jude was as sensual an experience as she could have hoped for, she had to confess, a flush of heat spreading through her at the memory. The glow had faded, though, as soon as they had separated and Jude's attitude had become even more pronounced. She had not asked, but she imagined he had tasted her independence in her blood. She had never relied on a man for anything, though she was perfectly willing to work with them and beside them, as long as they paid her the same courtesy. She would give Jude a chance, but if he did not accept that she would continue to fight and speak as she saw fit, she would tell him to find someone else to fight alongside. She would give him her blood to protect him, but she would not subject herself to that attitude.

The train pulled into the next stop, and passengers embarked and debarked. Looking up, Adèle recognized a familiar face. From the impressions she had formed as the day had gone on, she was looking at the vampire-half of the second most successful partnership formed last night. When Sebastien glanced her way, she nodded in greeting and waited to see if he would recognize her.

He did and moved through the car to her side.

"On your way back to Marcel's?" she asked unnecessarily, her voice pitched low so as not to attract the attention of the other passengers.

Sebastien nodded. "You, too?" he asked, in the same soft tone.

"Yes," Adèle confirmed. "I have a little work to get done before we start. You'll be there early, though."

"I know," Sebastien replied. "I thought I'd see if there was anything I could do to help."

Adèle laughed. "There's always something that needs doing. Marcel will put you to work in no time. Can you use a computer?"

It was Sebastien's turn to laugh. "Just because I was alive when Joan of Arc was burned at the stake doesn't mean I've stayed in that century. I've kept up with technology."

"Over five hundred years," Adèle commented. "I'm impressed. I wish all vampires were as forward-thinking as you."

"Jude?" Sebastien guessed.

"How'd you know?" she asked.

Sebastien grinned. "I've known him for about a hundred fifty years, though he's older than that, I think. I know all about his refusal to leave behind the era of his making."

"Any advice?" Adèle asked.

"Don't let him change you," Sebastien replied. "He thinks he wants a shrinking violet of a woman, but, at least from what I've seen, he'll be glad for you when it comes to battle. It'll take him a while to get used to the idea of fighting beside a woman – he may never get used to it – but he'll have no choice but to admit you're a capable fighter when he's been exposed to you long enough."

Adèle sighed. "Someday, I'd like to be able to stop fighting this battle."

"We'll beat Serrier," Sebastien said confidently.

"Oh, I know we will," Adèle declared. "I wasn't talking about that. I was talking about defeating the idea that because I'm pretty, I must be stupid or vapid or something. Men aren't judged that way. Why should I be?"

"You're absolutely right," Sebastien agreed. "If it's any consolation, I didn't judge you on your looks. Nor are women the only ones judged by their appearances. Young Orlando has been dismissed for a century because of his looks."

Adèle rolled her eyes. "Yeah, but neither of you is my partner. Jude is."

Sebastien lifted an eyebrow. "True. Do the other wizards look down on you? I didn't get that impression."

"Not the ones who know me," Adèle explained. "They know I'm in the Milice for a reason, and the ones I work with regularly – Alain, Thierry, Mathieu, Laurent – have seen my skills with magic and my intelligence often enough that they probably don't even look at me anymore. I mean, they see me, but they probably don't even take in my appearance. It's when I meet new people that I have a problem."

They fell silent for a moment. Finally, Adèle spoke again. "I hope I'm not intruding, but I couldn't help but notice some tension between you and Jean when you arrived yesterday. Is there a problem we need to know about?"

"It's ancient history," Sebastien replied, not wanting to think about Thibaut.

"Be that as it may," Adèle pressed, "I noticed a definite chill between you. Will it impact the alliance?"

"Not as far as I'm concerned," Sebastien said, his hand slipping into his pocket to finger the locket that held his only remaining link to his Avoué. "I can work with him."

"Good," Adèle replied. "We're going to have enough challenges to face without internal tension. Or, without adding to the internal tension."

"If Jude gets too obnoxious, say something to Jean," Sebastien urged. "He's a strong leader. He'll set Jude straight." Despite the history between them, Sebastien knew that Jean deserved the position of leadership he now occupied. Lombard had chosen well when he picked Jean to be his successor.

"I prefer to fight my own battles," Adèle replied haughtily.

"And so you should," Sebastien agreed, "but, as you said, we can't afford internal tension. If we're fighting among ourselves, we're not fighting Serrier. Let Jean do his job of keeping order among the vampires. That's what leaders are for."

"I'll think about it," Adèle answered finally, not wanting to refuse outright, but knowing it would take a lot before she reached that point. Perhaps if the chef de la Cour had been a woman she would have felt differently, but it would feel too much like failure to ask a man for that kind of help.

"You seem to get on well with Thierry," Adèle commented, changing the subject.

"I understand him," Sebastien replied simply.

Adèle frowned. "What do you mean?"

"I know what it feels like to lose someone you love. I can empathize with his loss," he explained.

"They weren't happy," Adèle observed. "I'm not saying he's grieving any less because of it, but their marriage wouldn't have lasted much longer even if she hadn't been killed. Aleth was a fine wizard, but she wasn't a very understanding wife."

"Why are you telling me this?" Sebastien asked.

"Because your loss is clearly a deep one. Thierry's is, too, but when the first rush of grief wears off, he'll remember all that was wrong between them. It won't erase his sense of loss, but it will temper it. You need to understand the whole story, not just the obvious part," she replied. "If I understand correctly, you'll feel his emotions when you feed from him. Maybe this will let you interpret them correctly and help him if he needs it."

"I don't know how much help I could be," Sebastien demurred. "We barely know each other."

"You might not be able to help," Adèle admitted, "but Alain could. They've been best friends for a long time, at least by the standards of mortals. He'll know how to help, but he's so caught up with Orlando that he might miss the need for his help. You can tell him if Thierry doesn't."

The thought made Sebastien uncomfortable. He had always considered what he learned from his prey as a secret told in confidence. The thought of breaking that confidence went against his ingrained sense of honor.

As if reading his mind, Adèle added, "He doesn't control his magic as effectively when his emotions are in turmoil. That's what hit you in the chest when you walked in: an emotional outburst that found a magical outlet. He could be injured or even killed if he goes into battle that way. You'd be protecting him."

Adèle's words triggered Sebastien's protective instincts. He could not have explained why it bothered him so much, but he would not allow Thierry to endanger himself unnecessarily. "I'll remember what you've said," he replied simply.

The train reached their stop and they descended onto the platform. On the train, a dark-haired young man frowned. He recognized the woman from various television images as one of the Milice de Sorcellerie. And the man was one of his own kind. What did a wizard and a vampire have to talk about? He did not know, but he thought maybe he should find out.

THE remote control flew across the room, crashing against the wall and falling to the floor in several pieces. "Fucking do-gooders," Serrier growled as he switched off the press conference with a wave of his hand. "Who does he think he is? Vampires' rights, protecting the Constitution, it's a load of bullshit, that's what it is. The Constitution says any person has the right to assemble. *Person*," he shouted, to no one in particular. "Vampires don't count. They're dead. They don't have the rights that we enjoy. And how did he know about their meeting and our presence, anyway?"

"He probably found out about the meeting the same way we did," Vincent pointed out, being careful not to utter Marcel's name when Serrier was in this mood. "As for how he found out about our people going there, your guess is as good as mine. He's always been canny that way."

The answer did nothing to appease Serrier, who looked around for something else to throw. "Nineteen wizards, dead or captured, and the only one who comes back to me knows nothing because he got knocked out before the battle ever began."

"How do we counter him?" Eric asked, trying to divert Serrier's anger. "What steps do you want us to take?"

Pascal paused to consider. "Nothing we could say in response to Chavinier's press conference would do any good," he said finally. "Even if we say that all we wanted was information, Chavinier makes us look bad by claiming that we threw the first spells. With Dominique unconscious through the whole battle, we have no way to prove otherwise. And we have no more information than when we started."

"Do you still want to find a vampire?" Eric asked, relatively sure nothing had been done in that direction since the last time they had met. For a hands-on general who took great pride in personally planning all their tactics, Pascal still required the occasional nudge. "Perhaps we could convince one to tell us what the meeting was about. If nothing else, we would know if there was something afoot we needed to counter. And if they were meeting to discuss the winter solstice celebration, or something equally innocuous, at least we'd know."

"It better not be something so trivial," Serrier growled. "It cost us too much to be something so inconsequential."

"Then the sooner we find out the better," Eric rationalized.

"Fine," Serrier said. "You and Vincent find me a vampire. I want to know what happened at that meeting."

EDOUARD COUTHON stalked the streets of Paris, looking for dinner and looking for information. Maybe the wizard and the vampire on the subway were just passing the time in idle conversation. It did happen occasionally, though not often enough for him to be comfortable with that explanation. Something was going on. He did not know what, but he had learned to listen to his instincts over the years. They had kept him alive against more mobs than he cared to count. He decided he would pay a visit to Miss Bouaddi's establishment. That would net him dinner and possibly information as well. He doubted any vampire in Paris was as well connected as she was.

Putting on his most innocent smile, Edouard crossed the threshold of Sang Froid, expecting to see the renowned procuress herself, but a man, a mortal, greeted Edouard instead.

"How may I help you?" François asked, surprised to see a vampire. He had expected business to be slow, the vampires all at the same meeting that kept Angelique away.

"I had hoped to talk with Angelique," Edouard replied with a disarming smile.

"Miss Bouaddi is unavailable," François explained with a disapproving frown. He did not know all the vampires in Paris by any means, but he thought he knew all the ones who knew Angelique well enough to address her so casually. "I am currently taking her place. How may I help you?"

"I'm seeking information and... disposable company," Edouard answered.

"You will find neither here," François declared coldly. "Company, yes, but not disposable, as you put it. For information, read the newspaper or watch the news on TV."

"But they so rarely cover the interests of vampires," Edouard retorted.

"If it's vampire business you're concerned with, I most certainly can't help you," François declared. "As you are surely aware, I am no vampire."

"And yet Miss Bouaddi trusts you," Edouard pointed out, drawling the name condescendingly.

"To run her business, not her life," François countered. Any vampire who spoke of disposable company was hardly trustworthy since Angelique had a firm policy that none of her employees were to be harmed, but François's reaction went deeper than that. Angelique had told him enough about the alliance and its genesis for him to feel confident that this vampire had been excluded for a reason. François did not know what the reason was, but he trusted Angelique and Angelique trusted Jean. That was enough for François. "I think you should look elsewhere for both your company and your information."

"This isn't over," Edouard hissed. "Angelique will hear about it."

"Feel free to tell her," François replied calmly. "If she feels I've overstepped my bounds, I will accept whatever consequence she deems fit. Until then, I think you should leave."

"And who's to make me?" Edouard demanded. "You?"

"I would never presume to take on a vampire," François said, "but I'm not the only one here." As he spoke, he gestured with one hand. Two of Angelique's bouncers stepped out of the shadows. Vampires themselves, but unmatched in the alliance, they were more than a match for Edouard. "These gentlemen are in charge of... pest removal."

François stepped back quickly before Edouard could lunge for him, leaving Roger and Pierre to deal with the irate vampire. They escorted him firmly out the door and into the street, leaving him fuming and swearing revenge.

AS soon as they were out of the room, Eric looked at Vincent and rolled his eyes. "'Find me a vampire.' Like I know where to find vampires," Eric complained. "They're less than mortal. What do I care about where they hang out?"

"I don't care where they hang out either," Vincent agreed, "but I seem to remember hearing about a brothel of sorts that catered to the desires of vampires as well as the desires of normal people. That might be a place to look. Even if we don't go inside, but just wait for a vampire to go in or come out, that would still let us find one to talk to."

"Do you know where this place is?" Eric asked dubiously. "I mean, it's a good plan, and now that you mention it, I remember hearing rumors about it, but I have no idea where it is."

"Right where you'd expect it to be," Vincent replied. "In the shadows of the Moulin Rouge with the rest of the sex shops."

Eric was impressed. It made perfect sense to put a business that catered to vampires in the one part of the city that had a booming night business. No one would think twice about people coming and going in the middle of the night. He wondered whose idea that was.

"Let's give it a try, then," Eric decided. "What's the worst that can happen? We spend a couple of hours and turn up empty-handed, right? And if that happens, we'll just look elsewhere."

Two hours later, Eric was wondering if those were prophetic words. They had seen plenty of people coming in and out of the shop that Vincent claimed catered to vampires, but none of them had the distinctive pallor that would have indicated their membership in that accursed race.

"You said they catered to normal people as well, right?" Eric asked Vincent when he got fed up with waiting.

"Yeah, so?" Vincent asked. "We don't need a normal person. We need a vampire."

"I know, but we're normal people. That means we could go inside, look around, maybe see if there are any vampires there. Maybe we could even hint that we were interested in meeting a vampire," Eric explained.

Vincent shivered.

"Not to do anything," Eric added quickly, "but if we can get one alone, we can get him or her back to Pascal."

"I guess it's worth a try," Vincent replied slowly, although he did not sound at all convinced.

"Do you have a better idea?" Eric wanted to know.

Vincent just shrugged, gesturing toward the door.

Feeling terribly conspicuous, Eric walked inside, Vincent right behind him.

"May I help you?" a cultured male voice spoke from their left.

Eric spun, resisting the urge to reach for his wand. "I... That is, we were looking for congenial company," he stuttered, feeling about twelve years old again.

"Congenial company is our specialty," the voice said as its owner stepped forward into the light, revealing a man of indeterminate age and lightly tanned skin. Eric hid his disappointment. Not a vampire. "Do you have a specific preference?"

"Actually, we were hoping to meet a vampire," Eric explained.

"Oh?" François asked, trying to place why the faces in front of him looked familiar. "And you expected to find one here?"

"We'd heard vampires came here when they wanted a snack," Vincent interrupted.

"Are you looking to be a snack?" François queried.

"Maybe," Eric prevaricated, trying not to let his revulsion show.

"I'm afraid you've come to the wrong place," François said apologetically, his nerves tightening as he finally recognized one of the two men. He was on the Milice's Most Wanted list. Angelique would be most interested to know that at least one dark wizard had been nosing around her place. "You might try one of the Goth clubs," François suggested, hoping to urge them on their way before any vampires arrived. "That's where people usually go when they want to meet a vampire."

Eric and Vincent left Angelique's place and headed to the suggested destination. When they reached the first club and looked at the line of people waiting to get in, it was quickly obvious that they would not be admitted. They were not at all the right type, in their simple jeans and T-shirts. Resigned, they settled down to wait again, hoping they would see a vampire going into or out of the club.

They waited an hour, shivering against the chill of the night air, unwilling to do a simple warming spell in case there were others around who could sense it. As capable as they were, they were only two. If Milice forces showed up, they would be captured or killed for sure. Finally, their patience paid off as they spotted a young-looking vampire and a young woman leaving the club together.

With a nod, Eric gestured for Vincent to follow them. They kept a generous distance, enough that they hoped not to be noticed. When the couple in front of them stepped into an alley, the two wizards followed to the entrance but did not go inside. They were not interested in whatever transpired between the two; they simply wanted to talk to the vampire when he was done.

Moans quickly filled the still night air, making Vincent and Eric look at each other uncomfortably. They knew, at least in theory, what was happening in the darkness, but to be witness to it, even if only to the sound of it, seemed voyeuristic.

When silence fell, they stepped deeper into the alley, totally unprepared for the sight that greeted them. The young woman who had been so vibrantly alive only minutes ago lay deathly still at the vampire's feet.

Fingering his wand in his pocket, Eric took another step forward. "I thought vampires didn't kill their prey," he observed.

The vampire grinned at him, blood dripping from his fangs. "Only those too afraid of their own shadows to remember what we were created to be," he replied, toeing the body at his feet.

Chapter 10

"WHY am I here?" Antonio asked Jean as they crossed the magical boundaries to Milice headquarters. "I didn't find a partner. I don't see what I can do to help."

Jean sighed. He knew this was going to be a problem with the unpaired vampires, but he had thought Antonio would be more eager. "Just because you didn't find a partner doesn't mean you can't help," Jean pointed out. "When the wizards approached us in the first place, they knew nothing of the pairings and the power to be found in those partnerships. Yet they needed our help. You can patrol the streets or listen in cafés and bars as easily as I can, with or without a partner, from dusk until dawn. And because you don't have a partner, you can help in a way I can't."

Antonio frowned. "How?"

Jean explained quickly about the interrogation and his role in it, the role he wanted to give to Antonio.

"And why can't you do this any more if it worked so well the first time?" Antonio asked.

"Because the bond between wizard and vampire makes it uncomfortable for my partner," Jean explained. "And for me," honesty compelled him to admit for the first time. "I can't explain why it is so, but biting that boy with Raymond looking on felt wrong. I tried telling myself it was because of the dark magic I could taste, but even though I wouldn't admit it at the time, it felt like a betrayal to bite someone else with Raymond watching. Even at that point, when we weren't getting along, Raymond felt it, too. Now that things are better, I need them to stay that way. And that means finding someone, namely you, to take my place in the interrogation."

They walked into the large conference room where Marcel planned to hold their meeting. Almost immediately, Raymond came to Jean's side. Jean introduced the wizard and the vampire. Raymond acknowledged Antonio with a nod and a brief handshake. Jean was pleasantly surprised. He had not been sure how Raymond would react to other vampires. He studied his partner closely, Antonio and everyone else in the room fading into the background. He could see circles under the wizard's eyes – *his* wizard's eyes – and a deep fatigue that bothered him in ways he was at a loss to understand.

"Did you sleep at all?" he asked sharply.

"For a couple of hours," Raymond replied. "I wanted to be ready to meet your mentor tonight, and that meant doing some reading. I can always sleep later."

"And if you're so exhausted that you can't hold your own in a fight? What then?" Jean chided.

"Then you're well rid of me," Raymond quipped.

"And if I don't want to be rid of you?" Jean's eyes narrowed dangerously. "We have too much to do, and you're too important to that effort."

"Then you'll just have to make sure I stay alive to do it," Raymond responded, touched by Jean's protectiveness.

"Damn straight," Jean muttered, thinking that Raymond clearly needed a keeper and wondering if the wizard would let him fill that role.

Sebastien's eyes scanned the gathering throng as he entered the conference room alone, Adèle having gone to take care of some paperwork before the meeting. He nodded across the room to Antonio, a gesture that could have included Jean if the elder vampire had been looking, but he was not, Sebastien noticed. His attention was fixed firmly on his wizard. Sebastien's gaze drifted on, over the various pairs already present, seeking his own wizard. He found Thierry almost immediately, his eyes drawn to the blond man like a magnet.

Thierry stood, deep in conversation with Orlando and Alain. Sebastien could not hear what they were saying, but everything about their postures proclaimed a deep camaraderie and solid friendship. He knew from Adèle that Alain and Thierry were long-standing friends, but he was fairly sure that Orlando had only recently joined them. That was based entirely on what he knew of the alliance, though, not on the way they were acting. Seeing the three of them together, Sebastien could detect no sign of division, nothing to suggest that Orlando was less a part of the circle than the other two. Sebastien desperately wanted to fit in that tableau, to have with Thierry the same sense of belonging that Orlando and Alain so clearly exuded.

As that thought crossed Sebastien's mind, Thierry looked up and met the vampire's eyes. He extended his hand to Sebastien, gesturing for him to join them, stepping back to make a place for the vampire in their circle. Alain and Orlando smiled in welcome, and Sebastien could tell it was genuine. Everyone wanted him to be a part of their circle. They understood that each pair was stronger together than they were apart. They all understood that, and yet, as he stood with the other three, listening to Thierry and Orlando ribbing Alain, he knew a vital connection was missing. They were not deliberately excluding him. Their smiles invited him to participate. Their laughter was contagious. He wanted to join in, to contribute to the teasing tone of the conversation. The jokes, though, came from a familiarity and an intimacy that Sebastien did not share with them. However much they wanted him there, he did not belong the way they did. At least not yet.

A commotion on the other side of the room drew Sebastien's attention. He smiled admiringly again as Adèle came into the room, but his smile faded when he saw the scowl on Jude's face. Having talked to Adèle on the train, he knew how much Jude's attitude bothered her. He silently willed Jude to stay where he was, with his like-minded friends, rather than crossing the room to bait Adèle. Unfortunately, Jude did not seem to get his message. Sebastien could not hear what Jude said to his friends, but he saw the younger vampire start toward Adèle. With a sigh, Sebastien turned back to the conversation that was supposed to include him.

"Look at her," Jude hissed under his breath to Colin, standing next to him. "She looks like a... a... I don't even know what she looks like," he finished finally. A part of him wanted to ignore her, to pretend that she was not even worthy of his attention, but his feet moved of their own accord, taking him across the room to her side.

"I see you decided to dress down for the occasion," he sneered.

Adèle glared at Jude. "I don't see what business of yours it is what I wear," she replied coldly. "I don't answer to you." She started to turn away, but he caught her arm, spinning her back around.

"Don't walk away from me when I'm talking to you," he spat.

"I didn't hear any conversation, only insults," Adèle retorted, forcibly stopping herself from slapping the arrogant vampire. "When you're interested in actually talking, I'll listen." She was about to start away again when Marcel came in and called the meeting to order. Trapped, Adèle resigned herself to enduring Jude's presence a little longer.

"Let's get down to business," Marcel said. "The sooner we can get this alliance functioning fully, the sooner we can turn the tide in this war. We've been simply holding our own for long enough. It's time to plan to finish it."

He looked across the room to Jean. "Did you find someone to help us with the interrogations?" he asked.

"I did," Jean replied, introducing Antonio, who bowed slightly with Old World charm.

"Good," Marcel said. "Antonio, you'll be working with Alain and Thierry, and their partners. I understand that Orlando and Sebastien won't be doing any tasting themselves, but I'm sure they can manage to look menacing, and the more people who hear what is said, the more brains we'll have to unravel all that we learn."

Alain and Thierry nodded, looking to their partners for confirmation. When the two vampires nodded, Alain and Thierry led them and Antonio toward the exit, intending to start immediately.

Marcel went on. "We need to draw up new duty rosters. If there are any partners that specifically want day duty, let Adèle know. She'll be in charge of organizing everyone."

"A woman in charge?" Jude muttered disbelievingly even as Jean spoke up.

"Angelique would be a good one to help with that," Jean suggested. "She runs an empire that puts the rest of us to shame."

David could not stop himself from rolling his eyes, even knowing that Angelique, standing nearby, would see. He was not sure what it said about the vampires that they were so openly accepting of Angelique and her profession. At least this task would mean that he was also working with Adèle. He admired Adèle's no-nonsense attitude. That would make this evening bearable, even if it did nothing to improve his situation in general.

"That sounds like an excellent suggestion," Marcel agreed, nodding to David to help as well. David joined Adèle and Jude, waiting to see who would volunteer for daylight duty.

Before Marcel could continue, Raymond spoke up. "Jean has arranged a meeting for tonight. We want to learn as much as we can about the partnerships that have been formed, and he thinks that his mentor might have information that could help us. He's agreed to meet with Jean and me tonight to see what we can learn."

"Good," Marcel said with a decisive nod. "Do I need to be there? I have often wanted to meet Monsieur Lombard."

"That's up to you," Raymond replied diplomatically. Marcel had never shown the kind of interest in the esoteric that Raymond had, and Raymond suspected that the conversation would quickly delve into realms in which Marcel had no expertise. He was not about to say that out loud, though.

"We shall see how things go, then," Marcel decided. "I may join you for a few minutes. For those of you who are left without specific assignments, your first task is to see Adèle and Angelique about your patrol assignments. Then you need to work with your partner to develop battle strategies. You all know your own strengths and weaknesses. Share those with your partner. He or she needs to know you as well as you know yourself so you can work together when we next go into battle. You have your orders. Get busy."

As the two wizards and three vampires walked down the hall, Thierry explaining the strategy from their interrogation of Dominique to Antonio, Alain dropped back a little to walk beside Sebastien. "Thierry spends so much time looking out for others that he sometimes forgets to look out for himself," Alain told the dark-haired vampire.

"Don't worry," Sebastien reassured him. "I'll watch his back."

SEEING that Marcel had dismissed the meeting, Angelique made her way quickly to Adèle's side, ignoring the two males also assigned to the task. She had learned long ago that arguing with those who saw only her henna-painted hands and lush beauty did no good. Instead, she proved herself quietly through her actions. She knew Jude, had seen how he treated Adèle, and how the wizard had reacted. David seemed to have the same attitude toward her. She would not argue with him; she would work with Adèle and show him, and Jude, how effective they could be.

"Do you have the current rosters?" she asked Adèle, ignoring Jude's brooding presence and David's frown.

"In my office," Adèle replied.

"Then we should set up there to take volunteers. We'll be able to plug them directly into the database."

Adèle nodded. "This way," she said, gesturing to the door. "A simple find and replace should ensure an equitable schedule."

"The more consistent we can be with days and nights, the more alert the pairings will be. It may take a few days to switch day and night for those whose schedules are changing, but it would be more difficult if their patrol times vary widely."

They reached Adèle's office. She sat down at her computer, pulling up a chair for Angelique next to her. David and Jude hovered in the doorway for a moment. "There are chairs in the conference room next door," Adèle reminded David without looking up. When she did not hear movement, she glanced at them. "I'm quite sure we can handle it on our own if you have other, manly activities to handle."

"Sarcasm doesn't become you," David said softly.

"Condescension doesn't become you," she replied tartly. "Either get in here and help or get out and leave us to do the work."

Jude moved into the room. "That wouldn't be prudent. Someone needs to make sure it's done right."

Adèle's eyebrows shot up. "And you are such an expert?" she challenged. "Here, come pull up the rosters and show me how you would adjust them."

"I am no secretary. I will dictate the rosters and you can record them."

"Can't type?" Adèle asked callously, "or can't write?"

Jude's eyes narrowed. "You don't know what you're talking about."

"Really?" Adèle queried.

Jude grabbed a pen and wrote his name on a pad, throwing it back on the desk.

"He knows his own name," Adèle said to Angelique. "I'm impressed. I didn't think he had it in him."

Angelique could not hold back her chuckle.

"Adèle," David scolded. "This is not helping."

"And your attitude is?" she challenged, rising from her seat. "I haven't seen you acting any better than that one."

"I didn't ask to be paired with a… a… harem wench."

"And I didn't ask to be paired with a male chauvinist pig!" Adèle shouted, slamming her hands down on the desk. "You two need to get over yourselves. We're fighting a war and your antiquated ideas are getting in the way."

"Antiquated?" Jude interrupted. "She knows some big words," he commented to David. "I'm impressed."

Adèle was around the desk in a heartbeat, face to face with Jude. "What is your fucking problem?" she shouted.

"Women who've forgotten their place," Jude sneered.

Adèle's hand was moving before she was even aware of it, fingers closing into a fist aimed squarely at Jude's jaw. If he had been mortal, it would have connected, but his vampiric reflexes brought his hand up to close around her wrist. They stood frozen like that, eyes clashing as they struggled, for one long second, then another, and another. Defiance shone on both their faces, but Adèle could feel another spark inside her as well. Mentally she shook herself, rejecting any attraction to someone who would treat her the way Jude had done, but she could not smother the spark completely.

"You don't really want to do that, do you?" Jude asked with deceptive stillness. The thrill of the chase was beginning to work its way through him. Adèle was not the first to think she could challenge him. He would enjoy teaching her otherwise, in as slow and thorough a way possible. By the time he was done, she would be purring like a big cat in his bed.

"Hell yes, I do," she spat, jerking her wrist back. "Get out," she ordered, pointing to the door. "You can come back when you've fixed your attitude problem."

Jude glared at her a moment longer before taking a step back. It would not hurt to retreat now. There would be plenty of time to tame her later. Adèle advanced on him, effectively shoving him out the door. When he was gone, she slammed the door behind him and turned back to face David and Angelique, ready to light into David next. Angelique caught her eye, though, and shook her head. Accepting the vampire's request, Adèle simply glared at David and then pushed away from the door. "I'm going to clear my head. I'll be back in a few minutes."

Angelique nodded and Adèle left, slamming the door again.

Angelique sighed and moved to the computer, searching for and finding the duty rosters. "Open the door and see if there's anyone they didn't scare off with their shouting. This needs to be done, so we'll have to do it," she told David pragmatically.

David did as she said, more than a little shocked by the ease Angelique displayed at the computer. She looked up and caught his bemused expression. "What?" she asked. "My tattoos didn't disable my hands or my brain. I know what I'm doing."

David watched in growing interest as Angelique took the names of the volunteers who came in over the course of the night and juggled the rosters for daylight duty.

"I think I owe you an apology," he said several hours later. "I seem to have underestimated you."

"I'm used to it," Angelique replied, never looking up. "You're hardly the first and I doubt you'll be the last."

"That doesn't excuse my behavior. Can we try again?"

Angelique looked up that time, seeing the boyish eagerness in David's face. "If you wish," she shrugged, returning to her work. She hit print and retrieved the sheaf of documents. "These are for Marcel, for his approval. If he signs off on them, you'll need to post them or distribute them, however you do it here."

David took the stack of papers, but he did not immediately leave. "How do you know all this?" he asked.

"I run Sang Froid," she reminded him. "You may not approve of that fact, but I still have to keep track of everything: schedules, salaries, expenses, income, supplies, benefits. I made the mistake, years ago, of relying completely on a manager so I was free to enjoy myself. He stole every penny I had. I swore to rebuild and to never again trust anyone else to run my business without my supervision. I have a truly reliable manager now who handles things during the day, but even with him, I check in to make sure his decisions are sound. Not all my decisions are good ones either, of course, but at least I know I made the choice, whatever the outcome."

"I see why Jean suggested you for this, then."

"This will not take all my time. The schedule's done unless there's a problem. I expect you to teach me your battle strategy so we will be able to work together outside these walls as well as within."

"I'll teach you what I know," David agreed, "but usually, I just follow orders."

"And I will too," Angelique replied, "but I have to know how to do so."

"These are finished, right?" David asked, rustling the papers in his hand.

"Yes," Angelique agreed.

"Let's take them to Marcel together and then maybe we could see if we could find somewhere to drill."

"I'd like that," Angelique replied, thrilled that David was finally giving her a chance.

ERIC looked at Vincent who grinned back. They had found a vampire with as few morals as they possessed. "We have a proposition for you," Eric began.

Edouard stepped over the dead body and advanced toward the two men. Neither of them moved, but he could see them tense. Good, neither of them expected their size to be a match for Edouard's vampiric strength. "And what is the nature of this proposition?" he asked.

"Our... friend would like to know a little more about vampires," Eric explained.

"You said a proposition," Edouard pointed out. "What's in it for me?"

"Our friend will have to explain," Eric replied quickly, "but he'll make it worth your while."

"And where, exactly, is your friend?" Edouard wanted to know.

"Near St. Denis," Vincent said.

"That's not close by. I don't know that I care to travel so far. After all, I need to get home before dawn."

"We can be there in a blink of an eye," Eric replied, "if you'll let us use our magic."

Edouard raised an eyebrow, intrigued. It seemed that more than one vampire in Paris would be talking to wizards tonight.

"Very well," he agreed.

Eric nodded at Vincent. As Vincent prepared to take himself back to their base, Eric cast the spell on himself and Edouard. Vincent followed a second later. They reappeared in another dark alley near the basilique St. Denis. Eric led them through an unassuming door. Nothing on the outside gave any indication that the interior walls of every building on the block had been pierced, providing a warren of rooms and halls of varying sizes to house Serrier's base of operations. He had other outposts, but this was his stronghold, so heavily warded that it was the only place Vincent let down his guard completely. He did not know how Pascal had managed to acquire an entire block of real estate without anyone knowing, and he did not ask or care.

The two wizards led the vampire into Pascal's meeting room. They motioned for Edouard to have a seat and Vincent went to find Pascal.

Edouard took the seat that was offered, looking around the room. He would reserve judgment, but he had a feeling he had found the rebel wizards. From what he knew of the Milice, those wizards would have tried to arrest him for murder rather than offering him some sort of deal in exchange for information.

A few minutes later, Vincent returned with another man, dark-haired, with a moustache and goatee. The man walked confidently up to Edouard. "My friends tell me you might be able to answer my questions," he said without preamble.

"I might," Edouard replied, "if I knew what questions they were. Your friends also mentioned making it worth my time to do so."

Pascal smiled. "I understand that you… enjoy your victims," he observed. "I imagine it might get difficult trying to avoid unwanted questions after a while."

"I move around a lot," Edouard replied with a shrug.

"And if I could offer you your choice of victims, to do with as you pleased, no questions asked?" Pascal suggested. "Would that make it worth your time to answer a few of my questions?"

Edouard pondered the offer for a moment. An unlimited supply of blood and no questions asked… "What would you like to know?" he asked, settling back in his chair.

Chapter 11

JEAN read Raymond's nerves in the tense set of his shoulders. "Stop worrying," he scolded gently. "What do you think he's going to do in a public place? If there is one thing that can be said about Christophe Lombard, it's that he's discreet. He will walk in, chat with the waiters for a moment, order an espresso, then sit at the table with us and drink it like he were any ordinary man. When we leave, the waiters will comment to themselves what a polite old gentleman he was."

"I'd rather they didn't remember us at all," Raymond said. "I sided with Serrier for a while, and I know how he does things. I don't know how he found out about the meeting last night, but he did, which means he wants to know what the vampires are doing. He's not going to give up simply because his first attempt didn't work. It wouldn't surprise me at all if he had his wizards out looking for vampires. I'd rather not come face to face with them when it's just the two of us."

"Christophe knows what battle we are fighting," Jean assured him. "He will not lead them to us. He's a canny old man, Raymond, not to mention being an old vampire. He'll take every precaution you could wish."

Raymond suppressed a sigh. It appeared the time for more truth had come. "Did you know that Serrier has put a price on my head?" he asked Jean. "500,000€ dead, double that alive."

Jean raised an eyebrow. "That's quite a bit of money."

"He wants to make an example of me, to show his people the cost of betrayal. If I seem paranoid sometimes, that's why. If they kill me trying to capture me, I won't care what he does to my body. I won't let them take me alive," he continued. "I'll kill myself before I'll let them torture me to death. Their cruelty has no bounds."

Jean could feel his hackles rising at the thought of anyone hurting Raymond. "It won't come to that. You'll never have to face them alone. And if we're outnumbered, get yourself the hell out of there."

"And abandon you? Like hell!"

"I didn't say abandon me. You'd go for help and come back for me," Jean said. "I've seen you do magic. You could be to Marcel's and back with reinforcements long before they could take me down. We don't have to worry about that tonight, though. All we need to think about tonight is figuring out these partnership issues."

Raymond nodded as they reached the café. It was neither the time nor the place to discuss it, but he knew, to his great surprise, that he would not be able to do as Jean asked, even to save his own life. He had never expected to feel this way about anyone, much less a vampire, but that seemed to be the hand fate had suddenly dealt him. He would stay on his guard, as always, and hope that Lombard did not inadvertently lead the dark wizards to this meeting. It was no longer merely his own life on the line. His vampire would suffer as well if he made a mistake.

"There he is," Jean whispered to Raymond when they entered the small coffee shop. A few days ago, Raymond would have been amused by the change that came over Jean at the sight of the elder vampire. Gone was the confident, even arrogant, leader of vampires that Raymond had come to know. In his place was a nervous, edgy soldier in the presence of a general. Looking around the café, Raymond's gaze landed on the venerable old man whose mien betrayed none of the age that the lines on his face or the white in his hair suggested, and he could understand Jean's nerves.

Jean led Raymond across the café, stopping next to the table, but not sitting down. "This is my partner, Raymond Payet," Jean began, introducing the wizard and the vampire, "and this is my mentor, Christophe Lombard."

Christophe rose from his seat and offered an elegant hand to Raymond who took it, refusing to let his nerves come through. "It is a pleasure to meet you," Christophe said to Raymond. "Jean tells me we share a love of books."

"He told me the same thing," Raymond replied, taking a seat when Christophe returned to his. Jean remained standing awkwardly by the table.

"Oh, do sit down, Jean," Christophe said with a sigh. "You wear me out sometimes, boy."

Jean dropped into a chair like a scolded schoolboy. Raymond had trouble containing his amusement, but he did his best. He and Jean were a team now, and until things were a little more solid between them, he did not think it wise to have too much fun at his partner's expense.

"I have been doing some reading today," Christophe said, turning to Raymond. "I have a few questions, if you don't mind my prying. They are a little personal, but the nature of this bond between wizards and vampires seems to be intensely personal."

"I will answer them as well as I can," Raymond assured him. "I want to figure this out as much as you do."

"I imagine you do," Christophe agreed with a small smile.

"What do you want to know?" Raymond asked, hoping to start the conversation.

"I have some ideas," Christophe explained. "When I talked to Mireille and her partner, Caroline, they described a certain rapport that they felt building between them, a compatibility, if you will, that linked them. Mireille even mentioned a feeling of compulsion, almost, that drove her to Caroline's side when they were separated. Have you felt either of those things?"

Raymond chuckled. "We did not get off to a very good start," he admitted. "I was having a hard time with the exigencies of the alliance…"

"Neither of us behaved well at first," Jean broke in, not wanting Raymond to shoulder more of the blame than was his to bear. "I'm not sure we would be the best ones to ask."

Christophe raised one regal eyebrow but did not comment. "What have you observed then?" he asked, changing the direction of his questions.

"Actually," Raymond said, turning to Jean, "we might be the best ones to ask. I mean, it would be next to impossible to distinguish what was the bond and what was simple attraction if we were to ask Alain and Orlando these questions, but given the way we started, anything we feel almost has to come from whatever is allowing my magic to protect you. Even when I was angry at Jean, at the alliance as a whole, I found myself crossing the room to where he was standing," he said, turning back to Christophe.

"And if he took his time coming to me, I almost always went to him," Jean added.

"Something about the bond pushes for exclusivity as well," Raymond continued. "I did not want Jean to feed from me at first, for various reasons, but it still bothered me to know that he was going to someone else. And when I had to watch him…" he trailed off with a shiver.

"It's not what it sounds like," Jean amended quickly, seeing the look of disapproval on Christophe's face. "We were interrogating a captured wizard and it seemed like a good idea to find out whether he was telling the truth. I tasted just enough to read his heart, that's all."

Seeing Jean's distress, Raymond chimed back in. "We've straightened things out now and found a vampire with no partner to help in the interrogations. We're learning through trial and error, but that's why it's so important to figure this out. The more we know, the less likely we are to make mistakes."

"I agree," Christophe replied gravely. "As I said, I have been doing some reading and I have some ideas, but I need to know a little more about the nature of magic the way the wizards understand it before I can be at all confident of my conclusions."

"The nature of magic," Raymond repeated with a laugh. "How long do you have, because I've spent my entire adult life studying it, and the more I learn, the more I realize how much I don't know."

Christophe chuckled. "I feel the same way about the nature of vampires. So, tell me what you have learned."

"Where to begin," Raymond mused aloud. "We teach young wizards that there is a difference between the elemental magic as an external force and magic that we do with our spells and charms. The external force is simply there, neither good nor bad, kept in balance by careful usage and work, and by our own practice of magic. The magic we do with our spells is internal, kept in balance by our own deeds. There are dark spells, magic whose sole purpose is to harm. The phrase 'dark magic' has gained popularity, especially with the recent war, but magic itself is not dark, only the way it's used. The problem is that with the war, we have spent our energy fighting rather than keeping the elemental magic in balance. Every day, the disequilibrium grows worse. It's only a matter of time until the imbalance starts to cause chaos in the natural world."

"And the external force," Christophe asked. "Is it finite?"

"The simplest comparison would be to something like a forest. It is finite, but it is renewable. That's one of the roles of wizards, to feed back into the elemental magic as much as we take out of it, to make sure that it stays in balance. And that's the problem. We're taking so much more out to fight than we can put back in."

Christophe nodded. "Is it… sentient, I suppose is the right word?"

Raymond frowned. "What do you mean?"

"Could the elemental magic do things, or encourage things, that would aid in its renewal?" Christophe rephrased. Before Raymond could answer, he caught the bored look on Jean's face. "You don't have to stay, Jean. I think we're perfectly capable of conversing without you."

Jean looked at Raymond to see his reaction to that suggestion. Jean did not share their fascination and so was not finding the conversation interesting at all, but he did not want to abandon Raymond either.

"It's fine," Raymond said softly. "Come back in an hour. I'll be here."

Jean frowned, their recent conversation about Serrier and his intentions toward Raymond fresh in the vampire's mind. "What if you finish sooner than that? I don't want to leave you here alone."

"I will wait with your partner until you return," Christophe interjected.

"In that case, I'll leave you to talk," Jean decided, rising from his seat.

When he had exited, Christophe turned back to Raymond. "He is a good vampire, but not much of a scholar."

Raymond chuckled. "The same could be said of most of my colleagues." Then he grew more serious again as he considered Christophe's question. "Capable of encouraging its own renewal," he mused aloud. "I've never thought about it, because we put so much effort into maintaining the balance ourselves, but there must have been a time when we did not know how to do that, and yet the balance was not so off that it destroyed the world. It's an interesting question, and you obviously have a reason for asking it."

"Symbiosis," Christophe said. "If I'm right, the vampire is protected from sunlight and the wizard from the effects of feeding, and from what you and the others have said, the symbiosis seems to be self-perpetuating. The protective, possessive instincts of the vampires have been stirred to life, pushing them to continue the bond even in the face of resistance. And you said yourself that you were drawn to Jean's side even when you wanted to be elsewhere. This is external, not internal, and your description of the elemental magic as an entity unto itself made me wonder if this bond could be something created to sustain it."

"I can see why this knowledge might have been suppressed," Raymond commented. "I can see quite a few wizards feeling coerced, even if by their own magic."

"Is it coercion?" Christophe asked. "Or does the inherent magic in each wizard find the right vampire, regardless of what apparent differences exist?"

"Alain and Orlando were attracted to each other before their bond. They're the only partnership that had a chance to form naturally. The others formed as a result of deliberate experimentation. There is no way to know what might have developed without that. I wouldn't have let Jean bite me because he was a vampire. It had nothing to do with his personality, his appearance, or anything except my own ingrained fears."

"What about the others?" Christophe queried.

"There seems to be a certain sympathy between most pairings. You said Caroline and Mireille felt it. Alain and Orlando certainly do. I saw one or two others that seemed mismatched, though. Adèle is a very modern woman, very independent, and I got the impression that her partner, Jude I think his name was, had a real problem with that," Raymond replied thoughtfully.

"Jude has a problem with anything, any idea, less than four hundred years old. He and a few of his friends have refused to leave the era of their making behind," Christophe explained.

"Then why would his match be Adèle? Why would her magic find a partner so antithetical to her nature? I mean, I can see Alain and Orlando together. Thierry and Sebastien seem well paired. Even Jean and I are as well matched as I can be with any vampire. Why would Jude match with Adèle? Why not someone like David Sabatier who is also relatively conservative?"

"It would depend on how deep the symbiosis goes. If it were only practical, it would make more sense, but this bond does not have its genesis in your alliance. It is older than I am, if my guess about Merlin and the vampire is correct. It is not a question of working together but of living together, it seems. How does this David feel about men?" Christophe wondered.

"You mean sexually?" Raymond clarified. When Christophe nodded, he continued, "As far as I know, he's only ever sought the company of women."

"The same is true of Jude, sexually. He prefers men as companions, women in his bed. Putting them together would serve the alliance, but not the symbiotic bond."

"I don't see Jude and Adèle as lovers either," Raymond laughed. "They could barely stand to look at each other."

"Perhaps he will temper her and she will temper him," Christophe suggested. "You said there was another mismatched pair."

"Angelique and David."

"Ah, yes," Christophe smiled. "The lovely Angelique. Appearances can be deceiving, as you well know. She is possibly the most business-savvy vampire in Paris. She looks like she belongs in a sultan's harem, and she was in fact taken from one when she was turned, but that does not negate the ruthlessly practical nature that lies beneath. It sounds as if David has misjudged her. When he sees her as she truly is, perhaps his opinion will change."

"Perhaps," Raymond acknowledged. "So, the pairings arise because of some underlying complimentary traits of the wizard and vampire. And the symbiotic nature pushes them towards a level of intimacy that would perpetuate the symbiotic state. It makes sense. Magic has to be regenerated and kept in balance. If something about the bond helps with that, it would explain a lot. Otherwise, I don't see the benefit for the wizards. The vampires get protection from the sunlight and in the alliance, we get new allies, but I don't see the personal benefits for the wizards."

Christophe grinned wolfishly. "You have obviously never had a vampire as a lover. Our instincts push us in ways you cannot imagine. If a vampire chooses to devote himself to you, you will never want for anything again as long as you live. We put things, people, on pedestals, building our very existence around the object of our affection. For me, it is books. For young Orlando, it will be his Avoué. For Angelique, it is her business. For Jean, up until now, it was Orlando - not sexually, but his world revolved around helping the youngling heal. Give your friend Alain a week and ask him if he has ever been treated so well in his life. Ask him if he would undo the Aveu de Sang if he could. He will tell you no and it will not be the magic speaking."

"You're so sure of it," Raymond said in amazement. The idea was so foreign to him, and yet even when he hated the idea of the alliance and all that it asked of him, he had felt the compulsion to be at Jean's side. Now that they had ironed out some of their differences, Raymond could not help but wonder how far the compulsion would take them. Christophe talked about the symbiosis as a lifetime bond. Would that bond be satisfied by a strong working relationship or by a deep and lasting friendship? Or would he and Jean find themselves pushed into a relationship of a different kind? His mind shied away from that. He was still having enough trouble letting Jean feed from him for the purposes of the alliance. He was not ready to contemplate having a vampire as a lover.

"I have had almost two millennia to observe my kind, and their interactions with mortals. I have only met, ever even heard of, a handful vampires in all that time who did not act as I have described. We have so much time before us after we are turned, and our instincts drive us to preserve that which brings us pleasure. I have seen those instincts change men when they were turned from uncaring beasts to rabid protectors. They did not lose their qualms about hurting those who would hurt their treasure, but the person they chose to protect lived in as much luxury as they could provide. I have never understood what went wrong in the few cases where our instincts did not take over. And in most of those cases, the threat of being outcast from the society of vampires was enough to keep them in line. I can think of only one case that truly went beyond the pale. He is destroyed now. I only regret that he caused such pain before he was destroyed." Christophe did not name Thurloe, did not indicate that he was in any way referring to Orlando's maker since that was Orlando's story to tell, but the underlying anger remained, even a century later.

"So it can go wrong?" Raymond asked.

"It can, I suppose, but only a few times in almost two thousand years is not too bad a record."

"Only a few times you know about," Raymond qualified.

"Granted," Christophe agreed. "How many wizards do you know about who have gone bad?"

"Touché," Raymond said, shaking his head.

"I have studied much, as have you. I have not found other cases of abuse from any reputable source since we became civilized enough not to kill our prey every time."

"I knew a boy who was killed by a vampire," Raymond confided, telling Christophe about the boy in his village.

"Do you remember the vampire's name?" Christophe asked curiously.

"I think it was Edouard," Raymond said. "I never knew his last name."

Christophe frowned. "I'm not aware of a vampire with that name currently residing in the city, but I will see what I can discover. Vampire society as a whole does not condone killing mortals. It makes us all look bad and it makes our lives that much more difficult. If a vampire is flaunting that convention, Jean needs to know about it."

"Why Jean?" Raymond asked. "Why not you?"

"I gave leadership over to him when he proved himself worthy of it. I have better things to do with my time. I have books to read, things to learn. I have no time for the petty squabbles that make up most of the duties Jean now bears. Would you want to be in Chavinier's place?"

Raymond laughed at that suggestion. "That will never happen. They will never forget that I sided with Serrier for a short time. I have more hope of winning this war single-handedly than I do of holding any position of authority within the Milice. I am only there at all because Marcel insists. The others would sooner see me dead."

"Maybe this will help them see your value as an ally," Christophe suggested. "Maybe it will even help them see the value of knowledge of every kind."

"We can only hope," Raymond replied fervently.

Chapter 12

ANTONIO raised his head and spat out the blood in his mouth. After questioning all of the dark wizards, he was beginning to understand why Jean had not swallowed any of the foul-tasting blood. The mere flavor of it was enough to turn his stomach without actually ingesting it. "He lies," he said when he had cleansed his palate.

"You do realize that every time he tells us that, you make your situation worse," Alain told Pacotte.

"Is there really anything I could say to make it better?" Pacotte countered with a bitter laugh. "You've already tried and judged me, and if I did tell you anything, I would be dead anyway, so what's the point?"

Thierry backhanded him, knocking the other wizard off the chair. "To keep me happy," he growled.

Alain started to reach for Thierry, to calm him, when Orlando swayed next to him. Alain cried out his lover's name and caught him as he collapsed.

"Shit!" Thierry muttered, throwing the binding spell over Pacotte again so he would not be aware of what was transpiring. "What's going on?"

He got no answer. Alain cradled Orlando in his arms, rocking him gently, as the other two vampires leaned over him solicitously. "What's wrong with him?" Alain asked, panic rising in his voice. He called Orlando's name again, trying to rouse the unconscious vampire.

"When was the last time he fed?" Sebastien asked Alain.

"Yesterday morning." Alain's eyes never left Orlando's still form as he spoke. He would answer Sebastien's questions, in the hope that the other vampire would be able to help, but all his attention was for his vampire, his lover.

"And when did you make your Aveu de Sang?" he asked.

"The day before that."

"Well, no wonder he's unconscious. He needs to eat," Sebastien explained. "Didn't anyone teach him anything?"

"He said he only needed to feed every two or three days," Alain replied anxiously. He was more than willing to let Orlando feed again, but it worried him to think that Orlando needed it so much.

"Normally, that's true," Sebastien agreed, "but this is not normal. The Aveu de Sang requires more nourishment than that, at least at first. Eventually, he'll be able to go longer, as much as two weeks, without feeding, but at first, he'll need you at least once a day." He paused for a moment to consider. "The protection from sunlight may not last that long. I didn't have that to worry about."

Thierry looked at Sebastien sharply, resolving to ask the vampire about that comment as soon as possible. First, though, they had to take care of Orlando.

"What do I do now?" Alain asked, calming a little now that he understood the reason for Orlando's state. "He's unconscious. He can't bite me."

"Is there some place private you can go? Once you're there, just scratch yourself enough to draw blood and put it on his lips. The taste will rouse him so he can feed properly," Sebastien assured him.

"Use our office," Thierry suggested. "I'm here and everyone else thinks you are, too. They won't bother you there."

Alain nodded and lifted Orlando into his arms. "You'll have to send us there. I don't want to carry him through the halls, and my magic won't work on him."

Thierry nodded and drew his wand, making sure to say the spell clearly so that Alain would know when to expect the dislocation. When the other wizard and the vampire had disappeared, Thierry looked at the dark wizard he had bespelled. With a flick of his wrist, he sent Pacotte back to his holding cell and turned back to Sebastien. "You seem to know a lot about the... what did you call it, Aveu de Sang."

"That's right," Sebastien replied, sure he was not ready to have this conversation. "And yes, I know a bit about it."

Antonio felt the tension in the air and decided this was a good time to make himself scarce. "Gentlemen," he said, drawing their attention but not their eyes, "it is getting late and I still have to feed before dawn. I want their foul taste out of my mouth. If you will excuse me, I will be going now." His unease augmented his usually subtle accent, making his Spanish roots more obvious than usual.

Sebastien and Thierry both nodded, but their eyes never completely left each other. Antonio slipped from the room, shutting the door behind him.

"It sounded like more than a bit," Thierry said when they were alone, not sure he was ready to hear that Sebastien had an Avoué in his past. He had seen the devotion between Alain and Orlando, even after such a short time. It bothered him for reasons he could not explain to think that Sebastien had once known that level of devotion, perhaps even felt it still. "It sounded pretty personal."

Sebastien's hand went reflexively into his pocket. He did not talk about Thibaut. Ever. To anyone. He had not since the man died almost four hundred years ago, leaving him alone. He was still not ready to talk about his Avoué, his heart, but running his fingers over the locket, he decided that maybe it was time he did. "It was personal," he agreed slowly. "I had an Avoué, a long time ago."

Thierry could hear the pain underlying those simple words. They called out to something inside him that he did not want to identify. He was not ready for a new relationship, however much his heart seemed to be demanding that he start this one. "Do you want to talk about it?" he asked.

"Not really," Sebastien replied with a short bark of forced laughter. "But I think you deserve to know."

Thierry held up a hand. "It's your choice," he assured the vampire. "I have no right to pry." He wished he had that right. He wished he had every right where Sebastien was concerned, but he could not say that. Not yet, maybe not ever. It would not be fair to Sebastien.

Sebastien did not address that comment. He was not ready to tell Thierry that the wizard could have whatever rights he wanted, and he did not think Thierry was ready to hear it. "His name was Thibaut. Unlike most of his friends, he wasn't scared because I was a vampire. I found out later that I was not the first vampire he'd met, or even the first he let feed from him, but I was the one he chose. I fell for him immediately. The taste of his blood was like nothing I'd ever known." Nor had he tasted its like since, until he met Thierry. That thought, though, he left unspoken as well. He was not ready to say it either, and he was sure Thierry was not ready to hear it. "We were together after that until he died."

"You miss him still, don't you?" Thierry asked, trying to decide what these new revelations meant.

"His death left a hole in my life that nothing since has filled." Sebastien did not add that Thierry's presence was finally easing that pain even if he had not, could not, replace Thibaut. It was too soon to think about a new relationship, especially with someone who had also recently suffered a loss. Yet another thing they did not seem able to talk about. He wondered if they would ever move out of this stalemate. They could work together, but they did not seem able to overcome the hurdles that would let them become friends, or, when they were ready, perhaps even more.

Thierry was not sure exactly how to respond to Sebastien's last comment, not ready to make the offer that would fill the hole. He knew about grief. He had known about it even before Aleth died, having watched Alain come to terms slowly with losing Henri and having seen what grief could do to an honorable man when Eric switched sides. He was not so sure, though, if his own experience could even begin to compare to Sebastien's. After all, he and Aleth had been estranged for some time before her death, and while he was still in love with the idea of her, he had not seen that side of Aleth since soon after the war started. He had known, though he had refused to accept it, that even the end of the war would not restore their relationship. Aleth had only died a few days ago; their relationship had been dead for almost two years.

"I don't know how to ask this without sounding crass," Thierry said. "From what Alain and Orlando have said, it seems that the Aveu de Sang is much like a marriage. I know that some people remarry after losing a spouse. Have you ever thought about finding another Avoué?" He was not sure why he was asking. He certainly did not want Sebastien to find someone else, but he was not ready to offer himself either. Certainly not so soon after Aleth's death. Maybe never.

Sebastien's immediate reaction was one of anger, but he knew Thierry was not trying to be cruel. "It doesn't work quite like that," Sebastien replied slowly, not sure he could explain the complex relationship. "There's an... expectation among mortals that you will get married, have kids, and spend a lifetime together. It's different for us. The lifetime of a mortal is a blink of an eye to a vampire. I spent fifty years with Thibaut, but I've been alone for five hundred. I made the commitment once, early in my life as a vampire, desperate for companionship and love after having lost all those I knew from before. We had fifty wonderful years together, and I would not change them for anything, but now I have to live with having lost him. I don't know if I could face losing someone like that again."

Alone for five hundred years. Hearing the vast emptiness in the vampire's voice, Thierry's instinctive reaction was to reach out, to comfort Sebastien, but he was not sure the vampire would appreciate the offer nor was he sure he was really ready to make it. The impulse was there, so strong that it was hard to deny, but he was afraid of what offering that comfort might imply.

"I'm sorry," he said, feeling incredibly helpless. Sorry did not begin to cover what he was feeling or what Sebastien undoubtedly needed. "I wish I could help."

Sebastien kept his expression from changing, but he could not stop the blow to his heart at Thierry's impersonal words. The wizard clearly did not feel the same connection that Sebastien had been feeling since he first tasted Thierry's blood. He suppressed a sigh. He would have liked a chance at winning Thierry's affection, but that was clearly not meant to be. He would have to be satisfied with his friendship.

Feeling increasingly uncomfortable, Thierry broke the silence. "I suppose we should report to Marcel, at least let him know what happened." It bothered him that they had not been able to get any cogent information.

Almost as much as it bothered him that he could not seem to make progress with Sebastien. He wanted to, desperately, but he simply was not ready.

RAYMOND looked up as Jean walked back into the café, his mind still struggling to take in everything he had learned that evening. If the eldest of the vampires was correct in his deductions – and Raymond could find no flaw in his logic – Raymond was looking at a life partner in one definition or another of that term. He knew next to nothing about Jean and yet his own magic was pushing him into a relationship with the vampire. He shivered a little. He had barely come to terms with the exigencies of the alliance. He had no idea how to handle this bond that was forming.

"Do I have something on my face?" Jean asked when he sat down.

"What?" Raymond stuttered.

"You were staring at me strangely. I thought maybe I had something on my face."

Raymond shook his head. "No, I was just thinking."

"I will leave you to talk," Christophe said, rising from his seat, "but before I go, Jean, there seems to be a rogue vampire who is willing to kill his prey. Edouard is his first name. If he is in Paris, you need to find him and set him straight. He endangers us all."

Jean nodded. "I'll look into it."

"See that you do." And with that, the elder vampire was gone.

"Did you figure some things out?" Jean asked.

"Yeah. Let's go for a walk. I'll tell you what we decided."

Jean agreed and they left the café, walking side by side through the darkened streets. Raymond stole glances at Jean out of the corner of his eye. The vampire's body was whipcord lean, his face rugged, but not overly so. He sported a hint of a moustache and goatee, an affectation that bothered Raymond in most men, but that seemed to fit Jean perfectly. His light brown hair was long, reaching his shoulders where it was pulled back into a tail. Some strands had worked themselves free and Raymond caught himself about to reach up and brush them back from Jean's face. The vampire looked younger than Raymond himself, but he was quite sure that appearances, in this case, were deceiving. Jean had not risen to his position of leadership in a matter of a year or two. He had heard several people refer to Jean as one of the eldest vampires in the city. He realized with a start that he was considering Jean, not simply as an ally, but the way he might consider a potential lover. A part of him quailed at the thought, but he pushed it aside. He had to consider Jean as an individual, not as a vampire. He owed him that much after the misunderstandings that had plagued the beginning of their partnership.

As they walked, Raymond struggled to find a way to sum up everything he had discussed with the elder vampire in as non-threatening a way as possible. The revelations that swirled through his mind had him feeling distinctly unsettled. For years, he had feared vampires because of what had happened to Jacques. He was beginning to understand that those events were a fluke, but the ingrained caution was not so easy to overcome. "Monsieur Lombard said that vampires often build their lives around their passion, whatever that was. He said his was his studies and that Orlando's would be Alain. Do you think he's right?" Raymond asked after several minutes of silence.

"I think that's often true, yes," Jean agreed, wondering what such matters had to do with the alliance. Had they wasted the evening on such esoteric matters that nothing practical had come out of their discussion? He would not put it past Christophe, but he had thought Raymond was more focused on the immediate situation.

"What is your passion?"

Jean considered the question, hoping this was leading somewhere. A week ago, he would have answered helping Orlando, but Orlando's care had passed into Alain's hands and would stay there for as long as the wizard lived, unless, of course, he proved unworthy, at which point Jean would do what it took to fix the problem. "I don't have one right now," he answered finally, an image of Karine flashing through his head. She would willingly have filled that spot if he had let her, but he had never allowed her to get that close. "Why do you ask?"

"We think the bond between wizard and vampire is a self-perpetuating one. If it triggers the possessive instincts of the vampires, it would prompt them to make their wizards into their passions and to act accordingly." Jean had no passion at the moment. That was the thought that resonated in Raymond's mind as he answered the question. Would that make Jean more likely to succumb to the demands of this bond between them? The thought both fascinated and repelled him. He could not begin to imagine what it would be like to find himself in that situation. It was enough to make him wish he were better friends with Alain. He could certainly use some advice on the matter.

"To what end?" Jean asked.

"We don't really know, but our theory is that the exchange of blood and magic between wizard and vampire must contribute to the natural balance in the world. Otherwise, there's no explanation for the almost compulsive need to be near our partners that many of us seem to be feeling."

Jean shivered, beginning to see the consequences could be far-reaching indeed. "No wonder this isn't widely known. Most vampires avoid any kind of long-term relationship with non-vampires because of the issue of mortality. We stay the same while generations of people live and die. I am over a thousand years old. That's thirty generations or more that have lived and died since I was made. The only way to stay sane is to let them go unnoticed. It's the same reason so few vampires form an Aveu de Sang like Orlando did. The loss when their Avoué dies is more than many vampires are willing to suffer. We prefer to seek sustenance anonymously and company among our own kind."

Raymond's heart sank. Not only were the vampires about to be faced with a commitment they had not asked for, it was one they would not want. He wondered what lengths they would go to in order to avoid that commitment. Could the alliance stand in light of this new information?

"How do we explain this to the vampires in such a way that they don't immediately go running for the hills?" Raymond asked.

Jean frowned. It bothered him that Raymond considered vampires so lacking in honor. "We keep our commitments," he growled, feeling the familiar, but unwelcome, frustration that had characterized his early interactions with his partner.

"Damn," Raymond said, hearing Jean's tone and realizing what he had said. "I'm sorry. That didn't come out the way I meant it."

"And how, exactly, did you mean it?" Jean asked, determined to stay calm and hear what Raymond had to say. They had come too far to go back to the sniping.

"I simply meant that this is a bombshell we're dropping on everyone, wizards as well as vampires, and we need to figure out the best way to explain it so that everyone accepts it and moves on," Raymond explained. "I never meant to imply that you would abandon the alliance."

Jean shook his head. "I have no idea," he replied honestly. "I can't even begin to think of a way to explain this rationally. We don't do this. We don't make these kinds of covenants, and suddenly most of the vampires in the city have made them without even knowing it. I wonder if we'd be better off saying nothing."

Raymond grimaced. He could see Jean's point, but... "Is that fair to everyone? I mean, they're going to start feeling the effects of the bond, and it's going to create confusion between their expectations and reality. And if that confusion endangers them, then it's also detrimental not only to them but to the alliance, which is what the partnerships were supposed to be about."

"What about the wizards?" Jean asked. "How will they react?"

"They'll probably be as upset as you seem to think the vampires will be. Practicing magic requires every bit of our reason to keep it under control. You saw what happened when Thierry lost control at the gare the other night. His magic went wild. If it had hit anyone other than Sebastien, it would have seriously injured them. The unreasoning passion that seems to affect both sides could affect our ability to maintain the necessary control."

Jean nodded. It sounded a little like controlling his instincts while he fed so that he took only what he needed rather than gorging himself and killing the person he fed from. "How will you explain it to them?"

"I haven't the slightest idea," Raymond admitted. "I was going to tell Marcel and leave it up to him. Plain speech is what I'm good at, not the kind of spin that Marcel gives to the press all the time. I thought it might help him, though, if we could give him some idea of what he should say to the vampires."

"I think that's my job," Jean pointed out.

"Yes," Raymond agreed, "but we need to present a united front. If the two of you don't appear to have it together at the leadership level, how can we expect anyone else to follow us?"

"Orlando said the same thing to me once before," Jean mused. "I guess we need to talk to Marcel, then." Even as he spoke, he was conscious of a desire to run away, as far away as he could possibly get from Raymond and this... covenant... that was forming between them. He suppressed the reaction, knowing he could not let any of the other vampires see it if he had any hope of convincing them that this was not a terrible turn of events. As soon as he could get away, though, he was going to Karine's, if only to prove to himself that he still could. He would work with Raymond to further the alliance because he had given his word, but he intended to choose how he spent his time away from the alliance, regardless of what Christophe and Raymond thought his instincts would push him to do. He might be a vampire, but that did not mean he had lost all self-control. He would choose who he wanted to be with, and right now, he wanted to be with Karine.

Chapter 13

ALAIN stumbled as he arrived in the office with Orlando in his arms. Years of practice had taught him how to keep his own balance during such a displacement, but he was not used to the extra weight he now carried. His disequilibrium sent them falling backward onto the couch, which suited Alain fine. He shifted Orlando so he was lying flat and looked around the room, trying to find something he could use to break his skin enough that he would bleed. Not bothering with the lights, he went to his desk, rummaging through the drawers to find something sharp. The contents went flying as he searched frantically for something, anything that would draw blood. Scissors, letter opener, this was an office, damn it! There had to be something!

His fingers finally found metal. He closed them around the object and drew it out. A paper clip. He was trying to save his lover and all he could find was a fucking paper clip. Fine! He would use that because he was not waiting any longer. He needed to see Orlando's eyes open again, to feel the vampire's dark gaze on him. Kneeling on the floor next to the couch, Alain unfolded the paper clip and forced the rough end to break his skin. It hurt. It hurt a whole lot more than Orlando's fangs, but that did not matter. All Alain cared about was bringing blood to the surface so he could feed Orlando.

Pulling Orlando into a tight embrace, he dabbed a bit of blood from his wrist and anointed the vampire's lips with it. When that got no reaction, he covered his finger with blood again and slid it between Orlando's lips so he could place the blood on his tongue.

The taste of blood roused Orlando from his stupor to a waking nightmare. He was back in Thurloe's dungeon, in the dark, restrained, blood being forced down his throat to keep him alive and heal him from the most recent round of torture. He had escaped that, damn it. Nothing could make him go back. He grabbed the arm restraining him, forcing it away, forcing his captor down. Enraged beyond reason, he pinned the still form and attacked, driving his fangs deep into the soft skin of the neck.

Orlando's attack was so sudden and so unexpected that Alain could not even struggle. He fell backward, his head hitting the floor as the vampire's body forced him down. Slightly dazed from the blow to his head, he started to call Orlando's name, to soothe him, but the fangs violently penetrating his skin changed the name to a cry of pain. Gone was the tender lover he had known and in his place was a vampire out of horror stories, feeding cruelly on him, taking his blood by force. That he would have, indeed had already, given it willingly was moot. His permission was not sought.

The hot rush of life-giving blood flooded Orlando's senses, bringing him out of his nightmare and back to reality. A reality where his actions were responsible for the acrid taste of pain and fear in the blood of the best person that had ever happened to him. He withdrew immediately in horror at what he had done, still crouched over Alain, panting. The desire to feed was still almost impossibly strong, but Orlando resisted it, pulling back more and huddling on the couch, sunk in the depths of despair.

Alain sat up warily, stunned and alarmed at Orlando's sudden transformation. Seeing his lover huddled in abject misery, his heart ached. Something had frightened or hurt Orlando badly enough to make him lash out blindly. Alain had no idea what he had done to cause that reaction, but he needed to find out what had happened so he could ensure it never happened again. Determined not to do anything else to startle Orlando, he cast an illumination spell, bathing the room and the two of them in a soft glow. "Orlando?" he said softly, his tone requesting an explanation.

"I'm sorry," Orlando said. "I'll go now. I won't bother you again." He stood up and started toward the door.

Alain locked it with a flick of his wrist. "You won't get far with the door locked," he pointed out reasonably. "Don't run from me. Talk to me."

"What's there to say?" Orlando replied bitterly. "I hurt you. I pinned you down and bit you without your permission. I broke our promise."

Alain struggled to his feet, still shaking from the rush of adrenaline he had felt when Orlando attacked, and went to his lover's side. Slowly, he reached out, waiting to see how Orlando would react. When the vampire did not rebuff his touch, Alain pulled him into a loose embrace.

"And that's totally unlike you. Why don't you tell me what happened to make you react that way? I need to know what not to do, just like I need to know what to do."

Orlando shook his head mutely.

Alain sighed and nuzzled the long locks. "You can tell me or I'll ask someone else. Sebastien seemed to have an idea about why you passed out. Maybe he'll know what set you off. Or Jean. I'll go to your elder vampire, the one who first mentioned the possibility of going out in daylight if no one else can help me, but I won't give up on you."

"You wouldn't!"

"Try me if you don't believe me. Up until now, you've been the epitome of gentleness with me. Something happened to change that and I think I deserve to know what I did wrong."

Orlando's laugh was bitter. "The only thing you did wrong was taking up with me. I'm damaged goods, Alain. I thought, maybe, I could do this, but how can I ask you to trust me when I can't even trust myself?"

Alain put a finger under Orlando's chin, lifting it so their eyes met. "You're not damaged goods. Don't put yourself down that way. As for trusting yourself, what made you stop?"

"I was hurting you. I could taste the pain in your blood."

"And you stopped," Alain pointed out. "You realized you were hurting me and you stopped. That's pretty trustworthy as far as I'm concerned."

"I should never have hurt you in the first place."

"Were you trying to hurt me?" Alain asked.

"Yes," Orlando admitted in a whisper.

"Why?" Alain asked as softly.

"I thought...," He could not say it. Alain did not deserve the comparison to the creature who had made Orlando. Alain was the complete opposite of that monster!

"What?" Alain prompted.

"I thought I was back in that bastard's control. It was dark. I couldn't see you. All I knew was that I was being held down and having blood forced between my lips. I couldn't go back." Orlando's whole body was shaking.

Alain wished Orlando's maker was still alive, because he wanted nothing more than to tear someone limb from limb, and who better than the monster who had broken the beautiful creature in his arms?

"You were unconscious. Sebastien said it was because you needed to feed, and that I should let you taste my blood, as it would wake you so you could feed. I didn't bother with the lights because this is my office. I know where things are. I was too focused on you to care about anything else. I'm so sorry I sent you back there, even for a minute."

Orlando was floored. Alain was apologizing to him? When he was the one who had hurt the wizard? "You don't have anything to be sorry for. I'm the one who should be apologizing."

"You were defending yourself."

"I hurt you!"

"And you stopped as soon as you realized it was me. Your rage wasn't directed at me, just at the situation. I still say you don't need to apologize, but I'll accept your apology if you'll accept mine."

"You didn't know. How could you when I hadn't told you?"

"So it was an accident on both sides. You'll learn to feel safe with me on even the deepest levels and I'll learn what not to do to trigger bad memories. We will make this work. It will just take time." Alain pressed a tender kiss to Orlando's temple. "Now, according to Sebastien, you should be hungry right about now."

"You keep mentioning Sebastien. What does he have to do with it?" Orlando asked.

"We were questioning Pacotte. You started shaking and then passed out. Sebastien figured out what was wrong and Thierry sent us here so I could take care of you."

Orlando's face fell. "I fucked that up, too, didn't I?"

Alain shook his shoulders gently. "You didn't fuck anything up. Pacotte wasn't going to tell us shit, even with the threat of the vampires. We knew that before we started, but we had to give him due process. We wouldn't have talked to him much longer even if you hadn't passed out, and he was the last one anyway. Stop blaming yourself for things you couldn't control. Sebastien said the Aveu de Sang will make you need to feed more often at first to cement the bond."

"I didn't know," he said softly.

This was not the first time Orlando had seemed unsure of things other vampires seemed to take for granted, but that was a concern for another time. "You need to eat," Alain said gently, drawing Orlando back to the couch. "Come." He tipped his head back, offering his neck to Orlando.

"No, I can't..."

"Why not?" Alain asked, raising his head. "You're not taking anything I don't want to give. You know I've enjoyed it every time –" a rakish grin illuminated Alain's face as he spoke, "– and I've never felt anything like what I felt two days ago. Not even making love with you could compare to the pleasure of feeding you. If you won't do it for yourself, then do it for me. Give me the joy of knowing it's my blood that sustains you, that I'm a part of you somehow."

Orlando trembled, hearing the plea. His hunger was growing more and more demanding, and Alain's complete acquiescence, his asking even, was not helping him stay in control. Still, he hesitated, his own fears holding him in check. The aftertaste of Alain's pain lingered on his tongue, reminding him of what he had done. He had no idea how Alain could possibly trust him, but neither could he resist the heartfelt words. Finally, reluctantly, he reached for Alain's wrist, starting to lift it to his mouth. At least this way, he would be less likely to injure his wizard again.

Alain shook his head. "Not like that," he said. "I want to feel your weight on me, your body against mine." He lowered their hands to his groin where his erection was already growing hard at the mere thought of being joined with Orlando so intimately again. "Can't you feel how much I want this?"

Orlando could not stop the stroke his fingers bestowed almost without his volition. Nor could he stop the rush of pleasure when Alain groaned and bucked his hips into the caress. He was at a loss to explain how Alain could trust him, want him still after what had happened, but then, he was at a loss to explain why Alain wanted him in the first place. The indisputable reactions of Alain's body, though, were proof of the inexplicable. Orlando would have fought his hunger, would have tried to control his need if Alain had shown even the slightest hesitation, but he was no saint. He could not fight both their desires. Moving his hand, he leaned over Alain, bringing their bodies into the full contact Alain wanted.

"You don't have to move your hand," the wizard murmured.

Orlando did not reply. That was a conversation for another time, when he was not desperately hungry and when the situation was not fraught with tension. He did, though, take the time to kiss his lover, letting the meeting of lips restore the balance between them.

Alain's mouth opened so willingly, so sweetly beneath his that Orlando lingered to savor it rather than stopping with the light kiss he had planned to bestow. His tongue darted out to tease its way inside Alain's lips, tracing their contours before he sucked Alain's lower lip between his teeth. The urge to bite, to taste, was strong, but he resisted. He would not mix a vampire's kiss with this one, especially when his control was already so shaky. Instead, he released the tempting flesh and delved deeper into Alain's mouth, exploring, teasing, arousing. He could feel the passion investing Alain's body, causing it to tighten beneath him. He settled himself more firmly against his lover's body, letting his weight press the wizard into the couch.

Alain shifted restlessly beneath Orlando. It amazed him what Orlando could do to him with a simple kiss. From the mere touching of their lips and the weight of Orlando's body against his, Alain was throbbing, aching for more. He needed Orlando. His lips, his fangs, his cock. He broke the kiss and threw his head back, baring his neck for Orlando's kiss.

Orlando gave up resisting, lowering his mouth to Alain's neck. Reverently, he dropped a tender kiss to the mark on Alain's neck, acknowledging, reaffirming the bond that had brought them to this moment. Then he moved lower to the wounds he had created earlier, when he attacked. The blood had clotted, blocking the flow, but they had not closed completely. Tenderly, Orlando licked away the soft scabs, cleaning and soothing the rents in Alain's flesh. He sucked gently, lips only, to see how deeply the wounds had closed. Almost immediately, fresh blood welled to the surface, filling him with Alain's desire. Gently, he lined his fangs up with the existing holes so that he would not add to the pain he had already caused.

Alain knew Orlando would take his time preparing his skin for the bite, but it did not ease his impatience. He wanted the connection between them restored, wanted the hurdle of Orlando's fears overcome so they could move forward. He arched into Orlando's mouth when he began to suck, feeling his blood begin to flow. When Orlando's fangs finally slipped inside him, he sighed at the feeling of fulfillment, of fullness. His hands moved of their own accord, one to Orlando's curls, urging him to drink as deeply as he needed, the other to his back, caressing gently before pulling the shirt free and slipping beneath it to find smooth skin.

Orlando tensed when Alain's touch added a physical dimension to the already powerful emotions coursing through him. He paused in his feeding to absorb the sensation, only continuing to draw sustenance when he was sure of his control. He had hurt Alain once. He had no intention of letting it happen a second time.

Alain felt the pause when he touched Orlando's skin and understood that he would have to go slowly. He wanted to slide his hand down, into Orlando's pants, and cup the firm globes, grinding their groins together. He wanted Orlando to strip them both naked and take his body as the vampire took his blood. The thought alone was enough to make him tremble and undulate invitingly beneath Orlando, even knowing that the vampire would almost certainly refuse. Instead of moving his hand lower, Alain worked it up until he could slide it around to slip between them and reach for Orlando's nipple.

The jolt that went through him when Alain brushed his nipple was more than Orlando could handle. His control wavered precariously. He grabbed Alain's wrists, drawing both hands over the wizard's head and pinning them there safely out of the way.

Alain whimpered when his wrists were restrained, leaving him with only the movement of his body to entice Orlando further.

Orlando sucked harder when he felt Alain start to move beneath him. He schooled himself to stillness, afraid to give in at all lest he lose control. He did not try to stop Alain's movements, though, nor to silence the sounds that left his lover's lips as his desire built. The taste was intoxicating, and Orlando drank deeply, Alain's trust as nourishing to his soul as the blood was to his body. His own desire grew with every mouthful of Alain's blood, with every undulation of his hips.

Alain struggled to stave off his release, not wanting the moment to end, but his body had other ideas, tremors surging through him as his climax hit. He thrust up against Orlando, wanting to take the vampire over the edge with him.

Orlando did not need the physical stimulation. The taste of ecstasy in Alain's blood was enough to send his own orgasm rushing through him. He tried to withdraw from Alain's neck before it hit, but he was not fast enough. When his release came, his fangs drove deeper instead, tearing Alain's skin as they did. The sounds coming from the wizard's mouth did not change. Nothing in his demeanor gave any indication that he had felt the damage, but Orlando felt it, a fresh surge of guilt washing through him as he gently laved the two larger wounds to close them. They would heal in a few days, as the marks on Alain's wrists had done, but Orlando would remember them even when they were gone. He had known it was dangerous to mix sex and feeding. Now he had proof. He could see the dangers all too clearly. He would make love with Alain every chance he got. He would feed when he needed to, but he would not mix the two.

He released Alain's hands and relaxed on top of the wizard, loving the safe feeling of his lover's arms around him in the blissful aftermath. He let that sense of security wash over him and settle deep in his soul.

Alain marveled again at the force of the emotions inspired by his connection to Orlando. Even when he and Edwige had been happy, it had never felt like this. As wonderful as it was, though, Alain sensed that it could be even better. The first time Orlando had fed this way had been incredible, but this time, with Orlando's body lying fully on top of his, with the additional stimulation of their erections rubbing together, even through their clothes, had been mind-blowing. They were already lovers. It seemed to him a logical step in their relationship to combine the two routes to intimacy, but Orlando's reluctance was palpable. He did not want to raise the issue right away, not so soon after the challenge they just had faced. The last thing he wanted was to pressure Orlando. Perhaps he could talk to Jean. The older vampire might be able to shed some light on the issue. If nothing else, Jean could tell him if there was some vampiric prohibition against feeding during sex.

"Orlando?" he said softly. "Maybe you should talk to Sebastien about the Aveu de Sang. We need to know what to expect so that something like your fainting doesn't happen again, maybe during a fight or some other critical time."

Orlando nodded but did not move immediately. He was too busy enjoying the comfort of Alain's arms and the pleasure of the solid body beneath his. Finally, though, he stirred with a grimace. "I need a shower and a change of shorts before I talk to anyone."

Alain chuckled. "There are facilities here you can use, and I'll get you a clean pair of boxers if you don't mind wearing mine."

"I don't mind, but why do you have them here?"

"Because I've crashed on this couch more times than I can count, often without it being planned. At least this way, I have clean shorts, even if I have to wear the other clothes a second day."

"What will you do for shorts?" Orlando asked.

Alain grinned and murmured a quick incantation. "Cleaning spell," he said with a laugh. "I can try it on you, but I doubt it will work."

"Probably not," Orlando agreed. "A shower's fine. Just show me where it is."

"I'll do better than that. Let me up and I'll join you."

Orlando would have thought himself sated after what they had just shared, but he felt his body stir at the thought. "I'd like that."

Chapter 14

"THERE was a meeting of vampires this morning," Pascal explained. "I sent several wizards to investigate, but only one came back, and with no information. I want to know what that was all about."

"A meeting?" Edouard asked. "I didn't hear anything. You're sure it was a meeting of vampires?"

"The report I got said that Bellaiche called a meeting of vampires and that a hundred or so gathered at the Gare de Lyon this morning for at least two hours."

"I'm insulted," Edouard said. "I wasn't invited. Then again, I'm hardly a scion of vampire society. Bellaiche probably doesn't even know I'm in Paris."

"Why is that?" Pascal inquired.

"I do my best to avoid notice," Edouard explained. "I don't fit their idea of what a vampire should be."

"Just as we don't fit the government's idea of what wizards should be," Pascal observed. "Are there others who feel as you do?"

"Undoubtedly, but we are not as organized as you. We rebel quietly, by avoiding our own kind and moving about as we need to."

"It seems our situations aren't all that different. Even though you couldn't give me the information I needed, it sounds like we could benefit each other. If we're successful, after all, we would lift the restrictions that make your life difficult as well."

"Really?" Edouard asked. "Tell me more."

"Our platform maintains that the magical should be the ones to determine the appropriate use of their own magic, not some outside government controlled by the non-magical."

"And you would place the vampires alongside the wizards?" Edouard challenged. "That would be a first. We have none of the privileges or protections that wizards receive under the current law."

"Not the fairest of situations, is it?" Pascal asked. "If we prevail, we shall have to see if we can redress that wrong."

Eric listened to the conversation in silence. He did not know who Pascal thought he was fooling, but he was certainly not deceived. The vampires' lot would not improve if they won the war, and Eric would not be surprised if it got worse. Pascal was not known for his tolerance of other races. He might say what he thought would get him the help he needed to win the war, but Eric was not so naïve as to think that he meant the first word of it.

ORLANDO looked apprehensively around the communal showers. The stalls had curtains on them, but those would do little to shield them from anyone who came in. "Are you sure about this?" he asked.

Alain grinned. "You keep forgetting I'm a wizard." He mumbled under his breath, casting a spell. "It's the same privacy spell Marcel used at the station yesterday morning. No one out here can see or hear what we do in there," Alain explained. "It's no one's business but ours what we do together."

"Well, in that case...," Orlando said, stepping into the stall. For a moment, the room was silent. Then an arm reached back through the magical barrier and grabbed Alain's sweater, pulling him into the shower.

Alain's grin split his face as he passed through his own magic into the shower stall. Orlando's own grin was unrepentant. "You were taking too long," he scolded.

"I'm sorry," Alain apologized facetiously. "It won't happen again."

"It better not," Orlando replied, beginning to remove his sticky clothes. Alain followed suit and in moments, they were both naked. Setting their clothes out of reach of the water, Alain turned on the spray while Orlando grabbed the soap off the ledge, though he knew Alain did not need it. He worked the bar into a lather and reached for his lover, determined to make up for the pain he had caused earlier. His foamy hands began exploring the now-familiar flesh, smoothing over it tenderly, the caresses having nothing in particular to do with hygiene and everything to do with desire. Rinsing away the lather, he let his touch linger on Alain's biceps first, cherishing the strength that was always restrained where he was concerned, before moving down to the long-fingered hands that never trespassed, never caused pain, but only brought pleasure. He lifted one hand to his lips and kissed each digit softly, sucking on them gently before releasing that hand for the other one.

"Let me touch you," Alain pleaded as Orlando's lips, but never his fangs, caressed the second hand.

Orlando lifted his head and smiled at Alain. Here was his chance to set things right between them, to restore the balance. He stepped forward, into Alain's embrace, and set his lover's hands on his hips. "Please do," he asked, his own hands returning to their explorations.

Alain caught his breath, his grip tightening involuntarily as the impact of Orlando's gesture sank in. The vampire trusted him to touch below the waist, not in the heat of passion as he had done the previous afternoon, but before passion had a chance to truly build between them.

"Putain," Alain groaned, pulling their bodies together, aligning their hips so their cocks rubbed together. Orlando moaned and pulled Alain's lips back to his, tongue invading to claim his lover's mouth as his cock would soon claim Alain's body and his fangs longed to claim the wizard's soul.

Alain leaned back against the wall of the small cubicle, letting it support him under Orlando's onslaught. His body, so recently sated from the feeding, responded ardently, shaft swelling, balls throbbing as if the recent orgasm had not occurred. On some level of his mind, barely functioning still despite the passion, Alain marveled at his reaction to Orlando. Even as a teenager, he had not recovered so quickly. He certainly had not expected to at his age, and yet his erection was as hard now, from their kiss, the brush of their bodies, and the thought of what was to come as it had ever been at the moment of release.

He broke away from the kiss, gasping for breath. "Merde, the things you do to me!" he exclaimed breathlessly.

Orlando grinned lustfully at his lover. Alain's lips were swollen, his hair wet and slick from the shower, his face flushed from the heat or passion or both, and the vampire felt his heart clench. He had no idea what he had done to deserve his wizard – for how could one damned deserve such grace – but he had every intention of cherishing the gift. "Shall I stop?" he teased.

"Hell, no!" Alain shouted. "Don't you dare!" He pulled Orlando's mouth back to his for another kiss, his tongue invading this time, running along Orlando's teeth and then deeper into his lover's mouth.

Orlando almost pulled back when he felt Alain's tongue against his teeth. He fought the instinct to let his fangs drop, knowing that, even full, the taste of blood would tempt him to drink, but he managed to control the impulse and let

Alain move as he pleased. He had denied the wizard one desire already tonight. He would not do so again if he could help it.

Emboldened by Orlando's acceptance, Alain let his fingers delve into the vampire's wet hair, twining around the silky strands. His other hand pressed Orlando's lower body even closer, fingers kneading one nether cheek gently. He struggled against the haze of lust that consumed him, trying to gauge Orlando's reaction to the caress, waiting to see if his lover would use his safeword. He did not want the vampire to withdraw as he had done earlier.

Orlando tensed when he felt the caress on his arse. Memories of other hands, cruel hands, grabbing him there, forcing his flesh apart in preparation for brutalizing him assailed Orlando. He broke the kiss and let his head drop to Alain's shoulder as he fought the memories. The bastard was destroyed. Orlando had seen to it himself, watching with great pleasure from the shadows as the morning sun burned his tormentor to dust inch by painful inch. The hand that touched him now had no intention of hurting, of raping. All he had to do was say the word, show the least bit of hesitation, and this hand would be withdrawn, to caress elsewhere or to fall at the wizard's side. Orlando knew that, and it gave him the strength he needed to let go of the nightmares.

"Orlando?" Alain asked softly in his ear.

The vampire raised his head and smiled. "Those things you said I do to you?" he replied. "Well, you do them to me, too. It's just taking me some time to get used to them."

"Do you want me to stop?"

"Hell, no!" Orlando replied with a grin, deliberately echoing Alain's earlier words. Then his face few serious again. "But if there comes a point when I do, I'll tell you. I promise."

"You'd better," Alain declared firmly. He would accept whatever limitations Orlando set without complaint, but he refused to do anything that would scare the vampire. Unfortunately, the only way he had of knowing what would scare his lover was Orlando's own words and reactions.

"THERE has been a… complication," Raymond declared, walking into Marcel's office with Jean in tow, "and it's going to require all your finesse to spin it."

Marcel looked up from the papers in front of him, detailing attacks and intelligence, trying to decide which of his sources had sent the most accurate information this time. "That sounds ominous," he remarked with deceptive calm. He had no desire to encourage the nervousness that he detected in Raymond's voice and in Jean's demeanor. "I take it the meeting did not go well."

"The meeting went fine," Raymond replied. "I learned quite a bit and we came up with a theory to explain some things we've observed, but the theory itself is unsettling."

Jean snorted. Unsettling was an understatement. "Try terrifying," he corrected.

Marcel raised an eyebrow. He had not expected such a comment from the heretofore unflappable vampire. "I think you had better start at the beginning."

Raymond recounted, as simply as he could, the theory he and Christophe had developed to explain the seeming compulsion that drew the vampires and wizards together, the symbiosis that benefited each party and the natural balance of the world.

Marcel listened in silence, trying to make sense of Raymond's explanation and of its implications. When the other wizard finished, Marcel sat silently for a moment, digesting all he had heard. "So, what you're saying is that the short-term, expedient partnerships we intended to create are going to have long-term, personal effects."

Jean flinched inwardly at the reminder, yet again, of how out of control his life had gotten. "The problem," he interrupted, "at least from our perspective, is that vampires exist for centuries, and most choose to avoid entanglements with non-vampires because of the inherent loss. When it does occur, it's a choice the vampire makes, like Orlando did. Most of the vampires, though, had no thought of anything permanent when they showed up to join the alliance. If this is not presented carefully, they may try to refuse the partnerships altogether, especially those who are less than happy with their partners. Jude, for example, might be willing to work with Adèle for a time, but I cannot see him being willing to commit to her outside of the alliance."

"And I doubt Adèle would be any happier about committing to Jude," Raymond added, "if the interactions I've seen between them are any indication of their feelings."

Marcel chuckled. "They do seem a little mismatched," he agreed. "I assume you brought this up with Monsieur Lombard. What did he think?"

"He seemed to think that blood did not lie, and that if they were paired this way, they were right for each other, no matter how they felt right now," Raymond replied.

"And that will only add fuel to the fire," Jean added, squirming mentally at the thought that he had no say in his fate. "We vampires tend to be an independent lot, not liking to be told what to do by anyone. I was surprised that no one who came to the gathering refused to participate simply because it was my idea."

"Will they try to back out if they know?" Marcel asked bluntly.

"We keep our promises," Jean replied reflexively.

Raymond laid a calming hand on Jean's arm. "No one's saying you won't," he assured the vampire, "but we have to consider the possibility that some of your independent friends may react... impulsively. What worries me is the effect that such actions would have on both the vampire and the wizard. If Monsieur Lombard and I are right, this... bond will eventually permeate many, if not all aspects of both partners' lives. And while I don't know how I feel about it on a personal level, I can see dangerous pitfalls at every turn for those who try to fight it."

Marcel pondered the problem for a moment. "I'm beginning to wonder if it would be helpful to even mention this to the others. If knowing is going to cause people to do dangerous or stupid things, wouldn't it be better to keep silent?"

"And if a wizard loses control because of the emotions inspired by the bond?" Raymond asked. "That could be just as dangerous as any of the possible complications from trying to avoid the bond. At least if they know, they can guard against that."

"If they don't reject it completely." Marcel fell back into deep thought. There had to be a solution. "Perhaps a comment about having noticed some... effects, and needing everyone to report any changes they notice in the way they're feeling so we can learn more. Would that be enough to make the wizards aware of the need for control while keeping everyone from overreacting?"

"Would it truly be overreacting?" Jean challenged. "I realize you don't have a partner of your own, but do you truly understand what this... bond means for those of us involved? If Raymond and Christophe are right, our lives are being turned upside down as we speak, and not just the vampires. Your wizards are about to find themselves with partners in ways they didn't want. What about those who already have lovers or even spouses? What about those who aren't looking for a relationship for whatever reason? What about Thierry, whose wife just died? How is this fair to any of them? And while I can see not telling them for the sake of the alliance, what about the sake of their sanity?"

"I'm not saying you're wrong," Marcel replied, steel in his voice, "but do you know what will happen if the alliance fails? If the war continues as it is now, the drain on the magical resources of the world will throw everything out of balance. Tides will change; seasons will begin to falter; the earth itself will tremble in protest. There will be disasters on a scale you cannot begin to imagine. Eventually, if it goes unchecked, there will be nothing and no one left. Then where will we be? We won't care about spouses or lovers; about relationships and those we've lost because we'll be so busy trying to stay alive that nothing else will matter. And if Serrier wins, the natural disasters might be averted, but do you think life will be any better for any but his wizards? If so, you are unbelievably naïve, something I would never have thought you to be. I agree that this is unfair. If I saw another choice, I would take it, but I have none. That was why I approached you in the first place."

"You both are right," Raymond pointed out calmly, though his heart twinged at the thought that Jean might be speaking of himself when he referred to those who already had a lover. "The fact remains that these bonds are being created, and are probably strengthened every time a vampire feeds from a wizard. Furthermore, if we are right, every time that happens, the magical balance is restored a little, giving us that much more time to win this war and set things back in balance properly. We have no idea how long this will last. It could be that the bonds are so strong, so prevalent right now because of the disequilibrium that Marcel spoke of. Perhaps when we can tend to things normally, they will become less necessary, less all-consuming. I don't know, but I do know that whatever we decide to do, we need to decide it now. And you are the ones who have to make that decision. Arguing about the fairness of it doesn't change a damn thing about the reality of our situation, from either side. So, Jean, what can we say that will make the vampires pay attention to their feelings and actions without causing a riot? And Marcel, the same question about the wizards?"

"Warn them that there may be side effects and ask them to report anything they notice to me," Jean said dully, knowing Raymond and Marcel were right. He might not like the situation, he might do everything he could to control his own feelings and actions, but he would not sabotage the one thing that had a chance of saving them all. "I don't see what else we can do."

"We will tell everyone the same thing," Marcel agreed. "The vampires can report any effects to Jean and the wizards to you or me."

"It could also be that as we learn more, we will find that the effects are not as universal as they seem. We are basing our conclusions on esoterica and a very limited sample of pairings. The more we learn, the better we'll be able to deal with whatever consequences there are," Raymond added reasonably.

"SIT still," Mireille scolded. "I can't do this right if you're squirming."

"My shoulder feels fine," Caroline insisted.

"The doctor said it would take a couple days to heal," Mireille replied. "And it hasn't even been one day yet. You can sit here and let me take care of you, or I'll drag you back to the medic and let him do it. And don't think I can't, either. Vampires are a good deal stronger than we look."

Caroline knew that all too well. The injury to her shoulder had not affected her eyesight. She had seen Mireille overpower the much larger male wizard they had dueled at the train station. If the vampire decided to drag her back to the infirmary, Caroline would have no choice but to follow. With a grimace she settled back on the couch at her apartment where they had spent the day. "Fine. Just be quick about it."

Mireille shook her head as she bent over her partner to tie the sling as the doctor had shown her. Caroline was as stubborn as she was beautiful, and that was saying something. She kept her hands gentle as she worked.

Caroline's eyes closed when she felt the tender touch of the vampire's hands. The day had been a strange one, with the forming of the alliance, the battle, her injury and Mireille's reaction, meeting the elder one, and then the sunlight hours spent in the quiet of her apartment getting to know her partner. A shiver went through her when Mireille moved her arm gently. It was better than it had been, but it still hurt. "Easy," the vampire murmured as she continued to work. The soft voice sent a shiver of a different sort down her spine. Mireille was such a study in contrast. Her soft hands and softer voice belied the strength she had shown during the fight.

Such softness had not been a part of Caroline's life in recent memory. The wizards she worked and fought with had no use for softness. To them, it was weakness. And in battle, that was true. Having such tenderness lavished upon her now reminded her of all she had sacrificed so that her colleagues would take her seriously. It was… refreshing, she decided, to relax and forget about always appearing strong. Mireille did not ask her to prove anything. She simply treated Caroline as another woman, with compassion, respect, and kindness. Caroline smiled. She could get used to this. "Thank you," she said, looking up at her partner.

Chapter 15

ALAIN braced his hands against the wall of the shower as Orlando surged into him. "More," he pleaded, the connection of their bodies grounding him, assuring him that he had not damaged their relationship in his office.

Orlando complied eagerly, letting the patent hunger in Alain's voice and actions soothe any concerns over treating his lover roughly. He knocked Alain's feet further apart to give himself better access, his hands closing tightly around Alain's hips to steady him as he plunged inside the clinging sheath again.

Alain pushed back into the urgent thrusts, encouraging Orlando wordlessly even as he pleaded for more. Harder. Deeper.

Seeing that Alain was steady on his feet, Orlando let his hands wander, feverishly seeking the places he had found most sensitive on his lover's body: the underside of his arm, the skin below his armpit where the hair thinned, the crease where his thigh joined his hip. He carefully avoided the normal erogenous zones, wanting Alain to see that even caught in this frenzy of passion, Orlando knew who he was with, who he was loving, and that this, like all their encounters, was personal, focused on them together.

"Fuck!" Alain cursed after a particularly well-aimed thrust. "So good. So close, Orlando. Just a little more."

Orlando nodded, though Alain could not see it. He leaned closer, his chin coming to rest on Alain's shoulder, seeking his lips. When the wizard turned his head, Orlando claimed the succulent mouth, his hands sliding lower, one to encircle the wizard's straining cock, the other to cradle his heavy sac. "Come for me, lover," Orlando whispered, his grasp tightening, his fingers massaging.

With a shout, Alain came, his essence spurting over the cool tile as his knees buckled.

Though his own release was tearing through him, Orlando caught Alain, supporting his weight as he thrust one last time.

"FINE," Jean said. "We'll do it that way. Hopefully, it will get us the information we need without making this situation any more complicated."

"It will work," Marcel said with more confidence than any of them were feeling. "We'll make the announcement the next time we all gather."

"Sooner rather than later," Raymond insisted.

"Tomorrow, the day after at the latest," Marcel promised.

Jean nodded. "Now, if you will excuse me, I have some personal matters to attend to. I'll be back tomorrow morning."

Before Marcel or Raymond could respond, he was gone, leaving the two wizards looking at each other with bemused expressions. "How are you holding up?" Marcel asked.

ALAIN kissed Orlando gently. "Talk to Sebastien," he said urgently. "Find out as much as you can about our Aveu de Sang. We have to know what to expect."

Orlando nodded. "I'll try to find him and see what he has to say. Will you come with me?"

"I can't," Alain said. "I have something I have to take care of for Marcel." He hated lying to Orlando, but he really did have something to do for Marcel. It was not, though, anything that could not wait. Still, he would do whatever it took to protect Orlando, even if that meant stretching the truth a little. "Do you want to wait for me in my office or meet me at home?"

"I'll wait for you here, if that's okay," Orlando decided. "I'd rather stay there than be in the apartment alone."

"Of course it's okay," Alain assured him. "I wouldn't have offered otherwise. Go find Sebastien. I'll meet you in my office when I'm done with what I have to do."

Orlando nodded and left the locker room in search of the other vampire. Alain waited until he was sure Orlando was gone and then went in search of a different vampire. Alain had questions, and he hoped Jean would have the answers.

Having no idea where in the maze of Milice headquarters he would find the elder vampire, he cast a quick searching spell and saw Jean leaving

Marcel's office, clearly on a mission. Alain hoped it was nothing that could not wait because he had every intention of intercepting the vampire.

Catching up with him just inside the front door, Alain called out Jean's name.

With a muttered curse, Jean turned to see who had called him. He was hungry and horny and all he really wanted was Karine's soothing presence. When he saw the blond wizard who was keeping him from his goal, he suppressed a sigh of impatience. Magnier was not the frivolous kind so surely there was a reason for this interruption.

"I need some advice," Alain said without preamble, seeing the impatience on Jean's face. "It's about Orlando."

"Wouldn't you be better off asking Orlando your questions?" Jean riposted.

"Probably," Alain agreed, "but he won't answer me. He just avoids the questions."

"And did it occur to you that maybe he has a reason for not wanting to talk about certain things?"

"Of course it did," Alain retorted, "but the fact that I don't know certain things is causing tension between us, which we don't need in the alliance, and which I don't want in my personal life either. Look, just answer a couple of questions about vampires in general for me. I'll draw my own conclusions from there if you don't want to tell me anything specific about Orlando."

Jean glanced up at the clock. "You have fifteen minutes. Use them wisely."

ORLANDO asked around until he finally found Sebastien in a lounge of some sort, perhaps a break room, to judge by the refrigerator, microwave, and snack machines that stood along one wall. He approached the older vampire hesitantly. "Sebastien? Do you have a minute? I could use some advice if you do."

Sebastien looked up and smiled, relieved to see Orlando on his feet again. "Well, you look better than the last time I saw you, so I guess your Avoué took proper care of you."

Orlando blushed a little, remembering just how well Alain had cared for him. "That's what I wanted to talk to you about. There seems to be a whole lot more to the Aveu de Sang than I realized, and I don't want to keep stumbling over problems that could be avoided."

"Very wise," Sebastien agreed with a nod. "Have a seat and let's talk. I'll tell you what I can. Some things seem universal while others vary a little from vampire to vampire."

"THERE'S an empty office down the hall where we can talk," Alain told Jean. "I'd rather not do this in the hallway, if that's all right with you."

"It's your fifteen minutes," Jean replied.

Alain scowled but walked down the hall to the empty room, unlocking the door and gesturing for Jean to precede him.

When the door shut behind them, Alain spoke again. "Is there some sort of prohibition among the vampires about mixing sex and feeding?"

Jean choked back a laugh. "That was blunt," he observed.

"You keep reminding me I only have fifteen minutes. I don't have time to beat around the bush."

"True. So, to answer your question, no. There is nothing in vampire law or tradition that keeps the two separate. In fact, many vampires prefer to combine the two. It makes both experiences so much more intense," Jean replied with a hungry smile. He had every intention of enjoying just such a combination as soon as he could get out of here.

"Then what's holding Orlando back?" Alain asked, more rhetorically than anything else.

Jean shook his head. "You'll have to ask him that question. All I can say is this: have patience with him. That he is with you at all is... a miracle, if you believe in such things. Let him give in his own time, even if it's slower than you would prefer."

"I FEEL like there's so much I don't know," Orlando began. "I barely even know what questions to ask."

"Start with what made you decide you needed to talk to someone in the first place," Sebastien suggested. "We'll go from there."

"What happened to me tonight?" Orlando asked. "I've never needed to feed more than every two or three days, and I've always known in plenty of time that I was getting hungry. Tonight, I was fine, and then I was unconscious. That could be dangerous, even deadly, if I'm alone or on a battlefield."

"The Aveu de Sang is strengthened by your feeding," Sebastien explained. "Surely you felt that. And so, for the first few weeks, you will need to feed often. Every day, maybe even twice a day."

"That will kill Alain!" Orlando protested.

"You're right. It should," Sebastien agreed, "but it won't. I don't know why it works, but you can feed from him until you're sick, every day, and he won't suffer for it. It's in the nature of the bond. Find a routine. In the morning before you sleep, or at night when you get up, and feed then, every day, for two weeks. After that, you should be able to return to a more normal schedule, although, by then, you may not want to."

"Why not?" Orlando inquired.

Sebastien laughed. "Feeding from your Avoué is even more addictive than making love to your Avoué."

"ONE more question," Alain said, "and then I'll let you get back to whatever you were about to do. It seems like Orlando doesn't know all the things he should. I mean, he knew about the brand, but not everything it symbolized. And then, he passed out because he didn't know that he would need to feed more often while the Aveu de Sang was new."

"That is an observation, not a question," Jean pointed out.

"Why doesn't he know what he needs?" Alain elaborated.

"Because when he came to me, he was already over a hundred years old. His maker should have taught him what he needed to know, but Thurloe was too concerned with his own twisted pleasure to teach Orlando anything more than how to stay alive. Orlando, though, didn't want to be treated like a vampire newly made and wouldn't let me teach him as I would one I had just turned. So he remains ignorant about anything outside his past experience. When I can do so without angering or belittling him, I fill in the gaps, but it often comes too late. You said he passed out. Is he all right?"

Alain nodded. "Sebastien was there and knew what was wrong. We took care of it."

Jean frowned. Yes, Sebastien knew what an Aveu de Sang entailed. He had stolen the one Jean would have claimed.

"ARE there other… side effects of the Aveu de Sang?" Orlando asked. "Other things I need to be careful about?"

"That's the only physical one," Sebastien replied, "but there are several less tangible ones that can be much more difficult to manage in the long run."

"What?" Orlando asked, cognizant of Alain's plea for more information.

"I already mentioned the sex. You'll probably find your appetite for it will increase. I think it's probably more from the intimacy of all the feeding than anything else, but it's an effect that doesn't seem to wear off, even when you no longer need to feed every day. In fact, you'll find that if you can stand not to have his taste in your mouth, a time will come when you could go as long as a couple of weeks without feeding," Sebastien commented.

Orlando nodded. He had already noticed that his desire for Alain was almost insatiable. "Will he feel the same? I mean, will the Aveu de Sang make him as eager as I am? I wouldn't want to… pressure him."

"I can't speak for your Avoué, but mine never found my attentions an imposition," Sebastien assured him. "Ask him about it if you're worried, but believe him when he answers you."

"What else?"

"Expect to feel possessive, protective, even jealously," Sebastien warned. "He won't give you cause to be jealous, but the rest of the world won't be so kind."

"Who would dare…?"

"Stop!" Sebastien interrupted before Orlando could continue. "If there is one thing vampire law prohibits, it is taking another's Avoué, so no one would dare try to take him from you. That will not stop other vampires, or other mortals, from looking at him appreciatively. Your priority is not them. They would not succeed even if they tried to lure him away from you. Your priority is controlling your reaction when it's irrational, keeping yourself from doing something stupid, because if you rashly challenge someone over a perceived slight, they will respond, even if they've done nothing. You know that much about vampires, I'm sure."

Orlando nodded slowly, anger still coursing through him at the idea that someone, anyone, would try to take Alain from him. "Anything else?"

"Is that not enough already?" Sebastien laughed.

"More than," Orlando agreed, "but I'd rather know it all now."

"The only other thing I ever noticed was that I could usually sense my Avoué's location. Not to the point of naming the room he was in, but enough to find him if we were separated at a fair. That sort of thing."

Orlando nodded. That could be useful if they were ever separated on the battlefield. "Thank you," he said. "That's given me a lot to think about. I appreciate you taking the time to talk to me."

"I know most of your time has been spent with Jean, but the rest of us are not bad sorts. You might even find that some of us would be your friend."

Orlando nodded again, ashamedly this time. He had avoided vampire society out of fear and mistrust for years. Perhaps it was time to remedy that. "I... I think I would like that."

JEAN glanced at the clock on the wall. "Time's up," he said, standing and heading for the door. He opened and then turned back. "You do realize, don't you, that he trusts you in ways he has never trusted anyone, even me? Show him you trust him the same way. He'll open up eventually."

Alain nodded. It was sound advice. He only hoped he could follow it amidst all the other demands the war and the alliance would place on them. When he looked up again, Jean was gone. Alain rose as well, locking the office behind him as he went to file the paperwork that was his excuse for not accompanying Orlando to talk to Sebastien. As he worked on the task, he found himself hurrying to finish, the longing to be with Orlando growing strongly again. The desire surprised him a little, since he had come twice already that evening, once from Orlando's fangs and once from his cock, but Alain did not question it, not when everything they did together felt so good.

Chapter 16

JEAN flew through the darkened streets, unconcerned at who might see him. He was a vampire on the prowl, and anyone with any sense would recognize that and avoid him. And anyone without that semblance of sense would be unceremoniously dispatched elsewhere because Jean would allow nothing to stand between himself and his destination. It was late, and he knew it, but that was not enough to stop him from seeking Karine. She would open the door to him as she always did.

This time, her eyes would be drowsy from sleep and her hair would be rumpled from the pillows, but she would be no less desirable for it. If anything, she would be more attractive, the only barrier between him and her body the fine lawn robe she wore to hide her nakedness as she answered the door. He would whisk her inside and into bed and she would not complain, offering her neck first, for she would sense his hunger, and as she was sating that hunger, she would offer him her body to sate another hunger, if that was his desire. Sometimes it was, sometimes it was not, but tonight it would be. Tonight he had something to prove, to himself if to no one else, and she was the means he would use.

He knew she would open the door and sate his hunger, and when he was replete, he would rise from her bed as he always did and leave her alone, missing him and waiting for his next visit, a day or a week or a month later. He knew she wanted more, and he wished he could give it to her. He envied Orlando, envied the relationship that was forming between his protégé and the wizard. Karine would let him mark her, if he asked. She would make an Aveu de Sang without thinking twice. She would do it, but he could not. She was not Thibaut, and could never be. Almost four hundred years had passed, but time did not matter to a vampire. Jean's heart was as tied up now in the memories of the young man he had never had the chance to love as it had been the day they met.

Banishing those thoughts, Jean climbed the steps of Karine's apartment building, ringing the bell and waiting for her to answer.

The door opened, as he had known it would, and she stood there in front of him. He had been wrong about one thing, he noticed as he stepped inside and shut the door. The robe was silk, not lawn this evening. "You should be more careful," he warned her. "You have no idea who might be knocking at your door."

"At three o'clock in the morning?" she scoffed. "Only you ever come to my door at this hour."

"And if someday it is not me?" Jean pressed.

"Why would anyone else come knocking on my door this late?" she challenged.

Jean was torn. He knew that part of the success of the alliance was in secrecy. On the other hand, not knowing about it could put Karine in danger. He did not love her, not as she desired and deserved, but he did not want anything to happen to her either. "It may seem like little enough to you that I lead the vampires, but there are those who would see me supplanted. I would not want you to get caught in a power struggle that involves you only because it involves me."

"It would bother you if something happened to me? I wasn't sure," she said lightly though the underlying bitterness was a slap in the face. As she spoke, she turned toward her bedroom.

Angrily, Jean grabbed her arm, spinning her around and into his arms. His lips descended on hers hungrily, punishingly. Not releasing her, he backed her toward the bedroom, his lips demanding, taking from her mouth as he would take from her body.

She struggled against him, even knowing it was futile. She was a slight woman and would have been no match for even a mortal man. Against a vampire, she was helpless. She had always known that, had always known that she would never best Jean in a physical struggle, that he could dominate her completely if he chose. He had never chosen to do so, and she had appreciated it, but now that appeared to have changed. She wrenched her lips away from his, intending to tell him, ask him to stop, but she never got the chance. Denied her mouth, his lips moved lower, seeking and finding the pulse of her neck, sucking there roughly, though his fangs did not pierce her skin.

Fiercely, her hands pulled at his hair, his rough touch fueling her passion as well as her anger. His head jerked back and their eyes met, blue clashing with brown. They fetched up against the wall outside her room, locked in an angry, erotic tableau. Suddenly impatient, Jean's hand slid between them, grabbing her peignoir and ripping it away from her skin, leaving her bare to his gaze and his touch.

Finding herself suddenly naked, Karine started to protest, but Jean's lips covered hers again, his tongue plundering her mouth. The protest died as she gave in to the passion exploding between them. She bit down on the invading muscle, hard enough to draw blood. Once, she might have worried about the effect his blood would have on her, but there was no room now for such thoughts. Her only thought was to inflame Jean's senses the way his assault was inflaming hers.

Karine's teeth scoring his tongue sent waves of lust through Jean. He knew his blood could not hurt her. He had not even bitten her yet, and he would have to drain her dry for his blood to have any effect at all. His reaction was entirely due to the reciprocal aggression. He tended to see Karine as passive, accepting what he offered, never demanding more. Now, she was demanding, and he had every intention of giving it to her.

Thwarted by the clothing Jean still wore, Karine tore at the button of his pants, uncaring when it popped off and flew across the room. Her only interest was in what lay inside. She ripped the zipper down and thrust her hand inside his pants, fisting him roughly.

Jean pulled back from her mouth as he felt her hand close around him, dragging over the skin with none of her usual tenderness. He pushed his pants down around his hips and thrust against her stomach forcefully.

"Do it," she hissed. "Fuck me right here. Right now."

He could not resist the crude words on her dainty lips. His hands cupped her buttocks, lifting her for his penetration. Without even checking to see if she was ready, he drove into her heat. Her head slammed back against the wall, baring her neck for his fangs. He took immediate advantage, his lips finding her pulse point, his teeth rending her skin as her hot blood splashed onto his tongue. His hips snapped forward again as he increased the suction on her neck, the rush of power making him dizzy with desire and bloodlust. With every thrust of his arousal, he sucked more blood, feeling her passion spiral out of control, the taste sending his in fast pursuit. Thrust, suck, thrust, suck. He wanted to continue forever, lost in Karine's heat, filled with her passion, but he could not maintain the tension in either of them.

Heedless of the damage he could do to her with his fangs, Karine rocked into Jean's thrusts, wanting him deeper inside her. Her head spun as he took her with cock and fangs, driving into her, inciting her passion, spurring her toward release. She wanted to linger in this moment, the only time when he was completely hers, but the sensations were overpowering, sending her senses spinning out of control. With a muffled sob, she gave in, her climax shuddering through her.

The taste of ecstasy in her blood was enough to snap what remained of Jean's frazzled control. His hips slammed forward one last time as his own release took him, his mouth sucking reflexively even as his jaws tightened.

They stood there, locked together at groin and at neck, breaths sawing in and out, as they struggled for control. Finally, Jean lifted his head, taking in the ravaged neck, the torn robe, the red marks on her arms and hips where he had gripped her with far more force than necessary. He knew she had been willing – he had tasted it in her blood – but she looked more like a rape victim than a woman who had just finished making love.

"I'm sorry, Karie," he murmured, his voice full of remorse. He lifted her more fully into his arms, his softening shaft slipping from her body. Cradling her against him, he carried her the rest of the way into the bedroom, laying her down gently on the bed. "Let me take care of you."

Karine was quiescent in his arms, withdrawing into herself after the uncharacteristic passion. She loved Jean, had loved him for ten years, but this was all she ever got from him: sex and feeding him. And even that was different tonight. He had never been so aggressive, so angry. As she lay on the bed where he placed her, listening to him in the bathroom running water, she tried to figure out what she had said or done that might have caused his outburst.

Riddled with guilt, Jean ran the water until it warmed, soaking a cloth to tend to her. She deserved so much more than he was capable of giving her. He knew she loved him. He had known it from the first. It sweetened her blood, made the taste damn near irresistible, even when he could not return the emotion. He used her, took advantage of her feelings to satisfy his own needs, every time he came to her. Tonight, he had gone one step further. He had abused her, abused her trust and her body, inexcusably. With a tortured sigh, he returned to the bedroom, determined to find a way to make it up to her.

Karine turned her head listlessly when Jean came back into her room. She let him remove what remained of her robe, let him wash away the blood on her neck and the semen between her legs. Gentle fingers traced the bruises that were already visible on her translucent skin, bruises that matched exactly the shape of the fingers now caressing them.

"There's no excuse for what I did," he murmured, leaning over to lap gently at the wounds on her neck, letting his saliva stop the bleeding and start them healing.

"Why did you do it?" she asked lethargically, her head tilting back automatically to give him access to her neck.

Jean winced. "You made me angry. I know you deserve better than what I can give you, but you never turn me away. You never tell me to leave. So I come back because you offer me things that no one else does."

"No one else spreads their legs for you when they let you feed?" she pushed.

His face tightened again, but he tamped down his anger. "No one else offers me a place to let down my guard and just be me," he replied shortly. "You don't want my power or my position. You're not plotting to replace me or angling for a better position through me. All you ask is my time and my tenderness."

"I've seen little enough of either lately."

"I know," Jean answered, shamefacedly. "It's just that things are happening, Karine. You watch the news. You know what's going on in the city."

He did not say it, but he did not have to. It was impossible to turn on the news without some mention of the war between the wizards. She blanched at the thought. "Are you...?" She did not even know how to ask the question.

"It's safer if you don't know," he replied gently.

Her eyes filled with tears. "This was good-bye, wasn't it? That's why you came. That's why..."

"No," Jean hastened to assure her. "That's not it at all. There's no reason why I can't still come to see you from time to time. Unless you don't want me to."

"You say that every time you come to me. Do you even listen when I tell you that I haven't changed my mind, that I want you to visit me?" she queried, starting to get angry again.

"Of course I listen. I come back, don't I? If I didn't listen, I'd stay away," he retorted. Feeling his anger start to flare again, he took a deep breath. "I didn't come to argue with you, Karine. I came to see you, to see how you were."

"To feed from me and to fuck me," she countered. "Just go, Jean. I love you, but I can't deal with you tonight."

"I'm sorry," he apologized again. "I wish I could be what you want me to be."

"You're everything I want you to be. That's why I love you. What I want is for you to feel the same way," she explained patiently, as if talking to a child. "I know. You can't force yourself to feel something you don't. And honestly, I'd rather you tell me the truth than lie to me. Just go, Jean."

He wanted to stay, to argue, but what good would it do? The only words that would end this stalemate were words he could not say. "I'll come see you again soon," he promised. He did not add, "If you still want me to," like he usually did. He would not insult her that way.

Rising from the bed, he straightened his clothes and started for the door.

Karine watched him go, a sinking sensation filling her. She jumped from the bed and ran down the hall after him paying no attention to her nudity. He had seen her naked more times than she could count. It did not even bear noticing now. Throwing herself in his arms, she kissed him one more time. "Be safe," she begged.

Jean hugged her tightly against him. "I can take care of myself," he assured her, giving her a final kiss.

Karine bit back a sob as she watched the man she loved disappear down the stairs and into the night. She closed the door and locked it, her eyes filling with tears. She wanted to believe his promise, but she could not shake the feeling that she would never see him again.

Chapter 17

ADÈLE paced the empty conference room furiously, her anger evident in every taut line of her body. How dare that insufferable, chauvinist vampire treat her like an inferior? How dare he judge her by standards so old they made Antiquity look modern? She was a woman of the twenty-first century, liberated, independent, self-sufficient. She did not need him or his superior posturing. He was a good-for-nothing scoundrel whose only redeeming quality was the beauty of his face. Oh, but what beauty! Despite herself, she could feel the desire building inside her along with the anger. Yes, he was an arrogant bastard, but he was a damn sexy arrogant bastard.

He had only fed from her once, at the Gare de Lyon, and she knew he would need to feed again before they went on daytime patrol. She almost... almost went back to her office to tell David and Angelique to put her only on night duty so she would not have to let him anywhere near her again. As much as she hated him, she knew that resisting his allure would not be easy if he fed from her. The feeling of his lips, his fangs, on her wrist had been undeniably erotic. She had not known what he was like at the time, but she did not think that knowledge would change his effect on her. She thought wistfully of Jean and the way he had looked at her, flirted with her. She imagined he would be a caring, considerate lover, as interested in his partner's pleasure as his own. She was pretty sure Jude had no such consideration. Sex with him would be the same power struggle they were already engaged in.

Scoffing at herself for her wayward thoughts, she tried to devise a strategy for dispelling the hostility between herself and her partner. They would never be able to function as a team if they could not resolve their problems, and the one battle they had already fought together was proof enough of how essential teamwork would be in this new alliance. This would not be each side fighting a common enemy more or less independently. This was a complete integration of two groups, and as one of the leaders of one of those groups, she knew it was her duty to set the tone. Yet Jude provoked her at every turn, as if he took pleasure in ruffling her feathers.

She reminded herself that his attitude was typical of his time, the macho warrior defending his territory, or perhaps the sportsman out for pleasure, but that did not make it easier to accept. She knew he had one use and one use only for women, and that was in bed. It was the double standard she hated. He wanted her modest and retiring in public, but she was sure that if they ended up in bed, he would want her unrestrained. The virgin and the whore. Well, she had news for mister arrogant vampire. She was neither, for him or for anyone. She enjoyed sex, when she had time for it, and did not mind expressing that enjoyment, but she also expected her lovers to treat her with respect, in and out of bed. That was, in fact, the one quality she demanded in a lover. He did not have to be suave or handsome or rich or strong or devilishly attractive or anything else. He only had to treat her as an equal, deserving of respect. Not pampering, not consideration, though she occasionally enjoyed that, too. She was a woman, after all. Those, though, were optional. He did not have to hold the door for her or pull out her chair. He only had to accept that she had the right to think for herself and make her own decisions. Her partner, though, seemed to think he was also her master. Well, he could think again. Arrogant prick! She would show him, one way or another. Before they ended up in bed.

ANGELIQUE stared intently at the field manual spread out before her. David had explained the strategy that she was currently studying and she wanted to make sure she understood it. Reaching for the patrol schedules they had just finished, she flipped open to the list of names in Mathieu Gatineau's company. "Let me see if I have this," she said, glancing at David sitting beside her as she began to assign members of the company to various positions on the page.

David listened with half a mind as Angelique talked through the indicated troop movements, her henna-painted hands drifting back and forth between the manual and the schedule. He still saw the tattoos, of course – they were impossible to miss – but he realized with no small shock that they had lost their stigma sometime in the last few hours. Instead of seeing them as a sign of infamy, they had simply become part of the woman he was coming to respect. As her sleeve rode up a little over a slender wrist, he saw that the design continued, disappearing up her arm into her sleeve, and he caught himself wondering how far the ink continued.

Angelique frowned imperceptibly when she saw the distracted look on David's face. She hoped it was just fatigue and not impatience or irritation, but she did not know him well enough to know for sure. Certainly, their conversation in Adèle's office had cleared the air between them a little, but she doubted it had laid all the wizard's concerns to rest. She would just have to keep proving herself until he accepted her for herself, with her true strengths and weaknesses as opposed to the ones he thought were there. For her own understanding, she continued to talk through the battle plan, even if David did not need to hear it again.

David listened to Angelique's explanation with one ear while his mind continued its evaluation of the charms he had not allowed himself to see before. The curvaceous form was more than pleasing to the senses, and the creamy skin looked as smooth as satin. He wanted to reach out and touch, but he doubted his advances would be welcome, especially after he had treated her so badly up until now. He would have to do better about that in the future, because he found himself wanting to have the right to touch, wanting to have his touch be welcomed.

"So if I'm reading this correctly, Guy and Jérôme should move down the left flank," Angelique continued.

"No," David interrupted.

"What?" Angelique asked. "But it says it right here."

"I didn't mean the movement," David hastened to explain. "I meant those two wizards. They don't work together."

"But they're in the same company."

"They are," David agreed, "and they've never given Mathieu a reason to switch them, but they refuse to work with each other. I heard, once, that they were lovers some time ago. Marcel didn't know about their history when he assigned them, and they don't let it get in the way as long as they don't have to work together directly. I've told Mathieu occasionally that he should have one of them transferred, but he doesn't see it that way."

Angelique nodded. "All right, then let's do it this way. Guy can go over here, and Charlotte and Jérôme can move down the left flank."

"Yes, that's it," David agreed, his eyes caught again by her hands, smoothing over the papers as she spoke. He realized with a start that the twinge he was feeling was jealousy, jealousy of the paper under her hands. Someday soon, he hoped, he would know what it felt like to have those hands on him instead.

CHARLOTTE flinched as she listened to her partner describe the fight they had just survived. They had been on a routine patrol, looking for hostile activity but not really expecting to find it. Marcel had intelligence – he always had intelligence – suggesting that the dark wizards were looking to establish a presence in the Quartier Latin, and she and Sophie Gasquet, her partner, had been among those assigned to patrol the area until further notice. Looking for anything to indicate that Marcel's intelligence was correct, they had worked their way methodically through the narrow, winding streets. Despite their caution, they had walked right into a group of enemy wizards as the rebels left an innocuous-looking building. She had attacked immediately, trying to use the advantage of surprise. It had worked for a few minutes, and the exchange of spells had been fast and furious. The two women were too outnumbered, though, for Sophie's strength to be of any assistance, and they had no choice but to retreat. Charlotte had provided enough cover for them to pull back safely, and they had headed back to headquarters to report what had happened.

Adrenaline still pulsed through her veins as she remembered what it had been like, ducking and running for cover as the spells hit all around them. Charlotte was still not convinced that Sophie had not been hit, but the vampire insisted that she was well, and her partner did not gainsay her. After all, what did Charlotte, or any of the other wizards, know about vampire physiology?

"You concur, then, with Charlotte's assessment?" Mathieu asked.

"I do," Sophie replied emphatically. "We didn't have time to see what they were doing there, but there were at least ten of them, and I've enough experience with human nature to know that they were up to no good."

Mathieu nodded. "I'll tell Marcel and we'll double the patrols in the area. I'll also recommend that any vampire/wizard pairing go on double teams. You were vulnerable tonight because Charlotte couldn't transport you out. I don't want that to happen again. Is that all?"

"Yes, sir," Charlotte replied with a salute. They were not true military and often let the stricter regulations slide, but Mathieu was her commander and she wanted that acknowledged.

"Dismissed," Mathieu ordered.

Charlotte and Sophie left his office, each lingering hesitantly in the hallway, unsure what to do or where to go next. "I could really use a cup of coffee," Charlotte said after a moment's searching for an excuse to keep her partner at her side. She did not question the desire to keep Sophie at her side, she simply acted on it. "Would you like to join me?"

Sophie considered the invitation for all of a half-second before accepting. "Coffee would be most welcome." She did not, and would not, tell her partner that she could not even taste the rich flavor on her tongue. Charlotte did not need to know that or she might not offer again, thus depriving Sophie of a way to keep her partner close a little bit longer. She could not have said, if pressed, why it was so important to have that opening with her partner, but she did not question her instincts.

They settled at a table in the Milice cafeteria, two cups of fresh coffee in front of them, each trying to find a safe topic of conversation. "Thank you," Sophie said eventually.

"For?" Charlotte asked sipping the hot liquid.

"For getting me out of there tonight. If I'd been alone, they would have caught me for sure." Sophie raised the cup to her lips, feeling the heat but unfazed by it. It would take much more than hot coffee to burn her.

"If you'd been alone, they wouldn't have bothered you," Charlotte countered.

"I'm not so sure," Sophie disagreed. "They were up to no good. Even if I hadn't been part of the Milice, they wouldn't have wanted witnesses to whatever they were doing. And alone, I would have been an easy target for their spells."

The thought of Sophie lying still on the cobbled streets, victim of a dark wizard's spell, sent a fresh heated rush of anger through Charlotte. They would not take her partner, not without taking her out first!

She blinked quickly, trying to clear her head. Where had that thought come from? Certainly, she was protective by nature, but she had never reacted that way at the thought of losing a member of her squadron. She would give everything she had to protect any of them, but the anger at the thought of something happening to Sophie was new. She had long ago accepted, albeit grudgingly, that not all of her comrades would make it through this war.

Feeling distinctly unsettled, Charlotte gulped the rest of her coffee and stood, breaking the lingering eye contact between them. "I... I should probably get some sleep. We're on patrol again tomorrow night and I want to be fresh."

Unsure what had happened to cause the sudden withdrawal, Sophie rose, nonetheless, and leaned forward to kiss Charlotte's cheeks in farewell, trying unsuccessfully to meet her partner's eyes to see what had changed.

Their cheeks touched and time seemed to slow. They drew back, moving so that they could complete the traditional embrace, eyes meeting again, though Charlotte's darted away almost immediately. Their faces came back together, lips brushing smooth skin. As they moved apart again, their heads turned and their lips met. Instantly, they recoiled, not in disgust, but simply in surprise, searching each other's eyes as they tried to understand what had happened. Neither spoke as the moment stretched between them. Finally, Charlotte took another step back. "Rest well," she said softly. "I'll see you when we go on duty tonight."

THIERRY'S cell phone chirped on his belt, startling him out of the half-sleep he had fallen into while waiting for Sebastien to return from his conversation with Orlando. He came instantly awake, automatically taking stock of his surroundings. To his surprise, Sebastien sat there in the shadows. He had not heard the vampire return, he who prided himself on being aware of what went on around him even when half asleep. Nodding to Sebastien, he flipped open his phone. "Dumont," he barked.

Sebastien watched as Thierry nodded several times, amazed at the way his partner snapped from sleep to wakefulness. He had spent several long minutes watching the blond wizard in repose. His eyes had caressed the rugged face and solid form, emotions stirring within him that had lain dormant for four hundred years, since Thibaut had breathed his last in Sebastien's arms. He had believed that part of himself dead with Thibaut, but it seemed some remnant of his heart still lived. This was not the vivid, all-consuming passion that had developed the moment he laid eyes on Thibaut and had lasted the rest of the man's life. Sebastien did not think he would ever have that immediate and eternal reaction again, but it was more than simple admiration for an attractive man, more than a passing fancy easily sated. The wizard who even now was clicking his phone shut decisively had caught Sebastien's interest. Unfortunately, the man would never be interested in him. He had just buried his wife. His *wife*. Even if his grief had not been so immediate, the wizard's preferences precluded the kind of interaction Sebastien suddenly desired.

"We just got tagged to back up a unit that's been attacked. Are you coming with me?"

"Wouldn't miss it," Sebastien replied. "Where are we going?"

"The quatrième. They're in the Marais, in the Place des Vosges. They've got Serrier's wizards cornered in one gallery, but they don't have sufficient numbers to finish them off. We're their reinforcements."

"Just us?" Sebastien asked.

"No, my squad will meet us in the Salle des Cartes."

"Lead the way," Sebastien gestured, still a little lost in the maze that was Milice headquarters.

They ran through halls, down stairs and past offices until they arrived at a large room whose walls were covered with maps, magically animated to show the location of all the wizards on patrol in the city.

"Impressive," Sebastien murmured.

"This way, we know where all our forces are so if anyone gets in trouble, we know exactly where to send help. Each wizard has a talisman, tagged to his or her magical signature and to this map. When we're on duty, we carry them on us somewhere. Off duty, we leave them here."

Sebastien nodded. "I wonder if something like that would work for the vampires as well."

"I don't know," Thierry replied, "but we should find out. After we finish this mission."

"Of course."

As they spoke, Thierry's soldiers filed in. He saw three other vampires, besides Sebastien, among their numbers. Laurent and... Blair, he thought the name was, Marie and her partner and Georges and his, neither of whom Thierry had met yet.

"I met Blair," Thierry said softly to Sebastien. "Who are the other two vampires?"

"Geneviève Iserin and André Perrot."

Thierry nodded his thanks. "Listen up, people," he said, raising his voice. When silence fell, he began his explanation. "First, welcome to Blair, Geneviève and André. And of course, to Sebastien, though I've told him that already. Now, our mission for tonight. Lt. Raynaud de Lage and her squad have a group of rebel wizards cornered but insufficient force to take them out." He moved to the map, indicating the square where the standoff was taking place. "This is our insertion point, right outside the Place des Vosges. Once there, you know the routine. Capture if you can, but kill rather than let them escape. Any questions?"

None were raised. "Marie and Georges, make sure Geneviève and André get there. I'll take Blair with me. Laurent, if you'll bring Sebastien along?"

"Yes, sir," the three wizards replied.

"On my order, then," Thierry said as the vampires switched places for the displacement. "Three, two, one, jump!"

Thirty wands flashed in unison, thirty voices murmuring the incantation. And in the blink of an eye, thirty-four bodies disappeared from the room to reappear in formation just outside the Place des Vosges. The four paired wizards reclaimed their partners and the unit fanned out slowly across the square. They could hear and see the flurry of spells exchanged between the two sides, zipping back and forth like so much gunfire.

"How many?" Thierry asked softly when he and Sebastien reached the other unit's position.

"Thirty still standing, sir," Lt. Catherine Raynaud de Lage reported.

Thierry glanced at Sebastien. "Can the vampires get behind them if we draw their fire this way?"

Sebastien looked around the square. "If you can get them to focus on that corner of the Place, I think we can get in from the other."

"How many vampires do you have with you?" he asked Catherine.

"Six."

"And we have four. That's ten against thirty. I don't like those odds."

"They're spread out," Sebastien countered, watching the continued exchange of spells. "We wouldn't take them all out, just a few. It's not as if you're going to be here doing nothing. If we can get their wands away from them, they can't hurt us anyway."

"If you're sure," Thierry replied slowly.

"I am."

"All right. Let's do it." With a wave of his hand, he ordered the wizards to the left, drawing the focus of the rebel wizards with them. Sebastien led the vampires in the other direction, their forms fading into the shadows as they slunk toward the enemy's vulnerable flank.

"Get their wands away from them," Sebastien said, "and then drop them. Don't bite them, though, if you can help it. They taste foul with the dark magic coursing in their blood."

The others nodded and followed Sebastien's lead, ghosting up the gallery until they reached the first of the dark wizards. Silent as wraiths, they struck from behind, sending the wizards' wands flying as they attacked. One of the dark wizards managed a shout of alarm before he fell, drawing the attention of the others.

"Merde!" Sebastien swore under his breath as the remaining wizards turned. Almost immediately, though, three of the dark wizards collapsed as spells from Thierry and the others hit their unprotected backs.

One of the dark wizards barked an order for half the company to face the square while the other half faced the vampires. Seeing that the new attackers were not carrying wands, he sneered. "Is Chavinier so desperate that he's sending unarmed civilians against us now?"

Sebastien grinned, the moonlight glinting off his fangs. "Who said we were unarmed?" Then he attacked, closing the distance between them before the commander could speak again. One hand caught the man's wrist in a tight grasp, forcing the hand to open until the wand fell. The other hand clamped around the man's throat until lack of oxygen sent him to unconsciousness. Out of the corner of his eye, he could see his comrades doing the same.

When he had subdued the commander, he shouted to the remaining wizards. "Drop your wands or you're next." Six of the wizards did so, raising their hands in surrender, but one did not comply, shouting, "Abattez!" as he leveled his wand at Justin. The spell hit the vampire, causing him to stumble backwards a few steps. Before any of the vampires could react, a woman's voice repeated the spell and the rebel wizard fell to the ground, dead.

"All clear," Sebastien shouted to Thierry.

A few moments later, Thierry was at their side, surveying the situation. Four wizards dead from Milice spells, two from the vampire's attack – the commander and one who had not wanted to surrender to Blair – and twenty-four prisoners.

"Good job."

"Thanks," Sebastien replied. "It was a team effort."

"You're alive! But how...?" Catherine's voice broke into their conversation and they turned to see her running her hands over Justin's chest. "The spell hit you. I saw you go down."

"What happened?" Thierry asked as he and Sebastien joined the other pair.

"This is Justin Molinière, my partner. He was hit with a killing spell. I saw him go down, but now he's here and unharmed," Catherine explained.

Thierry frowned. He, too, had heard the spell cast, but had assumed it missed since all the vampires were accounted for.

"We need to take this to Marcel," he told Catherine. "Laurent!"

Almost immediately, Laurent was at his side. "Sir?"

"You're in charge of getting the prisoners in custody and the mess cleaned up. I need to take Lt. Raynaud de Lage and her partner back to base."

"Yes, sir," Laurent replied, turning to give orders to move the prisoners.

"Catherine, if you'll bring Sebastien back with you, I'll see to your partner."

Catherine bit back a protest. She knew Thierry was her commanding officer, knew he would take as much care of Justin as he would of his own partner, but she was still reeling from the shock of thinking the vampire lost to her, and the idea of being separated from him, even momentarily, had every instinct she possessed revolting. She knew she could not transport Justin herself, but the thought of anyone, even Thierry, pointing his wand at her partner for any reason was almost more than she could bear.

"Do it quickly," she requested, murmuring the spell that carried her and Sebastien back to Milice headquarters.

Chapter 18

LT. CATHERINE RAYNAUD DE LAGE ran a critical eye over her partner as soon as he materialized next to her captain. It was not that she did not trust her commanding officer, but to know that another wizard – any wizard – had pointed a wand at her partner so soon after she had watched a killing spell hit him in the chest was almost more than the fiery brunette could stand. She knew it was her mother's Spanish blood that made her react the way she was doing, but that knowledge did not in any way alleviate the reaction. She wanted nothing more than to reach out and wrap her arms around him. She had a feeling, though, that neither Justin nor Thierry would appreciate that reaction.

"Your report, Lieutenant," Marcel asked when they met in the briefing room.

"Sir, we encountered a group of rebels in the place des Vosges. Realizing we were outnumbered, we called for backup and tried to pin them down. Captain Dumont and his team arrived and we drew their fire while the vampires snuck behind them and brought them down."

"We had a little help," Sebastien inserted. "We were ten against thirty. We couldn't have done it alone."

"That's not what has you so flustered, though, is it?" Marcel asked the usually collected lieutenant.

"No, sir. During the final part of the battle, one of the rebels cast an *Abattoire* spell on my partner. But, sir, he didn't go down. Justin, I mean, my partner. The spell hit him. I saw him stumble, but by the time I got there, he was on his feet like nothing had happened." Her eyes cut to the right, raking over her partner again, trying to understand how the most lethal spell in their repertoire had not done more than stun her slender partner. She had never known it not to work, but she would have been less surprised if her captain's partner, larger, stronger, more solid, had survived than her own willowy vampire. She knew he was stronger than he looked; she had seen the vampires fight. His appearance, though, brought out every protective instinct she possessed. Again, the urge to enfold him in her embrace washed through her, rocking her on her heels.

Marcel frowned. "Thierry, see if you can find Jean and Raymond. We need to figure this out."

The burly blond leaning in the corner moved to follow orders, but his own partner stopped him.

"What is the spell?" Sebastien asked. "The one that didn't work."

"It's a very simple, but very effective killing spell," Marcel replied. "It attacks the brain stem and stops the heart and breathing, instantly killing the target. It's a spell we avoid using except as a last resort."

Sebastien nodded. "That's why it didn't affect Justin. We're already dead. Oh, our bodies give the appearance of life. We're conscious and all that, but we're not alive in the same way as non-vampires. We can be hurt by conventional means, although feeding will heal us almost instantly, but really, the only way to destroy us is to starve us or expose us to sunlight. And now, even the sunlight isn't a problem for those of us with partners."

"It makes sense," Justin agreed, speaking for the first time from his place at Catherine's side. "I'm sure there are spells that could hurt us, maybe even destroy us, but they won't be the ones that would simply kill a wizard. Something that burned would probably work just as well on a vampire as on a wizard, if it burned us badly enough. But even then, it would have to burn us so badly that we couldn't survive long enough to feed."

"How is that possible?" Thierry asked. Even as he asked it, a part of him was relieved. He had been concerned about the vampires – who was he kidding? *his* vampire – going into battle with no defense against the dark wizards' spells except the speed and agility of the Milice operatives protecting them. They were not impervious to every spell, but it sounded like they had a built-in defense mechanism against the worst of them.

Sebastien shrugged. "That would be a question for a scholar, not for me. Jean might know. If he doesn't, old monsieur Lombard certainly would, but I won't be going to ask him."

"That won't be necessary," Marcel intervened. "We'll ask Jean when he and Raymond come back on duty, and if he doesn't know, we'll send Raymond to meet with monsieur Lombard again. They've already had one interesting conversation. I'm sure they'd be willing to have another one."

"Better him than me," Sebastien muttered under his breath. He had met Christophe Lombard twice, once when he was a newly-made vampire, and the impression had lingered with him all this time, reinforced again when the old vampire had summoned him to help forge the alliance. Despite the tense situation with Jean, dealing with him was, in Sebastien's mind, far preferable to dealing with the senior vampire.

Thierry heard the muttered comment and smiled, meeting Sebastien's eyes with a sympathetic look. Sifting through dusty tomes in search of information was not Thierry's pastime of choice, and from all he had heard of monsieur Lombard, he was one to appreciate that sort of knowledge.

Marcel took a deep breath, his mind reeling with all that remained to do and discover. The report he had just received demonstrated yet again the wisdom of the alliance with the vampires, but he could not rid himself of the worry that Raymond's earlier revelation had spawned. Considering this as good a time as any to start spreading the word, he turned to the two commanders. "One more thing before I dismiss you for the night. I need you to get word to any of your people who have formed pairings. Obviously, the partnerships that have formed have magical properties, but we don't know what all those properties are yet. We need to have everyone alert to anything... unusual they might be feeling so we can determine what side effects there may be besides the obvious protection from sunlight."

Both wizards and both vampires nodded their understanding of the orders, though they did not ask what the effects might be. Catherine glanced at Justin.

A shudder ran through the two vampires suddenly, bringing frowns to Catherine's and Thierry's faces. "What is it?" they asked almost as one.

"Dawn," Sebastien replied. "We always feel it when the sun rises."

Thierry nodded in understanding. "I remember Orlando talking about that, the first morning. You know the sun can't hurt you anymore."

Sebastien shook his head. "We don't know how long the effect will last, so we can't say that with any certainty."

"Orlando described being able to feel the effect of Alain's magic surrounding him, insulating him, I guess," Marcel interrupted. "Can you feel the same thing?"

"I did," Sebastien replied, "when we left the gare yesterday and during the night tonight, but the feeling is fading. That might mean that the protection is also fading."

"Just twenty-four hours?" Thierry said in disappointment. "That isn't a very long-lasting effect."

"It's almost certainly a product of how much blood we ingest," Justin suggested. "I can't speak for Sebastien, of course, but I know what I drank yesterday was more like a snack, because I didn't know Catherine well and because other vampires had already bitten her. It could be that if we fed more deeply, the effect would last longer."

"Rather like not being hungry the next morning after a large meal," Catherine commented.

"It makes sense," Sebastien agreed. "Now we just have to figure out if this magic is subject to logic."

"Another thing to tell the partners, then," Marcel said. "Not only should they watch for side effects, they should pay attention to how long the magic protects them and how long they fed each time."

"There may be other variables, too," Thierry added. "The strength of the wizard's magic, for example. I'm afraid this is going to be another trial and error situation."

"And we should probably not use Alain's and Orlando's experience as much of a guide," Sebastien observed. "The Aveu de Sang which binds them changes everything else about their relationship."

Thierry frowned. "In what way?"

"Every way," Sebastien repeated. "For example, there's a finite amount of blood I can drink from you before it kills you. Orlando could gorge himself on Alain regularly and it wouldn't hurt him. The magic that is the Aveu will sustain him regardless of how much Orlando drinks. That isn't true of the other wizards. We can't just say, 'Well, drink your fill before you go out on patrol each morning, just to be safe,' because the wizards' bodies couldn't handle it. Alain could, but not anybody else."

Thierry shivered at the thought of Orlando and Alain, at the need the Aveu created and the intensity it added to their feeding. He knew from talking to Alain that his fellow wizard found the experience incredibly fulfilling, incredibly arousing, an experience to repeat as often as possible. Despite feeling disloyal to Aleth for his thoughts, Thierry longed to feel a similar intimacy. It had been so long since he had felt the kind of closeness Alain had described, and in his heart he ached to be held, to be comforted in his grief. He doubted letting Sebastien feed from him would be enough to provide that comfort, but maybe it would be a first step.

"Something else to consider, then, in making the patrol schedules," Marcel declared. "Perhaps we should give any pairing a day shift off between any two day shifts, so the wizard has time to recover enough to feed the vampire again."

Sebastien and Justin both nodded. "That would probably be enough time."

"I'll review the schedules Angelique and David brought me and see if any changes need to be made. In the meantime," Marcel added, smothering a yawn, "we've all been on duty for far too many hours. Get some rest and report back for your next assigned patrol."

The four operatives filed out of the briefing room, splitting immediately into their respective pairs as Catherine and Thierry each returned to their offices to finish up their reports, their vampires walking alongside them.

When Sebastien and Thierry returned to the wizard's office and went inside, Sebastien looked around critically. The volets were still shuttered for the night, and he hoped that with them closed, it would be safe for him to rest there.

Thierry flopped down on the couch, exhaustion clear on his face. "This has been an... exciting few days, hasn't it?" he commented, trying to keep Sebastien close a little longer.

Sebastien nodded and sat down next to him. "You can say that again. In fact, I can't remember a more exciting string of days since I was turned. And I'm not even sure that compares."

Thierry felt curiosity stir at the mention of Sebastien's becoming a vampire, but he could not find the strength to ask about it. Instead, he simply closed his eyes, drifting in that state of semi-awareness that so often preceded sleep. He thought wistfully of his bed before deciding that it required too much energy to get there, magically or non-magically. That thought made his eyes fly open. "You can't go home, can you?"

"I don't know if I could or not," Sebastien replied honestly, "but I'm not going to take the chance. There might have been a time when I had a death wish, but that time has passed. I'll just stay here if you don't mind me using your couch. I've slept in far worse places in my lifetime."

Thierry wanted to nod and accept Sebastien's easy declaration. There was no hint, no suggestion in the vampire's words, but Thierry did not need a request to know that he could make it possible for Sebastien to return to his own lodgings, to his own bed. He reached for the sleeve of his shirt, pulling it up past his elbow, revealing the tender flesh of his inner arm to Sebastien. "You should eat so you can go home and be comfortable."

Sebastien's eyes stayed riveted on the tempting flesh as a double desire shot through him – the desire to taste Thierry's blood again and the desire to be close to the alluring wizard – but he forced himself to demur. "You're already exhausted. This will just make it worse. I'll be fine here until nightfall and then it won't matter again until tomorrow morning. I'll feed then."

Well aware of the irony of asking for something he had wanted to avoid, Thierry shook his head. "I'll be just as tired tomorrow as I am today. It's been months since I had any kind of break and it will be the end of the war before I get another one."

Sebastien opened his mouth to protest again.

"Just bite me already, damn it," Thierry said before Sebastien could speak, "so we can both go home."

"What do you mean 'both go home?' There's nothing keeping you here."

Thierry snorted. "Yeah, like I'd be able to get any rest at home knowing you were cooped up here. Take what I'm offering, Sebastien."

Accepting that the offer was genuine, Sebastien moved forward with an eagerness that belied his verbal reluctance. He lowered one knee onto the couch next to Thierry's hip, but the angle was awkward. "Lay your arm along the back of the couch," he suggested.

The blond wizard did as his partner asked, stretching his arm out so that it was pillowed by the cushions and easily accessible to the vampire's fangs. He forced himself to remain relaxed. He had offered this, maybe even wanted this, though he was not completely sure of that. He knew there was nothing to fear, that Sebastien would not hurt him. All that remained was to quell his instinctive reaction. This was a routine they would share for months to come. Thierry firmly believed that the vampires' participation would tip the scales, would be the edge they needed to win the war, but it would not happen overnight. And even once the war was over, there would still be pockets of resistance that would need to be rooted out, clean-up to be done.

Thierry was enough of a student of history to know that the work did not end with the surrender of the enemy. In some respects, the fighting was the easy part. The trials and investigations afterward were often more time-consuming, more difficult, than the war itself. That was not his current concern, though. His current concern was the vampire who loomed over him, lips hovering centimeters above his skin. Unable to bear the tension of waiting any longer, Thierry reached across his body and let his hand find Sebastien's head, fingers exploring the thick, dark mane that fell almost to the vampire's shoulders.

The touch startled Sebastien. His head swiveled toward Thierry, turning the touch into an inadvertent caress. He stifled his moan at the sensation as he looked questioningly at his partner.

"Go ahead," Thierry urged. He took a deep breath, struggling with the admission that hovered on his lips. "I want you to."

There. He had said it.

Fresh desire washed over Sebastien as he searched Thierry's face. The wizard was not lying to him. He knew there would be no point anyway. Sebastien would taste any lie in his blood. He was tempted to tease, to ask Thierry if he had developed a blood fetish all of a sudden, but he did not know the blond man well enough to know how he would react, and he wanted what Thierry was offering too much to risk having it spoiled by an untimely comment. Instead, he nodded and lowered his lips to Thierry's arm. He would drink his fill if he could, but he would also monitor Thierry's fatigue closely. Not only had his partner become important to him, Thierry was clearly one of the lynchpins of the war effort. Adèle's words came back to him. *He doesn't control his magic as effectively when his emotions are in turmoil. He could be injured or even killed if he goes into battle that way.* She was convinced Thierry would not take care of himself if left to his own devices. Grimly, Sebastien promised himself that Thierry would no longer be allowed to neglect himself. He would make sure his wizard got the rest he needed even if he had to make it happen himself. And feeding less, but more often, would be one way to keep an eye on Thierry's state.

Hand still cradling Sebastien's head, Thierry tensed reflexively, then sighed as Sebastien's lips brushed his skin, the vampire's thin moustache teasing alluringly over the sensitive inner skin of his arm. He had not understood Alain's eagerness to let Orlando feed from him, had even questioned whether Alain had somehow been coerced into accepting Orlando's attention, but he was beginning to realize what his friend must have felt. When other vampires – Orlando, Jean, the others when the partnerships were formed – had bitten him, even to some extent when Sebastien had fed from him the first time, it had been impersonal, almost clinical, and had left Thierry untouched, almost repulsed. This was not like that, though. There was nothing impersonal about Sebastien's lips on his skin, Sebastien's tongue preparing him.

On the contrary, it was the most personal contact he had experienced in almost two years – since Aleth moved out. They had seen each other, worked together in that time. Thierry had even tried to discuss their problems, but she had always brushed his efforts aside, saying they needed to focus on the war and on staying alive. Their issues could wait, she said, until the war was won. And now she was gone. And in her place, offering a closeness she had denied him, was a vampire. No, Thierry corrected himself. Sebastien. *His* vampire. The slide of fangs into flesh caught him in the middle of that realization, and the pleasure of the connection settled into him, a bone-deep sense of belonging that had been missing from his life.

Thierry's eyes stayed riveted on the sight of Sebastien feeding from him. He could not help wondering what was going through the vampire's mind as he fed, wondering what the vampire read and did not read in his blood. He wished he had the same opportunity for insight that he gave his partner every time Sebastien tasted him, but he knew of no magic that would let him read minds. A shiver ran through him as he realized how much he was enjoying the connection to Sebastien. A part of him longed for that connection to continue, but he knew it was only fleeting. All Sebastien needed from him was sustenance, and having offered the vampire that, there was no reason for him to linger when he was done. Sebastien could leave and wander safely where he pleased, protected for a little while longer. He would come back, Thierry knew, and the connection would be restored for a time, but in the end, it was only temporary, and the loneliness that had haunted him would return.

The mix of emotions that assaulted Sebastien's senses along with the rich flavor of Thierry's blood was overwhelming. Sebastien struggled to sort them out even as he felt the wizard's magic surging into him and wrapping around him. He could taste the pungent regret and grief that he already knew haunted Thierry's soul, but beneath it was a bitter loneliness, one far deeper than should have developed in the few days since his wife died. It was a loneliness that tugged at Sebastien's heart. It was a loneliness he understood, one that came from prolonged separation. He knew, from Adèle, that Thierry's marriage had been in trouble, but he now wondered just how long it had been that way. How long had his partner been alone? And why had no one done anything about it?

Sebastien could not answer those questions, but he added another resolution to his list of promises concerning Thierry. His wizard would only be alone if he wanted to be. Sebastien would not force anything on him, physically or emotionally, but he would offer Thierry his friendship, his companionship, and perhaps, together, they could find a way to heal the rough edges of their hearts, because, if he was not mistaken, obscured by the more overpowering emotions, Sebastien tasted acceptance, maybe even a silent plea to be comforted. He would wait for Thierry to give him some more definitive sign before addressing more than the loneliness, but he would watch – carefully – for any indication that Thierry wanted or needed more from him than simple friendship.

Chapter 19

ANGELIQUE rose from her seat and replaced the field manual on the shelf where David had found it earlier. She could feel her hunger growing, and she found herself fancying another taste of her partner. His attitude had improved greatly over the course of the evening, persuading her to let down some of her defensive shields. She could begin to see him now as a man instead of only a challenge to face. He had short, strawberry blond hair and bright blue eyes with a light dusting of freckles across the bridge of his nose. He was not a handsome man in the way some of her former lovers had been. He could not compare to Errol Flynn or Laurence Olivier, but he had a boyish charm overlaying a masculine strength that she was coming to greatly appreciate. His appearance might not demand a second look the way Orlando's or Sebastien's did, but she was glad she was getting that second look anyway. She had missed his charm the first time.

She moved back to the table where David was still sitting, but instead of taking her seat again, she stepped behind him, her hands settling on his shoulders, rubbing firmly with an expertise learned from her years in the sultan's harem.

Angelique's touch startled David, but the massage felt too good to stop, hitting all the pressure points along his neck. He could feel the tension of the last few days, and the last two years, seeping away as she worked. His eyes closed and his head fell back, almost of its own accord, coming to rest against the smooth plane of her stomach. He had no idea of what Angelique was asking for or offering, no sense of what her deft but innocuous caresses were suggesting. The shiver that ran through him could have just as easily been from the draft in the old building as from the sensuality of her touch.

Angelique smiled as she felt her partner relax. It was so much more… pleasurable to feed from a willing victim than from a reluctant one. She knew what David's reluctance tasted like, though he had not tried to refuse her. She hoped that his change in attitude toward her would let her taste his willingness this time. She worked her hands up from his shoulders, past the collar of his shirt to the skin of his neck, still massaging, deliberately not softening the touch so she would not spook him. She doubted he was ready for an all-out seduction, nor was she sure she wanted to take that step just yet, but she was not opposed to his sensing some of the benefits that could come of such a choice at a later date. David's throat, as he leaned back against her, was too tempting to ignore entirely. She ran her slender finger from his collar to his jaw and back down to the pulse she could see throbbing beneath his skin. Her fingers lingered, learning the rhythm, her own heart settling to beat in time. Letting the hand that was still massaging cradle David's head, she stepped back enough that she could bend and taste the skin over his pulse.

David moaned when he felt her lips and tongue on his neck and realized what she wanted. Perhaps if she had asked with no preliminaries, he would have hesitated, but his body had already relaxed under her gentle massage and not even the thought of her fangs in his neck could shake the feeling of rightness that enfolded him. He raised his chin a little more, giving her permission.

Angelique caught the gesture and its implications and felt the thrill of his agreement all the way through to her core. She did not immediately bite, though, despite her fangs' prompt appearance. This was not a one-time encounter, pleasurable but brief. This covenant with David had to last the duration of the war at the very least, and that meant building a relationship based on trust and mutual respect. It also meant doing nothing to cause David to change his mind about letting her feed from him. She knew from previous lovers that many men took time to grow used to being taken rather than doing the taking, because her fangs claimed them as surely as any man had ever claimed her. Although the mutuality was a requirement, she knew enough of male egos to introduce the concept subtly. Besides, she *enjoyed* the anticipation, almost as much as she enjoyed feeding. Her hair fell forward across David's chest, long dark locks contrasting with the beige sweater he wore. She had cut it short once, soon after leaving the harem, because the slave master in the harem had delighted in using it as a means to bend her to his will, but she had long since let it grow again, the silky fall proof that she had conquered her past and lived now on her own terms. She had even come to enjoy the feeling of a man's hands in her hair again. David, though, was too lost in what she was doing to reach for it. That was fine. She had time to educate him to her ways.

Angelique's tongue flicked over stubbled skin, tasting the lingering hint of soap and aftershave where David had clearly shaved before coming to Milice headquarters, but that had been at least twelve hours before. The prickle of whiskers did not bother her at all; it only served to remind her that her partner was male. His scent filled her nostrils, a cool mint from his aftershave, a light musk of his sweat, and underneath it, the smell of blood, a siren's call she was finding it harder and harder to resist.

"Angelique."

The sound of her name on his lips ended her attempts to linger. Her fangs found his skin and pierced the unblemished expanse, his hot blood flowing into her mouth. She swallowed eagerly and sucked in more.

David caught his breath when he felt Angelique's fangs penetrate, felt her lips and mouth drawing on him powerfully. The shiver that wracked him this time had nothing to do with the cold and everything to do with her proximity, her actions. This feeding bore no resemblance to the hurried one yesterday at the Gare de Lyon. That perfunctory interaction had left David resigned to repeats at regular intervals, not dreading them exactly, but seeing nothing there to anticipate. Now, though, Angelique's hands moved in his hair and on his chest respectively, her lips and teeth beckoning, enthralling, seducing. And his whole body responded. Beneath her hand, veiled by his shirt and sweater, his nipples peaked. Inside his pants, his cock hardened. He felt his entire body swell with desire, pulsing in time with the pull of her mouth on his neck.

Angelique smiled as the rich flavor of desire coated her tongue. In six hundred years, she had never grown tired of that taste, not since she realized that her supernatural strength gave her the upper hand in choosing what to do about the desire directed her way. Later, she would have to consider what to do with this man's desire, given all the complexities of their relationship, but for now, she would simply enjoy it, enjoy the thrill of feminine power that came from evoking and controlling David's passions.

"I NEED to get some things from my apartment," Alain told Orlando as they were leaving Milice headquarters. He hesitated for a moment, wondering if he dared invite Orlando to go back there with him, to the cold closet he inhabited. He was not sure he wanted Orlando to see how empty his life had been in the last two years. The important thing now was how much that was changing – had changed – in the past five days.

"Do you need help?" Orlando offered, not wanting to impose, but wanting to see Alain's personal space. The office he shared with Thierry was professional space, with little of Alain's personality apparent. Orlando wanted to see how Alain lived, what he considered comfortable. Orlando knew his own apartment was small and cramped, with little to make it a home, yet Alain had said he preferred Orlando's place to his. It made Orlando worry about how Alain had been living. He could do nothing about Alain's past, but Alain's future was his, and he had every intention of making it a good one. With that thought in mind, he hoped there would be something at Alain's place that he could bring with them to help make his apartment their home.

Alain debated how to answer as they walked toward the subway, but ultimately, he did not want to hide anything from Orlando, even the barren wasteland that his life had become after the death of his family. "There isn't much to move," he admitted, "just some clothes and a pan or two, but you're welcome to go with me." The thought occurred to him that seeing, knowing how empty his life had been might help Orlando realize just how much he enriched the wizard's life. "I'd like you to come."

The smile that lit Orlando's face at the words assured Alain he had made the right choice. Their lives were intertwined now, the good and the bad. It would take time to learn about each other, to cement the foundations for their future, but the decision was made. All that remained was to take the steps. "Let's go, then. The sooner we get my stuff, the sooner we can go home. I could use a few hours sleep."

"Would you rather go after you sleep?" Orlando asked.

Alain thought about it. Delaying his return to his apartment was incredibly tempting, but he knew that seeing the barren space would raise questions in Orlando's mind, and retelling the hell that had led him to the studio apartment the size of a postage stamp would be incredibly difficult. "No, let's go now. It'll be easier to face knowing we can go home together afterwards."

Orlando accepted Alain's words without questioning him, but he could not help but wonder why Alain seemed to dread going to his apartment. It had not escaped his notice that Alain had never once used the word home in connection with his own apartment, only with Orlando's. He would ask later, if the opportunity presented itself, but in the meantime, he would be as supportive as he could. "I'll guard your dreams while you sleep."

Gratitude shone from Alain's eyes as they reached the métro and made their way down to the train. They spent the ride mostly in silence, hands joined. Periodically, one or the other would squeeze their clasped hands gently. Alain's grip tightened as they neared the Anvers stop. He hated going to his apartment, alone or with others, hated the empty space, yet he had nothing to fill it that would not make the pain worse.

Orlando grew progressively more concerned as he sensed Alain's growing tension. What could be so bad as to have Alain so clearly ill at ease? He did not know the answer, but his protective instincts were kicking in. Whatever demons awaited Alain in his apartment, Orlando would stand at his wizard's side as he faced them.

Alain released the wards on his apartment, listening for the click of the latch before pushing the heavy door open to the modified studio that was his current residence. He hated this place, hated that his life had been reduced to this, but he needed things inside, which meant crossing the loathed threshold. "Come on," he said as much to himself as to Orlando. "The sooner we get my stuff, the sooner we can get the hell out of here."

"What can I do to help?" Orlando asked, eyes darting around curiously. It was immediately clear that this place meant nothing to Alain. The walls were desolately bare and starkly white. While the furniture stated clearly that someone lived in this space, nothing gave any hint to the owner. No pictures, no mementoes, not even any books. Just a fold out bed, a ratty armchair and a spindly iron table and chairs.

Alain thought about what he had in the flat and what he cared enough about or needed enough to move to Orlando's. "Grab the clothes from the closet," Alain said, gesturing across the single room to the storage space. "I'll get what I need from the kitchen."

Orlando opened the closet and began pulling out articles of clothing, stacking them on the couch. He saw a suitcase on the floor of the closet. Kneeling down, he pulled it out so he could put the clothes in when a plain cardboard box caught his eye. It was taped shut with no label so he had no idea what was inside, but something told him it was important. He lifted it out and turned to face Alain. "Do you want to take this box?" he asked.

Alain looked up from the kitchen drawers on the other side of the efficiency and blanched when he saw what Orlando held. He grabbed the counter to steady himself against the onslaught of memories and emotions. He had packed that box the day he buried Edwige and Henri, the day he lost Eric, the day his other best friend had turned from him in anger and bitterness, betraying their friendship and his allegiance by switching sides in the war. "I..." he began, unable to mute the stab of pain even two years later.

The anguish on Alain's face was more than Orlando could stand. He set the box carefully on the couch and went to his lover, wrapping the man in his arms. "Talk to me," he pleaded. "Tell me what ghosts linger here."

"None," Alain replied. "The only horror here is the emptiness. I couldn't face the memories any more, couldn't face what I had done, so I got rid of everything that reminded me. I threw away what I could, but the things I couldn't are inside that box. I can't look at them, yet I can't get rid of them.

They're dead weight around my mind and heart, dragging me down, keeping me alone."

"Not anymore," Orlando interrupted emphatically. "I can't change your past, but you're not alone anymore."

"I know," Alain replied, his face buried against Orlando's neck as he struggled to regain his composure. "You came here with me. You're holding me now, and it helps more than you can possibly know."

"You don't ever have to open that box, if that's your choice, but I hope someday you'll see that we're strong enough together to face even that. In the meantime, I know you'll tell me what you can."

Alain nodded. "I will, but not here. I have to get out of this place before it sucks the life out of me. You've given that back to me, and I don't want to lose it."

Orlando's fingers floated up to the mark on Alain's neck. "You won't lose it. You won't lose me. We made a promise."

Alain turned his head and pressed a kiss to Orlando's fingers. "Remind me when I forget that," he requested. "I've been alone for so long that I've forgotten how to be with someone."

Orlando laughed sadly. "You've forgotten and I've never known. What a pair we make!"

"That's right," Alain agreed. "We're perfect for each other."

Orlando's smile deepened, losing its sadness. It thrilled him to hear such sentiments. "Do you have what you need?" he asked, needing to get Alain out of this empty space and back to the apartment they were making into a home.

"Yes. Let me just stuff it all in a bag. I'll send it straight to your apartment, and then we can go there."

"It's not my apartment," Orlando corrected. "It's our apartment and we're going to make it a home." He looked around him again at the impersonal décor. "We've both been trapped in the past for too long. It's time to look forward now, instead of back."

Alain knew it was not as simple as that, but he hoped Orlando was right, that they could overcome their pasts and move forward with a fresh start. He knew, though, that it was far easier to say than to do. His conversation with Jean had already demonstrated that. Even so, just hearing Orlando express the sentiment was heartening. "Having a home again is the best thing I've heard in a long time." He packed his suitcase quickly, clothes, a pan, a knife, a cutting board, and transported the bag and the box to Orlando's apartment. "Let's go home."

They left Alain's apartment and the wizard set the wards again, though nothing of value to him remained inside. He would give notice to his propriétaire as soon as he could. This was one stage of his life with which he would gladly cut all ties.

When they arrived back at Orlando's apartment – their apartment – Alain opened the suitcase to retrieve the cooking utensils and started toward the kitchen. Orlando stood in the living room awkwardly for a moment before Alain's voice broke into his thoughts. "Come talk with me while I make something to eat," the wizard called.

Orlando went to the kitchen and sat at the table as Alain opened cabinets and the refrigerator and pulled out food he had bought the day before. Orlando relaxed into the welcome domesticity of the scene as Alain made himself an omelet. They chatted about inconsequential things while Alain's attention was divided between their conversation and the cooking. When he sat at the table with his meal in front of him, he took a deep breath and brought up the elephant in the living room.

"The box…," he sighed, "it's all I have left from the first forty-four years of my life." He fell silent, eyes blinking against his memories. Orlando did not prompt him, did not push. He simply reached across the table to take Alain's hand in his. "I lost everything that day," Alain said finally. "Everything but Thierry."

Privately, Orlando thought Alain would have more luck getting rid of Orlando himself, Aveu de Sang and all, than he would getting rid of Thierry, but he kept his observation to himself and waited for Alain to go on with the tale.

"I guess the first thing to explain is about Edwige and me," Alain said slowly. "Ours was not a conventional relationship by then. We had married because of Henri, though I like to think we loved each other in our own ways, but by the beginning of the war, we were sleeping in separate beds, separate rooms. We divorced, but we continued to live in the same house because we didn't want Henri pulled back and forth between us. All we were to each other, though, was Henri's parents. We were no longer lovers, no longer in love, but we still shared a house, a life built around the perfect child. I don't know how long we would have sustained our unusual family, but at the time, we were making it work because we loved Henri enough to rub along together as his parents." Alain smiled sadly as memories of his son assailed him: Henri's birth, bringing him home from the hospital, his first tooth, his first steps, his first word, his first day of school. Alain blinked back tears.

"I wish I could have known him," Orlando said softly. "He must have been an amazing boy."

Alain could only nod, too overcome for the moment to speak. He took several deep breaths before continuing. "The war had just started and Thierry and I had gone on a recruiting mission. We were supposed to be gone three days, but we finished early and came home. I don't know why he came with me to the house. He and Aleth weren't having problems then, at least not that anybody besides them was aware of, but he came home with me first. The smell of death, of dark magic, was so strong we sensed it before we ever got inside. Once we did..." he trailed off, the remembered sight of Edwige and Henri lying dead on the floor, faces contorted with the agony of what had been done to them before they were killed more than he could stand to describe.

Orlando tightened his grip on Alain's hand, knowing already what had happened. "You found them dead," Orlando continued for him.

Alain nodded, struggling against tears. The sight was too much for Orlando to bear. He rose from his seat and moved to stand behind Alain, embracing his wizard from behind. "You're not alone anymore," he swore. "You never have to face this by yourself again. I'm here, and I always will be."

Alain drew a deep, steadying breath before pulling Orlando onto his lap. "And that's what's keeping me sane right now." He took up the thread of the tale again. "We found them and the wizard who'd tortured them. He was still there in the house. I went a little mad, I think. All I cared about was killing the man who had killed my son. I cast every spell I knew at him, determined to hurt him the way he had hurt them. It's all a blur now, but I know I would be dead if it weren't for Thierry. He kept the other wizard's spells from hitting me, from killing me, while I took him down."

"Thierry told me about that fight," Orlando said when Alain paused. "He told me about your friend."

"Eric," Alain agreed sadly. "I killed his family and in doing so wrecked Eric's life as badly as my own, worse perhaps. Not only did he lose his family, he lost his friends."

"He made a choice," Orlando contradicted. "He did not have to leave. You did not force him out. That was his choice."

"A choice he made because of what I did." Alain's voice broke. "He and I were almost as close as Thierry and I are. He's a little younger than us, but we fit together. We knew each other inside and out. We'd even worked out a code of sorts, a way to check on each other without saying the words. In hindsight, it was probably silly, but it was our thing, a prescribed string of names. Each name had a significance. We simply worked the name into the conversation. Flamel was usually a question because he referred to being worried. Merlin was the best answer, giving the all clear. Morgana meant betrayal, Niniane meant we were injured, Paracelsus was success. There was a whole list. At the funeral, when he was so cold to me, I asked him how he was, but he wouldn't speak to me at all so I asked him if he remembered our conversation about Flamel, hoping to remind him that beyond the anger and grief, we had a friendship, a loyalty worth saving. He glared at me with such hatred and spat out that Morgana had the better idea. Everything in his tone, his stare accused me of betraying our friendship, our loyalty. Two days later, he defected. We haven't heard from him since except for the occasional report of his rise through Serrier's ranks. It haunts me, Orlando, that I couldn't sway him, that my actions sent him running to the opposite camp."

"It was an accident," Orlando reminded Alain. "I know you. You would never, *never*, hurt an innocent bystander deliberately. Hell, you're even the good cop in your interrogations with Thierry. If you'd known they were there, you would have taken precautions, but you didn't know. You can't carry this burden." He could see that his words were not reaching his exhausted wizard. "You need to rest. We'll talk more later. For now, I want to hold you in my arms as you sleep." He rose to his feet to allow Alain to move.

Alain nodded, the combination of physical and emotional fatigue leaving him completely drained. He made to rise as well, but even that was beyond him. He sent a pleading glance in Orlando's direction. Immediately, his vampire was at his side, pulling him to his feet, into a tender embrace. Orlando wrapped an arm around Alain's waist, urging his lover to lean on him for support. "I'm just so tired," Alain said softly.

"All the more reason for you to rest," Orlando replied, guiding Alain to their bedroom. He helped the wizard sit, then knelt to remove the man's shoes. Pushing gently on Alain's shoulders, he tipped his lover backward onto the bed, climbing in next to him. "Sleep. I'll be here when you wake."

Alain tried to nod, to show he understood, but his eyes were drooping as surely as if someone had cast a sleeping spell on him. Giving in, he settled into Orlando's embrace and slept.

Orlando watched while Alain slept, pondering everything his wizard had revealed intentionally and unintentionally. He had known some of it before, had known about Edwige and Henri, about Eric and his family, about the spell gone awry. He had not known that Alain had been so caught in his despair that he had been careless. He owed Thierry a debt of gratitude for having kept

Alain alive then, a debt he would be sure to acknowledge the next time he spoke privately with the other wizard. He had not tasted anything like a death wish in Alain's blood, but he would pay more attention when next they fed. He would not lose his wizard to despair, not now that he had finally found someone who saw beyond his curse to the man he was. He wondered what the failure of his marriage had done to Alain. He had tasted Alain's determination and commitment each time he fed. To be forced to accept that all the commitment and determination he felt were not enough to salvage his relationship with his wife must have been a terrible blow, yet they had gone on, finding a way to provide some stability for their son. Orlando wished he could have known the boy. Any child of Alain's surely would have been extraordinary. That could not happen now, but he hoped Alain would eventually share those memories with him.

He hurt for Alain, knowing what Henri's loss must have done to him. No more, Orlando swore to himself. He would look out for Alain from now on. Nothing would be allowed to hurt him again. He knew that meant protecting not just Alain but Thierry as well, since Thierry was all Alain had left. The last thing Alain needed was to lose his only link to his past. He shifted next to his lover, trying to get comfortable for the hours of stillness that would come while Alain slept. As he did, he wondered suddenly if he needed to have a care for himself as well. He had never cared whether his own existence continued or not. His destruction would not hurt anyone, even himself, and while he had not actively sought it out, he had never given any thought to his own safety. He reached for the brand on Alain's neck. Had that changed? Would Alain miss him if he was gone? He was unused to thinking about himself, about his own worth. If anything, he had always felt that he had none, that his own existence counted for nothing, maybe even less than nothing. He had lived with that knowledge for over two hundred years, but he was beginning to believe that might have changed.

His conversation that morning with Alain suggested that perhaps his presence had become as necessary to his wizard as the wizard's presence was to him. He was not ready, yet, to put a name to that emotion, not when he had pushed all emotion aside for so long, but some emotion was undeniably building in him. Did that mean it was building in Alain as well? If that was the case, then he had someone else to add to his list of people to protect: himself.

His thoughts lingered briefly on the code Alain had described, wondering if it was worth learning it, but he ended up deciding not to bother. If it was something only Alain, Thierry, and Eric had used, bringing it up now would only stir up painful memories. He could always ask about it later if he saw that others were using it.

Orlando let himself drift into the semi-conscious state that passed for sleep among the vampires. He was not tired, did not need to rest the way Alain did, but since he did not intend to venture from his apartment without Alain at his side, there was no reason to stay completely alert either.

The setting of the sun roused him enough to look at the clock. Six o'clock. Alain had been asleep for eight hours. Orlando wanted to give him more time, but he knew they were expected back at Marcel's and he could feel his desire for his Avoué growing within him again. Knowing now that he could not hurt his lover by feeding as often as the desire took him, and knowing that he needed to feed often, he would not question his hunger. "Alain," he murmured, nudging his lover awake. "I need you."

Alain woke from a dreamless sleep to the unsurpassable feeling of Orlando's lips trailing across his skin. It took a moment for the words to penetrate his sleepy brain. "Again?" he asked, surprised, since it had not been much more than twelve hours since Orlando had last fed.

Without lifting his mouth from his lover's skin, Orlando replied, "Sebastien said I should feed every twelve hours for a time. He also said I couldn't hurt you, no matter how often I fed. The Aveu de Sang protects you."

Still half asleep, Alain reached for Orlando, his hands finding the hem of the vampire's sweater and pulling it off, seeking the buttons of his shirt underneath. He wanted as much contact between them as Orlando would allow.

Jean's words warred with Orlando's fears. *Consider how much more powerful feeding and making love would be if you put them together.* A part of Orlando wanted that, wanted the increased intimacy, wanted to give in to Alain's clear desire, yet fear held him back, immobile. Only that morning, he had attacked Alain, albeit unknowingly. Experience had taught him that even with the careful application of his saliva to close them, the wounds he had inflicted that morning, when they rubbed together so intimately, would take several days to heal. How could he even consider something that might cause Alain even more pain?

Feeding from your Avoué is even more addictive than making love to your Avoué. Sebastien had spoken with such calm, such confidence. He had not said flat out that he mixed the two pleasures, but the implication was clear, as was his obvious pleasure in the memory.

As Orlando lay there, frozen by his fear, Alain's hands were busy, opening Orlando's shirt to reveal his smooth chest. When he realized that Orlando was not helping, he released his lover long enough to pull off his own sweater and turtleneck, allowing their bare skin to touch.

"No," Orlando muttered, pulling back. "It's not safe." He met Alain's eyes. "I know what you want. A part of me wants it, too, but we can't, Alain. I won't allow anything to hurt you, including me, and I can't guarantee that I won't. I'll make love with you and then feed from you, or feed from you and then make love with you, but I won't combine them. I can't. I would be destroyed if something happened to you, if I hurt you."

Alain sighed in frustration. It was so clear to him, so patently obvious, that what little pain might accompany a loss of control on Orlando's part would be insignificant when compared to the pleasure to be had in combining the two paths to intimacy, but Orlando could not seem to see it.

"I won't do to you what he did to me," Orlando finished hoarsely.

Those words silenced Alain's protests, possibly the only ones that could have. He knew – to the depths of his being, he knew – that Orlando would never hurt him the way he had been hurt, but he also knew that saying those words to his vampire would be pointless. Only time and trust would heal those wounds.

"Then don't," Alain said simply, leaving Orlando to interpret them as he wished. He stopped his attempts at undressing them, though. He had promised not to pressure Orlando into more than he was willing to give, and he would do his best to keep that promise. Instead, he tipped his head back, offering his neck to his vampire.

As always, Alain's trust, Alain's acceptance, amazed Orlando. He hoped he would always be worthy of that trust. In the meantime, he would be as gentle as he could with Alain, using the existing wounds to feed rather than making new ones. He looked down to find the incisions only to see unblemished skin. Frowning, he tilted Alain's head the other way, but the only mark on the wizard's neck was the brand that marked him as an Avoué.

"Did you do a healing spell?" Orlando asked softly. "The bite marks from this morning are gone."

Alain frowned. "No, it never occurred to me to do that. I don't think of them as injuries that need to be healed. If anything, I want them to linger, points of pride that you want me, that you chose me."

Orlando's heart melted at the words. "We chose each other," he amended. "But that doesn't explain why the only mark on your neck is the Avoué brand. There's no sign of where I bit you."

Alain ran his fingers over his skin, searching for the bites, but Orlando was right. There was no indication he had ever been bitten. Frown deepening, he looked down at his arms, where Orlando had bitten him before. Granted, those marks were older than the ones on his neck, but it had only been a few days. There should have been some indication still. That skin, too, was free of marks except for the tiny H tattoo on the inside of his right wrist. "I don't understand," Alain said finally.

"Nor do I," Orlando admitted.

"Could it be part of the Aveu de Sang?" Alain asked.

"I don't know. Sebastien didn't mention it, but maybe he didn't think of it. He did tell me I couldn't hurt you, no matter how often I fed. Maybe this is part of that."

"You can ask him, or I can, the next time I see him. It doesn't matter now. What matters is feeding you so we don't have a repeat of last night," Alain declared. "Come, Orlando. Feed from me."

Chapter 20

THE pleading tone of Alain's voice was enough to make Orlando flush with desire and a newfound sense of his own power. He had seen Alain at the alliance summit at the Gare de Lyon. He had watched the wizards – most of them – fall in line at Alain's request. He had fought at Alain's side during the brief skirmish. He knew how highly respected his lover was. He knew how powerful his wizard was. Yet Orlando had reduced him to begging. Alain had given him control of their intimate interactions from the beginning, instinctively at first and then because Orlando needed it, but this was different. This was not Alain ceding control to Orlando. This was Alain dependent on Orlando for his pleasure. As alien as the concept remained to him, Orlando knew that Alain enjoyed having him feed. He wanted it as much as Orlando needed it, and he had even before they made their Aveu de Sang. With the heady rush of power firing his heart and body, Orlando lingered over Alain's neck, nuzzling the smooth skin, tickling gently, barely resting his fangs against Alain's skin, only to withdraw a moment later before returning to prepare another patch of skin as if to bite there.

"Tease!" Alain ground out when Orlando's fangs caressed him then withdrew a third time. The vampire had not even bitten him yet and Alain was already hard. He had no idea how he would survive the feeding when he was already aching for release before they had even begun. "Do it," he pleaded. "Let me feel you inside me. I want you, mon ange. Bite me, please."

Angel. Hearing that word on Alain's lips did things to Orlando's heart that he would have sworn impossible. He understood a little better now what darkness had shadowed his lover's life, but it still amazed him that he, reclusive vampire, creature of the night, could somehow ease that gloom. Giving Alain what they both desired, he ceased his teasing and sucked forcefully on Alain's neck, calling blood to the surface. When the skin turned livid from his attentions, he let his fangs slide beneath the surface of his wizard's skin, tasting the blood that had welled up at his call.

Alain's back arched off the bed as Orlando sucked at his neck and then bit him. The connection between them slammed into place as it had done every time they were together this way, even the first time in the cemetery when Alain had not known what to expect. The first time, he had feared the touch of Orlando's fangs, but not since. Now he could not get enough of them. If he had been able to think rationally, he would have been grateful for the magic of their Aveu de Sang, which made it possible for them to share these moments as often as the mood struck them without worrying about the effect on him. Such a logical progression, though, had been beyond him from the moment Orlando's fangs touched his skin. He threaded his fingers into Orlando's long curls, reveling in the added sensation of the silky hair brushing his knuckles, teasing the backs of his hands. He wanted to let them wander, to return pleasure for pleasure, but he resisted the temptation, promising himself time to indulge his desires later, when they made love.

With the blood at the surface of Alain's skin already, Orlando did not have to exert much pressure to draw it into his mouth, his lips attached only lightly to his lover's neck, his fangs only breaking the skin, rather than driving deep as he had done before. He had learned finesse in the century since his escape from his maker, though he felt like it all disappeared each time he fed from Alain. Not this time, he promised himself. This time, he would use every trick he had learned over the years to make this as enjoyable as possible for his lover, to make this a prelude to making love as he knew Alain wanted to do, even without the flavor of desire already clouding his senses.

He pushed aside the desire, his and Alain's, and focused on feeding, on grazing Alain's skin with his fangs, on lapping at the blood that flowed onto his tongue, on ghosting his lips over and over the little piercings, tantalizing his lover in every way he knew how.

Alain squirmed on the bed, wanting more than Orlando was giving him and yet marveling at the control his vampire was exhibiting, teasing him so masterfully. This was yet another side to his lover. He had seen Orlando insecure, passionate, angry, bitter, sad, but never so deliberately seductive. "More," he begged. "Give me more."

Orlando let his mouth settle over the mark he had left, sheathing his fangs once more in Alain's neck. Immediately, the richness, the succulence of the wizard's blood assaulted his senses. The heady flavors inundated his body, sending his desire spinning out of control. He struggled to control his esurience. He had fed only half a day before. There was no reason for him to be this desperate for more. Yet there was no denying the desperation that took him, that urged him to gorge himself on the nourishing blood. He drank deeply, hurrying now despite his earlier pledge, knowing that he needed to sate his physical hunger before his, or Alain's, sexual hunger slipped their traces and overran his restraint.

Feeling Alain's passion beginning to spiral out of control, Orlando pulled away from his wizard's neck, breaking the connection, panting for breath as he tried to bring his own passion back to manageable levels.

Immediately, Alain uttered a groan of protest. "Don't stop," he pleaded.

Orlando smiled and leaned over to kiss his lover. "If I stop, we can make love," he pointed out in what was supposed to be a reasonable tone of voice. It came out sounding as desperately hungry as Alain's plea.

We could do both hovered on Alain's tongue, but he bit back the words. "Please," he said instead. "Make love to me."

Orlando shook his head. "No, but I'll make love with you."

Alain's head jerked up as he met Orlando's eyes for a moment, trying to ascertain exactly what the vampire was offering.

"I trust you," Orlando insisted, though he was not completely comfortable with what he was offering. That was irrelevant. He was denying Alain something the wizard clearly desired by not feeding as they made love. Giving Alain this was the best he could do. He only hoped it would be enough.

If Orlando's offer had sent lust shooting through Alain, those words sent love soaring through his heart along with a deep determination to be worthy of Orlando's trust. His vampire might be lifting the restrictions, but Alain had not forgotten what he knew of Orlando's past. He would take advantage of Orlando's offer so that his lover knew he appreciated the gesture, but he would not push too hard. They had time; they could move forward with deliberation. Little by little, caress by caress, Alain would show Orlando all he had been missing.

"Lie down beside me," Alain requested, turning onto his side so that they could lie face to face, neither one on top or on the bottom, but rather equal partners in their pursuit of pleasure.

Orlando shifted so that he was lying next to Alain. His nerves jangled uncomfortably at giving up his position of power, but he reminded himself that Alain had never hurt him, had promised that he never would hurt him, and had, furthermore, respected Orlando's fears at every turn. He had tasted the goodness of Alain's heart. He could trust his wizard not to suddenly change simply because he had offered some control.

Alain drew Orlando into a gentle embrace, seeking his lips, taking them in a tender kiss, trying to reassure Orlando of the wisdom of his decision.

Orlando, though, was far beyond gentle, turning the kiss hungry, possessing Alain's mouth with all the passion that had built between them as he was feeding.

Alain moaned edaciously, his hands coming up to Orlando's head, pulling their mouths even more tightly together. Their tongues tangled in a passionate knot, slipping back and forth from mouth to mouth. Alain could taste traces of his blood in Orlando's mouth, and it only added to his desire. He would not have believed a week ago that he could find the taste of blood, much less his own blood, erotic, but tasting it now, knowing why it was there, sent his passion soaring almost out of control. His hands flew over Orlando's back, kneading, grabbing, holding. Alain's ravenousness caught Orlando by surprise, and for a moment, he could only lie still in his wizard's embrace. Then his own hunger pushed to the fore, and his hands began to move, mirroring Alain's, flying across the wizard's skin, tweaking sensitive spots, digging hard when Alain's hands sent tremors through him.

Their lips parted on a gasping breath only to seek each other again, blindly, eagerly. Their hands slowed their frantic explorations, settling finally over well-loved places, kneading, caressing, touching, to set off a symphony of moan and sighs.

Alain's fingers returned over and over to Orlando's distended nipples, playing with the tips, circling the large disks around them. The whimpers and moans that fell constantly from his vampire's throat emboldened him. Breaking their kiss, he slid his lips down his lover's jaw to his collarbone, careful only to kiss and lick rather than nibbling, Orlando's fear of being bitten vivid in his memory. Orlando might not have set any limits this time, but that did not keep Alain from being aware of where they had been before. He would start with familiar gestures and move on from there if Orlando seemed comfortable.

Alain's hands and lips worked their magic on Orlando, sending him back into the realm of bliss where desire ruled and all that mattered was making each other feel good. Wanting to return the pleasure his wizard was bestowing on him, Orlando ran the fingers of one hand through Alain's blond hair while the other hand slid between them, seeking Alain's dusky pink nipples. The gasp that accompanied his caress made Orlando smile even as he tweaked the taut peak again, hoping to elicit another moan.

Wanting access to the rest of Orlando's chest, Alain pushed gently on his lover's shoulder, rolling him onto his back and rising over him. It did not occur to him until he felt his vampire freeze that the position might be another of Orlando's scars. "Easy," he soothed. "You know I won't hurt you."

Orlando lay still, panting with fear now instead of desire. He chanted Alain's name silently, a litany intended to slow his racing heart and steady his frantic nerves. His wizard had never been anything other than gentle with him. That was not going to change now. He knew that in his head. Now if he could just get his body to believe it.

Alain pushed up on one elbow when Orlando did not relax as quickly as he had hoped. He cupped the vampire's cheek in his hand. "Look at me," he murmured. When the ochre eyes opened, Alain dipped his head and kissed his lover softly. "Focus on me," he instructed. "Just me. Nothing else exists outside our bed. No past, no future, just us, just this moment and our lovemaking."

Orlando clung to the reassuring hand, trying to do as Alain asked. He concentrated on the caring blue eyes that hovered just above his face, directly in his line of sight. This was his lover touching him, his Avoué, not his creator. Slowly, he was able to relax, to focus again on the gentle touch of Alain's hand, on the tender kisses the wizard bestowed upon him. "Just us," he whispered finally, hoping Alain would understand.

Alain pulled his knees under him so that he could sit more stably. Keeping his gaze fixed on Orlando's face, he trailed his fingers over his lover's chest, lightly caressing, tantalizing. Then he let them drift lower, teasing across Orlando's returning erection and away, down his legs and back up again. "Touch me," he urged.

Orlando acquiesced, running his hands over Alain's chest as the wizard had done to him. As his desire mounted again, his eyes drifted shut from the pure pleasure of what he was doing.

Seeing that Orlando was with him again, Alain reached into the nightstand and pulled out the lube Orlando kept there. He wanted to be patient, but his body was throbbing, empty, begging to be filled. Gently, he pressed the tube into his vampire's hand, hoping Orlando would prepare him quickly.

Orlando's eyes flew open when he felt the tube being pressed into his hand. He looked at Alain, who spread his knees wider, giving Orlando access to his cleft and his tight entrance. Suddenly eager to feel Alain's heat again, he coated his fingers and slipped his hand between his lover's legs, pausing long enough to roll the heavy sac in his palm. Then, his fingers moved back further, seeking the pathway that would lead to bliss.

Alain shifted again, reaching back to spread the globes of his arse to help Orlando. One finger slipped inside him, slowly but firmly, stretching him gently. He took it easily, still open from their interlude in the shower. "More," he urged, rocking down against Orlando's hand.

Orlando complied, adding a second finger next to the first. Alain hissed in pleasure, moving faster against the questing fingers. Orlando started to push up, to roll Alain beneath him so they could be joined as they both so clearly desired, but Alain's hand stopped him. "Lie back."

Orlando sank back against the sheets, consternation clear on his face as Alain swung a leg over his body so he was straddling the vampire. The wizard scooted back until he could align his lover's cock with his entrance. Slowly, he sank down, taking Orlando inside him as he did. His back arched at the stretch, but it was a welcome burn, assuring him that they were now one in a way surpassed only by the intimacy of feeding.

For a moment, Orlando watched, transfixed by the passion that transfigured Alain's face. Then his hands began to move again, sliding over his wizard's chest and down to close around his cock, matching his strokes to the rise and fall of Alain's hips.

Alain moaned with pleasure at the touch of Orlando's hands on his body, bucking up into the tight fist that surrounded his cock. He called on every trick he had ever learned to bolster his self-control, not wanting this moment to end, certainly not wanting it to end so soon. No trick, though, no mental games could distract him from the immediacy, the potency of Orlando's erection filling him, Orlando's hand touching him. They moved together in a timeless rhythm that all too soon had their tempo accelerating and their hips stuttering toward completion. As one, they gave up the struggle and gave in to their desires.

Alain collapsed forward into Orlando's welcoming arms. The vampire rolled him gently to one side, disengaging reluctantly to cradle the body of his lover against him. He burrowed into Alain's embrace, not wanting to lose the closeness of their loving. He trembled a little when he thought of what they had just done. Not the sex in itself, but the configuration. It was a huge step for him, letting someone be above him that way. He had taken it, though, and survived unscathed. More than unscathed. He was thoroughly sated. Smiling, he pulled Alain closer, if that was possible, and settled down to rest until they had to rise to go back on duty.

Alain accepted Orlando's snuggling willingly, thrilled that his boldness had not driven Orlando away. There had been a few tense moments, when he was not sure if Orlando would allow the change of position, but in the end, he had accepted it and, by all appearances, enjoyed it. He smiled. Little by little, he would show Orlando all the things he had been missing all these years, and hopefully, someday, they would be able to love one another completely without fear. He glanced at the clock and seeing that they had a couple of hours until they went back on duty, he settled against Orlando's side, a quick flick of his wrist setting the alarm to alert them in time.

Chapter 21

JUDE'S scowl had deepened steadily as the day wore on. He had returned to his partner's – the word a curse in his mind – office before dawn, intending to feed so he could return home, but she had not been there. He had found Angelique, looking most well-fed, and her partner, looking well-fucked, though Jude doubted it had been more than feeding. Angelique did not look mussed enough for it to have been more, and the office was in the same shape as when he left. Even so, it had added to his frustration. Angelique was able to leave and go about her business. He could not. His frustration had increased as all over Milice headquarters, in the rooms where it was safe for him to be, he saw vampires coming and going, protected by their partners' magic while he was condemned to skulking in corners or hallways where the sun did not shine. The clouds that hung over Paris that day gave him a little more freedom, but not enough that he dared venture out.

Night fell, but still Jude stayed, determined to confront Adèle at the first possible moment. He was not hungry, particularly, certainly not enough to hunt, but he wanted the protection her blood would afford him. When another hour passed and she still had not arrived, he broke down and consulted the duty rosters that Angelique and David had finished the night before. Painstakingly, he examined the names until he found his own. His eyes traced the curves of the letters in her name, learning the shapes so he would recognize it again. Nine o'clock. She was supposed to go on duty at nine o'clock. It was – he turned to the clock, working through the process of reading it – seven o'clock. Two hours. Two more hours cramped up in this fucking office, waiting for her. He was tempted to leave and come back, just for the change of scene, but he wanted to be here when she arrived and he had no idea if she was one to come early.

He paced the confines of the office restlessly, the heat of his anger transmuting slowly to a cold rage. Finally, he heard footsteps coming down the hall, the click of the heels a rhythm he already recognized. He stepped behind the door so he would not immediately be visible to her when she came through the door.

Adèle opened the door to her office in a much better frame of mind than when she had left the night before. Eight hours of sleep and some time spent pampering herself had restored her equilibrium and left her once more in charity with the world. In her current mood, she was even willing to put up with her partner, though she hoped the time apart would have softened his mood as well.

She closed the door behind her, starting toward her desk when hard hands closed roughly over her upper arms, pinning her face first against the door. "Where were you?" her partner's voice growled in her ear.

Remembering her determination to work with Jude, Adèle did not struggle. "I was off duty. I went home," she replied as calmly as she could.

"You left me," he ground out, his mouth close by her ear. The stirring of the air from his words raised gooseflesh on her neck. "You stranded me here."

Adèle frowned, though she knew he could not see it. "What do you mean? You don't need me to leave."

Her words sparked Jude's anger again and he spun her around, his hands returning to her biceps to pin her against the wall again. "Don't mock me," he barked. "You know I need your blood to move in daylight and you left without letting me have any."

Her own anger flaring in response to his, Adèle closed her hands around his wrists, pushing up on them to make him let her go. They did not budge at all. A frisson of fear shot through her as she realized that she was physically helpless against him. Though it went against her nature, she also acknowledged that she owed him an apology. She had not realized her magic had worn off so quickly, given how long Alain's had lingered in Orlando, but that did not excuse her from checking with him. "I didn't know the effect would wear off so quickly," she explained as calmly as she could, trying to assuage Jude's fury. "I'm sorry."

"Words mean nothing," Jude retorted, tightening his grip.

"Release my wrist and you can feed as you wish," Adèle suggested, the necessity of the alliance at the forefront of her thoughts. She could not be the cause of her partnership failing.

"I don't want your wrist," Jude replied, harshly grabbing her chin and forcing it upward so he could access her neck.

Instinctively, Adèle fought him, striking at him with her freed hand hard enough to knock any mortal man on his arse. Jude barely budged, though he grunted harshly as he absorbed the force of her blow. She already knew that using a spell on him would be pointless, and she doubted her physical struggles would amount to much, but her pride demanded that she fight him, that she protect herself from his attack. "Is this how you build the alliance?" he taunted. "By fighting me?"

"And you build it by forcing me?" she retorted, constraining herself to stand still in his grip. Marcel had formed this alliance, and she owed him far too much to scuttle it. She had spent the day pampering herself while leaving her partner trapped here, however inadvertent that was on her part. If this was the price she had to pay to put things right between them again, she would do it.

"I shouldn't have to force you," Jude pointed out harshly. "This was part of the agreement."

Not like this, Adèle thought as she consciously made herself relax in his grip. Maybe if she stopped fighting, he would gentle his touch as well.

The fangs that penetrated the fragile flesh of her neck were anything but gentle, wringing a distraught cry from Adèle's lips. Instinctively, she struggled for a moment before forcing herself back to stillness.

Jude sucked forcefully, filling his mouth with the life-giving blood, relishing the chance to dominate his wizard. He was not sure when he had decided she was his, but the thought felt right as he pinned her against the wall, drinking his fill of her.

Adèle's fear subsided slowly as she realized Jude was not going to hurt her more than he had already done by his rough penetration. As he continued to feed with no thought for her comfort, her anger transmuted to disdain that he could not do this without violence, that he had turned what she knew instinctively should have been a beautiful, sensual experience into a meaningless exchange of blood.

Adèle's fear and anger had only aroused Jude, firing his own emotions, but the condemnation that flavored her blood brought him up short. This was supposed to show her that he was a force to be reckoned with. Instead, it seemed to have had the opposite effect. Frustrated, he finished and pulled away, opening his mouth to say – he did not know what.

As soon as Jude pulled away, Adèle jerked her leg up, catching the vampire off guard and slamming her knee into his balls. "Ask next time," she said, shoving him away as he doubled over in pain.

Gasping, bent over in agony, Jude retaliated the only way he could, his hand striking out to hit whatever he could reach, landing sharply on her arse.

Not wanting to end up back within Jude's reach, Adèle kept walking, refusing to consider the effect that his hand on her bottom had created. She had seen Alain and Orlando together; she knew what this partnership *could* be, but it seemed she had gotten the short end of the stick in her partner. He had no interest in her beyond the protection her blood could give him. She would come to terms with it, accept it and move on, because that was the way she did things, but a part of her deeply regretted what could have – should have? – been.

MIREILLE nudged Caroline's uninjured shoulder. "Wake up," she urged softly. "It will be time to leave soon."

Awareness returned to Caroline slowly. "How long have I been asleep?" she asked drowsily.

"About twenty hours," Mireille replied. "You obviously needed the rest. How does your arm feel?"

Caroline paused to evaluate her condition. "Better, I think," she answered finally. "Sleeping helped."

"Good. I was worried about you." She hesitated, knowing she needed succor before they went on duty again, but unsure if she dared ask.

Caroline smiled, extending a hand to her partner. "Sit here beside me," she invited, unconcerned that she was still lying in bed wearing only the thin camisole and panties she slept in. Her sleep-fogged brain clearing, Caroline tried to calculate when her partner had last fed. It had been at the Gare de Lyon, right after the firefight with Pacotte's company. That had been at least twelve hours before she got to sleep, and she had been asleep for almost a day. That meant close to thirty-six hours since Mireille had eaten. "Do you need to feed before we go back on duty?" she asked solicitously.

"Our shift ends after sunrise tomorrow so I probably should," Mireille replied. "I can still feel your magic, but it is weaker than it was, and we might not have time once we're on duty to allow for it then. Are you well enough for it?"

"If I am fit for duty, I'm fit for you to feed. That's part of my duty now."

Mireille's face fell. She wanted to be more than just duty to her partner, who had already come to mean more than that to her.

"Damn," Caroline swore, seeing the look on the vampire's face. "I didn't mean that they way it came out. I meant that if I'm not strong enough to give you what you need, then I have no business being on patrol with you either. We're a team, and that means looking out for each other. You looked out for me yesterday and last night when the healing spell knocked me out. Now I want to look out for you by offering you this and my full abilities by your side. That's my duty as a soldier, but it's more than that. It's my responsibility to a teammate. I want to do this."

Caroline's words mollified Mireille to some extent, though she knew it had gone far beyond responsibility for her. Still, it was a start, and she would build on that. Accepting Caroline's offer, Mireille moved to sit on the bed, trailing her fingers up the bare arm toward her wizard's shoulder.

Caroline looked up, startled, but she did not pull away from the unexpected touch. It had been a long time since anyone had simply touched her, and she found herself enjoying the gentle attention, her eyes fluttering shut so she could dwell purely on the sensation.

Mireille hesitated before accepting the invitation she thought she saw in Caroline's gestures. She wanted whatever Caroline was offering, and more, but that did not mean she should or could take it all right away. She had not had many relationships in her long years, but she had learned patience from them. Limiting herself to continuing the gentle caress she was already bestowing, Mireille lowered her head to the wizard's neck, lips coming to rest against satin-smooth skin.

Caroline's eyes flew open when she felt the vampire's lips on her neck, but she did not push Mireille away. The top of the red-gold head filled her vision as she tried to decide what she was feeling. She was surrounded by soldiers day in and day out, wizards, male and female alike, who had hardened themselves to deal with the reality of war, or else professional soldiers who came to give them advice and support. The only gentleness she had known in two years was her own, until Mireille. The vampire had taken more care of her in the last day and a half than anyone had since Caroline left home, and she discovered that she liked it, liked having Mireille close. Her fingers threaded into the long locks, holding the vampire's head to her throat. "Go ahead," she urged. "Take what you need."

Mireille wondered on how many different levels Caroline intended her offer, for the vampire had the habit of using her feeding to appease her sexual needs as well, her present employment making it difficult for her to maintain a relationship to see to those other needs. Tentatively, she stroked her hand down Caroline's side as she prepared the skin of her partner's neck, paying close attention to the wizard's reaction. When Caroline did nothing to stop her, she trailed her fingers along the underside of the other woman's breast, just as her fangs penetrated Caroline's neck.

Caroline arched beneath the combined sensation of Mireille's fangs sliding into her vein and Mireille's fingers teasing her breast. Once again, the vampire had surprised her, and once again, she found herself enjoying the sensation. No man had taken the time to touch her the way Mireille was touching her. They – her male lovers – had always gone straight for her nipples or else had kneaded at her breasts, almost roughly. Mireille's touch was light as a feather through her thin camisole, riveting her attention on the vampire's caress, to the exclusion of all else, even Mireille's fangs which rested, unmoving, inside her.

When Caroline did not push her hand away, Mireille grew bolder, circling Caroline's breast until she reached the edge of the camisole, sliding it down to bare the wizard's skin. She wished she could look as well as touch, but she was too enraptured with the flavor of the woman's blood to pull away. It was sweet, but not cloyingly so, like the flavor of a fine Royal Tokayi wine, rich and full, offering nourishment and pleasure, especially with the undercurrent of desire that ran through it. She drew more deeply, beginning to suck in earnest as her fingers danced across Caroline's exposed breast, teasing her sensitive nerves as her teeth and lips teased the arch of the wizard's neck.

Caroline trembled with passion, warm and smooth beneath her skin, making her undulate against the sheets, seeking more contact with Mireille's softness. The rhythmic pressure of the vampire's lips sent frissons of desire through her, her body arching against Mireille's fangs as she had previously arched against her lover's erection. The feeling of being filled was nearly overwhelming, the added sensation of the delicate fingers enough to have her on the cusp of exploding.

"Miri," she whispered as she came on a sigh, her body going suddenly limp with satiation.

Mireille withdrew her fangs, tenderly laving the punctured flesh with her tongue to speed its healing, her own passion still engaged. Lifting her head, she looked down at Caroline's flushed face. With trembling fingers, she stroked the beautiful face and shoulder-length blond hair, shorter and paler than her own. The grass green eyes opened, glazed with sated desire, and met Mireille's own hazel orbs. Caroline must have read something in Mireille's eyes, for she raised her hand slowly and rested it against the vampire's face. "Can I... do something for you?"

"Kiss me," Mireille replied softly.

Caroline nodded and pushed up on one elbow, completely unselfconscious despite her bared breast, letting her lips brush across the vampire's, the slightest hint of her blood lingering to titillate them both. Mireille sighed into the light pressure, letting go of the passion still sparkling in her blood and settling into blissful afterglow.

"Thank you," Mireille murmured, withdrawing slightly.

"Not yet," Caroline countered, pulling Mireille's head back to hers and kissing her again. When, a moment later, she lay back on her pillow, she looked up at the vampire as if seeing her for the first time. "I think," she said after a moment, "that I should be thanking you."

Chapter 22

JEAN sat in his living room, the drapes pulled tightly shut. He glared at the flicker of sunlight that danced around the edges of the curtains. Once again, he was trapped inside by its rays. It had not bothered him in centuries, this confinement. He viewed it as the equivalent of the nighttime rest required by mortals. Then, two days ago, he had tasted freedom, had walked outside in the daytime. All his placid acceptance of his lot had disappeared in that moment, feeling the warmth of the sun without worrying about being burned.

It would have been bad enough, he was sure, under any circumstances, but now he was wracked with guilt. He chafed against the limitations that trapped him in his apartment instead of allowing him to go to Karine's side and apologize. He knew what he had done was inexcusable. She might not have uttered a protest, but that did not mean she deserved the way he had treated her. He considered himself a gentleman, for all his humble roots, and he had prided himself on never mistreating a lady or a child. That attitude had often put him at odds with others of his kind, especially in less enlightened times, but he had stood firm in his choices. Until yesterday.

Yesterday, he had broken every precept by which he had lived and led. He had all but raped the closest thing to a lover he had known in four hundred years. She deserved better than that, deserved someone who could love her the way she wanted. In the back of his mind, the theories Raymond and Christophe had presented echoed like a death knell to all of Karine's hopes. He wished there was a way to change that, to at least give her what he had already been giving her. She had earned that much of his regard. Yet he did not see an option for it. All he could foresee for her was abandonment. He hoped she would accept it and move on, but she had not yet, though he had told her time and again he would never be able to give her what she desired.

He would have to go to her eventually, try to repair the damage he had done, but not yet. It was too soon, for both of them. He needed to give her time to heal, and he needed time to see what he could, in all honestly, offer her. Or if the time had come to finally sever those ties for good.

There was another complication now – Raymond – and it only added to his guilt. He had gone to Karine not because he actually wanted to see her but to prove that he could, that Raymond's blood and his own instincts were not stronger than the force of his will. Any other time, he would have waited much longer before going to see her again simply to keep her from imagining their interactions meant more than they did.

He had proven his point, to himself, but at what cost? Would Karine ever trust him again, and even if she did, could he trust himself? He was afraid the answer to that was no. Rising from his seat, he began to pace the confines of the small room, a sign of agitation he would never have allowed himself had anyone been present. Rarely did he even allow it when he was alone. Too much depended on his perfect self-discipline. The vampires were not an orderly lot, and they preyed on weakness, wherever they found it, even among themselves.

He had a weakness now, Jean knew, though he did not see anything he could do about it. Raymond's blood had shown him a world that had been closed to him until two days ago. A world that was closed to him right now because he had let his pride get the better of his common sense. He had fled from Raymond the night before without feeding from him, and so now he was stuck inside until nightfall. He toyed with the idea of calling the wizard, of somehow finding his number and asking him to come by on some pretext so that he could feed, but that would be pointless. He had gorged himself on Karine's sweet blood during the night. Even if he could find Raymond – and he was not sure he could – it would do him no good. He could not feed again yet without making himself sick.

Forcing himself to reclaim his seat, Jean closed his eyes and rested his head against the back of the couch, trying to sort out his feelings. Memories of Raymond's reaction when he had tasted the dark wizard in the train station kept flitting across his mind, and that led to thinking about their conversation at Milice headquarters, where they had made their peace. Jean had promised not to make Raymond watch him feed from someone else, and he had kept that vow, but he could not help feeling that he had betrayed the wizard anyway. He had no formal relationship with his partner, only the military alliance, but the guilt he felt when he thought of Raymond had nothing to do with alliances and everything to do with the kind of intimate, personal connection Raymond and Christophe had posited must exist between the matched pairs.

Uttering a string of curses fit for a sailor, Jean rose and resumed his pacing, waiting impatiently for the sun to set so he could be about his business again. Perhaps if he kept busy with the alliance, he could forget these niggling doubts.

"DO you have any particular characteristics in mind when you choose your prey?" Serrier asked conversationally as he walked beside the vampire through the corridors of his lair.

"It depends on my mood," Edouard replied, "but unless I'm in the mood for a fight, I generally prefer women. Men are too much trouble. I like them young, too. They're so much sweeter that way, before life takes its toll on them."

Serrier nodded thoughtfully. It seemed his henchmen had found the perfect vampire for their cause. "I think we can oblige you." A quick order sent one of his wizards out into the night, and a few moments later, the man returned with a struggling teenager in his arms. "Will she suit?" Serrier asked.

Edouard looked at the girl, abject terror written on her innocent face. "Admirably," he replied with a hungry leer. "Leave us. I need no further assistance."

Serrier bristled at the order, but motioned for the other wizard to withdraw. The wizard did as he was ordered, pushing the girl toward the corner away from the door. As Serrier left the room, he turned back and cast a surveillance spell so he could watch what transpired within. Too much was riding on this vampire's help for him to be deceived in any way.

Inside the room, Edouard smiled at his adolescent victim. The wizard who brought her had indeed chosen well. He considered toying with her, weighing his pleasure in tormenting her against his hunger. In the end, his hunger won out. Moving with preternatural speed, he caught her arm, pulling her into a cold mockery of an embrace. She squirmed against him frantically, but her feeble movements were no match for his strength. His fangs scored her skin, bringing blood to the surface. She cried out in fear and pain, her struggles only adding to Edouard's pleasure. He licked at her skin, tasting the sweet blood tinged with her panic. Eyes closing with the sublimity of his power over her, Edouard paused to savor the moment, the thrill of the chase firing his blood already.

"Please," she begged, reading his savoring as reconsideration. "Don't hurt me."

Edouard looked into her dark eyes and stroked her smooth, glossy hair. "It won't hurt for long," he promised, opening another cut with his fangs. She struggled again, but more weakly this time, as if she was coming to understand that it would not avail her. Edouard smiled cruelly, licking the blood from the most recent cut before rending the flesh of her neck and drinking deeply.

The flavor of her torment, her pain, her dread filled his senses. He could smell it on her, feel it in the tremors that wracked her, hear it in her agonized whimpers, but most of all, he could taste it in her blood. Sucking hard, he flooded his mouth with her life force, drinking deep, feeling himself grow more powerful as she grew ever weaker.

He tore his lips away from her tender, tempting flesh. This was going too quickly. He was alone, in a safe place, with his ideal victim. He should not rush this. He should linger, should enjoy every minute of her torment rather than rushing for the climax because despite the wizard's offer, he did not know when he would have such an opportunity again.

Glancing around the room, Edouard wished wistfully for a bed, but the lack did not matter. He did not need one. Grabbing the collar of his victim's blouse, he tore it down the middle, baring her sweet young flesh to his eyes. " No," she begged, "please don't."

He laughed at her pleading, feeling the terror rolling off her go straight to his head. And his loins. This was the thrill he had been missing: being able to toy with his prey. One hand keeping her immobile, he ran the cold fingers of the other down her neck and over the swell of her small breasts. He wondered idly if she would fill out more as she grew older or if she had reached her adult figure. At a glance, he would judge her about eighteen, maybe nineteen. Almost the age he had been when he was turned.

He spun her in his arms and pinned her again the wall, lifting her so her chest was level with his mouth. Her abject pleading increased, but the words fell on stony ground. There was no pity left in Edouard's heart and her fear only added to his enjoyment. His lips played across her skin in a parody of lovemaking, his fangs leaving behind one cut after another until her pale skin was pink with blood and saliva.

Her fear mounted, growing frantic as she changed from simple pleas to bargaining, asking Edouard what he wanted in exchange for her freedom. He laughed and lifted her higher, fangs moving across her belly, grazing constantly, then stopping to pierce deeply just above her navel. "Blood," he replied, lifting his head after drinking deeply. "The price for your release is your blood."

She nodded, as if considering his request. "And if I give you my blood, you'll let me go?"

"Oh, most definitely," Edouard agreed. "I'll have no use for you once I've drained you dry."

The new spike of terror and screams at his words only sweetened her blood. "But you said you'd release me," she babbled.

"I will," Edouard answered. "I never said I'd release you alive."

Her tears began to fall in earnest as he ripped open the pants she was wearing. Her babbling changed from pleas to prayers, but Edouard ignored them, focusing on the creamy flesh of her thighs, mutilating them as he had her upper body. He knew her greatest fear, besides dying, was that she would be raped first. Lowering her so her feet touched the ground again, he pressed her against the wall with one hand, opening his clothes so they would not get stained. He leaned into her body, letting her feel the pounding erection. As he had hoped, another layer of terror entered her blood. With a cackle, he humped against her stomach as his fangs returned to her neck.

He sucked forcefully, drinking like a parched man at an oasis, his hips moving in time with his lips. He tasted the change in her blood even before he felt it in her body, the last gasp of breath. As he sucked it in, he climaxed against her bloody stomach, his semen adding to the mess. Taking a step back, he let her fall to the ground, sated for the moment. As sweet as it had been, though, he knew he would need more soon.

Wiping himself clean with the remains of her shirt, he buttoned himself back up and left the room. The wizards could deal with his mess.

"OUR young spy has sent us some interesting information," Marcel told the assembled captains and their partners as they sat in their morning briefing, half ready to go off duty, the other half coming on. "It seems Serrier has found a vampire."

"Who?" Jean asked sharply, the emotions that had ridden him hard all of the previous day barely controlled under the best of circumstances. Hearing there was dissension in his ranks certainly did not qualify as good news. If that was the case, he needed to know about it now so he could deal with it.

"Dominique didn't give me a name," Marcel replied calmly. "Either he doesn't have it or didn't think it safe to send. His description, though, is of a young man, barely in his twenties, with dark hair, pale skin, and incredibly vivid blue eyes. Does that ring any bells?"

Jean shook his head. "No, but I'll keep my ears open. It could be someone newly arrived in the city or newly turned. I didn't extend the invitation to the alliance to every vampire. Just to my friends. The ones I could trust to listen and participate. I wanted it to get off the ground before we let just anyone in the door." He did not look at Sebastien as he spoke, sure he would see reproach on the other vampire's face.

"A vampire of that description visited Sang Froid last night," Angelique said softly. "As did two of our enemies. My manager had never seen the vampire before and did not get his name, but he was concerned enough by his attitude and behavior to report it to me."

"What did he want?" David asked, suddenly protective.

"Disposable company was the way he put it," Angelique replied with a moue of disgust. "Congenial company is our forte. Disposable company is not." She was surprised by the tone of David's comment. Was he worried about her?

Jean's frown deepened. Christophe had warned him of a vampire who was flaunting their traditions. He hoped this was the same one. He hated to think he had two rogues on his hands.

"What about the wizards?" Alain asked. "Did your manager say what they wanted?"

"To meet a vampire, apparently. He did not oblige them either," Angelique assured them.

"So Serrier's after information?" Thierry hypothesized.

"That or a guinea pig," Raymond agreed. "If he's figured out about the alliance, he'd want to know everything he could about vampires. Their strengths and their weaknesses. And he isn't above experimenting to find out."

"We need to warn everybody," Jean declared. "Both to be wary of this rogue vampire and to be on the lookout for dark wizards. If Serrier is taking prisoners, he may not stop at one."

"He almost certainly won't," Raymond interjected. He thought wistfully of his own privacy and then shrugged. The alliance and its success were more important than his comfort. "It might not be a bad idea for people to go home in pairs," he suggested. "And preferably a wizard and a vampire. If Serrier goes hunting for vampires, our allies could be in trouble should his people catch them alone. They have no defense against magic."

"That's asking a lot of everyone involved," Marcel pointed out. "Are you sure it's a good idea?"

"Make it voluntary," Thierry suggested. "Tell everyone the dangers. Tell them we recommend traveling in pairs for safety, and then let them decide." He avoided looking at Sebastien as he spoke, not wanting his partner to see the sudden desire on his face. He had only to close his eyes to see the vampire in his apartment, and the vision was surprisingly enticing.

"There's no reason a wizard can't escort his partner home, then use a displacement spell rather than more conventional transportation, if they're not comfortable staying," Caroline pointed out reasonably, though she knew she would be asking Mireille to stay. "We can't convey our partners, but we haven't lost the ability to transport ourselves."

"And then what?" Sebastien asked, bristling a little at being treated like he was helpless. "The wizards come back to meet us before we leave? Isn't that a little like house arrest?" He was not so worried himself about being confined – he would simply ignore the edict if he felt like it. Then he thought about Thierry. Would the wizard look out for himself? Perhaps the idea of sharing an apartment was not such a bad idea after all.

"As I said," Thierry responded, "make it voluntary. Make sure everyone understands the situation and then if people choose to go out alone, vampire or wizard, they do so at their own risk."

Marcel nodded. "We'll inform everyone, make the recommendation, and leave it up to them to decide. David, will you see to it that there are wizards assigned to make sure any unpaired vampires who want it get to and from headquarters safely?"

"We'll add it to the duty rosters. We still have them on file, don't we, Angelique?" David agreed.

The vampire nodded.

"Good. Anything else the night shift needs to report?"

Jean, Raymond, Alain, Orlando, Mireille and Caroline all shook their heads.

"Good. Adèle will be returning from patrol soon. We'll debrief with her when she gets back. In the meantime, get some rest before your next shift. Day patrol, any questions about your assignments before you get started?"

David, Angelique, Thierry and Sebastien indicated none. "Good. Dismissed."

The ten operatives rose from their seats, splitting into pairs. "Jean," Marcel called. "A moment of your time."

Jean looked back at Marcel still sitting at the head of the table. "Wait for me?" he asked Raymond softly. The wizard agreed and stepped outside the door.

"I didn't want to ask in front of everyone since I felt it was not for us to handle without your permission, but how do you want to deal with this vampire? There was also a second report, a new report this time, of a twenty-year old girl found in the jardin de Luxembourg this morning. S he'd been savaged by a vampire. I'm going to assume this is the same one Serrier has recruited because that's preferable to thinking we have two vampires out of control."

Jean's face hardened. "There's only so much I can do until I know who it is," he said, "but I'll make the rounds tonight and see what I can learn, and while I'm out, I'll remind everyone that killing does not help our cause. I know what people say about our kind, but we are, on the whole, far too sensible to deliberately make our lives more difficult."

Marcel raised his hands to ward off the protest. "I know that. If I doubted it, I would never have approached you in the first place. We must make sure, though, that the actions of one do not destroy our efforts for the rest. Can you bring him to heel?"

"It will take time," Jean answered honestly. "Because we have not had the protection of civil laws, we have developed our own code over the years. Despite my best efforts, killing a mortal in and of itself is not a punishable offense in any formal way. Only when it endangers other vampires. That is difficult enough to prove that rarely is a trial convened for such an offense. Rather, we meet for crimes against other vampires. The procedures are thus: we must prove to the gathered host that the vampire's behavior endangers us all. That will take careful evidence."

Marcel listened, fascinated. "I had no idea you had your own courts."

"We meet only when needed, which is rarely, but we do have ways of governing ourselves."

"So you need evidence that this vampire's actions hurt all vampires," Marcel clarified. "Take Raymond with you tonight when you make your rounds. He might have some insight or think to ask a question that you might not see. His wealth of knowledge astounds me."

"You don't think, like the others do, that he's a spy or a weak link?" Jean asked.

"No," Marcel replied emphatically. "He is, in many ways, the strongest link because he knows firsthand the cruelty we are fighting. We have all seen the results. He had to endure the process. If we win this war, he will succeed me some day. Not in the Milice, for I pray we will not be needed, but certainly in l'ANS."

"L'ANS?"

"L'Association Nationale de Sorcellerie," Marcel explained. "It's an organization for the education and advancement of wizardry. It's how I ended up with this job. As its president, I was well-known, an influential figure in public policy. When the war broke out, our President asked me to lead the newly formed Milice against the rebels. It seemed the least I could do since I had insisted that he form it in the first place."

Jean nodded. He had not followed current events except in how they affected his own people for so long that he had paid little attention at the beginning of the war. By the time he had realized the implications of the war on vampires and on the whole world, Marcel had been well-established as the leader and Jean had not questioned his right to the role. Feeling the unease that came with the dawn and knowing he had lost his protection against the sunlight, he excused himself to Marcel, promising to bring the results of his inquiries to the next day's briefing.

To his relief, Raymond was indeed waiting for him outside the conference room. "Thank you for being patient," he offered.

"If Marcel called you back, I'm sure it was important," Raymond replied with a shrug.

"It was," Jean agreed. "Is there somewhere private we can go? I'll tell you what he said." He flushed a little, uncomfortable. "I'll need to feed as well if I'm to leave. The sun has risen."

"The effect of the magic is gone?" Raymond asked.

"Yes. Since yesterday morning. Perhaps because I didn't feed deeply from you the day before."

Raymond nodded. A part of him wanted to urge Jean to take what he needed, if only so they would not have to do this so often, but another part of him remembered all too well the boy in his village. "We can go to my office. It's small, but no one ever comes in there but me."

"Not even Marcel?" Jean asked, the older wizard's words fresh in his mind as he followed Raymond through the maze of corridors.

"If Marcel needs me, I go to him," Raymond explained. "I would never make him come to me."

"He thinks highly of you," Jean observed.

Again, Raymond nodded. "More highly than I deserve."

Jean frowned. "Why do you say that? You're obviously an intelligent, well-educated man, probably better educated than the others in the meeting this morning, yet you denigrate yourself."

"You don't know what I've done," Raymond protested as they walked into his office.

Jean looked around. It was small, as Raymond had said, but it was also very clearly this wizard's. The walls were lined with shelves full of books, many of them ancient if Jean was any judge. Even more books were stacked along the walls, the bookcases too small to hold the bounty of Raymond's scholarship. Jean had not been in the other wizards' offices, but he doubted he would find such evidence of research in their space. "No," Jean agreed, "I don't know what you've done. I can't draw that kind of detail from what I taste in your blood, but I can know you on another level, and while I did feel anger and regret, I also tasted the basic goodness of your soul. I have tasted evil in my lifetime, and you do not have that in you."

Ill at ease with the topic, Raymond changed the subject. "What did Marcel want to talk to you about?"

"The rogue," Jean replied. "He felt, and rightly so, that dealing with him was my responsibility, but he wanted to ask my plans."

Raymond wanted to know, too, but he did not know if he should ask. Fortunately, Jean did not seem to require prompting.

"He suggested I take you with me tonight when I go to see what I can learn. It seemed like a good idea. Will you come with me?" Jean requested.

Taken by surprise, Raymond did not answer right away. "Why?" he asked after a minute.

"To be another set of eyes and ears, to be proof of the alliance to those who question, to add your voice, your logic to mine if we must convince others of our point of view. To be at my side should our enemies attack. To be at my side."

Even more surprised by the answer, Raymond nodded slowly. "Where do you want me to meet you?"

"Why don't you come to my apartment," Jean suggested. "Thierry's and Caroline's ideas were valid ones, and while I need to feed to get home, I have had a thousand years or more to grow used to 'house arrest' as Sebastien called it."

"That isn't necessary," Raymond began. "If you want to go out, I could..."

"You could nothing right now," Jean interrupted. "You have been up all night and I am about to add to your fatigue, at least in the short term, by feeding from you. You're going to escort me home and then get some sleep. I may no longer be mortal, but I do remember how bad sleeplessness can make you feel."

"As you say," Raymond had to admit. He glanced around the small space. There was even not any place for them to sit while Jean fed.

Chapter 23

A WAVE of Raymond's wand rearranged the stacks of books, and a murmured incantation transformed them into a comfortable couch.

"Your books!" Jean protested. Though he understood, on a conscious level, that books were no longer the commodity of his youth, he had been raised to think of such tomes as more precious than gold, and to see his partner, a scholar, treating them with such disregard was shocking.

Raymond laughed. "It's magic, Jean. With a wave of my wand, they'll be back as they were before. If I wasn't sure of that, I would have changed something less valuable, my desk or something." Even as he spoke, though, he catalogued Jean's reaction. His partner was not a scholar if his interest in Raymond's conversation with monsieur Lombard was any indication, but he did have an appreciation for books that was rare outside the realm of academia.

Jean flushed uncomfortably. "You must think me a royal idiot, or at least an ignorant fool."

"Neither," Raymond insisted, "simply unused to magic. I forget that what's normal to me isn't normal. I can't remember a time without magic. My mother was a wizard, as was hers, and so dependent on her magic that I doubt she could have done anything without it. Cooking wasn't done on the stove but with a wave of her wand. Cleaning didn't require a mop or a vacuum, just a flick of her wrist. I need a couch, I make one and turn it back into whatever it was later, when I don't need it anymore or need the books more."

Jean shook his head. "I cannot begin to imagine a life like that. Before I became a vampire, I was a seminarian, taught to believe that magic did not exist. Becoming a vampire convinced me that it did, but even so, the magic in my world is the magic that keeps me animate, or else it is external magic, like what binds Alain and Orlando together." He walked over to the couch, running his fingers over the velvet-covered cushions. "It feels so real."

"It is real," Raymond assured him, "as real as the books were before. If you really want an explanation, I'll try to give it to you in layman's terms, but you needn't fear it will collapse under your weight." To prove his point, he sat down on the newly made cushions and patted the space next to him to encourage Jean to join him.

Jean shook his head. "You'd lose me before you finished the first sentence," he replied. "I'll just trust that you know what you're doing." He sat gingerly next to Raymond, not because he was afraid the couch would crumble, but because he remembered what made the couch in the first place. He did not want to damage the books.

Taking a deep breath, Raymond unbuttoned the sleeve of his shirt and pushed it and his sweater up to his elbow. "You said you needed to feed," he offered uneasily.

ADÈLE led her patrol back into base, dismissing them to find their rest. She still had to meet with Marcel, to let him know that there had been no incidents while they were out. She imagined the other team leaders had probably checked in already, but her circuit last night had been one of the longer ones.

When the rest of her team was gone, she turned to Jude. "Can you get home safely?"

Jude sneered. "I do not need a woman's protection."

"That wasn't what I meant," she protested. "I have to report to Marcel, and then I have some other things to take care of before I go off duty. I just want to make sure you didn't need to feed again before you left."

"Now you think to ask that," Jude scoffed. "Where was this concern yesterday when I was trapped here all day?"

"I answered that question already," Adèle snapped. "I'm still learning about the demands of this alliance just as you are. I'm doing my best to make it work."

"Feeble best," Jude muttered.

Adèle's hands went for his neck before she could stop herself, catching him in perhaps his most vulnerable spot and using it to pin him to the wall. "Do you need to feed?" she growled, knowing she had only succeeded because she had caught him off guard and that even now, he could probably throw her across the room if he decided to.

"No," he replied tersely.

"Then get the hell out of my sight," she spat, releasing him and turning to walk away. She had taken two steps when a hand on her arm spun her around and cool lips closed tightly over hers. She did not struggle. She already knew she could not break free of the vampire's grasp and saw no reason to humiliate herself by trying. Instead, she stood perfectly still, letting him kiss her, but not responding at all. When he pulled back, she slapped him hard, the blow landing this time. "I'm not interested," she lied as she stalked off.

She knew it was a lie, but she was not about to admit that she was attracted to the golden-haired vampire despite his deplorable attitude. She put up with enough shit at work. She refused to have any in her personal life. She was sure sex with him would be explosive, but it would merely be sex, and she had long since lost interest in one-night stands or casual affairs whose only purpose was getting laid. She had other, better things to occupy her time. Like giving Marcel her report so she could get some sleep. Alone. In her comfortable, but empty bed. "Damn it," she muttered. "I'm not doing this."

JEAN stared down at the pale skin of the wizard's arm. His partner had little more color in his skin than a vampire, but Jean could detect the warmth that ran beneath this alabaster surface, a warmth that was missing from the pale flesh of his vampire kin. "I won't take much," he promised. "Just enough to get me safely home."

"No," Raymond insisted. "If you do that and there's any delay, the sunlight could destroy you. Feed normally. You've assured me it will not hurt me. I have to trust you in that, and this is the best way to begin."

"Are you sure?" Jean asked. "I don't want to make you uncomfortable."

Raymond considered his answer for a moment and opted for complete honesty. "There's probably no way around that at this point, but my fears are my problem. If I let myself be ruled by fear, I would still be in Serrier's camp simply because I was afraid of what he would do if he caught me again."

Jean's face hardened. "He won't. I won't let him."

Raymond smiled gently. "That's easier said than done unless you plan on never leaving my side."

"Your apartment is protected, isn't it?" Jean wanted to know. If it was not, he and Raymond were staying here until Marcel could correct that oversight.

"Of course," Raymond assured him. "I'm as safe there as I am here."

"Then it's simple. When we're on duty, we're together anyway. Once we're off duty, I'll go with you for anything you need to do, then you can take me home, and go home yourself, straight to your apartment. That way, you'll either be with me or in a protected place," Jean suggested logically.

"It's all right," Raymond said. "I've been taking care of myself for months now, ever since I joined the Milice."

"I know you have," Jean assured him, "but there are two of us now. Wouldn't it make sense to watch each other's backs? We both have enemies, personal enemies as well as the more general enemy we are fighting. Why not combine our forces, at least when we are away from our strongholds?"

Raymond pondered the suggestion. "I could weave wards around your apartment. The difficulty would be in tailoring who could come and go. For my own apartment, I can simply allow or not allow entrance once I see who's there, but you cannot manipulate my magic that way. I could easily allow any vampire to pass the wards, but we know there is at least one vampire we would want to keep out. Without knowing him, though, it would be difficult to exclude him."

Jean considered the problem. " Could you set it so that only known vampires could come in?"

"Eventually," Raymond replied, "but it would require a spell to identify each vampire who could enter."

"I'm not so worried about the vampires," Jean said after a moment. "There are few, if any, who could best me. I would be more concerned about being cornered by a wizard with ill intent."

"Who would visit you besides me?" Raymond asked. "Wizards, I mean."

Jean thought for a moment. "Perhaps Alain. Orlando was once a frequent visitor, and if that continues now, I'm sure Alain will come with him."

Raymond knew Jean was protective of Orlando – he had seen it the day they met – but now he wondered about the exact nature of their relationship. It was obvious to Raymond that Alain and the other vampire were lovers. Did Jean resent that? His tone was even, but Raymond did not know his partner well enough yet to interpret that. Was it truly an indication of acceptance or was it rather a studied attempt at casualness to keep Raymond from seeing how deeply the situation bothered him? It depended in part, he was sure, on what the relationship had been previously between the two vampires. Had they been lovers and Jean now found himself jilted? The thought shocked him because it was so far from his usual train of thought. He squelched further reflection on the topic, including the spurt of jealousy at the thought of Jean in the arms of the younger vampire, trying to concentrate instead on what other wizards might visit Jean.

"Thierry?" he suggested after a moment.

"I would be surprised," Jean answered, "if only because his partner knows he would not be welcome. I will work with him, but I will not welcome him into my home."

Raymond would not willingly admit to the curiosity he felt at hearing this confession, at getting this glimpse into his partner's personal life, and so he could not ask for more details, but he filed the information away for later, wondering if Thierry knew more and if he would tell the other wizard if he did know. He could only speculate at what might have set the two vampires at odds. Unfortunately, his speculation once again took a sexual bent, and he imagined the torrid clench followed by an explosive argument that led to an irreparable breach. Telling himself that such thoughts were ridiculous – and that jealousy based on such conjecture was even more ridiculous – Raymond dropped his gaze to his arm. "You should feed so we can go. I'll put up the wards when we get to your place. I can always tweak them later if they need it."

Jean nodded, turning his attention back to the warm, pale skin that had caught his attention before. He lifted his hand and trailed his finger down the smooth flesh from the bend of Raymond's elbow to the fold of his wrist.

"Don't," Raymond pleaded. Despite the paths his thoughts had been taking, he was still barely able to consider allowing Jean to feed. Thinking of any other level of intimacy was too much. His fears were still too strong. "Don't try to make this anything but functional. I know what monsieur Lombard said, but I can't…"

Jean looked up and met the wizard's gaze. "Neither can I," he replied regretfully. "It was aesthetic appreciation on my part, nothing more."

Jean was such a mix of contrasts, Raymond thought randomly as Jean spoke. He claimed to be a simple man with no interest in anything esoteric, yet he was more respectful of Raymond's books that he, a scholar, was. The wizard wondered idly what had happened to make Jean the man that he was. The things his partner must have seen in his lifetime! He wanted to ask, to share in those experiences, to know his partner on a different level. Objectively, he recognized it as the bond he and the elder vampire had conjectured must exist between matched pairs, but his objectivity did not serve to dampen the growing curiosity. The twinge of jealousy returned, the thought of the string of lovers that must have filled Jean's past combined with the vampire's resistance to anything more than a professional relationship sparking the uncharacteristic emotion.

Jean closed his hand around Raymond's wrist and lifted it to his lips, tongue preparing the tender skin quickly and efficiently. As soon as that was done, he slid his fangs into the soft flesh, sucking softly to draw blood to the surface. It flowed into his mouth immediately, the flavor he was already coming to identify as uniquely Raymond filling his senses. He could taste the fear, the anger, the regret, the intelligence – all the characteristics that made his partner the complex individual he was – but underneath it all, he thought he caught a hint of something new. He almost dismissed it because it seemed so contrary to all he knew about his wizard, but the more he concentrated, the more he was sure he tasted the first tendrils of trust in Raymond's blood.

Chapter 24

SEBASTIEN stood at Thierry's side, staring at the lights on the large screen. "Tell me again how this works," he requested.

Having anticipated the request when Marcel gave them their assignments, he reached in his pocket and pulled out a small carving. "This is my repère," the wizard said, handing it to Sebastien. "Whenever I have it with me, it creates a blip on the screen there, letting anyone who looks know where I am. The map is usually set for Paris, but it can be expanded to a larger area, to show l'Ile-de-France, for example, or even the whole country. Of course, the bigger the area, the less detail in location, but you get the idea."

"So it's the talisman," Sebastien said, "that shows up on the board."

"Yes," Thierry agreed, "but only when it's animated by my magic. If you're holding it, it won't work. It works in my hand, my pocket, my cape, not in anyone else's."

Sebastien examined the carving more closely. "A falcon!" he exclaimed. "Did you choose this or was it random?"

"I chose it," Thierry replied. "I've always thought they were magnificent birds."

"Amazing," Sebastien breathed with a sigh. "What are the chances?"

"Chances of what?"

"You carry a falcon in your pocket for protection of sorts. When I was a mortal, I was a falconer. I trained the birds for the lords of the land," Sebastien explained softly. "And you're right. They are magnificent birds."

Feeling uncomfortable at having yet another tie with Sebastien, Thierry retrieved his repère and slipped it back into his pocket.

Seeing Thierry's unease, Sebastien changed the subject. "So your talismans are animated by your magic. We have no magic, though. Can we make this work for the vampires?"

Thierry considered the problem. "Every living being has a unique aura. Perhaps we can tie the spell to that." He closed his eyes and focused his magical senses, seeking to identify the aura of the man standing next to him. He could feel the wizards going about their business in the room and in the hallways outside, but Sebastien was a complete blank.

"Damn," Thierry swore softly. "Why can't I find your aura?" He ran his fingers through his hair, mussing it most attractively, Sebastien thought irrelevantly. He tried to focus on the problem at hand, but his eyes kept straying back to the adorable picture Thierry made with his blond hair adorably disheveled.

"I don't know," the vampire replied hastily, realizing Thierry was looking at him expectantly. "Jean might."

"Or Raymond," Thierry added grudgingly. He did not like the other wizard, or trust him, but he could not deny that the man's knowledge was sometimes useful.

Sebastien was tempted to ask why Thierry seemed not to like the other wizard. He had seen little of Raymond in the days since the alliance had formed, but he had seen nothing to make him dislike the man. Thierry, though, clearly did.

Thierry shook off his frustration. It was pointless, anyway, and Raymond was off duty, so he would have to use his own resources to solve the problem. He did not have Raymond's scholarly background, but he was no lightweight either. Logical thinking was the basis of all his strategy. "If identifying you magically won't work, maybe we can do it biologically," he thought out loud.

"Biologically?" Sebastien asked.

"Sure," Thierry replied. "They use DNA evidence in the courts all the time to identify people. Maybe we can tie the spell to you that way."

"How would you get the DNA into the talisman?" Sebastien queried.

Thierry grabbed a pen. "We'll find a better repère for you when we know this works, but let's try it. Give me strand of hair."

Willing to give it a try, Sebastien reached up and pulled free a couple of hairs, handing them to Thierry. The wizard wrapped them around the pen and cast a tracking spell on them. A second spell changed the view on the screen to show only Milice headquarters. Thierry's name showed up immediately in the

Salle des Cartes, as did the other wizards in the room, but there was not even a blip on the screen next to where Thierry was standing.

"Damn," he muttered, "that didn't work either."

Sebastien stared at the screen, willing his name to appear, though he was sure it would not. If it was going to, it would have already done so. "Could it be because I'm not really alive anymore?"

Thierry considered the question, but realized quickly that he had no answer for it. "That's a question for the philosophers, not for me," he replied, "but that might be part of it. Let's think about this logically. You say you're not really alive, and I remember Jean making a similar comment to Alain, so what gives you the appearance of life? Because you certainly don't look dead to me."

"Blood," Sebastien said bluntly. "As long as we can get enough blood to drink, we remain animate."

Thierry shuddered, not at Sebastien's comments, but at the sudden implication that occurred to him. He would be willing to bet a small fortune that the vampires were animated by some kind of blood magic. It would certainly explain why they required blood to stay alive. For as long as he could remember, every reputable wizard he had heard speak on the subject had reviled blood magic as evil. "If we're going to have to use blood to make this work, we need to talk to Marcel first," he told Sebastien. "I can't do blood magic without his approval."

"What's so different about using blood?" Sebastien asked.

Thierry fought off visions of sacrifice and altars, dark magic and evil spells flashing through his mind. "It's dark magic," he replied with a shudder.

Sebastien saw the revulsion in Thierry's face. It bothered him on one level that the magic that granted him a continued existence was so repulsive to his partner, but Thierry did not seem to be rejecting him, only the magic. "Perhaps we shouldn't worry about it, then," he suggested.

"No," Thierry disagreed. "I may not like it, but if it's the only way to provide the vampires the same protection we have, then it's worth asking. If he says no, maybe we can do a generic spell, one that won't identify who, but will at least identify location. It would be less useful, but not useless."

"If you're sure," Sebastien replied.

"We'll let Marcel decide," Thierry declared. "If he thinks it's safe, we'll try it."

As they walked back toward Marcel's office, Thierry reflected on the new knowledge that not only did vampires need blood to survive, but were actually kept alive in their way by blood magic. It should not have come as a surprise to him, but he had never thought about it. Glancing surreptitiously at his partner, he tried to digest the information. In the end, it changed nothing, he realized. If he had known it before they formed the alliance, he might have hesitated, but not now. Sebastien was his partner and had proven his loyalty more than once by fighting at Thierry's side. That outweighed any other consideration.

Knocking at Marcel's door, they waited for his call to enter.

Seeing who was outside, Marcel smiled warmly. "Have you come to report success?" he asked.

"Unfortunately not," Thierry replied. He quickly explained about the absence of auras and the failure to make the hair work.

"And your theory?" Marcel wanted to know.

"That it only works on living creatures," Sebastien explained. "For all that we appear alive, it's magic, not biology that keeps us that way."

"So what do you recommend?" Marcel queried.

"The only solution we've come up with that might work for an individualized talisman would require using blood," Thierry answered. "Sebastien's explanation makes me think that vampires are kept viable by blood magic. I didn't dare experiment with that kind of dark magic without checking with you first."

Marcel chuckled. "I can hear Raymond now. Magic itself is neither good nor evil, he would insist. Only the way it's used deserves that kind of value judgment."

Thierry scowled. "Raymond doesn't get to make those decisions."

"No, he doesn't," Marcel agreed. "That falls to me. I find myself agreeing with him, though. If blood magic were inherently evil, then vampires would be inherently evil, yet we've allied ourselves with them. Are our allies evil, Thierry?"

Thierry squirmed uncomfortably, put on the spot by Marcel's logic. "No," he replied firmly. "I don't believe that. If they were, I doubt they would have made the alliance in the first place, and if they did, some hint of their perfidy would have shown by now."

Sebastien had almost protested Marcel's question, but he realized after a moment that the question was rhetorical, intended to force Thierry to look at the gap in his own logic. He smothered a sigh of relief at hearing his partner defend him and his kind.

"And while I haven't researched it," Marcel added, "I'm fairly sure that the magic that lets your blood protect your partner would also be considered blood magic. We have to stop judging so bluntly if we're to build a future for our kind. We lost many, as we did Raymond at first, because of our narrow views of right and wrong. Raymond came back when he saw that Serrier's methods were far worse than our inflexibility. Others have not, and that's not something we can afford to let continue. A simple tracking spell on a few drops of Sebastien's blood and a piece of stone cannot hurt anything, not when its intention is to protect him. That's what we have to focus on, Thierry: the intention behind the spell, not the spell itself."

Thierry took a minute to digest this information. "Then I guess we should see if it works," he said finally.

"Let me know if it does," Marcel replied. "I'll take care of informing the others. Let that decision come from me, not from you."

"So how do we do this?" Sebastien asked when they were back in the hallway.

"Let's go to my office," Thierry said. "I know what Marcel said, but I'd rather do this in private than in the Salle des Cartes. If it works, we'll deal with the prejudices later."

Sebastien nodded and followed Thierry back to the wizard's office. They shut the door behind them, enclosing them in the privacy of the small space. Sebastien lifted his wrist to his lips, intending to break the skin to draw blood.

"Don't," Thierry said, stopping his partner. "One of the unfortunate attributes of blood magic is that the person casting the spell has to draw the blood and it can't be their own. It lends itself to abuse, as you can imagine." He started looking through his desk for something he could use to draw blood.

Sebastien could, far too easily, but this was different. "Mine is freely given, and I know you won't take any more than necessary." He waited until Thierry looked up and met his eyes. "There is no evil in what we do together."

Thierry dropped his gaze to continue his search. Finally, he found an ornamental dagger, deep in the drawer, which he kept as a letter-opener. "I know," he said. "I do know that. What do you want to use as your talisman?"

Sebastien considered the matter. "I don't know what to use. Does it matter what it is?"

"No," Thierry replied, "although at least among the wizards, the spell seems to be stronger if the tracer is special to them. After all, if everyone used a paper clip, how would you know which was yours?"

Sebastien chuckled. "I can see how that would be a problem. If it doesn't work, it won't matter, but if it does, I doubt you'd want to have to recast the spell just so I could have a better talisman."

"I'd rather not," Thierry agreed. "I'll do it once, since Marcel said it was all right, but I don't imagine I'll ever be completely comfortable with blood magic."

Instinctively, Sebastien's hand sought the locket in his pocket. He had not been separated from it since Thibaut died. He could use it for this, but Thierry had said the wizards left their talismans when they went off duty. He wondered if he could stand to do that. "Would I have to leave the repère here when I went off duty?" he asked. "I have something I could use, but I'd rather keep it with me."

"It's more a matter of privacy than necessity," Thierry explained. "The repère will continue to track you whether you're on duty or not. If you don't mind always being on the map, there's no reason why you can't take it."

Sebastien nodded. "Could you give me a minute?" he asked softly.

Thierry frowned, confused, but stepped out into the hall, giving his partner the requested privacy.

Inside, Sebastien pulled the locket out of his pocket and stared down at it. It was his most prized possession, the lock of hair inside the only connection he still had, other than his memories, to his dead Avoué. All he had to do was close his eyes to see Thibaut as he had been the first time he laid eyes on the young man who had become the center of his world. His mind told him that four hundred lonely years had passed since then, but his heart pulled up the memories as clearly as if it had been yesterday. He had arrived in Paris only weeks before and was still finding his way around, welcomed warmly by the vampire community and beginning to finally feel at home. He had been prowling the streets, looking for someone to feed from and had seen Thibaut, standing on the Pont Neuf, bathed in the moonlight. The man had turned and met his gaze boldly, brazenly even. "You're a vampire," he had said without hesitation. Sebastien had admitted it, though softly in case others were nearby with a less tolerant attitude than his current companion's. Thibaut had offered his hand and led Sebastien to his lodging, offering much more once they were in private. The attraction was instantaneous and a few weeks later, at Thibaut's insistence, Sebastien had burned the brand into his neck that marked the mortal as a chosen one, an Avoué.

That same night, Thibaut had pressed the locket into Sebastien's hand, saying that since he could not brand Sebastien as the vampire had branded him, he would claim him another way. He had not been without it since that day, his testament to the love that had sprung up between them unbidden and endured long after Thibaut's life was spent.

Another memory rose up to replace the first. Thibaut had aged well, but at the time of his death, he looked his years. Seventy was not so old in modern times, but at the turn of the seventeenth century, it was ancient. Lying in the bed from which he would not rise, Thibaut had offered his neck to Sebastien one last time. When Sebastien had fed, only his vampire limitations had stopped the tears welling within him. Thibaut had cradled his face and whispered, "Do not mourn for me over long. We have been blessed with a full mortal's life and I do not regret a moment of it. When a seemly time has passed, find another love. I want to know you'll be happy again."

Sebastien had protested, but Thibaut was implacable and Sebastien had given the promise, as traitorous as it had seemed. He had not kept it, though. He had taken people to his bed, men and women alike, but it had been about release, not about love. None of them had moved him deeply enough to consider returning to them. He felt bad enough about being with them once. He could not see letting them into his life for longer. Now, though, the locket taunted him, reminding him of his unkept promise. Had the time finally come to let Thibaut go, to let himself move on? His heart seized at the thought, but even then, the flavor of Thierry's blood teased his senses, and he forced himself to consider it. Thibaut had told him to do this, wanted him to do this, and had not intended for it to take four hundred years. The wizard was a very different man than Thibaut had been, stubborn where Thibaut had been conciliatory, strong where Thibaut had been soft, buffeted by life where Thibaut had still been young and mostly naïve, reticent where Thibaut had been eager. He knew Thierry wanted him as a partner in the alliance. That had not been in doubt from the first time Sebastien had fed, but there was a big difference between that and what Sebastien was considering now. Would Thierry even be willing to discuss a different kind of relationship? Sebastien did not know if it was a risk he wanted to take. The locket mocked him, mocked his doubts. *It is time*, it seemed to say.

Lifting the cool metal to his lips, he kissed it. "You were right as always, my love. It's time to move on."

Opening the door, Sebastien motioned for Thierry to come back inside. "Thank you. You can use this as my repère." He offered the locket to the wizard, trusting that Thierry would take good care of it.

Chapter 25

THIERRY stared down at the locket Sebastien pressed into his palm. "This is exquisite workmanship," he observed admiringly. "It looks ancient!"

"Not quite ancient," Sebastien contradicted, "but definitely old. Late Renaissance, to be precise. It was a gift, and I'd like to think the giver would be pleased that it will help protect me now."

"A family heirloom?" Thierry asked.

"No, a bonding gift from my Avoué." Sebastien unlocked the clasp to reveal the lock of hair and a tiny miniature. "Thibaut."

Thierry examined the picture carefully before shutting the locket, remembering what Sebastien had said about how much time he had spent alone. For four hundred years, the vampire had kept this locket. And now he was using it as his repère. Thierry could not help but wonder what that meant. He was beginning, slowly, to understand the level of commitment the locket represented. He had only to look at Alain to see how... all-encompassing the Aveu de Sang could become. To know that the feelings lingered in Sebastien even four hundred years later drove that point home yet again. The vampire had already made it clear that he was not interested in another covenant of that magnitude, and Thierry thought he could understand why. "Are you sure you want to use this?" he asked.

"The spell won't change it, will it?"

When Thierry shook his head, Sebastien replied, "Then yes, I'm sure."

Thierry nodded and set the locket carefully on his desk. "Let me have your hand."

Sebastien held it out, letting Thierry move it so his fingers hovered an inch above the locket, ignoring the immediate desire he felt from Thierry's skin against his.

Thierry's hand trembled as he retrieved the dagger. He was not at all comfortable with what they were about to do, the ingrained avoidance of blood magic hard to overcome. Taking a deep breath to steady his hand and his nerves, he pricked the tip of Sebastien's finger, watching in transfixed fascination as the carnelian drop welled from the wound. One drop fell to land on the locket. He squeezed out a second and a third drop before lifting the finger to his lips to lave the wound.

Sebastien tensed as his finger approached Thierry's mouth. He was not concerned about what his blood would do to the wizard – he would have had to drain Thierry dry before his blood would have any effect – but he was less sure about the effect Thierry's mouth on his hand would have on him.

Attuned as he was to the magical vibrations in the room, Thierry fancied he could taste a bit of the power that kept Sebastien alive in the drop of blood that fell on his tongue from the pinprick he had inflicted. To his surprise, and despite his qualms, nothing in the taste repelled him, unlike the acrid scent that seemed to accompany many of the killing spells and other dark magic that Serrier and his minions trafficked in. He sucked a little harder, his tongue ghosting over the pad of Sebastien's finger, trying to get a better sense of the magic.

"Thierry," Sebastien husked, though in protest or encouragement he could not have said. His body reacted immediately to the feeling of Thierry's mouth on his skin, nerves tingling, heart beat and respiration speeding up. His soul reacted just as immediately, throwing up pictures of Thibaut, pointing out his infidelity, his unworthiness. Thibaut had given his whole life to Sebastien. Was it so unreasonable to ask Sebastien to do the same? Thibaut's voice seemed to answer his question this time, the beloved tone echoing in his heart. *I want to know you'll be happy again.*

Sebastien's voice broke Thierry's concentration, and he suddenly became aware of the situation again. Flushing, he released his partner's finger and focused back on the task at hand. He murmured an incantation binding the blood to the locket and the locket to the locator screen. A soft glow surrounded the necklace for a moment and then was gone. He let out the breath he had been holding and smiled. "I think it worked. Shall we go check?"

Sebastien nodded, biting back the overwhelming desire to pull Thierry into his arms and kiss the wizard. He reminded himself that his partner had only recently lost his wife and that just because he was ready to move on did not mean Thierry felt the same way, despite what Adèle had implied about the state of their relationship before the wife's death. He had waited four hundred years. He could wait a little longer if it meant having what he needed and wanted in the end.

They walked back through the maze of corridors to the Salle des Cartes, and there on the map, next to Thierry's name, was Sebastien's. "It worked," Thierry repeated. "As long as you have the repère with you, you'll show up on the map."

THE air was cold and crisp when Alain and Orlando left Milice headquarters, walking down the street to the nearest métro stop. They descended again into the warmer, staler air. "I would almost prefer the longer walk," Orlando commented as the darkness surrounded them again.

Alain smiled. "I've often felt that way after a night on duty. Let's go home and we can sit on your balcony and enjoy the sun."

"Our balcony," Orlando insisted as they stepped onto the train. "We both live there now."

Ignoring the other commuters on their way to work instead of home, Alain leaned over and kissed Orlando lightly. "Keep reminding me until that becomes automatic," he requested.

The kiss caught Orlando by surprise and by the time the shock wore off, Alain had pulled back and was talking again. "I will," he promised, when he heard his lover's words.

They left the train and the subway, walking up past the cemetery to Orlando's street. "Let's stop here for a minute," Alain suggested as they walked past the bakery on the corner.

Orlando followed Alain inside as the wizard purchased a baguette and two croissants. The next store netted them a rack of lamb, and the *Casino* provided vegetables for a side dish. Orlando watched the display of domesticity with a bemused air. It had been so long since he had thought of such things.

When he had everything he wanted, Alain smiled at Orlando. "We can put this in the oven for a few hours and have dinner when we wake up."

Orlando grinned at that, running a hand down Alain's back, stopping just above the swell of his buttocks. "Who said anything about sleeping?"

Alain's answering grin was wolfish. "In that case, let's go home!"

Orlando laughed and left the corner store, heading toward their apartment. Knowing there was nothing breakable among Alain's purchases, he had no qualms about pushing his lover up against the door as soon as it shut behind them.

Alain let the bags fall from his hands to encircle Orlando's waist, though the vampire needed no encouragement to press closer. "Need you," Alain mumbled against Orlando's lips as he took them in a deep kiss.

"You have me," Orlando promised, pulling back gently after a moment. "Let's get your dinner on so we can do other things."

Alain almost protested when Orlando pulled back, but his lover's words made sense. He retrieved his bags and headed into the kitchen, the vampire trailing behind him. They settled the bags and Alain dug out a roasting pan, rolling the lamb in fennel and cracked pepper before setting it in the pan.

"Do you think Thierry was right?" Orlando asked as his lover prepared his meal.

"About what?" Alain asked, looking up from cutting the potatoes he planned to roast along with the lamb.

"About Serrier coming after the vampires when he realizes."

"Yes. He has no scruples," Alain declared. "He'll do anything he can think of to weaken us. I'm more worried about the rogue vampire, myself."

"Why?" Orlando asked. "There's nothing he can do to any of us that we can't counter."

"I was thinking more in terms of him stumbling on the effects of our blood and revealing our advantage to Serrier."

Orlando nodded slowly. "But what would that change? Yes, he'd know we're fighting with you, and yes, he'd know we can move in sunlight, but it still doesn't affect our other abilities. His killing spells won't work on us any more in the daytime than they do at night," he added, remembering the first part of the briefing, where Marcel had revealed the vampires' apparent immunity to the *Abbatoire* curse.

Alain shrugged. "It might not change anything, but the less he knows, the harder it will be for him to combat our attacks."

"I can see that." He paused for a moment. "Will the other teams take Thierry's advice and travel as pairs off duty?"

Alain dumped the vegetables into the pan and covered it with foil. Switching on the oven, he considered Orlando's question. "Some pairs will," he decided upon reflection. "Adèle won't. She can't abide her partner. I don't know about David. His attitude seems to have improved. Raymond would, I think, since it was his suggestion in the first place, but Jean seemed hesitant."

Orlando laughed. "Jean is used to being king of the hill. He's been the leader of the vampires for as long as I've known him and he wasn't new when we met. The idea that he might need someone else's protection is completely foreign to him."

"Surely he sees the logic of Raymond's argument, though. He isn't stupid or he wouldn't have kept his position for so long," Alain declared, sitting down across from Orlando while he waited for the oven to finish heating up.

"I could be wrong," Orlando agreed. "It's happened before. And as you say, Jean's not stupid." He trailed off, thinking about the disparate personalities that made up the leadership of the Milice. "What about Thierry?"

"I don't know," Alain replied honestly. "He's a bit of a hothead sometimes, so he might resist on principle, although he did seem to think it was a good idea. Of course, it's not just his decision, either. Sebastien seemed pretty averse to the idea."

Orlando shook his head. "I don't know Sebastien. I'd never met him before the meeting at the station. He and Jean have a history, obviously, but that doesn't tell me anything about him as a man."

The oven dinged to announce it was hot. Alain rose and slid the pan into the oven, setting the timer for three hours. Turning back to Orlando, he smiled rakishly. "That's enough politics for now. I can think of much better ways to spend our downtime."

"Oh, you can?" Orlando asked with an answering smile. "Care to enlighten me?"

"Come over here and I'll do my best," Alain promised.

Orlando's grin widened and he went swiftly to Alain's side. "Now that I'm here, what are you going to do with me?"

Alain wrinkled his brow as if considering the question. "Well," he drawled, "I suppose I could start by kissing you."

Orlando stepped closer to Alain. "I think you should," he agreed huskily, tipping his head and offering Alain his mouth.

Alain tilted his head immediately, capturing the curved lips with his own, relishing their sweetness and the novelty of being offered control, however temporarily, of their interactions. He was sure Orlando was not conscious of it at all, but to Alain, it was another sign of the growing trust between them. He took heart from that. It might take time, but eventually, Orlando would trust what they shared enough to stop weighing every action before he reacted.

Orlando relaxed into Alain's gentle embrace which belied the hunger in his kiss. And that contrast gave the vampire the courage he needed to press his lover against the counter, their bodies touching from knees to mouths.

"I want you," he murmured against Alain's lips.

"You have me," Alain promised, rocking his hips forward into Orlando's. "I'm all yours."

"All mine?" Orlando asked softly.

"In every way," Alain replied, his voice husky from the force of his emotions.

Orlando's heart leapt in his chest. "Does that mean I can do whatever I want to you?" he teased.

"Anything," Alain agreed. He did not mention – he did not have to – that he had already allowed Orlando privileges that no one else had ever been granted. The brand on his neck was the most obvious sign, but the bite marks on his neck that had not quite faded were yet another example.

Orlando felt his knees tremble at the thought of Alain's overwhelming trust in him. With shaking hands, he clasped the wizard's hips and turned him to face the counter. "Like this," he murmured, reaching for the oil Alain had drizzled on the vegetables before putting them in the oven.

Alain pushed his hips back against Orlando's groin. "Any way you want," he reiterated, rubbing against the erection he could feel in his lover's pants. He doubted Orlando even remembered the conversation from a few days ago when their lovemaking had started in the kitchen before moving into the bedroom, but Alain remembered it, remembered how Orlando had been worried about hurting him despite Alain's constant reassurances that he would not. Those fears had clearly been laid to rest since then, another little victory over Orlando's past.

Orlando did remember the incident, though, remembered how he had balked at what now seemed such a trivial choice. He did not waste his time cursing his past, but he did pause to appreciate how blessed he was now in his choice of lover. He was quite sure most men would not have been as patient with his many hang-ups as Alain continued to be. Grinding himself against the wizard's buttocks, he reached forward and tore at the buttons of his lover's shirt, his hands delving frantically beneath the fabric in search of skin.

Alain arched into Orlando's urgent touch, a low moan escaping his lips. It had only been a few hours since they had last made love, yet he craved Orlando's touch like they had been separated for months. "Hurry," he begged.

Orlando could not resist the pleading tone of Alain's voice. One hand lingered to pinch and pull at Alain's nipples while the other went to the waistband of the wizard's trousers, opening them swiftly and delving inside eagerly.

Alain lifted one hand from where it braced him against the counter to push his pants down over his hips, baring his buttocks to his lover. "Hurry," he repeated. "I need you inside me."

Orlando fumbled with the lid of the oil, tipping the bottle enough to splash oil on his hand. He did not bother trying to put the cap back on. That was beyond him at this point. His only concern now was his lover and their mutual pleasure.

His fingers dove between Alain's nether cheeks, probing urgently, encouraged by the eager moans and unrestrained movements as the wizard pushed back against his hand. His fingers slid inside the tight entrance, leaving behind the slippery oil to ease his way. He searched for and quickly found the little bump that brought his lover such pleasure. He worked it swiftly, wanting Alain to know the same desire that was coursing through the vampire's body.

Alain was with him, body, mind and soul, rocking his hips against Orlando's questing fingers as hard as he could. Bracing himself on one hand, he reached down to pump his hard cock in time with Orlando's thrusts. The vampire batted his hand away, replacing it with his own, working Alain both inside and out. Alain felt his balls draw up in prelude to his release. "Stop," he gasped, surprising Orlando into stillness. He turned his head to capture the vampire's mouth in reassurance. "I want you inside me when I come," he murmured against his lover's lips. "I want us to come together."

Orlando relaxed when he heard the request, sliding his fingers out from where they were buried deep inside Alain's passage. He slicked his erection quickly and surged into the still tight hole, his fears easing the rest of the way when Alain pushed back against him, impaling himself on the vampire's shaft.

Both hands braced on the counter, Alain rocked back to meet every one of Orlando's thrusts, nearly mindless now in his need for release. Hoping he could keep his balance, he moved one hand behind him, to reach for Orlando's hip, and then further back to cup the clenching muscles that drove the vampire inside him. He did not think, in his passion, of Orlando's fears, Orlando's past, as his hand closed over flesh he had never before touched. His only thought was urging Orlando on.

The feeling of Alain's hand on his buttock caused Orlando's rhythm to falter for a moment, but nothing could quench the rising tide of desire he was feeling, not even that unfamiliar touch. And once he relaxed into it, once he realized that Alain only intended to encourage him, the caress had the desired effect, spurring Orlando on to greater efforts to release their pent-up lust. Lowering his head to Alain's shoulder, he sucked hard on the curve of muscle, keeping his fangs drawn up by force of will alone.

The pull of Orlando's mouth on his skin was all it took to trigger Alain's release. Behind closed eyes, he dreamed of the day when it would be Orlando's fangs as well as his lips that would tease his skin as they made love.

Feeling the tremors that wracked his lover, Orlando increased the tempo of his thrusts, wanting to augment Alain's passion and to join him in release. His harsh grunt as he came was accompanied by Alain's hoarse shout. Trembling, Orlando leaned against Alain's sweat-sheened back, knowing he had to be pressing the wizard uncomfortably against the edge of the counter. He tried to pull back, but his muscles refused to cooperate, refused to move him even an inch from his lover's side.

Finally, Alain shifting beneath him made Orlando force himself to move, at least enough so that Alain's stomach was not pressed against the edge of the counter. "Shall we move somewhere more comfortable?" he suggested in a husky whisper.

Alain's grin over his shoulder was inviting. "Oh, most definitely," the wizard agreed. "We've taken care of one hunger, and my dinner's in the oven, but we haven't seen to yours yet."

Chapter 26

MARCEL leaned back in his chair and twirled his wand between his fingers, a sure sign that he was lost deep in thought. He had meant what he told Thierry about blood magic and he would stand by those words, but the news his captain had brought certainly complicated his life. He was sure Raymond would not protest, not given the wizard's attitude toward knowledge and magic in general, and he was fairly sure Alain would go along with it simply because Alain would do anything to keep his partner – Marcel snorted silently, his lover was a better description – safe. The others, though, could well be more hesitant.

Mentally scanning the duty roster, he settled on David and Angelique as his test pairing. David was conservative enough that Marcel would be able to see how well his arguments would work in swaying the doubtful, but open-minded enough that he could be convinced with well-presented logic. He also seemed to be developing a decent rapport with his partner, something that would be essential if the wizard had to draw his partner's blood. He wondered how much of that rapport was real and how much was magical, at least if the suppositions Raymond and monsieur Lombard had developed were accurate, but he had no way of determining that and no intention of rocking the boat by asking. Shaking his head at how complicated his simple alliance had become, he pushed the button on the intercom and called David and Angelique to his office.

An hour later, David left Marcel's office with his head reeling. He felt like his world had just been turned upside down. Blood magic... Marcel expected him to do blood magic. He had followed every argument Marcel made, understood every bit of logic, but the deeply ingrained prejudices that had filled his upbringing as a wizard had all surged to the fore as soon as Marcel mentioned drawing blood to link the repère to the locator board. He glanced over at his partner of five days. She meant far more to him than she should have in such a short time, something David attributed to the unique intimacy forced upon them by the sharing of blood. There it was again. Blood. It seemed he was already doing blood magic, however inadvertently, simply by protecting her from the sunlight. Of course, he cast no spells that way, did nothing actively magical. It was her magic acting on his blood that allowed the protection, yet it still occurred. He was involved in blood magic already. Would one spell to allow her to be linked to the board that protected them all by keeping track of them while they were on duty be so terrible? Marcel said Thierry had already performed the spell with no ill effects. David was not sure that was a recommendation, since he had always considered the other wizard far too reckless for anyone's good. Still, it was proof that he would not get thrown out of the Milice and into jail for the spell. Marcel would never have allowed Thierry to do something that heinous.

Angelique walked alongside her partner, not sure where they were going, but knowing that wherever it was, she needed to be at his side. She had felt that way quite a bit in the past two days, more so than before, and she was not sure how she felt about that. She had never liked being dependent on someone else, especially a man, for anything, and to find herself clinging to one now was... bothersome, to say the least. She only hoped it was temporary, brought on by the newness of the situation and the partnership. Once she knew better what was expected of her, this dependence would fade, leaving her confidently independent once again.

Each lost in their own thoughts, David led Angelique back to his office. Opening the door for her, he followed her inside, shutting the door behind them. "Let's get this over with," he sighed.

Angelique frowned. "I don't have anything here to use as a talisman. Marcel said the spell was more effective if the object meant something to me, right?"

David nodded curtly, not liking anything that might delay the inevitable. He had his head wrapped around the necessity of doing the spell, but he had no idea how long that would last. "Let's go, then," he said curtly.

Angelique's frown deepened. She already knew, though he had not said it aloud, what her partner thought of her occupation. Rubbing his face in it seemed like a very bad idea, but everything she had of value, monetary or sentimental, was in her apartment above her business. She thought about suggesting that David wait for her here while she went home to get something she could use, but after the meeting that morning, she doubted the wizard would let her out of his sight. She sighed. "I have to go back to Montmartre. Anything I could use is either in my office or in my apartment. I assume you'll want to come with me."

David grimaced. In all honesty, it was about as low as possible on his list of things to do, but this war had made him do a lot of them anyway. This was just another in a long line. "Let's go," he said. "The sooner we get there, the sooner we can get back and get this done."

They checked out of Milice headquarters and headed north on the métro to Montmartre where Angelique ran her business. She greeted several of her employees as she walked in, all of whom seemed surprised to see her in the daylight hours. She assured them that everything was fine and promised she would be back to check in with them more fully later. As she spoke to them, she firmly ignored the waves of disapproval she felt radiating from the man at her side. She would not change what she did to earn her living, for him or for anyone. She knew the value of the service she offered, even if David would never see it. He would get used to it or he would leave. The choice was entirely his. The alliance gave him certain claims on her time, just as it gave her a claim on his blood before a day shift, but it gave him no say in her personal life, and she intended it to stay that way, certainly as long as his attitude remained.

"Wait here," she told him when they reached her office. She might have brought him this far out of duty and for safety's sake, but she had no intention of letting him taint her home with his negativity.

David frowned as Angelique shut the door behind her, leaving him alone in the windowless room. It felt stifling to him, despite the relatively cool temperature. His thought darted back and fort from one unwanted image to another. Angelique's henna-painted hands. Her dark head as she sank her fangs into his neck. Her… employees. His mind provided lascivious images of all that went on behind closed door in Angelique's… establishment. *Establishment*, he repeated sarcastically. Whorehouse was more like it. All his misgivings returned full force as he was forced to face the reality of her livelihood. Yes, she was far more independent and intelligent than he had first given her credit for, but at the end of the day, she still sold people for a living, a reality he found repulsive.

Upstairs, Angelique opened her safe and drew out an antique lacquered box of Middle Eastern origin. Reverently, she opened the lid and gazed on the treasures within, each a gift from a special lover, each a token of a special time in her life. She ran her finger over the mother of pearl comb that had been a gift from al-Marbruk, one of her sultan's guests. She had not been one of the sultan's personal concubines, being too dark for his tastes, so he had offered her to visiting guests as part of his hospitality. Most had been little more than a job for the evening, but one guest had lingered, requesting her presence night after night. He had been the closest thing she had to a lover in those days, and his patronage had probably saved her life. Before he left, he made it clear to her sultan that he expected to see her again on his next visit. His goodwill being something her sultan wanted to keep, he had refused her services one night to another visitor who had brutalized another concubine so badly that she had eventually died of the injuries. Angelique shuddered at the memory, her fingers moving on to the brooch her maker had given her. He had turned her and stolen her away from the harem, taking her with him from Persia across Turkey and eventually into northern Italy. They had stayed together for some time, until her need to be truly independent became overwhelming. He gave her the brooch as a parting gift, saying she could always sell it for seed money for her business. She had never been that low, though she had used it as collateral to get the money to start her business. There were other objects as well: a jeweled pin that Louis XIV had given her, a diamond pendant from the mayor of Paris during the Empire, and others, but while special, they were less meaningful than the first two. Her hand hovered back and forth between them, trying to decide which one to use as her repère, finally settling on the comb. Its giver had protected her once simply by his favor. Now his token of esteem would protect her again. Removing the comb, she closed the lid and set the box carefully back in the safe, spinning the lock and checking to make sure it was secure.

She looked around her haven one more time before descending the stairs to her office again, steeling herself to face David's opprobrium. He could be as disapproving as he liked. She knew her own worth and it did not depend upon his acceptance of her.

She had just shut the door behind her, preparatory to dealing with David when a knock sounded. "Come," she called, turning her back to her partner.

Isabella Barbier, one of Angelique's best employees, stuck her head in the door. "Do you have a minute, Miss Bouaddi?" she asked. "I'm sorry to disturb you, but monsieur Roche said I'd have to check with you."

"You're not disturbing me," Angelique replied at her most soothing. Isabella was also one of her most flamboyant, theatrical employees. "What can I do for you?"

"It's my sister, Miss Bouaddi," Isabella explained. "She's having a baby and my mother can only stay with her for a few days or she'll lose her job. You know what the situation is – we've talked about it before – but my sister can't possibly stay home by herself with a new baby just after she gives birth. I need a few days, maybe two weeks off, just until she recovers from the delivery enough to take care of herself."

David watched the exchange sullenly, not listening at all to what the woman was saying. He saw only the tight, low-cut blouse and short skirt that sat so low on her hips David could see the ring that pierced her navel. He was quite sure that if she bent forward at all, her breasts would fall out of the shirt and her arse out of the skirt. He supposed she was attractive, in a florid, overblown way, but he saw only the skimpy outfit, far too minimal to be appropriate in the chill October weather.

When the woman left, David scowled at Angelique. "Do you have no shame, making her flaunt herself like that? She's probably freezing in this weather."

Angelique turned slowly, the frustration that had been growing since they left Milice headquarters coming to the fore. "First of all, Isabella chooses to dress that way. I have no requirements for my employees' attire. Secondly, you haven't the slightest idea what you're talking about," she said hotly.

"Don't I?" David challenged. "Are you going to tell me you don't sell that poor girl and the others like her to the highest bidder every night?"

Angelique snorted, though not in amusement. "Like I said, you haven't the slightest idea what you're talking about. I know what you're thinking. Procuress is the nicest of the words going through your head. Pimp. Whoremonger. Those are the ones you're really thinking. You know what? I don't give a damn. Judge me if you think you have the right, but judge me for what I actually do, not for what you think I do. Did you ever bother to ask me what I do? The only thing I sell is blood. I'm not naïve. I know some of my employees choose to make additional arrangements with the vampires who purchase the right to feed from them, but that's between them. I have no part of it, whether money changes hands or not. And before you condemn me or them for that, consider the alternative. Consider where Isabella and some of my other employees would be if I didn't offer them the salary and benefits I do. They'd be on the streets, selling themselves there, with all the dangers of rape and abuse and disease that they're protected from here. Instead, they have a safe, clean place to work where all they have to do is let a vampire bite them. That's a pretty damn good deal. So take your holier than thou attitude and shove it up your arse."

David had the good grace to flush in embarrassment as he realized the erroneous conclusions he had jumped to. He opened his mouth to apologize, but she was advancing on him, her face set with anger. "Get out. I can't deal with you right now."

"But the alliance…"

"You can stick your precious alliance next to your attitude for all I care right now," Angelique retorted. "Get out."

"But…"

"I said, get out," she repeated, reaching for his shirt, intending to remove him forcibly. He raised his hands placatingly and began backing toward the door.

"We're still on duty," he protested. "What do I tell Marcel?"

"Tell him that I'll be back when I think I can deal with your attitude without killing you," she replied.

"But won't you need to feed?"

"I'm sure I will, but I don't need you for that," she reminded him. "All I need you for is protection from the sunlight, and since I'm home, I don't need that until the next time we're on patrol."

"But you promised..." David insisted, the irrational surge of jealousy sweeping through him enough to halt his progress toward the door.

"I promised not to feed from any other wizard, which I won't. I have no desire to associate with any wizards right now. And I think your behavior has pretty much negated any promises I did make. If you want my loyalty, if you want me to only feed from you, maybe you ought to think about giving me some incentive to do so. I certainly don't see any right this minute. Now, I'll tell you one more time: get out."

David backed the rest of the way out of the room, flinching as the door slammed shut in his face. He lifted his hand helplessly, as if to knock, but he knew that was folly. He had been in the wrong and there was no denying it, but Angelique was clearly in no state of mind to hear anything he might say. He hoped she would come around sooner rather than later because Marcel would not be happy with him otherwise. Grimacing at the thought of explaining her absence to the general, he made his way back through the front room of the building, looking more carefully as he did, seeing what he had missed before. While the woman in Angelique's office had been dressed like a common prostitute, most of the men and women in the public room were dressed casually, not at all like someone for sale.

THE fire in Orlando lit anew at hearing Alain's words. "How did you know?" he asked softly, for while he had felt the desire to feed growing for some time, he had also intended to let Alain sleep first.

Alain grinned, turning in Orlando's arms so they were face to face, their half-clothed bodies rubbing together enticingly. "Because I'm eager to feed you." He had given up wondering how his attitude had changed so completely from their first meeting, when the thought of Orlando's fangs in his flesh was as repulsive as it was attractive. The reason did not matter, be it a side effect of the Aveu, of the magic that let his blood protect the vampire from the sun, or simply a side of himself he had heretofore not explored. He only cared now about assuaging the need that had grown inside him with the same insistence as his sexual desire: the need to nourish his lover. "Take me to bed."

Orlando grabbed Alain's hand, not needing any further encouragement, and led him across the little hall into their bedroom. The bed was still a jumble of sheets and blankets from the night before, when they had last made love. They ignored the mess, though, pushing the covers aside in their eagerness for one another. Alain pulled the shirt over his head as he toed off his shoes. He was tempted to reach for his open trousers and push them down as well, but he was afraid Orlando would protest, and he did not want to mar the harmony that reigned between them. Instead, he lay down and opened his arms to his lover.

Alain was more alluring, if possible, Orlando decided, half dressed than he was completely naked, the play of shadow from his unzipped pants revealing as much as it hid, giving the impression of complete debauchery. Lowering himself onto the bed next to his lover, he kissed his wizard's kiss-swollen lips tenderly.

Alain returned the kiss ardently, hands moving up to cradle Orlando's head, fingers threading into the silken curls. He thought he could spend hours just touching his lover's dark hair, letting the soft strands run across his palms and twine around his fingers. The war did not give them that leisure, but Alain held onto the hope that with the alliance beginning to truly function now, it would only be a matter of time before Serrier was defeated. Then, he would take the time denied to them now and spend hours lingering over each patch of Orlando's skin, each curve of muscle and jut of bone.

The tenderness in Alain's touch moved Orlando to the depths of his being. No one, not even Jean, had ever cared about him the way Alain seemed to, and that tenderness eased his battered heart a little more. Wanting to return the devotion in kind, he lowered his head to the wizard's neck, nibbling at it with his lips. He felt Alain's hands tighten in his hair and knew not to tease so he bathed the sensitive skin with his tongue, preparing it for his fangs. When his lover arched his head back, offering his neck without hesitation, Orlando could delay no longer. His fangs slid beneath the surface, drawing life-giving blood into his mouth.

Alain's blood had always been sweet to him, but it was even more saporous than usual with the flavor of satiation added to the mixture that was already indelibly imprinted on Orlando's mind and heart. He had tasted Alain's release in his blood every time he fed, but this was different. Instead of tasting the burst of passion, he tasted the lingering contentment, the muted joy that came after the moment of completion, and that was new, and incredibly heady. It rocked him to his core to realize that he could bring his lover not only release but also this tranquility that suffused him now. There was another new flavor that lurked beneath all the others, something Orlando did not recognize and could not identify. He dismissed it as unimportant, though, focusing instead on keeping the rhythm of his sucking gentle to suit the mood he tasted in Alain's blood.

Beneath the dulcet lash of Orlando's tongue and teeth, Alain floated on a haze of satiated bliss, each tender pull of the vampire's fangs lulling him deeper into relaxation. He could almost feel himself drifting along on the sea of contentment, swamped by tender emotion. He had enjoyed each time he and Orlando had come together this way, from the first tentative interaction in the cemetery to the exploratory feeding on the couch in the living room, from the first time Orlando fed from his neck to their passion-filled encounter the night before. Nothing came close, though, to the depth of feeling that accompanied this moment, this feeding. Every possessive, protective instinct in him swelled to the forefront of his consciousness, leading him to wrap his arms snugly around his lover's shoulders, holding him close.

The unidentified flavor in Alain's blood grew stronger as the feeding continued, though Orlando came no closer to identifying it. Eventually, he gave up, simply relishing the richness it added to the already beloved taste. Instead, he concentrated on lavishing pleasure on his lover, his hands seeking Alain's, fingers twining with his wizard's, locking them together in another small way.

So focused was he on the emotions rocking his heart, Alain's release caught him unaware, flowing through him and out with all the inevitability, yet all the smoothness of the tide. He gasped as his cock twitched suddenly, releasing its load in long, gentle waves. His hands tightened imperceptibly on Orlando's shoulders before he relaxed back into the pillows with a sigh.

Orlando's sigh mingled with his lover's as he raised his head, bestowing one last, healing lick on the pierced skin. He sat up then and reached for Alain's pants, sliding them down and off so his wizard could sleep more comfortably.

Bereft of his vampire's touch, Alain's arms sought Orlando automatically.

"Shhh," Orlando soothed. "Let me undress and I will join you."

Alain nodded, eyes closing as sleep bore down on him now that his twin desires were slaked.

Orlando stripped quickly and slid in bed next to his lover, resting his head in the crook of Alain's shoulder, hand smoothing gently up and down the lightly furred chest until the wizard's breathing evened out as he slipped into slumber. Orlando's eyes closed as he let himself fall into reverie.

Chapter 27

RAYMOND had no real thought of where he expected his partner to live, but if pressed, he would have guessed near Montmartre since that seemed to be where there was a concentration of clubs and other businesses that would appeal to a vampire. He would not have guessed the upscale area that Jean now led him to. The rue d'Anjou was right off the rue du Faubourg St-Honoré, one of the most fashionable streets in the city! Somehow, that was not the image Raymond had built of his partner.

"The huitième," Raymond commented as they stopped in front of one of the buildings while Jean sought his keys. "I'm impressed."

Jean chuckled. "It was much less trendy when I moved here," he admitted. "In fact, it was practically wilderness. When these buildings started going up, I agreed to let them tear down the cottage I was living in if they would deed me one of the apartments in the new building. I've been here for almost two hundred years."

Raymond shook his head. "You speak of centuries the way other people speak of decades."

"That's the life of a vampire," Jean shrugged, unlocking the heavy door. "When I was turned, Paris was the Ile-St-Louis and the Ile-de-la-Cité. My apartment's on the third floor."

They climbed the sweeping stairs side by side, the building being too old for an elevator. Jean's door was one of only two on his landing, instead of the three or four that were common in a building this size, giving Raymond another inkling that there was more to his partner than met the eye.

The door, when it opened, revealed a large apartment that could well have been a museum except for the absence of protective covers and barriers. A glance at the walls revealed the old style silk wallpaper, much as graced the walls of Versailles, in a pale blue that reminded Raymond of the summer sky. The floors were elegantly patterned parquet. Every piece of furniture in the large salon looked as if it came straight from a museum. Knowing he was staring but unable to help himself, the wizard went from piece to piece, examining each, marveling at the workmanship. "This must have cost a fortune!"

"Not so much when they were new," Jean reminded him. "These were good quality everyday items when I purchased them. It's their age that makes them valuable now. I also didn't furnish my home all at once. I've had time to collect the perfect piece here and there as I found them. I'm still missing a few things, but I don't know that I'll ever find them now."

"Like what?" Raymond asked, wondering what could possibly be missing from this showplace.

"I have a set of Limoges china," Jean replied, "but I'm missing the tureen. The pattern was discontinued some time ago, so I can't even get a modern substitute until I find an original. Little things like that. I have all the big pieces, furniture and fixtures. It's the small things, a lamp, a vase... things I remember seeing in one salon or another and not having the means to acquire at the time."

Raymond shook his head, seeing his partner in an entirely new light. He had imagined the other man to be uncultured, but the opposite appeared to be true.

"Would you like to see the rest?" Jean asked, gesturing toward the hallway.

Raymond nodded mutely, wondering what other treasures awaited him. Jean led him down a long hallway with several doors to each side. "Kitchen," he said with a dismissive gesture. "It's not at all modernized since I have no need for it." A little further down, he pointed out the toilettes and salle de bains. "I had running water installed for a bath, but the fixtures are purely functional." He opened the door at the very end of the hallway. "This room, however, might interest you."

Raymond followed his partner in and gaped even more than he had in the salon. "This is..." Words failed him as he stared at the floor to ceiling bookshelves that covered every wall. "I thought you weren't a scholar," he accused.

"I'm not," Jean replied. "Most of these are popular texts, not even great literature, but rather entertaining stories that caught my eye when they were written. Some of the others were gifts, from the writers themselves or from others thinking to curry my favor by offering a tome I mentioned wanting to read. Still others are part of the mantle I wear, records of vampire law and history that I keep safe for those who would consult them. Most of those are still at monsieur Lombard's since he actually consults them regularly and I don't, but I keep some volumes here for those who would rather not beard the lion in his den."

"May I?" Raymond asked, approaching one of the shelves.

"Of course," Jean offered. "You will gain much more enjoyment from them than I do, I'm sure."

Raymond glared at the vampire sharply. "I think you play dumb so people will underestimate you. You've devoted too much space to books, even if they're popular fiction as you put it, to get no enjoyment from them."

Jean had the good grace to look shame-faced. "You've caught me. So, are you going to tell everyone the truth?"

"And spoil a perfectly good ruse that could quite possibly work to our advantage?" the wizard asked incredulously. "Do I look that stupid?"

Relieved, Jean laughed. "I'm so glad someone else sees it that way."

"Does anyone know the truth?"

Jean shrugged. "Orlando's seen my library, of course, and even helped me look for things before, like when we first started the alliance. We always believed wizard's blood was poison, you know. I don't know if he's put together the extent of my deception or if he just accepts it because it's me."

"You've very close," Raymond said slowly.

"He's the little brother I never had," Jean replied firmly. "Maybe when I first met him, I might have considered a different relationship, but not now. Not in a long time. Alain is far better suited to him than I would have been anyway." Despite the conviction in his words, Jean could not stop the pang of regret at the thought of what might have developed between him and his young friend under different circumstances. For the thousandth time or more, he cursed the sorry excuse for a vampire who had so brutalized Orlando that he was only now learning to trust again.

"Alain is a… good man," Raymond said finally. "We don't always agree, but there's no doubt about his integrity or his loyalty. He'll take good care of Orlando."

Jean was not sure exactly what he heard in his partner's voice, but he sought to ease it nonetheless. "So are you, mon ami. And some day he'll open his eyes and see it."

Raymond shrugged. "It doesn't matter. I don't need him to like me, just to help keep me out of Serrier's clutches." Looking around the room, he forced his thoughts back to the reason he was there. "I should set the wards and let you rest."

"Set the wards," Jean agreed, knowing the protection they would offer was essential. If Serrier sent his people after a vampire, Jean would be their first target if only to deprive the vampires of his leadership. "But don't feel like you have to rush off. As long as I've fed, I don't require rest, just walls to protect me from the sun. And now, I don't even need that."

Raymond smiled, sure that Jean was just making the offer to be polite, then turned his thoughts to the business of protecting his partner. "Is there just the one door?" he asked, making himself abandon the library for the time being.

"Just the one," Jean agreed, "but there are windows in almost every room. Only the bathrooms don't have windows."

"I'll need to ward those as well," Raymond declared, "but it's generally best to start with the door and build the rest of the wards from that. I haven't been able to find a reason for that, but every text I've read, every experiment I've done bears it out. The spells are more effective if they're cast first on the main entrance to the house or room."

Jean nodded, trusting Raymond's expertise. He stood quietly and watched as the wizard chanted old, arcane spells. It took a moment, for it had been centuries, but as he listened, the vampire realized that much of what he was hearing was in the French he had spoken as a young seminarian, a millennium ago, rather than the modern language that surrounded him now. And then he realized that while understandable, the pronunciation was off. When Raymond had finished, for he did not want to disrupt his partner's concentration, he commented, "I understood that. That was the language I spoke when I was turned. I never thought I'd hear it again."

LYING in bed next to Alain, Orlando's mind floated in the semi-conscious state that passed for sleep among the vampires. He never completely lost awareness of his surroundings, of the warmth of Alain's body next to his, but his thoughts wandered aimlessly, without direction, from emotion to emotion, sensation to sensation, all of them centered around his Avoué. It made sense, a disconnected part of his brain reflected, since Alain had become the center of his life. Warring with the joy Alain brought him were the memories of his past that haunted him always, but especially at times like this, when his thoughts escaped his conscious control.

He could feed his body being invaded, feel his flesh tear as his maker brutalized him with the handle of the whip he had just finished using to beat him. Blood poured down his back to mingle with the blood that seeped from his anus. He begged for mercy, though he knew it would avail him not. The bastard had no concept of mercy. Orlando lost track of how long that torture lasted, but when he was hanging limp in the chains that held him to the wall, too weak to fight anymore, the offending object was removed to be replaced by his creator's penis, as thick as the whip handle and almost as hard. Orlando struggled again, resisting another violation, another rape. He was bound at wrists and ankles, though, spread out against the wall for his master's pleasure.

The sensation of Thurloe's semen invading him, mingling with the blood from his beating, made Orlando retch, his empty stomach heaving as it tried to expel its contents. His maker released him finally from the wall, though the chains around his ankles and wrists remained, and dragged him into the next room where a young girl lay bound. Grabbing her wrist, the monster punctured it and forced it against Orlando's lips. He tried not to swallow, but his instincts were too strong, and once the sweet blood hit his tongue, he could not resist. He drank and drank until he felt her life-force ebbing. He pulled away to spare her life, only to hear his creator's maniacal laughter. "If you will not finish her, then I will," he said, taking up the limp limb and sucking out what remained of the girl's blood. The sight of Thurloe bent over the dying girl's body, covered in Orlando's blood and his own fluids, was enough to make Orlando feel sick again. He fought down the nausea, though, not wanting the girl's sacrifice to go to waste. Some day, he would be strong enough to fight the bastard and escape. Someday, Thurloe would not win.

The sound of the kitchen timer penetrated the nightmare, bringing Orlando back to the present. Not wanting to disturb Alain, Orlando slipped from bed and silenced the alarm, pulling the lamb out of the oven so it could cool a little. He went to the bathroom to wash away the remnants of the dream, needing to clear his head before facing his far too perceptive lover. Reliving his captivity in dreams was bad enough. He did not want to relive it in words as well.

Stirring restlessly, driven by a featureless morass of terrified dreams, Alain reached for his lover, seeking the comfort of the vampire's body. Finding only empty space, he opened his eyes, the sense of dread from the dream following him into waking, leaving him disoriented, and more than a little confused. Without Orlando at his side to ground him, he did not immediately recognize his surroundings, which only added to his panic. He could not shake the feeling that Orlando was missing somehow, lost or taken against his will. "Orlando!" he called frantically.

In the bathroom, Orlando would have preferred a few more minutes to compose himself but he heard the incipient panic in Alain's voice and it triggered his protective instincts strengthened by the Aveu de Sang. Stepping out of the bathroom, he crossed back to the bed. "I'm here," he said, forcing a smile. "I was just taking your dinner out of the oven."

Alain told himself it was a perfectly reasonable explanation, but he could not shake the sense of threat, of panic, that had awakened him, that lingered still. He reached for Orlando who, thankfully, moved willingly into his arms, letting the reality of the physical connection reassure him on a deeper level than words alone could do. He could not explain what had triggered his irrational fear, for he knew logically that he should not have felt that way. His logic, though, had nothing to do with his emotions upon waking alone or his profound relief at finding Orlando safe.

Alain's arms around him soothed the last of the horror that lingered from Orlando's nightmare, and he let himself relax completely into the wizard's embrace. His maker was destroyed a hundred years ago, and Alain was here now, offering safety, tenderness, devotion. Thurloe had no power to hurt him anymore. Orlando knew it would take more than that reminder to cease the tormenting dreams, but he finally allowed himself to hope that a lifetime of Alain's embrace could achieve that feat.

The urgency was fading with Orlando in his arms, but Alain did not want to go through the upheaval of the last few minutes again. Nuzzling Orlando's neck tenderly, he requested, "Promise me you'll be here when I wake up, every time I wake up. Promise me I'll always wake up in your arms."

Emotion rocked Orlando deeply at hearing Alain's request. He knew he was important to his wizard, but this was more than mere importance. This was... he had no word, he realized, for what he was feeling. He knew only that he wanted to always feel this way. "I promise."

Relief surging through him, Alain sought Orlando's lips blindly, sealing their promise with a kiss. His hands slid down Orlando's back, cupping the naked flesh as he had done earlier in the kitchen, pulling the vampire toward him.

Orlando flinched and pulled away. His nightmare, though fading, was still far too fresh for him to accept his lover's caress. "Don't," he said softly, his voice firm despite the quiet tone.

"But..." Alain protested.

Orlando shook his head. "You promised. Nothing more than I was comfortable with. If that's a problem..."

"It's not a problem," Alain interrupted quickly. "You just didn't mind earlier, in the kitchen and so I thought it was okay now."

"It was okay earlier in the kitchen," Orlando agreed, "but not now, please." He rose from the bed, turning to find a pair of boxers to pull on. "Your dinner's getting cold. You should eat it." Not looking back at Alain, he grabbed a pair of the wizard's pants and threw them toward the bed.

More than a little confused, Alain climbed out of bed as well and pulled on the pants. He wanted to press Orlando for an explanation, but he feared that would be counterproductive. The vampire trusted him because he had always given his lover the time and space he needed. Alain understood, at least theoretically, that Orlando had suffered terribly and had never let go of that abuse. With a sigh, he walked into the kitchen, hoping the vampire would join him while he ate. The kitchen was empty, though.

Alain found a plate and served himself a piece of lamb and vegetables. He wanted a glass of wine, but he had not bought any and they would be back on duty in a few hours. Settling for a glass of water, he took his plate and went in search of his lover.

On the balcony, Orlando stared blindly at the façade across from his apartment, not even taking note of its colors or the gentle sunshine. His thoughts were all turned inward as he wrestled with his conscience and his fear. Alain was right about one thing. He had not minded feeling his lover's hands on his buttocks as they made love in the kitchen before sleeping. In fact, he had enjoyed feeling his lover urging him on. The nightmare, though, had brought back all his insecurities. He had no idea why Alain wanted him, why he had agreed to accept the Aveu de Sang. In moments of calm, it did not matter. Orlando cared only that Alain had accepted it and did want him. The nightmare, though, was dragging him back into the pit of self-doubt, of unworthiness, that he was only beginning to escape, making him fear those motivations, fear that desire could fade, that the end of the alliance would end Alain's willingness to put up with him. He had learned enough at Thurloe's hands, though he had resisted every lesson with every breath, that he could keep Alain entranced with those wiles, but that was not the relationship he wanted.

He wanted… he wanted a true relationship with his Avoué, wanted Alain to stay with him of his own free will, not because Orlando had beguiled him into it. He wanted to be accepted for himself with all his insecurities and problems. He had heard the devotion in Sebastien's voice when he spoke of his dead Avoué. Orlando wanted that, wanted to know that Alain felt for him the same lifelong commitment that Sebastien's Avoué had obviously felt for the other vampire.

Alain walked into the living room and found it empty as well, the open casement revealing Orlando's location. He went to the window and looked outside. The vampire leaned on the railing, his expression pensive, even forlorn. "Would you like company?" Alain asked softly. "I can bring a chair out here if you'd rather not come inside."

Orlando looked up on hearing Alain's words, so lost in his thoughts that he had not heard the wizard approach. "Don't bother. I'll come in," he replied.

Alain stepped back to let the vampire inside, wishing his hands were free to embrace his lover. He thought about trying to kiss Orlando anyway, but his lover was past him and the moment was lost. Feeling incredibly stilted, Alain moved to the couch, setting his plate and glass on the low table. To his relief, Orlando came and sat down next to him, but the vampire did not break the tense silence, and Alain did not know where to begin.

Sitting next to his wizard, Orlando cast about for something to say, hoping Alain would speak, would say something, anything, to start the conversation going again. Maybe if he did, the vampire would be able to say what he knew he needed to.

The silence stretched uncomfortably as Alain ate, until he could stand it no longer. "What do I need to do?" he asked. "How do I make this right between us?"

Orlando flinched. "I don't know," he replied honestly. "You're suffering for my fears and I don't know how to stop it."

Alain shook his head. "I'm not suffering, Orlando," he insisted. "How can you think that when you have brought life back into my existence? You saw my apartment; you know what my life has been like the last two years. You saved me from that." He took a deep breath, trying to decide how much to divulge. "Do you know why I came to the cemetery to meet you that first night?"

Surprised at the seeming non sequitur, Orlando shook his head.

"Marcel told Thierry and me both about the meet. I insisted on being the one to come, not for the reasons I gave them, but because if you had been treacherous, I didn't have anything left to live for, and Thierry did. His marriage wasn't in very good shape, but as long as they were both alive, there was hope for reconciliation."

Orlando blinked a couple of times. He had known Alain was lost, but he had not realized just how deep it had gone. "And now?" he asked softly.

"I'll meet you anywhere, anytime," Alain quipped.

Orlando chuckled. "That's not what I meant."

Sobering, Alain nodded. "I know. And now, I wouldn't do anything I could avoid to put myself in harm's way. We're at war, and danger is an unavoidable part of that, but I have a reason to live now. You're my reason to live now. I'm a patient man, Orlando. I'll give you the time you need to deal with your past. I just need your help to know what's okay and when it's not."

Orlando sighed. "That's the problem," he explained. "I didn't know it wasn't all right until it happened, until I froze up. I wish it were as simple as telling myself that you would never hurt me. And I do know that, truly, but there seems to be a difference between knowing it and acting on it. And I don't know what to do about it."

"The first thing to do about it is to remember the safeword we discussed," Alain declared. "I won't be offended or hurt if you use it. I want you to use it if you need it. That's why we agreed on it, and using it actually shows me that you trust me to stop when you say it."

"I forgot," Orlando answered honestly, cringing slightly at the thought that he had disappointed Alain. "I panicked and pulled away instead of using the safeword. I'm sorry."

Alain sighed in frustration. "Stop apologizing, please," he asked softly. "You don't have to be perfect. I'm certainly not, and I don't expect it from you either. We've only been together five days, only known each other for six. It's normal for there to be bumps in our relationship, even without our difficult pasts."

A thought struck him. "Did something happen while I slept, something that upset you?"

Orlando blanched, thinking of his dream and his reluctance to talk about it.

Seeing the color fade from Orlando's face, Alain reached for his lover's hand. "Tell me," he requested gently. "I can't change your past, but let me share in it."

"Don't ask that of me," Orlando pleaded. "You don't want to go into that hell."

"I won't force the issue," Alain promised, "but it might help me to understand. It's a part of who you are now, and I want to know everything there is to know about you."

Thinking of all he had suffered, of the shame he still felt at his imprisonment and failure to escape on his own, Orlando cringed. He did not want to share that with anyone, even with Jean who knew the worst of it and never seemed to judge him. This was his Avoué, though, his lover, the man with whom he would live for the rest of the wizard's life, and that meant building a real relationship, not one based solely on appearances or casual acquaintance. Orlando's thoughts on the balcony came back to him, his desire for the kind of commitment Sebastien had obviously had with his Avoué. Perhaps this was the first step down that road. "If you're sure," he mumbled.

Honestly, Alain was not sure at all. He knew only a little of Orlando's past, but enough to know that the rest was, as the vampire had said, hellish. He had no real desire to know more than that. It would not make him any more careful of Orlando than he already was – he was not sure that was even possible – and he feared it would make him hesitant to touch his lover at all lest his touch evoke the wrong memory. He pushed aside his doubts. "Have you ever truly talked about it?" he asked. "I mean, I know Jean knows a lot of it, but that's because he was there. Have you ever just unburdened all the fear and anger and hate?"

"No," Orlando replied. "Jean knows, the worst of it anyway, but I've never talked about it. I wanted to forget it, to move on, and he respected that."

Alain heard the implied criticism, that Jean respected Orlando's wishes in a way Alain did not, but he pressed anyway. "Did it work?" he asked instead.

"Until recently, yes," Orlando retorted.

"Really?" the wizard challenged. "Where is your normal life by vampire standards? Where are the lovers and friends who have filled your days in the last hundred years?"

"Bastard!" Orlando spat, trying to move away. Alain caught his arm to keep him there. "You know you're the only lover I've had and that Jean is my only friend!"

Alain pulled Orlando against him, holding him despite the vampire's struggles. "Then maybe it's time to stop pretending nothing's wrong and really face what happened," he said softly. "You're not alone anymore. I'm here with you, and I'll always be here. As long as I live, I'll be here. Let me help you exorcise these demons once and for all."

Orlando's struggles eased as he heard Alain's words, Alain's offer. "Do you really think talking about it will help?"

"Probably not right away," Alain admitted, "but we can't keep ignoring it when it interferes with our relationship. It's not going to go away on its own, angel, however much we'd both like it to. It hasn't in a hundred years, and it's not going to now. If you'd rather talk to Jean than to me, I'll try to understand, but I think you need to talk – really talk – to someone."

"Let me think about it," Orlando requested.

"Will you at least tell me what happened while I slept?"

"I had a nightmare," the vampire replied flatly, "and not even a particularly bad one compared to some, but it still spooked me." He sighed. "I told you before: I'm damaged goods."

"And I told you before that you're not," Alain insisted hotly. "I won't press, but think about what I said, please."

Orlando nodded. "I will." He glanced up at the clock on the wall, looking for a way to change the subject. "Finish your dinner. We're back on duty soon."

Inwardly, Alain cursed the Milice for cutting short this moment, this opportunity to keep Orlando talking, but he knew his duty all too well. They would just have to come back to it later.

Chapter 28

CAROLINE woke slowly, vaguely surprised to feel a body next to hers. As the haze of sleep cleared, she remembered all that had happened that morning: the debriefing at the change of shift, Thierry's suggestion that the wizards and vampires travel in pairs even off duty, Mireille's easy acceptance of her invitation to stay. Knowing the vampire did not need sleep the way she did, she had encouraged her partner to feel at home, to enjoy the television or the computer or any of the other amenities Caroline's apartment could offer, but Mireille had declined, following the wizard to the bedroom and the bed, unselfconsciously stripping down to her underwear. Even that had been removed at Caroline's hesitant offer of a nightgown. Much to Caroline's delight, once she realized the vampire planned to share her bed, Mireille did not even blink at the filmy swath of white silk Caroline produced from a drawer. The garment veiled Mireille's luscious body, but did nothing to hide it. Through the filmy veil, she caught tantalizing glimpses of rosy nipples topping the lush mounds of the vampire's breasts, taut with desire and pressing against the cloth, and of the nest of curls at the apex of the long, milky thighs that beckoned to her relentlessly. "Your turn," Mireille had husked when she was attired for bed, turning Caroline's attention away from the vampire and back to herself.

Caroline undressed as well, slipping into an equally sheer black chemise, aware the whole time of Mireille's eyes on her body. By the time she climbed into bed, she was flushed and throbbing. She had barely touched the soft sheets when her partner's hands reached for her, sliding over, then under her diaphanous shift, sending tendrils of desire along her skin to pool low in her belly, a deep, pleasurable ache. She had tried to reciprocate, but Mireille had stilled her hands, telling her to lie back and enjoy. She wanted to protest, to insist that the vampire let her return the pleasure she was bestowing, but Mireille's lips silenced her before she could give voice to the words.

By the time those lips left hers to skate over her skin, veiled by her shift, Caroline was so lost in desire that she had lost the ability to protest. "You can take it off," Caroline had offered when Mireille continued to taste her only through fabric, but Mireille shook her head, leaving Caroline achingly frustrated even as she grew more aroused. She had almost reached for the hem herself to pull off the annoying garment when Mireille's fingers slid beneath the cloth to dance along her thighs, urging them gently to part. Caroline had obliged immediately, opening herself completely to her partner – her lover, she corrected herself, for after this morning, there was no doubt that their relationship had changed. Tender fingers had explored her most sensitive flesh as the vampire's lips continued to tease her nipples through the black silk, completely soaked from her saliva. Caroline had thrashed on the bed, wanting more, until finally Mireille's fingers had slid inside her to fill her, pressing firmly against the walls of her passage even as her thumb caressed the tight nub hidden within her folds. Caroline had tried to hold back, to prolong the pleasure, but Mireille's ministrations had been inexorable, pushing Caroline higher and higher until she felt herself flying, completely unconnected anymore. The next thing she remembered was waking in her new lover's arms.

Deciding she had been selfish long enough, Caroline nuzzled Mireille's neck, rousing the vampire. "Will you let me return the pleasure you gave me this morning?" she asked when the hazel eyes opened to meet hers.

"Gladly," Mireille replied, "but tomorrow, when we get off duty. As much as I would enjoy it now, I really must go to monsieur Lombard to see how he is doing without me there."

Caroline frowned, her memories having rekindled her passion along with her desire to take care of her lover, but she respected Mireille's dedication. "Then we should get ready and go. I'd invite you to join me in the shower, but that would only delay our departure."

Mireille hissed as she fought the desire to agree. "Ask me when we get off duty. I'll say yes and gladly then."

Caroline's eyes sparked. She swore she could smell the flare of Mireille's passion. She wanted nothing more than to push the vampire back on the bed and bury her face between her partner's legs so she could better savor the scent, but she already knew the answer to that was when they got off duty. With a groan, she rose from the bed and started toward the bathroom. "I'll be out in ten minutes."

"You'd better be," Mireille joked, trying to ignore the sight of her wizard crossing the room in only the little scrap of black silk that did nothing to hide the creamy buttocks revealed as Caroline departed, "because I'm joining you in fifteen."

Caroline leaned against the doorjamb as desire swamped her again, weakening her knees. "Don't tempt me," she ground out, making herself step into the bathroom and shut the door.

Mireille slumped back on the bed, hands trembling as she fought to stay where she was, to stop herself from following Caroline into the shower and taking what they both so clearly wanted. Duty warred with desire, but she had worked for monsieur Lombard too long, subjugating her needs to his. She might break that habit some day, but not today. She closed her eyes, body aching and empty. Even the feel of the silk on her skin as she shifted restlessly on the bed fired her blood. She had known lust before, but never to this uncontrollable degree. Knowing she would never be able to fulfill the duties that awaited her without some relief, she stripped the gown over her head so that only the sheets and the cool air caressed her skin. And then her own hands. Closing her eyes, she let herself imagine it was Caroline's hands that stroked her curves, that tweaked her nipples and teased her folds.

In the shower, Caroline forced her mind away from her body's needs, using a meditation trick she had learned as a student to calm her jangling nerves and force her mind to the matters that would occupy her night. Monsieur Lombard, first, because she would not let Mireille go alone, and then the Milice. Feeling herself settle, or at least getting herself under control, Caroline left the shower and dried off. Wrapping one towel around her body and another around her dripping hair, she went back into the bedroom to tell Mireille that the shower was free.

The sight that met her eyes undid all her meditation. Mireille lay naked on the bed, legs splayed wide, touching herself as Caroline desired to do. "Fuck this," she muttered, going to Mireille's side. "Let me," she demanded, pulling the vampire's fingers from her body and replacing them with her own.

Mireille's eyes flew open, green and hazel clashing, then melting as Caroline lowered her head to kiss the vampire. Their lips melded together as Caroline worked her fingers inside her lover's passage, twisting, stroking, tantalizing. She wanted Mireille as mindless as she herself had been that morning. She wanted to touch and taste every inch of the bounty spread out before her, but she knew there was no time for that. Soon, she promised herself as she worked to bring her partner release as quickly as possible.

"Turn around," Mireille gasped. "I want to touch you, too."

Eagerly, Caroline shifted on the bed, pausing only long enough to lick delicately at the strawberry-colored nipples that beckoned so earnestly. The moan that escaped Mireille at the sensation made Caroline determined to revisit that pleasure as well when they had time to linger. For now, though, she moved on, settling her hips near Mireille's shoulders and cocking one knee so she was as open to her lover as the vampire was to her.

Mireille's mouth watered as Caroline stretched out next to her, spreading her legs for the vampire's pleasure. She wanted – how she wanted! – to bury her face in the blond curls and lick and suck on the tender flesh. Her fangs had dropped, though, before Caroline joined her and she feared she would not be able to taste without biting, and that was not a step to take without some serious conversation beforehand. If she had known they would end up like this, she would have kept her fangs retracted, but feeding and sex were so powerfully linked for her that she would never be able to pull them in now. She would have to wait for another time to please herself and her lover that way, but that did not preclude other avenues of pleasure. With a smile, she returned her fingers to the depths that had welcomed them the night before.

The vantage point of her new position gave Caroline ideas. This relationship with Mireille had caught her off guard in many respects and she found herself lagging behind her partner in matters of intimacy, copying what the vampire had done to her rather than taking the initiative herself. This time, though, she was not going to wait for Mireille to act. Sliding her fingers from her lover's eager body, she lowered her head and lapped at the tender flesh damp with Mireille's essence. Keeping in mind the caresses she liked best, Caroline set out to lavish as much pleasure on the vampire as her lover had earlier bestowed upon her.

Mireille had already been close to release when Caroline came out of the bathroom. The touch of the wizard's fingers had set her teetering on the edge of release. Feeling her lover's lips and tongue on her center left her whimpering in mindless need until the tip of Caroline's tongue flicked over the tight bud of flesh hooded by her folds. Eyes rolling back in her head, her body tightened then released in a rush, her juices flowing copiously, slicking Caroline's chin and mouth.

Caroline tasted the sudden rush, lapping at the folds like a kitten with so much cream. The flavor only added to the sensations spinning through her from the thought of having brought Mireille to climax. A gasp tore from her as the vampire's fingers shifted inside her, calling forth her own orgasm, leaving her once again limp and panting at her partner's hands. At least this time, she knew she had brought Mireille the same joy.

They lay there for several minutes, catching their breaths, restoring their control, until the buzzing of the alarm clock startled them. "I guess it's time to get up," Caroline sighed, turning off the offending appliance. "I need another shower."

Mireille shook her head. "Wait your turn," she teased, rising from the bed and giving her lover a view of her curvaceous body as she walked toward the bathroom.

Caroline chuckled as she drank in the sight of her partner. Falling back on the bed, she pondered the unexpected turn their relationship had taken. Marcel had said to notify him of any unusual behaviors that might be associated with the sharing of blood and magic, but surely this did not apply. After all, this was between her and her partner. What did it have to do with anyone else?

Nothing.

Getting up and going to the closet to dress for the night, she cast a cleaning spell to avoid the time to take another shower and decided there was no reason to mention their newfound closeness. She had been lonely and Mireille assuaged her need for company, for tenderness. It was as simple as that.

And something the men would not understand and might well ridicule. No, it was definitely better for this to stay between the two women. Pulling an outfit from its hanger, Caroline whistled tunelessly under her breath as she dressed for the night, a little smile tugging at the corner of her lips.

THE end of the shift was rapidly approaching, and Sebastien could feel his restlessness increasing. It had been an interesting day, with setting up the repère and watching Thierry in Marcel's absence. It was a side to his partner Sebastien had not seen before. He had seen Thierry lead a patrol and orchestrate a battle, but this was both more and less. More because Thierry was in charge of all the patrols, not just his own. Less because he gave only the most general of orders. He sent a patrol to one location or another, but each commander then had to make the rest of the decisions. Sebastien saw their patrol go out, too, without them, and saw Thierry's frustration at being unable to accompany his team. "Laurent's more than capable," Thierry told Sebastien when the patrol winked out. "I've already recommended him for a promotion, but damn it, it feels wrong to send them into danger while I sit here and twiddle my thumbs."

"Who does command go to in Marcel's absence and yours?" Sebastien asked, wondering if Thierry could go with his team.

"Alain."

"And when he's not on duty?"

"He's called in," Thierry explained. "Likewise, if he were on duty and had to leave and I was not. We haven't had a situation yet when all three of us were unavailable. Marcel has a whole chain of command worked out, but it's never been an issue."

"You could call him," Sebastien suggested, "if it bothers you that much to let the patrol go without you."

Thierry shook his head. "No, he was on duty and in command last night and will be again tonight. It wouldn't be fair to call him unless it was an emergency. And he's got something else to concentrate on now, too."

Sebastien could not quite decide what he heard in Thierry's voice at that last comment. "Does that bother you?" he asked with deceptive innocence.

"No, of course not!" Thierry replied. "I'm thrilled to see him happy again."

Sebastien raised an eyebrow, making Thierry flush and glance away. "Fine, I wasn't thrilled at first. It happened so fast that I wondered if he'd been coerced somehow."

"It happens that fast sometimes," Sebastien defended Orlando and Alain, thinking about his own first meeting with Thibaut. "The lightning bolt, the coup de foudre."

"I know," Thierry agreed. "I should know better than most because it was the same way, or almost, when I met Aleth, but she was another wizard. I knew what she was capable of and not. Orlando is a vampire and I'd heard stories," he raised his hand to forestall Sebastien's protest. "Now I know they're just stories, but I didn't know it then and Alain's actions seemed to fit with every legend I'd heard of vampires controlling people through their bites. They'd known each other only a little more than twenty-four hours and Alain had a brand on his neck. At less than thirty-six hours, he was rushing me out the door so they could become lovers. Alain set me straight, though, and I *am* happy for them. I'm not going to disrupt what little time they have together just because I prefer field work to paperwork."

"You're a good man, Thierry Dumont," Sebastien declared.

"I don't know about that," Thierry demurred, "but I do my damnedest to be a good friend."

Sebastien smiled and glanced at the clock. "Only an hour left until the briefing. Do you expect Marcel back?"

"He didn't know," Thierry replied. "Alain and I can handle the meeting if he isn't."

"I have no doubt," Sebastien assured him. "I just wondered about the situation with David."

"I'll take your advice and speak to Jean about it. He already said he would be making the rounds tonight to see what he could learn about the rogue. Marcel told me that before he left, so I wouldn't assign Jean any other tasks if Marcel didn't make it back for the briefing. Hopefully, he won't mind adding one more stop to his list."

"It may not even be an extra stop," Sebastien amended. "More than one vampire goes to Angelique's for information as well as nourishment."

"Is that how you found out about the meeting?" Thierry asked curiously since he knew Jean had not planned to invite Sebastien. He had not asked exactly why, deciding it did not matter for the time being.

"No," the vampire replied. "I still prefer to hunt for myself rather than paying for blood. I came home from hunting that night to find a message under my door." He chuckled. "A summons actually, from monsieur Lombard, who informed me of the meeting and that I would be attending. When I asked why, he didn't answer, just repeated his insistence that I go. Nobody denies the old man without a damn good reason and I didn't have one, so I went. You know the rest."

"I'm glad you came," Thierry said softly, remembering his frustration at his difficulty in finding a partner.

"So am I," Sebastien replied, his thoughts focused on his revelation earlier in the day. He wondered if he dared ask about his partner's late wife. The wizard had mentioned her. Surely that gave Sebastien permission to ask. "You mentioned your wife."

"Aleth," Thierry interjected, not sure he wanted to talk about her, but Sebastien had told Thierry about his Avoué. It seemed fair enough. "We met by accident, fell in love, then fell apart. I blamed the war when it first started, but it was deeper than that. I told myself and everyone else that we were just going through a rough patch, that we'd fix things when the fighting ended, but honestly, I doubt we would have. Things had gotten too complicated. We'd grown too far apart. If she hadn't been killed, all that would have been left was dividing our things between us. Now I have to decide what to do with her things."

"I'm sorry," Sebastien said softly, trying to imagine what he would have felt if Thibaut had changed his mind. Even now, the mere thought was nearly debilitating.

Thierry shrugged. "I try not to think about it," he admitted. "It's easier just to focus on the war and the alliance. The issues her death raised don't need my attention now, and you and the Milice do. There will be time to deal with the rest later."

Sebastien did not know what to say to that so he let the subject drop. He pondered what Thierry's comments might mean for Sebastien's own hopes, but he had no way to decide. He hated the cliché that only time would tell, but it was unfortunately accurate in this situation. Patience, he reminded himself. He had waited for four hundred years. He could wait a few more months if that was what it took.

Chapter 29

ORLANDO looked across the room at Alain and Thierry, trying to master his wildly fluctuating emotions. He had been out of sorts since waking from his nightmare. The conversation with Alain had not helped, and they had left the apartment without feeding or making love as had become their habit. In many respects, that bothered Orlando more than anything else. According to Sebastien, he should have been hungry for his lover, and the lack of need concerned him. Was something wrong with the Aveu de Sang?

And then, as soon as they walked in to the briefing room, Thierry had pulled Alain aside without more than a nod in Orlando's direction. He had thought he and the other wizard had begun to form a friendship, but apparently, he was mistaken. He knew the two wizards were friends, not lovers, and only that knowledge held him back, but it raised a different desire in him, to have a friendship like the one they shared, a meeting of equals that transcended everything else and provided a bone-deep connection that nothing could shake. He saw that connection when he looked at the two men, saw how profound their trust in one another was.

A part of him clenched jealously every time Thierry touched Alain, but he trusted his Avoué. He even trusted Thierry, he realized, to stand at Alain's side and protect him, no matter what. A part of him recognized how foolish his jealousy was, for Alain had given him no cause to doubt him and every reason to trust him. If one of them had reason to doubt the other, it was surely Alain, given the way Orlando had behaved that evening. Rationally, he knew his reactions were out of proportion with the situation, but he could not completely control them. They were a by-product of the Aveu de Sang, according to Sebastien.

"He is no threat to you," a voice murmured in his ear. "Your wizard is his best friend, and Thierry only wants to see him happy. And while you will have to take my word for it, he understands that you make his friend happy."

"I believe you," Orlando replied, "but that seems to make no difference to my reactions. I want to go over there and drag them apart, drag Alain somewhere private and..." he trailed off as he realized he was speaking to a vampire he barely knew.

"And do unspeakably erotic things to him," Sebastien finished. "You don't need to watch your words with me. There is little, if anything, you will experience with your Avoué that I have not known."

"How do I fight this?" Orlando asked plaintively. "How do I deal with these emotions? I can't expect him not to go out in the world. He has responsibilities, and his insistence on honoring them is one of his most admirable traits. I can't ask him not to be himself."

Sebastien nodded in agreement. "Time," he answered slowly. "As the Aveu de Sang settles into place, as you grow used to it and its demands, your emotions will level out and you will be better able to deal with the reality of his life." It did not occur to him to mention that feeding while having sex would speed the process. It did not occur to him that two people so obviously in love would abstain from combining those two pleasures.

On the other side of the room, Thierry was explaining to Alain what had occurred with David and what course he intended to follow in his attempts to limit the damage.

"What were they doing at her apartment in the first place?" Alain asked.

"Getting something to use as her repère," Thierry replied, realizing he had started his story in the middle.

"Then it worked?" the older wizard asked. "You figured out a way to connect them to the locator map?"

"We did, but it's complicated. The only identifying characteristic we could find was blood," Thierry explained.

Alain did not bother repeating it, did not ask if Thierry was sure. They had been indoctrinated since their formal training began about the dangers of blood magic.

"Marcel approved it," Thierry added, seeing the antipathy cross his friend's face.

"I didn't doubt that," Alain hastened to say. "I know you wouldn't do something like that without his approval. So what now?"

"Marcel explained it to a few people on the day shift, but I think he expected to be able to explain it to the night shift himself," Thierry replied.

"He told me he'd explain it so it wouldn't be me changing the rules, but he's not here."

"Did he tell everyone?" Alain asked.

"No, just David and a couple of others, I think."

Alain nodded. "Then we can leave it until Marcel returns to make the announcement himself. I'll talk to Orlando privately and see if he and I can get his repère functional, too. That'll give Marcel another success story to point to since David didn't do his job." He scowled at the thought, but he knew Thierry had already handled it in the short term, and it would be up to Jean and Marcel to handle it in the long term. "Stupid fucker," he muttered nonetheless.

Thierry chuckled in rueful agreement. "Let's have this meeting," he said to his best friend. "I'm ready to go home."

"And will you be taking Sebastien with you?" Alain teased.

Thierry caught himself just in time to stop the blush that threatened to stain his cheeks. "That'll depend on him," Thierry replied seriously. "I don't want to impose on him or invade his space." Before Alain could reply to that, Thierry had turned and asked everyone to be seated for the briefing. Alain took his place, resolving to speak with Thierry again later. He thought he saw something in his friend's eyes, something he had not seen in some time. First, though, he had to make it through the briefing.

"We have a problem," Thierry told them after they had dealt with the issues of patrols and intelligence. That finished, he had dismissed the patrol leaders, leaving just himself and Sebastien, Alain, Orlando, Jean and Raymond around the table. "I've handled this end of it, but Jean, I could use your help with the rest."

"What's the problem?" Jean asked, surprised his help was being sought so openly.

"David screwed up," Thierry said flatly, "and Angelique sent him packing. I've already dealt with him, but I'm hoping you can persuade her to give him another chance."

"What did he do?" Jean asked warily. "She isn't one to hold a grudge unreasonably, but she has a couple of touchy areas."

"I didn't hear what he actually said," Thierry replied, "but I'm pretty sure he insulted her choice of business."

Jean sighed. "I was afraid of that. I'll talk to her and see what I can do, but she's very sensitive about the services she provides." He met the eyes of each wizard at the table one by one. "She only sells blood," he told them. "That's the only transaction she enacts. Some of her employees choose to offer more on the side, for a fee or because they enjoy it, but Angelique isn't involved in that. She refuses to be. Outsiders think of it as a brothel, but a restaurant would be a better comparison. Make your selection off the menu, eat your fill, pay your bill."

"We're not judging her," Alain assured him. "We'd just like her to accept David's apology and rejoin the alliance."

"Will he apologize?" Jean asked.

Thierry snorted. "After the arse-kicking I gave him, he'll do whatever I tell him." Alain and Raymond both chuckled. They had witnessed Thierry dressing down someone more than once, and the burly captain was not exaggerating. They had never known a soldier to balk after one of Thierry's lectures.

"I'll talk to her tonight," Jean promised. "I planned to stop there to see if anyone knows anything about our rogue anyway. It'll be simple enough to speak to Angelique privately as well." He met Thierry's eyes seriously. "I can't promise anything. Vampire society is not like the Milice. I lead more by example than by decree, except in the rare case when vampire law has been violated. My participation in the alliance does not force anyone else to be here. If she refuses to come back, I can't compel her."

"We understand," Alain assured him, "and we know you'll do your best. Anything else?"

Raymond debated for a moment mentioning that Jean had offered to teach him the correct pronunciation of some of the older spells, but he did not actually know yet if these lessons would make any difference in the effectiveness of the spells. Until he did, he would keep it between him and Jean rather than get people's hopes up over nothing.

When no one said anything, the meeting broke up, the various partners going about their assigned duties. Thierry caught Alain's eye as the other wizard was about to leave. "Laurent's still out with my patrol," he told Alain. "Let me know when they get back."

"I will," Alain promised, "although you're worrying for nothing."

"I'm sure you're right," Thierry agreed, "but they're still my team and I want to know they're safe."

"I'll call you as soon as they check in."

"Thanks." He left the briefing room, heading to his office. To his surprise, Sebastien followed him. He waited until they were inside with the door closed to inquire. "I'm just dropping off my repère," he told his partner. "You don't need to wait for me."

Sebastien tried to decide how to frame his response. He had spent most of the briefing debating what he should do when his shift ended. His stubborn streak, his independent core, demanded that he go home alone, but he was not alone anymore, he reminded himself. He had a partner now, a partner who was as vulnerable to a vampire attack as Sebastien would be to an attack by a wizard. Not only that, said partner had caught Sebastien's eye on another level.

"I thought perhaps we should go home together," he suggested. "Your argument this morning was a good one."

The intimacy of that statement shocked Thierry. He had honestly not expected his partner to agree. At the most, he had hoped Sebastien would eventually let him put up wards on the vampire's residence. He had certainly not foreseen this! His mind raced. His studio was well warded, but tiny and a mess. Aleth's death left him another option, though. He could take Sebastien back to the little villa he and Aleth had bought in Boulogne, just outside the city limits of Paris. Aleth had been meticulous in her organization. Her house – Thierry's house – would be spotless, if he could stand to go there again. "My house is already warded," he heard himself say before he realized he had made the decision. "It'll be the simplest for now," he added. "I can... I can put up wards at your place later if you'd rather."

Sebastien did not need to taste Thierry's blood to sense the nervousness in the other man. Unfortunately, he had no way of telling if those nerves were a sign of a returned interest or something completely unrelated. "Your house will be fine," Sebastien replied, leaving the length of his stay and the question of his apartment open for later discussion. For now, though... "Let's go soon," he asked. "I'm ready to be elsewhere."

Thierry pulled his repère from his pocket and slid it into a box in his desk drawer. "I'm ready," he told Sebastien. "It's a bit of a train ride to the house. Is that okay or should I ask Alain to send you out there?" It occurred to him, not for the first time, that it would be much simpler if he could transport Sebastien the way he did himself. A wave of his wand and a quick incantation and he could go wherever he pleased. To take Sebastien with him, though, required much more planning.

"The train ride doesn't bother me," Sebastien replied, "unless you're in a particular hurry. I'm not accustomed to magical transportation anyway."

Thierry considered the question. On the one hand, the time they spent on the train, unprotected from outside magic, was time they were in danger. On the other hand, he was not overly eager to arrive at the house he had shared with his wife in the company of... his new partner, but it was more than that. Thierry had tried denying it, to no avail. He enjoyed Sebastien's company, sought it out, even. He had not felt this way since he first met Aleth. He was not quite ready to put a name to the emotion that drove him, for it was far too complex for any simple word, but this was much more than bringing home a professional contact for a business dinner. And despite their separation, that seemed far too much like betraying Aleth's memory mere days after her death. "The train's fine," he decided, delaying the inevitable a few minutes longer.

"CAPTAIN!"

Orlando did not react immediately, not used to hearing Alain called by his rank. Only when he realized his wizard had turned around did he stop.

"Yes?" Alain asked.

"We've got a patrol under attack in the 15ème," the other wizard reported.

"Copé?" Alain demanded sharply, knowing that Thierry's patrol had been assigned to Montparnasse.

"Yes, sir."

"Shit!" Alain swore. "Come on," he said to Orlando. "Thierry'll kill me if anything happens to his patrol."

Orlando followed Alain in silence as they raced through the corridors to the Salle des Cartes. To Alain's relief, his patrol was already assembled. He studied the locator map for a moment, deciding on strategy. He was about to give the orders when he realized he would not be able to accompany his patrol. "Fouquet," he said, turning to his lieutenant, "you'll have to do this without me. I'm on duty here until Marcel returns."

Lt. Hugues Fouquet nodded, thrilled at this chance to prove his abilities. His impulsiveness in the past had kept him from promotions given to the younger captain. This was an opportunity to show he could be trusted with command. He listened carefully to his superior's orders. The plan was simple enough. Get in, get Copé's patrol out of trouble, and get back to base, taking down as many of the dark wizards as possible in the process.

Orlando listened to the discussion in silence. The plan was a good one, he thought. Alain's company would drop in behind the attackers and catch them in a pincer movement with the squadron already there. What surprised him was that Alain was not going. When he asked, Alain explained succinctly about the chain of command, adding in a softer voice his concerns about his lieutenant's rashness. "Do you want me to go with them?" Orlando offered. "I can keep an eye on him for you."

Alain wanted absolutely nothing of the sort, but he dared not say that to Orlando. The last thing his vampire needed was to feel coddled, regardless of where the impulse came from. Turning down the perfectly reasonable request would require justifications Orlando would surely not care to hear. On the other hand, perhaps knowing that Alain's partner was there would help temper Fouquet's impulsiveness. "They don't know you well enough yet for me to give you command," Alain replied softly, "but I can make it clear your input is to be seriously considered before any changes in the plan take place."

Turning back to his squadron, he added, "I'm sending my partner with you as well, since he isn't part of the command structure here. If you're in doubt, listen to him. Lieutenant, I'll need you to include him in your displacement, please."

"Yes, sir," Fouquet replied, hiding the tinge of resentment at the suggestion that Alain did not trust him completely. He did not mind having the vampire along. He had heard how a group of vampires had broken the stalemate a few nights ago when Catherine and her patrol were trapped in the Marais. He only wished this particular one had not been sent to keep an eye on him.

Orlando moved to stand next to the wizard who had spoken. A part of him was nervous about going into battle without Alain, but this was why he had joined the alliance, and he would honor his promises to the best of his abilities.

At Alain's signal, the team deployed, leaving Alain standing in the room with only the wizard assigned to monitoring duty. It was, he realized with a pang, the first time he and Orlando had been separated by more than a room since the day after they became lovers. It had been one thing to know Orlando was talking with Jean somewhere in the city before going home. It was another thing entirely to know that his lover was in danger without being at his side. Alain reminded himself that while hot-headed, Fouquet was a formidable wizard with an uncanny ability to survive difficult situations. He would make sure Orlando came back unharmed. His eyes stayed pinned to the board, watching his patrol appear according to plan. He could not track Orlando directly since they had not had time to create a repère for the vampire, but he could track the general movements of the squadron. The first order of business when Orlando returned, he decided, besides kissing his lover senseless, would definitely be to get a repère made.

Chapter 30

SPELLS were flying furiously as the backup team materialized behind the attacking dark wizards. Lt. Fouquet assessed the situation and realized this was a battle they could not win. "Fan out," he ordered. "We've got to give Copé a chance to regroup. As soon as they're clear, we get the hell back to base. This is now a rescue mission and that's it."

"Yes, sir," the other wizards agreed.

He turned to Orlando. "I've heard that vampires are faster and stealthier than mortals. Can you get behind them and tell Laurent to get his patrol out of there?"

Orlando surveyed the scene. "It'll take a few minutes," he replied, "since I'm not familiar with this area of the city, but I can work my way through the side streets."

"Do it," Fouquet ordered. "Do you want me to send a wizard with you?"

"No," Orlando demurred. "He'd just slow me down."

Fouquet nodded, hoping Alain would not have his arse for this. "Make sure one of them gets you back to base."

Orlando nodded and then ran, using every heightened sense he had to navigate the unfamiliar streets and avoid their enemies. He had just reached the holed-up patrol when he heard a pained shout. "Laurent's down!" he heard a voice shout.

The blur that moved past him at those words could only have been another vampire. Orlando looked on in horror at the scene unfolding before his eyes.

"Laurent!" Blair cried, cradling his bleeding, gasping partner in his arms.

"We've got to get him out of here and back to base," a wizard told Blair. The vampire did not even look to see who had spoken.

"No... time," Laurent choked. "Too late."

"No!" Blair protested. He looked up at the wizard. "Isn't there something you can do? Anything!"

The wizard shook his head, recognizing the symptoms of the spell that had hit Laurent. If a medic had been on hand the moment it hit, maybe, but now, Laurent was right. It was too late.

"Damn it!" Blair swore. "You can't just leave me." Eyes hardening, he made a decision. "There's another choice, Laurent," he said urgently. "Let me change you. Let me make you a vampire."

Laurent could feel his breath leaving him as his throat closed, but he nodded. Blair's head went immediately to his neck, the now familiar intent providing some measure of comfort and the prick of teeth was fleeting.

Blair sucked hard and fast, draining every drop of Laurent's blood. When there was almost none left, he slashed his wrist with his fangs and pressed it to Laurent's mouth. He could feel the wizard sucking weakly. "Take more," he urged. "You can't hurt me."

Laurent heard Blair's words and tried to do as his partner said. He forced his throat to work around the constriction, the blood dripping into his mouth and into his stomach. His vision blurred as consciousness deserted him. He could feel the darkness closing in, but he knew that becoming a vampire meant dying to be reborn again so he did not panic. His trusting gaze met Blair's as he faded, anticipating seeing those eyes again when he awoke.

Blair watched Laurent's gaze go blank, watched the wizard's chest still. He counted the seconds that passed. One. Two. Three. Four. Five. As they ticked by, he began to grow alarmed. Ten seconds, fifteen at the most, and the change should have been completed. Twenty seconds passed with no reaction, then thirty. "No!" he screamed, pulling the wizard's body into his arms. "No!"

Orlando could not stand it. He stepped from the shadows and hailed another wizard. "Lt. Fouquet says to get everyone back to Milice headquarters."

The stunned wizard shouted the order to retreat as they could, before turning back to Orlando. "What about...?" she asked, gesturing to the two forms on the ground

"Can you send back both Blair and Laurent's body?" he asked.

Marie nodded.

"Then do it, and I'll need help as well."

Marie cast a spell and Blair disappeared, Laurent's body still held tightly against his chest. Another spell and Orlando was back in the Salle des Cartes. He glanced around, not seeing Blair, but immediately finding Alain. Heedless of the onlookers, he crossed the room, wrapping his arms around his lover.

"What is it?" Alain asked. "What happened?"

"Laurent's dead," Orlando said, his voice monotone with shock. "Blair tried to save him, but it didn't work. His blood didn't turn Laurent like it should have."

Alain blanched at Orlando's words. Keeping an arm around his lover as the Salle des Cartes filled with the returning patrols, he led Orlando toward his office. "I've got to call Thierry," he murmured, his grief at Laurent's death overshadowed by his need to offer comfort to his best friend and to assure himself that Orlando was unharmed.

As soon as the door to Alain's and Thierry's office shut behind them, Orlando pulled his lover into his arms, heedless of the wizard's need to call his friend. He had a need, too: to prove to himself that his partner was alive and well. His lips closed over Alain's, claiming them. He inhaled his lover's scent as their tongues twined together, his wizard's body pressed tightly against his own.

Alain could not help but react, everything else subsumed in his relief that Orlando was unharmed and in his arms again. His fear and grief burned away in the face of the overpowering passion he felt for his lover. His arms encircled the slender body, thanking Merlin and all the gods that Orlando had not been the one struck down.

As wonderful as it felt to have Alain in his arms, Orlando needed more. His conscience pricked him, though, reminding him of Thierry waiting for news of his team. "Call Thierry," he gasped, pulling his lips free from Alain's. "Hurry. I need you."

Nodding, as desperate in his desire as Orlando, Alain grabbed his cell phone and punched in Thierry's number by rote. He forced himself to focus, to concentrate on Thierry and Thierry's reaction to the news. He had been the bearer of bad news to families in the past, and he knew that his own emotions needed to be under control when they spoke.

"Dumont," Thierry's voice barked across the line.

"Thierry, it's Alain," the wizard said. "Orlando just came back with your patrol. There was an ambush…."

"Who?" Thierry asked tonelessly.

Alain's eyes closed as he struggled for control. "Laurent."

"Shit! Fuck! Putain de merde!" The curses streamed out of Thierry's mouth. Alain held the phone away from his ear as the vituperation poured across the connection. When the outburst stilled, Alain fitted the phone back to his ear and said, "I'm sorry, Thierry, but there's nothing anyone could have done. They tried."

"I'll be there in a few minutes," Thierry said slowly.

"Don't," Alain stopped him. "You just got off duty. I can take care of your patrol tonight, and you can handle the rest in the morning. Get some rest, Thierry. You need that more than you need to be here."

Thierry did not reply, but when the line went dead and the other wizard did not immediately appear in their office, Alain decided his best friend had listened. He flipped his phone shut and looked back at Orlando. "Fuck," he muttered, running his hands through his hair. "It never gets any easier."

"I don't think it's supposed to," Orlando replied softly, coming to lean on the desk next to where Alain stood. "If it gets easier, it means you've stopped caring." He tipped Alain's chin up to meet his eyes. "Don't stop caring."

"When did you get so wise?" Alain asked with a pained smile.

"When I met you."

Alain's smile widened a little at the words. He leaned forward and kissed Orlando softly, the desperation of a few minutes earlier absent for the moment. "I was worried about you," he admitted.

"It was awful," Orlando acknowledged, head bowing as the memories flooded back. "Lt. Fouquet asked me to get around the battle and tell the others to get out as soon as they could. I got there easily enough, just as Laurent went down. He was bleeding and gasping for breath. Blair got there almost immediately, but it didn't seem to matter. The other wizards told him there was no hope, but he tried anyway, tried to turn him. It wouldn't have been life as Laurent knew it, but it would have let them stay together. Laurent agreed, but it didn't work." Orlando lifted luminous eyes to Alain's face, the implications of Blair's failure crippling him. "It didn't work."

Alain stroked the smooth cheek, trying to ease the pain of Orlando's memory. He could think of nothing to say. His own mortality, present and future, was something he lived with, something he accepted every time he went into battle. If they survived the war, he and Orlando would have many years together, magic offering greater longevity to him than was normal for humans, but one day, he would die. No amount of hoping or pretending could change that.

"Don't dwell on it," Alain urged. "We can't know what tomorrow will bring. All we can do is make the most of the time we are given, each moment, each day. I only had ten years with Henri instead of his lifetime. I'll never stop missing him, but I can't – I won't – regret the time I had with him."

Orlando's eyes prickled with unsheddable tears as he nodded, pulling Alain back into his arms. "I need you."

"My body, my blood are yours," Alain promised. "Take what you need."

Orlando's hands trembled as he reached for Alain's sweater, pulling it over his head, stripping him bare to the waist. Alain lifted his arms, willingly facilitating his disrobing, needing the confirmation that Orlando's actions would provide as much as the vampire himself seemed to need it.

Another time, Orlando would have lingered on that expanse of flesh, caressing, kissing, nibbling, but he had no patience for lingering tonight. He needed Alain and he needed him now. Ripping his own shirt off, buttons flying in the process, he urged Alain up onto the desk, knocking aside everything in their way. "Now," he insisted as he reached for the buttons on Alain's trousers.

Alain lifted his hips, as eager as Orlando. He leaned back on his elbows and spread his legs, watching avidly as his lover stripped off the rest of his clothes. "Now," he echoed, lifting his heels to the edge of the desk so that he was spread wide for Orlando's penetration. "Take me now."

Orlando stepped closer, hand falling to his erection. It took every ounce of willpower he had not to simply slam into the offered portal, but he knew what that felt like and no amount of desperation, no degree of frenzy, could persuade him to hurt Alain that way.

"Lube," he ground out.

"Don't need it," Alain insisted, his mind on only one thing: feeling Orlando inside him. "Please."

Orlando shook his head. "I won't take you dry. *He* delighted in doing that to me, in making me feel every tear, every abrasive thrust. I won't do that to you."

The pain in Orlando's words was a bucket of ice water on Alain's need. Still, he was thrilled that Orlando had trusted him with such a revelation after his earlier refusal to talk about the vampire who had turned him. Focusing his mind until he could picture their bedroom clearly, he whispered a summoning spell and handed Orlando the necessary tube. "Hurry," he pleaded. "I don't need much preparation."

Orlando slicked up two fingers, working them inside Alain's body as quickly as he dared. Knowing he would not resist his lover's pleading for long, he added more lube hurriedly, scissoring his fingers to stretch the tight muscles.

"Enough," Alain said, sitting up halfway and reaching for Orlando. "I need you now."

Orlando pulled his hand back, using the lube on his fingers to slick his throbbing shaft. He stepped closer in between his lover's thighs, one hand on Alain's chest pushing him back onto the desk as he lined his cock up with the pulsing entrance. Alain's desirous groan gave Orlando pause until the wizard lifted his hips, speeding his impaling faster than the vampire would have dared.

Alain understood that Orlando did not want to hurt him, but lust spurred by fear was riding him hard, and only Orlando inside him could ease that desperation. He pushed up against the vampire's still-cautious thrusts. "Stop holding back," he insisted.

Orlando's desire warred with his fear, as he slid ever deeper into Alain's body. He obviously was not hurting the wizard, and that appeased his greatest concern. Giving in to his desperate lust, he increased the speed of his thrusts until he was pounding into his lover's channel.

Alain gasped when Orlando's control snapped. Words of praise and encouragement spilled from his lips as he felt himself claimed, conquered, as never before. It was exactly what he needed to dispel the fear that had held sway the entire time Orlando was gone. Abdicating any semblance of mastery over himself or the situation, he strove for his release, flexing his sphincter to massage Orlando's driving cock, hoping to bring his lover as much pleasure as he was deriving from their frenetic coupling.

Orlando lifted his eyes to Alain's face, needing the sight of the beloved visage contorted with pleasure to remind himself that his wizard was safe, that tragedy had, for once, spared him. The deliberate, rhythmic contraction of Alain's sheath sent him soaring, shattering what little remained of his control. Unable to hold back any longer, he climaxed with a hoarse shout, reaching between their sweaty bodies to tug insistently on Alain's cock. Almost immediately, the thick shaft disgorged its load, coating his fingers with sticky fluid. He lifted his hand to his lips, licking it clean. He still could not taste it like he could Alain's blood, but he thought he caught a hint of saltiness.

When he had swallowed every drop, he lowered his head to Alain's chest, thankful when his lover's arms encircled him, holding him close. He rested there for several long seconds, letting the peace and tranquility soak into his soul. At moments like this, he could almost – almost – believe that he was not as damned as he had always thought, that his existence could perhaps take a turn for the better. With a sigh, he lifted his head, looking down into Alain's cerulean eyes, feeling a different desire blindside him as suddenly as his lust had. He nudged at his wizard's chin, urging him to tilt his head back.

Alain's eyes flew open when he felt Orlando's lips on his neck. Did the vampire mean to...? Before he could even think the question, he felt Orlando's fangs brushing his skin. "Yes," he hissed.

Orlando's hesitations melted in the face of Alain's patent desire. Still buried inside his lover, he slid his fangs into the wizard's neck, tasting again the contentment he had tasted before, the subtle hint of something else he still could not identify but savored nonetheless. This time, he could also taste the residue of Alain's fear. The flavor was bitter, but fading, assuring the vampire that his actions were not the cause. Grief was mixed in as well, reminding Orlando of the wizard they had lost that night. He sucked more deeply, needing the connection to Alain, the connection Blair had lost with his partner. Life-giving blood flowed into his mouth, strengthening him, sustaining him, comforting him.

Even sated as he was, having Orlando feed from him like this, naked, entwined, Alain felt his desire reawakening. He shifted restlessly beneath Orlando, rubbing their bodies together, his stirring cock brushing Orlando's belly.

Orlando froze for a moment when he felt the desire build in Alain's blood and the corresponding physical reactions. He was too far gone, though, to withdraw completely as caution told him he should. It felt too good to be buried inside his lover. He did not have to worry about his own self-control, not when he had assuaged his passion already that evening. Alain would almost certainly climax again, but he always did when Orlando fed. The only thing changed by their current position was the increased feeling of intimacy. He drank more urgently, hoping to bring his lover as much pleasure as possible.

Alain stirred more deliberately beneath Orlando, seeking friction on his swelling shaft. He could still feel the stretch of his lover inside him, though the thick shaft was quiescent now. He wanted to feel it stir within him, to have it swell again with the same desire that flowed in his own veins, but he contented himself with the thought that Orlando was still lodged within him rather than pulling away. The steady beat of his heart echoed the rhythmic suction against his throat, his pulse beginning to pound not only in his chest, but throughout his body. He gasped when Orlando's fangs drove particularly deep, his body arching up and his seed spilling out of him again, adding to the stickiness between their bodies.

Orlando trembled when he felt Alain's climax hit, riding out the waves of pleasure. He had tasted them before, each time he had fed deeply from Alain, but he never grew tired of the flavor. He thought he could willingly spend eternity lavishing this kind of pleasure on his lover. He licked the wizard's skin carefully to close the wounds, laying his head on Alain's chest again, reluctant to let reality intrude. He knew they would have to rise soon so Alain could return to his duties, but he wanted to linger just a little longer in this moment in time.

Chapter 31

THIERRY closed his cell phone, staring blindly at the wall.

Dead.

Laurent was dead.

He had sent his lieutenant into battle without his captain's assistance and now he was dead.

Looking across the living room at his partner, his guilt redoubled. If it had not been for Sebastien, for Thierry's hope that Sebastien would let the wizard ward his apartment, Thierry would almost certainly have gone after his patrol when he got off duty. Loyalty to his team would have driven him to it despite Alain's words, and Laurent's death might have been averted. Thierry did not delude himself that he was so powerful that he could have stopped Laurent's death single-handedly, but he had years of experience and a knowledge of strategy that Laurent had not possessed. He might have made a different decision, deployed his troops in a different formation that would have kept Laurent out of harm's way. Furious at himself and at the situation, he threw his phone across the room, watching it slam against the wall and shatter into pieces.

"Thierry?"

Sebastien's voice broke into Thierry's thoughts. He turned angry, haunted eyes to his partner.

The look on Thierry's face caught Sebastien by surprise. He had never seen such anger or regret on his partner's face, even when talking about his wife's death. "What happened?"

"Laurent's dead."

Sebastien knew his reaction was unworthy of him, but his first thought was gratitude that Thierry had not gone out with his patrol. He was sorry to hear about Laurent, but his relief that it was not Thierry was overwhelming. He did not know what he would do if he lost his partner. He had lost one partner, one lover, and it had nearly destroyed him. To lose Thierry now, so soon after finding him… The thought did not bear contemplation, though it was a shock to realize that he was already thinking about Thierry in the same way he thought about Thibaut. That reflection triggered another. Was someone helping Blair? He would ask Thierry about it, but not right away. First, he needed to tend to his own partner.

"Being there wouldn't have changed anything," Sebastien said soothingly, crossing the room to join Thierry on the couch.

"It might have," Thierry replied defensively, trying to remember what he knew about Laurent personally, whether the man had a family, a lover, anyone who would need to be notified. He was sure Alain would check on that, but it seemed unfair to ask his friend to do his job for him. Frustrated, he realized he did not know, had not taken the time to know Laurent on a personal level, and now he would never have the chance. "I might have made a different decision than Laurent did, might have avoided the ambush entirely or turned it back on the attackers. Laurent's good, but he doesn't – didn't – have my skill at strategy."

The correction brought another scowl to Thierry's face. He simply could not imagine his second-in-command being gone. He had finally gotten Laurent trained, used to thinking the way Thierry did often enough that he no longer had to explain every detail. Who was he kidding? He would train a hundred new lieutenants willingly if that would bring Laurent back.

It was not that simple, though. Nothing ever was, but his guilty conscience insisted that this was far more complicated than it should have been. He should simply have let Sebastien go home and joined his patrol. He had not, though. His own desire to keep his partner close had outweighed his duty and he had given in. Sitting on a couch he did not recognize in a house that was only his in name, he admitted to himself that he wanted Sebastien with him, there and everywhere. And it only added to his guilt, because he knew – he *knew* – that before Sebastien, he would have gone out to join his patrol. Even if it had changed nothing, even if Laurent had still died, he would not now be sitting here feeling the weight of his absence, the weight of his dereliction of duty. Oh, Marcel would not see it that way. His actions would never be questioned by anyone outside this room. In fact, he would be surprised if Sebastien questioned his actions. That did not make him feel any better. If anything, it made him feel worse, knowing that no one else understood.

"So you have two choices," Sebastien said, interrupting his thoughts. "You can sit here and mope or we can go out and do something about it."

"Do what?" Thierry asked in frustration. "Laurent's dead."

"But the ones who killed him aren't," Sebastien pointed out. "I imagine you would feel at least a little better if they were."

Thierry gaped at him for a moment. "Are you serious about this?"

Sebastien nodded. "And I think I know someone else who would be willing to help us, if you don't mind having another vampire along."

It took a minute to follow Sebastien's train of thought. "Blair," he declared.

"Yes," Sebastien agreed. "A vampire who loses someone special often reacts... badly," he explained, remembering his own desperate thoughts after Thibaut's death, his own contemplation of suicide in the hopes of being reunited with his love beyond this world. "Having something to do, being able to release his anger and frustration, might help keep Blair from doing something rash."

Thierry chuckled despite his grief. "And going after Laurent's killers with just the three of us isn't rash?" he asked.

Sebastien smiled back. "I think you might find that the rest of your patrol would like to go with us, too."

Thierry's grin turned feral. "Let's go. By the time we get back to base, they may all be gone."

"Get yourself there and send someone back for me," Sebastien suggested. "It'll take less time than riding the train."

"You don't mind?"

Sebastien shook his head. "Go. I'll be waiting for whomever you send."

MIREILLE hurried down the hall to Caroline's office. She had heard that a wizard had been killed, a wizard with a vampire partner. "Who is with the vampire whose partner was killed?" she asked without preamble.

Caroline looked up, surprised. "What?"

"A wizard was killed on patrol. Somebody said he had a partner. Who is with that vampire?" Mireille responded insistently.

"I don't know."

"We need to find out. He or she shouldn't be alone. Vampires who lose someone special are known to behave... rashly," she explained.

"Let's go," Caroline said. "We'll find out."

She led Mireille through the halls to the infirmary where deceased as well as injured wizards were generally taken. A medic met them at the door.

Caroline explained who they were looking for, and the medic pointed them to the final cubicle. The two women approached quietly, a soft smile passing between them as they each remembered the last time they were in this particular space. "Let me go in first," Mireille said softly. "If he overreacts, he's less likely to hurt me than you."

Caroline frowned, not liking the idea of Mireille being in danger at all, but she acceded to her partner's request.

Mireille pulled aside the curtain and stepped inside. The vampire on the floor did not even look up, his body bent protectively over the wizard in his arms, as if he could shield his partner from all harm that way. She recognized Blair, but he was not a vampire she knew well. She cast about in her memory for anyone he might be close to, but he had been in Paris such a short time that she was not sure he had formed any friendships here. "Blair?" she said softly, kneeling at his side.

"Why didn't it work?" Blair answered without looking up. "Why couldn't I save him?"

Mireille had no answer for that question so she simply rested a compassionate hand on his shoulder. "You should let the wizards see to him," she suggested.

"No!" His shout was emphatic, and loud enough that it brought Caroline through the curtain from the hallway. Mireille gestured to her that all was well. Caroline nodded but did not step back outside.

"He said he wanted me to turn him," Blair continued after a moment, as if his outburst had never taken place. "It's never not worked before when someone wanted to be turned." He turned plaintive eyes to Mireille. "Why didn't it work?"

It was the same question he had been asking himself since he realized that he had not succeeded, that Laurent was gone despite his best efforts.

Laurent.

Blair lowered his head again, pulling his partner's body close to his chest. Had it really just been days since they met? Blair had trouble believing it. It felt like he had known Laurent for years. From the first taste of the wizard's tangy blood, he had known that Laurent was different, special. His eyes closed as he remembered.

Laurent approached them slowly, him and Fabienne and Paul Bertrand. They turned wary eyes on the wizard and he stopped several feet away.

The wizard cleared his throat. "I'd like to seek a partner among you," Laurent said formally.

Fabienne looked over to Jean. She caught his eye and he nodded reassuringly. So she straightened her shoulders and took the few steps to stand in front of Laurent.

"I'll try," she said.

The concern on her face was clear, but Laurent nodded, pulling off his leather jacket and unbuttoning his sleeve. The other two vampires came to stand behind her as she took his proffered wrist. "Go ahead," he said, steeling himself.

Fabienne dipped her head and sipped. Blair could see how little she took, how careful she was being. She pulled back within a second and shook her head.

"Thanks," Laurent said weakly, not sure what he was expecting. Fabienne gave him a lop-sided smile and stepped back.

The two vampires looked at each other, each waiting for the other to act. "Oh, for Christ's sake," Fabienne exclaimed. "C'mon Blair, just do it."

The black man blinked at her and then looked at Laurent, who held out his wrist. He stepped forward and clasped Laurent's wrist lightly. He was as careful as he knew how to be when he bent his head and bit. If this did not work, the wizard would have to offer his wrist again and again until it did. Blair did not want to make it any more painful than necessary.

Blair lowered his mouth to Laurent's wrist, first inhaling the scent of his skin and barely suppressing a shiver as he tried to sink his fangs as delicately as possible to taste Laurent's blood. Although he had heard Jean's description, nothing could have prepared him for the warm wave of feeling enveloping him, strengthening him, comforting him, wrapping around him until he felt invincible.

He pulled back, raised his dark eyes to meet glittering blue and was completely swept away. It was like the world melted away and left only this man and his magic, sweeping in and around, enveloping Blair's soul.

"Blair? Hey, Blair?" Fabienne stepped up next to him and snapped her fingers in front of Blair's face, breaking the gaze.

Blair blinked and came back to himself. "It worked."

Fabienne nodded. She and Paul stepped away as Blair remained still, holding Laurent's wrist gently.

"I didn't expect to find a partner," Laurent said, studying the smooth planes of the man's dark face.

"Me, either," Blair said quietly, fingers lightly caressing the skin of Laurent's wrist.

"I want to help the cause," Laurent asserted, voice businesslike. "Alain's a good man, and I trust him. I've always thought there would be a way to find allies…"

Blair tilted his head as he listened to Laurent talk, enchanted by the musical rhythm of his voice. He could still feel the mesmerizing pull of Laurent's presence… he quite simply did not want to move away. He was fascinated.

Orlando appeared at his side and looked at Blair. "Everything all right?" he asked quietly.

Laurent broke off in mid-sentence. "We're partners."

Orlando looked to Blair, searching his face. After a long moment they both nodded in agreement. "Excellent," Orlando said. "We're trying to get the people who are paired all in one place." Blair nodded again and Orlando moved to the next cluster.

"Don't talk much, do you?" Laurent asked.

Blair raised a shoulder in comment and remained still, watching Laurent.

"I guess we should walk over there," Laurent said, looking at Blair, then at his wrist, then back at the vampire.

With a tilt of his head, Blair offered a cautious smile, but he did not release Laurent's wrist. Laurent cleared his throat and looked at Blair so oddly that the vampire reluctantly loosened his fingers, immediately missing the buzz of feeling that had been swimming in his veins, although a supremely warm protective power remained.

Laurent shrugged into his jacket and walked away, leaving a thoughtful Blair to follow. While Laurent immediately started talking with other wizards, Blair remained withdrawn, occupied by the new thoughts of Laurent that swamped him.

Those thoughts had not stopped swamping him, not in the four days that had followed, not in the hour since Laurent died in his arms. He had howled his grief on the streets during the fight that had taken Laurent from him. He had whispered his grief in the silence of the infirmary after one of the other wizards had transported him here. He wanted to sob his grief into the arms of a friend, but he had none here in Paris, and even if he did, he knew the tears would not come. He turned a bleak gaze to the vampire at his side.

Mireille remained kneeling at Blair's side through the silence. This was not the first time she had sat vigil with another vampire, and she knew the effects would not soon wear off. She did not know how many years ago monsieur Lombard had loved and lost his Avoué, but she knew what month it had occurred. Even now, all these many years later, he left Paris and returned to his Avoué's gravesite to mourn. She knew many would scoff at Blair's emotions, citing the short time he had known his partner, but glancing up at her own wizard, Mireille knew that, in this case, time truly was irrelevant. Four years, four centuries, could not create a bond any deeper than the one she already shared with her partner. Only the magical bond of an Aveu de Sang would surpass what she and Caroline already shared.

Troubled by Blair's silence, she reached for his shoulder again. To her surprise, he turned into her arms, his partner's body sliding gently to the floor. She opened her embrace to him, hoping it would provide some comfort.

Caroline watched the scene in helpless silence. She did not know Blair and knew nothing about the way vampires grieve, so she was no help in either respect. She simply hoped her presence was a support for Mireille. When the other vampire moved toward her partner, Caroline's hand flew automatically to her wand, jealous fear driving her to protect what was hers, but Mireille simply opened her arms to the grief-stricken man, and Caroline forced herself to relax. She scolded herself silently for her reaction, reminding herself that she and Mireille had made no promises outside the alliance and that even if they had, her partner was offering comfort, nothing more, to a fellow vampire in the face of an incomprehensible loss. Her reaction had no place in this room, or any other, she told herself firmly.

The soft arms that closed around him provided comfort, but they were not the arms that Blair craved. There had been nothing soft about Laurent, other than perhaps his heart, but even that was hidden beneath the brusque exterior his partner had shown to the world. The leather jacket was as much a shield as any ward Laurent had cast around his apartment. Blair had recognized the brusqueness as the defense mechanism it was the first time he tasted Laurent's blood, but he had only slowly been coming to see what lay behind it. Each time he fed, he had seen more, felt more of who his partner was – had been. Laurent had not been insensible to the effects of his feeding either, and they had come together explosively more than once. The thought of having to hunt again, of having to search again for sustenance for body and soul brought all the grief crashing down on him again. He pulled away from Mireille and reached for Laurent, burying his face against the cold flesh of his partner's neck.

Chapter 32

A RUSTLING at the door caught Caroline's attention. She tore her eyes away from the painful tableau in front of her and turned to see Thierry and Sebastien hovering in the entrance. She stepped back and joined them. "Laurent's partner," she said redundantly.

Thierry nodded. "How is he?" He could not see Blair's face, only the curve of the vampire's back as he clutched at Laurent's lifeless body.

"I don't know," she replied honestly. "He hasn't moved from Laurent's side since we got here."

"He won't," Sebastien elaborated, "unless we give him a reason to."

Caroline blanched. "A reason?"

"We're going after his murderer," Thierry said bluntly. "I wasn't there to stop his death. I will avenge it."

"I'm going with you."

Thierry looked over at the vampire who, though he looked up, still cradled Laurent's body. "That's why we're here," he assured the vampire. "We knew you'd want to go with us."

"How do we find him?" Blair asked, finding something outside his grief to focus on.

"Magic leaves a trace, like a fingerprint," Thierry explained. "If you'll let me, I can do a spell on Laurent to see that fingerprint. Then, a tracer spell will lead us to his killer."

Every instinct Blair possessed rebelled at the thought of anyone pointing a wand at Laurent.

"It wouldn't hurt him, even if he could feel it," Sebastien promised, understanding Blair's hesitation. He had seen it when Thierry cast a spell on Alain at the gare a few days before.

"It's just an identification spell," Thierry added. "Would it help if I cast the spell on someone else first, so you can see how it works?"

Blair would have preferred that, but he told himself he was being ridiculous. Laurent was dead. Nothing the wizard could do would hurt him now. Something in his demeanor, though, must have given away his hesitations, because Thierry looked at Sebastien. "Will it bother you to let Caroline cast the spell on me?"

Sebastien tensed, but he appreciated Thierry asking first and knew it was the right step to take to help Blair. He nodded shortly, steeling himself to watch a spell, however harmless, directed at his partner, the protectiveness he had not felt since Thibaut died coming to the fore once again.

Caroline knew exactly the spell Thierry wanted and cast it easily, the sparks of her magic dancing around the other wizard for a moment until a pale luminescence arose. "That's the signature," she said for the benefit of the vampires in the room.

Thierry smiled his thanks, then turned to Blair. "A perfectly harmless spell," he repeated. "Is it all right if I try it on Laurent now?"

Blair nodded.

Thierry glanced at Sebastien who also nodded. If Blair was giving permission, they had to take him at his word.

Thierry cast a final glance at Blair before reciting the spell. Catching a trace of magic, he grinned ferally. "Now we see where it leads us." He cast the second spell, the one that would send the misty light toward its source. To everyone's surprise, the light immediately settled around Blair.

"Damn," Thierry cursed. "All I get is your magic, Blair. When you tried to save him, it must have erased the trace of the wizard."

"So what do we do now?" Blair asked flatly, seeing his hope for revenge dwindling.

"I have no idea," Thierry replied. "I didn't even think about your magic."

"Blair," Sebastien said, drawing their attention, "when you tried to save Laurent, could you taste the spell that killed him, or the taint of it?"

Blair considered the question. He had not thought about it at the time, too caught in what he was doing to think of anything else, but now, looking back, there had been an odd taste in Laurent's blood. He nodded.

"Can you do the identification spell on his blood?" Sebastien asked Thierry. "Maybe you could get the trace from there."

"It's worth a try," Thierry replied, every hesitation he had about blood magic gone in the face of his anger and grief over Laurent's death.

Blair raised his wrist to his lips.

"No," Thierry said quickly, stopping him. "I have to draw the blood or the spell won't work." He looked around and saw a needle lying next to the bed in the small cubicle. He picked it up and took Blair's upturned wrist, puncturing the skin so that blood welled to the surface. "Let it fall to the floor," he directed, "so the spell only affects your blood, not you."

Blair flipped his wrist and massaged the limb so that more blood welled, enough to send several drops onto the tile. Thierry cast the spell again and watched the familiar luminescence appear, a slightly different blend of colors than when he had cast it on Laurent's body. That was good. That meant he had a chance of finding his lieutenant's killer. The tracer spell was next, and the light moved toward the door, hovering there, waiting for Thierry to follow.

"Be careful," Caroline instructed behind them. "Getting yourself killed over this won't bring Laurent back."

"We know," Thierry said, turning to face her, "but this has to be done." Gathering the two vampires with a glance, he added, "Wait an hour, then tell Alain. If we're not back by then, he'll know what to do."

Caroline shook her head as they disappeared out the door. She would give them a few minutes, but she was not going to wait an hour to tell Alain.

JOËLLE MORVILLIERS closed the door behind her with a satisfied smile. She had earned Serrier's recognition tonight, bringing down one of Chavinier's lieutenants. She had hoped for an even bigger prize when she led her patrol against Dumont's, but the captain had been notably absent from the battlefield. Still, her spell had taken out the head of the patrol, leaving them in disorganized chaos even when the second patrol arrived. Even better, she had lost fewer of her troops than any patrol that had gone against Chavinier's forces this week. For some reason, casualties had skyrocketed in the past few days, more and more wizards being captured or killed with each battle. Serrier was at a loss to explain it or to counter it, a fact that had left him fuming. The reports of wizards with superhuman strength were causing the most alarm. Serrier's first thought had been the vampires, but the reports had come from day patrols as well as night patrols. Even Serrier's pet vampire had been at a loss to explain that and so the idea had been dismissed. She had seen some evidence of that strength today, but their greater numbers had kept Dumont's patrol pinned, and the reinforcements, when they arrived, had only been interested in rescuing the other patrol, not in taking out her squadron. Serrier had ordered a meeting of his most successful captains for tomorrow morning to discuss ways of dealing with the new advantage the government supporters had suddenly developed. She was beyond thrilled to have been ordered to attend, though she honestly did not know what she could suggest beyond increasing the size of any group that went out.

The thought that despite having carried the day today she would have nothing to contribute tomorrow had her nerves jumping. Serrier was not known for his patience, and his favor was as changeable as the tides. She would worry about that tomorrow, though. For now, she wanted a drink, a meal, a bath and her bed, preferably in that order.

Opening the tantalus, she mixed herself a Campari and tonic, pausing for a moment to appreciate the deep red color, so close to the color of the blood she had spilled that night. Silently toasting her success and Copé's demise, she took a sip and sighed her appreciation of the slightly bitter flavor.

Glass in hand, she wandered in to the kitchen, opening the refrigerator to see about something to eat.

AS they followed the tracer spell, Thierry cast another spell, to identify the charm that had killed Laurent this time. That the wizard had lived long enough for Blair to try to save him told Thierry that his lieutenant's killer had not used an *Abbatoire* curse, since that killed instantly. What he found, though, chilled him to the bone. The spell was a nasty piece of work, intended to cause bleeding in the stomach and lungs, leaving the wizard in debilitating pain as he drowned in his own blood. Thierry's eyes narrowed. Whoever had cast this was not simply a combatant in a war. He was a sadistic bastard as well, but he was about to pay for it. Thierry would see to that!

"Watch yourselves when we find this salaud," Thierry warned. "He didn't just kill Laurent. He killed him slowly and painfully. And if he did it once, he'll do it again."

Sebastien frowned. Thierry was warning them, but of the three of them, the wizard was most vulnerable to attack. He would watch Thierry as well as himself when they found this salaud.

HAVING finished her dinner, Joëlle set the plates in the sink to tend to later and walked down the hall toward the bathroom. Turning on the water, she went into her bedroom to undress. She had just pulled on a robe when the door to her apartment burst open. She grabbed her wand and spun to face the intruders.

"How did you get in?" she hissed when she saw Dumont along with two other men. Her wards should have kept out any wizard, even her own kind.

"Brute force," Thierry replied, his wand in his hand, reminding himself that beautiful woman or not, her magic had killed Laurent in a deliberately painful way.

At the wizard's side, Sebastien measured up his opponent. She was tall for a woman, slender and elegant in her white silk robe. If he had passed her on the street, he would have found her attractive, but the snarl that marred her features and the knowledge of what she had done, the pain she had deliberately inflicted on Laurent that caused anguish in turn to Sebastien's partner, was enough to erase any such sentiments. He saw only a cold-blooded killer, one who undoubtedly would be happy to see the three of them join Laurent.

"Drop your wand and surrender," Thierry ordered. "You're under arrest for the murder of Laurent Copé."

"It's not murder when you're fighting a war," Joëlle spat, trying to decide who to take out first. Dumont was the only one carrying a wand, but the air of menace around the other two men was palpable. Whoever they were, whatever their reasons for being there, they were clearly as much of a threat to her as Dumont. Still, he was the known quantity. Better to start with him. She aimed and cast an *Abbatoire* spell. As much as she would enjoy seeing Dumont suffer, she did not want him to have time to cast a spell as he died. To her surprise, the man to Thierry's left stepped between her and the other wizard, taking her charm directly in the chest. She watched, horrified, as he staggered, only to continue advancing. Before she could say another word, the other man's hand closed around her wrist, crushing the bones. She cried out in pain as her hand lost all feeling and her wand fell to the ground.

"I should do to you what you did to Laurent," Thierry spat, watching as the woman writhed in Blair's grasp.

"Don't," Sebastien and Blair said simultaneously.

"Don't lower yourself to her level," Sebastien added.

"Her death is mine," Blair declared, baring his fangs as he faced the woman who had stolen his partner away from him. "I should make you bleed," he said to Joëlle. "I should prolong your death the way you did Laurent's until you beg for surcease. I gave it to my partner. Don't think you'll be so lucky."

"Don't dishonor Laurent by doing something he would abhor," Sebastien murmured so softly that only Blair's preternatural hearing could pick up the words.

He flinched. Visions of tearing her throat out, of making her bleed as she had done to his partner filled his mind, but Sebastien's words held him back. "You are not worth my soul," he said after a moment, snapping her neck with an efficient twist of his hands. Her weight sagged and he let her fall to the ground unheeded. "This isn't over," he said, turning to Thierry. "I won't rest until every one of them is dead or in prison. I won't be able to go out in the daylight when the last of Laurent's blood wears off, but I will hunt at night, and every one I kill will be one less for you to worry about."

The urge to protest was strong, but Sebastien understood Blair's grief. If fighting this war in his own way helped ease that, the vampire would not question it. He shook his head at Thierry, discouraging his partner from speaking.

"Let's get back to base," Thierry said simply. "I don't want Alain to send out the cavalry."

The two vampires nodded and they started back toward Milice headquarters, each lost in his own thoughts. Blair's only focus now was finding a patrol to go out with until dawn. He would hide away again from the sunlight, prowling the streets at night, a weapon in the hands of the Milice commanders. When there were no more dark wizards, he would decide what would happen next.

Sebastien and Thierry would have been unnerved to realize how closely their thoughts moved in sync. Each one contemplated all that had happened, from Laurent's death through the execution of his murderer. As they moved through the darkened streets, they faced the very real possibility of finding themselves in Blair's shoes some day, each hoping desperately that it did not happen, that they survived the war long enough to see what might come of the startling new feelings growing between them.

One other thought occupied Thierry's mind: Alain would surely demand an explanation, even if Marcel did not. He could face his general if it came to that, but he dreaded facing Alain's knowing eyes and probing questions.

Chapter 33

"WE need to go by my apartment before we start," Jean told Raymond as they left Milice headquarters. "There are certain tokens of my leadership whose display could be used to good effect tonight. I don't wear them on a regular basis, but it won't hurt to subtly remind my peers of my authority in this case."

Raymond nodded, impressed again at the cunning his partner possessed beneath the carefree façade he projected. They arrived at Jean's apartment and Raymond waited patiently in the living room while Jean went to collect what he needed. It sufficed for the wizard to close his eyes and he could see Jean's bedroom as clearly as if he stood there with his partner. Each room in the vampire's apartment contained some marvel, some treasure, but the bedroom was definitely the crowning jewel. He had gone there last, the day before, after warding the rest of Jean's home. The room was not large, but it was stunningly decorated, the centerpiece and focal point of the room being the large, four-poster bed.

Set up on a dais against the far wall, the heavy mahogany was draped with a canopy and curtains of black brocade, the two tones of the cloth providing the most subtle of patterns. The pattern carried over onto the walls, painted an equally dark shade with the slightest bit of gray to break the monotony. Raymond had stared at the arresting sight, speechless, for several long seconds before Jean recalled him to his task. He had flushed, hoping the vampire would not read more into his fascination than a historian's interest in an artifact, resolutely pushing aside the image of Jean's pale skin against the dark sheets. That image returned to haunt him now. He did not know, had not asked, what signs of leadership Jean intended to don. It could be something as simple as a ring or a necklace, some token passed from generation to generation of vampire chef, but that knowledge did not stop Raymond from imagining his partner slipping out of the casual jeans and sweater he had been wearing into something more elaborate for the task to come. The vividness of that image, of the sweater and jeans coming off, startled Raymond enough that his eyes flew open and an involuntary gasp escaped his lips. He had always been rather flexible when it came to the gender of his lovers, but this... this was not simply a question of being interested in a man. This was interest in a vampire! Despite his reservations, despite his fears, or perhaps because of them, Jean had always handled him carefully while they were feeding, and after their fight, the wizard had stopped noticing side effects from the loss of blood. Perhaps this was not as impossible as it seemed, except for one thing. Jean had to be interested in him as well, and so far, he had shown no signs, at least that Raymond could identify, of being so inclined.

The door to Jean's bedroom opened and his partner stepped out, interrupting Raymond's musings. The vampire had changed clothes, a realization that sent a shiver down the wizard's back as he saw again that image of pale skin against the dark furnishings. His eyes raked Jean's appearance, trying to see what would be the marks of leadership they had come back to get. The jeans had been replaced by a pair of dark pants, wool perhaps, topped by a silk shirt the color of ripe wheat or the fields of colza that grew around his home town of Laon. Hanging around his neck was a gold medallion of indeterminate age. That, Raymond decided, was the reminder Jean wanted the other vampires to see.

"May I look at the pendant?" he asked, rising from his seat and approaching his partner.

Jean nodded and held the heavy disk out for Raymond's inspection. The carving on it was Celtic, the scholar in Raymond recognized immediately, but not of any pattern he had seen before. He studied it more closely, trying to make sense of what he saw.

"It tells a story," Jean said without waiting to be asked, "the story of how vampires came to be. At least, that's what monsieur Lombard told me. I can't read it and neither, apparently, could he. Its ownership confers leadership over those of our kind."

"Fascinating," Raymond murmured. "I would love to know what it says."

"You and I and half my peers," Jean chuckled. "Perhaps, when the war is over, you will have the leisure to study it in peace. Who knows, maybe a wizard will succeed in unlocking its mysteries where vampires have failed."

"If we both survive this, I would relish the opportunity," Raymond replied, releasing his hold on the medallion.

"It's a date," Jean quipped. "Now, shall we see what we can do about the rogue? One battle at a time, after all."

Raymond signaled his agreement and followed Jean once again, north to Montmartre. "It seems like I just made these rounds," the vampire commented with a sharp laugh, "not even a week ago to call my kind to a meeting."

"They listened to you then. Let's hope they listen to you now."

Jean agreed and led Raymond into a bustling café. He didn't see anyone he knew right away, but he motioned for Raymond to have a seat at one of the tables while he made his way to the bar. A quick word with the bartender answered his question and he joined Raymond at the table.

"Laetitia will be here soon," he told his partner. "She's due in at nine."

Raymond nodded and ordered an espresso from a passing waiter. If nothing else, it would help them blend in, and he figured Jean was not looking to stand out, at least not here. A few minutes before nine, a tall, slender woman with honey brown hair walked in the door. "There she is," Jean murmured, not moving from his spot.

Raymond sipped the hot drink and waited, curious to see how Jean would handle the situation. The wizard was under no illusion that his presence was anything other than politeness on Jean's part and protection for the vampire if they ran into any of the dark wizards. Raymond had no standing in the vampire community and no real desire to gain any.

Laetitia spoke with the bartender, turning in surprise to look at the two men seated in the back corner. She nodded emphatically and disappeared into the back of the café. Raymond frowned. "Don't worry," Jean assured him. "She'll be with us momentarily. Everything with vampires is a question of power. Making us wait is her way of reminding me that I'm on her turf here. If I went chasing after her or demanded her immediate attention, she'd gain even more because I played into her hand. She'll come to us in time because of who I am and I'll be in control again."

Raymond shook his head. "I had no idea it was so complicated."

Jean chuckled. "You're not alone. We taught intrigue and power play to all the great houses of Europe, but only Louis XIV of France ever truly mastered the game. Only he had the longevity to appreciate its subtleties, and I'm not sure even he could have played against the vampires of his day, only against the rest of the aristocracy."

"Something else for you to teach me," Raymond observed. "Wizards live longer than the average mortal if our lives are not cut short by some spell. I wouldn't want to accidentally cause you to lose face." It only occurred to him after the words left his mouth that he was thinking not only of the alliance but of a longer association as well.

Before Jean could reply, the door to the back of the café opened and Laetitia came back out, making her way to the table where the two men sat. "Twice in a week," she said softly to Jean as she took the seat he pushed out for her. "One would think my help was worth something."

Jean's lips curved into a smile, but Raymond noticed it did not reach his eyes. "Did you help?" he asked coldly. "I didn't see you at the gare the other night. Or maybe you no longer consider yourself my friend."

Laetitia shifted uncomfortably in her chair, not wanting to have that discussion. Her eyes settled on the medallion around Jean's neck and she shifted again. "What can I do for you tonight?"

"Nothing," Jean replied. "I merely thought you should know there's a vampire in Paris killing people."

"You don't think…"

"No, I don't think it's you," Jean interrupted. "I wanted you to know about it. It's in all of our best interests to see him stopped."

"How do you figure that?" Laetitia demanded. "It's not against our laws."

"True," Jean agreed, "but part of what you missed by not coming to the meeting I called is an initiative to grant us equal rights and protection under French law. And if that happens, then killing anyone will be illegal for us. Rogues like this one endanger that for all of us."

Laetitia opened her mouth to comment, but Jean waved her to silence. "Before you say you don't care, think about this. You run this café anonymously, hoping that no one in the neighborhood realizes it's owned and run by a vampire. Most of your customers probably know you're a vampire, but they probably don't realize that you're the patronne. What would happen, currently, if they found out? What would happen if your neighbors found out?"

"You wouldn't!" Laetitia hissed.

"No, I wouldn't," Jean agreed. "I'm not about to put a vampire out of business for any reason unless he or she violates vampire law. But if this initiative is successful, it won't matter. They won't be able to drive you out. And if they try, you'll have recourse under the law, just like any other café owner. Imagine it, Laetitia, not having to hide what you are anymore."

Laetitia pondered Jean's words, her fingernails tapping rhythmically on the table. "Fine, I see the advantages of your initiative. What do you want from me?"

"Information if any comes to you," Jean replied. "The rogue has to be stopped. I have a description of him, but no name. I know he's in Paris, but not where. I'm not asking you to go searching for him yourself, but if you hear anything, I want to know about it."

"Agreed," Laetitia responded after a brief pause. "Information, I can do."

"And if you change your mind and want to hear the rest of what the meeting was about, you know how to find me," Jean added, rising from his chair. Raymond rose with him and followed him out of the café.

"You don't think she'd be more inclined to ask if you mentioned the benefits of the alliance?" he asked as they walked toward their second stop.

"She probably would be," Jean admitted, "but as I'm sure you noticed, there's more going on here, with her, than just the alliance. She's power hungry enough that she would come if I told her, but I'm not positive she would stay with the alliance, and I'd rather not have her breaking her word, not for her sake, but for the perception of vampires in general within the Milice. Her defection, if it happened, would hurt us far more than the kept promises of all the others."

"That, unfortunately, is probably true," Raymond agreed, thinking of the way he was still treated by the majority of the Milice. His work on their behalf was consistently overshadowed by his initial decision to side with Serrier. "So what's our next stop?"

"Somewhere, and someone, very different," Jean replied. "The goth clubs are popular hunting grounds for vampires because the people who frequent them want to meet my kind. They'll also be the first place any witch hunt starts because of that reason. The vampires who go there for food or pleasure need to be warned for their own protection even if they have no information to give us."

That made sense to Raymond as he followed Jean up to one of the clubs. The bouncer recognized Jean as a vampire immediately and gestured for him to come to the front. Jean nodded and Raymond followed him.

"Are you sure your friend wouldn't be happier elsewhere?" the bouncer asked, looking Raymond's conservative attire over disdainfully. "He ain't gonna fit in here at all."

Jean arched an eyebrow, his eyes glittering dangerously. "He's with me," he replied coldly.

The bouncer shook his head, starting to refuse. Jean stepped forward, pinning the big man to the wall. "I said he's with me. You really don't want me to tell my vampires that our friends aren't welcome here, do you? They might reconsider their patronage."

Before the man could reply, the manager came outside. "What seems to be the problem?" he asked conciliatorily.

"Buster here doesn't want to let my partner come inside with me," Jean said bluntly. "I was just explaining to him that alienating the chief vampire in the city could be very bad for business."

The manager took one look at the threat in Jean's eyes and conceded. "That surely won't be necessary," he assured the vampire. "Any friend of a vampire's is welcome here."

"Make sure you tell your staff that," Jean informed him. "I think you'll see a lot more of us moving with mortal company over the next few months, and we won't be going anywhere our friends aren't welcome."

"I'll make it very clear," the manager promised, leading the men inside. "What can I offer you to make up for the inconvenience?"

Jean gestured for Raymond to choose whatever he wanted, but Raymond demurred. He was on duty. Alcohol was definitely not the best choice. The manager left them alone after making them promise to seek him out if there was anything he could do. Raymond was inwardly impressed at Jean's changeable disposition. He seemed to know just the right note to hit with each person he talked to. When another vampire joined them in a few minutes, he felt his opinion rise even more. Unlike with Laetitia, Jean spoke to this vampire without any of the confrontational attitude, relating the news of the rogue without preamble. The other vampire's reaction indicated to Raymond right away that he understood the implications.

"Do you have a description?"

Jean outlined the information they had.

"I think he was here a couple of nights ago," the vampire told Jean. "He was bad news. They found the girl he left with in an alley. I don't think they reported it since it would be bad for business, but I was still here when it happened."

"Did you get a name, Julien, or anything else that could help us locate him?" Jean asked.

Julien concentrated for a brief moment. "I was standing near the bar when he picked up his *date*. I think he told her his name was Edouard. He's a piece of work if this is the same guy. He looks like he's a kid, sweet and innocent, barely old enough to get in a place like this. Nobody will ever suspect him just from seeing him."

Raymond froze, hearing that name. He had no way of knowing for sure if it was the same vampire who had killed his friend when he was a teenager, but the name was the same. He did not interrupt to mention it, but he would talk to Jean about it before the night was over.

"If he comes back in, I need to know about it," Jean said. "You know how to reach me. I can be here in a matter of minutes."

Julien promised to let Jean know if he saw Edouard again. "I didn't get a chance to tell you the other night," Julien continued, changing the subject, "but I think what you're doing with the Milice is wonderful. I don't know what I can do since I didn't find a partner, but you have my support if you need it."

"If you can help us find this Edouard, you're already helping," Jean assured him. "Beyond that..." Jean turned to Raymond.

"There was at least one squadron of wizards that didn't make it that night because they were on patrol and didn't get back in time," Raymond offered. "If you want to try, you might find a partner in one of them. And even if you don't, you could still go out at night with a team."

"I'll think about it," Julien promised.

"We have one more stop to make," Jean told Julien with a smile. "We'll be waiting for any new information you get."

Leaving the club, they walked down the Boulevard de Clichy toward the Moulin Rouge and Angelique's establishment. They knocked and were admitted by Angelique's manager. He greeted both men with a welcoming smile.

Jean introduced Raymond, then asked, "Is Angelique in?"

"In her office," François replied, "and in a bitch of a mood."

"We heard all about that," Jean responded with a rueful smile. "I'll see what I can do to coax her out of it."

"If anyone can, it'll be you," François answered confidently.

"I hope you're right," Jean laughed, leading Raymond toward Angelique's office. He tapped on the door and it swung open to admit them.

"I don't want to hear about it," she declared, taking one look at the two men.

"We're not here to talk about David," Jean assured her calmly. "We have bigger fish to fry."

Chapter 34

ANGELIQUE frowned, anger set aside in the face of Jean's serious concern. "What's going on?" she asked, shutting the door.

"Are your security cameras working?" he asked in reply.

"Yes, of course," Angelique assured him.

"Can you pull up the tape of the vampire who came in seeking 'disposable company'? I want to see who he is."

"Give me a minute," Angelique requested. She went to the door and called François to her office, asking what time the other vampire had come. His reply in hand, she pulled up the recording from that night and skimmed through to the approximate time. Finding the scene, she froze it and stepped back so Jean and Raymond could see. "What's going on?" she repeated.

Jean did not reply right away, studying the face on the screen. He already had the description from Angelique before, so it was not so much the other's features that interested the senior vampire but his expression. This... creature – for Jean did not even want to dignify his behavior with the name of vampire – was responsible for at least two deaths in the past few days, and Jean wanted to see if it showed on his face. What he saw chilled him. If this Edouard had been ugly, warped, misshapen somehow, it would have been easier for something of his evil would have showed on his face, but no sign appeared, other than the deadened eyes. In those, Jean saw more than he wanted to know. No remorse, no emotion whatsoever, colored the pale blue orbs. "Watch out for him," Jean said softly. "If he comes back, get word to me immediately, but don't leave him alone with any of your employees. He's killed twice already in just a few days. I wouldn't put it past him to kill again."

Angelique nodded. "I'll do what I can," she promised, "but I won't put François at risk either. If he gets nasty, he'll be thrown out on his arse just like anyone else."

Jean smiled. "Always the blunt one," he said with a smile, then his face turned serious. "He has to be stopped, Angelique. I don't have to tell you what kind of repercussions this could have for all of us, but especially for you and the other entrepreneurs. People won't wait to see which vampire is responsible. They'll ostracize us all at the least. At worst, we'll be persecuted again the way we were in the past."

Angelique nodded, staring at the face on the screen. "All for his irresponsibility," she murmured. "If the consequences of it weren't so grave, I'd drag him out in the sun myself and just leave him to burn."

Jean chuckled. "I had the same thought, but that isn't our way, not unless he commits a crime against one of us. So far, he's been smart enough to avoid that. It doesn't mean, though, that we can't work a little peer pressure on him. He needs to know that we won't tolerate his killing, even if it isn't strictly against our laws."

"Maybe it's time to make it against your laws," Raymond suggested, intervening in the conversation for the first time. He needed to speak with Jean about this vampire, but he preferred not to do so in front of Angelique. As he was still learning the rules of Le Jeu des Cours, he did not want to do anything that might endanger his partner's status through his own ignorance.

"I've tried," Jean replied, "but when we aren't given the protection of mortal law, it's a hard sell to convince my kind that we should protect them."

"Then maybe Marcel's policy of secrecy concerning the alliance is not the best policy," Raymond observed. "Maybe it's time to introduce the bills in the parlement that would protect your kind in exchange for your agreement to abide by our laws. Then you'd have legal recourse to stop the kind of witch hunt this Edouard could provoke."

"It isn't too soon?" Jean asked.

"It's not my decision to make," Raymond pointed out, "but we stand to lose far more to any kind of racial cleansing than we would by letting Serrier know about the alliance. I'm not talking about revealing everything, only that the vampires are fighting on the side of the government and that in return, the government should acknowledge their rights as citizens."

"If you're going to discuss the alliance, I'd appreciate you taking the conversation elsewhere," Angelique interjected peevishly. "Right now, I don't particularly trust any wizard, not with 'mine' as an example. I don't want anything to do with that close-minded bastard."

"Come now, Angelique," Jean chided gently. "There's no need for name calling."

"No need?" Angelique hissed. "Tell him that. Until he gets his head out of his arse and apologizes, I don't want anything to do with him or the alliance. This deal with the rogue is different. That affects me, alliance or not, but the rest... I don't want any part of it for now."

"He's willing to apologize," Jean assured her. "You just have to come back so he can."

Angelique considered it. She hated the implications of what David had said, hated the suggestion that she somehow took advantage of the employees she worked so hard to protect. She wanted to say to hell with him and the alliance and everything that was not a part of her business. The words would not come, though, no matter how she tried to say them. She simply could not walk away from the promises she had made or the inexplicable pull that drew her to David even when she wanted nothing to do with him. "Not tonight," she decided. "Maybe not tomorrow. I need a little time to cool off or else I'm likely to hurt him. I'll let you know when I'm ready, but even then, he's going to have to come to me."

"That's all I can ask," Jean replied. "We'll leave you to your business then. We still have some tasks of our own to attend to."

Raymond looked at Jean, surprised, but held his tongue. He had expected his partner to do more to influence Angelique, but it seemed the vampire chief had no intention of bringing his authority to bear. Keeping his own counsel, he bade Angelique a good evening and followed Jean back outside. "I thought this was our last stop," he commented. "What other business do we have?"

"None," Jean responded, "but to leave after her declaration with no suitable excuse would be to lose face in the game. Even with my 'friends' I have my role to consider. Pressuring Angelique will not help. I have known her for centuries, and she will not be persuaded beyond what I did tonight. To linger would only have made us all uncomfortable for no reason."

Raymond shook his head. "I can see why it takes decades and more to learn this game of yours. So where to next?"

"Back to my apartment," Jean answered. "I want to drop off the medallion and change back into more comfortable clothes. After that, it's up to you."

Dark, erotic images flashed into his mind. Raymond shook his head, reminding himself it was the effect of the bond and not any real interest in his partner that drove such thoughts. "We'll see," he evaded, starting toward the subway.

The ride back to Jean's apartment passed in silence, each man lost in his own thoughts. While Jean went into his bedroom to change, Raymond busied himself studying the books in his partner's library, hoping to find something of interest to distract him from visions of the vampire in his room. Despite the wealth of knowledge in the room, he found his thoughts straying outside his conscious control, found himself wondering if Jean's skin was as pale everywhere as on his face, if the skin of his chest was smooth or covered in a dusting of hair like his chin. When Jean joined him in the library, Raymond looked up with a smile, the warmth of his thoughts carrying over into his expression. "I didn't want to say anything earlier, but do you remember the story I told you about the boy in my village?"

"The one who was killed by a vampire?" Jean asked. He noticed the unusual expression on Raymond's face and paused long enough for his body to absorb the reaction to the look. With a suppressed frown, he reminded himself of all his resolutions concerning Karine.

"Yes," Raymond replied, his smile fading at the lack of reaction from Jean and from the seriousness of their conversation. "His name was Edouard, and from the sound of the vampire we're dealing with now, it might be one and the same."

"It's certainly possible," Jean agreed. "You didn't recognize him from the video at Sang Froid?"

"No, but I never met him at the time. My friend was very secretive about it all, mentioning his name but never wanting any of us to meet him, almost like he was afraid we'd steal the vampire away." Raymond shuddered again at the thought.

"You said they'd been associated for some time before he died. I'm not sure if that's a good sign or a bad sign."

"What do you mean?" Raymond asked, curiously.

"He killed his victim outside the bar almost immediately," Jean explained. "That could mean he's escalating, which isn't good, because if he is, the murders will get more and more brutal, and probably more frequent."

"I see how it's a bad sign, but how could it possibly be a good sign?"

"It means he was once capable of feeding without killing," Jean replied. "Perhaps enough of that humanity remains to persuade him to change his ways."

SERRIER walked into the darkened room. "Did you enjoy your plaything last night?"

Edouard opened his eyes, the shadows no impediment to his enhanced sight. "Very much."

"I'm glad," Serrier replied. "I've upheld my end of the bargain. Now it's time for you to uphold yours. I need information. I need to know why the vampires met last week. My forces are being decimated by opponents of extraordinary strength. If half the battles hadn't been fought during the day, I'd think Chavinier had formed an alliance with your kind. Maybe that's it, maybe it's not, but I need to know who my people are fighting."

"What do you want me to do?" Edouard asked defensively. "I already told you I'm an outsider in their circles."

"What you do is up to you," Serrier replied coldly. "But if you don't keep your end of the bargain, I'll make sure that a recording of you with that girl is released to the local police. You won't be safe anywhere in Europe when the identity of the serial killer vampire gets out."

"Serial killer?" Edouard challenged with a frown.

"Oh, yes," Serrier assured him, "because if you don't cooperate, I'll make sure plenty of other young girls are found with the same marks on their bodies as you left on your last victim. You'll be blamed whether you were involved or not."

Edouard's eyes narrowed. He should have known better than to trust a mortal, and a wizard at that. "I'll do what I can," he spat, "but think carefully about crossing me, human. I can do things to you that will make the tortures I inflicted on that girl look like child's play."

Serrier felt the chill of that threat, but he let none of it show on his face. He was not one to show weakness. Ever. "Don't threaten me, boy," he replied coldly, his ire summoning sparks of magic to dance around their heads. "You may be stronger than I am physically, but you have no concept of the power I can command. Do your work like a good little vampire and I'll see you rewarded. Cross *me* and you'll regret it forever."

WITH a deep sigh full of fatigue and frustration, Marcel let himself into his office and slumped in the chair, all of his one hundred ten years weighing on him as he thought about his day and the demands of the government officials wanting to know when the war would be over. He had not dared tell any of them about the vampires, not wanting to risk the secret getting out prematurely. Taking another deep breath, he summoned Alain to his office, wanting to know what had transpired during his absence.

To his surprise, not only did Alain and Orlando come to his office, Thierry, Jean, Sebastien, and Raymond joined them as well, along with a vampire Marcel did not know by name.

"What are you still doing here?" he asked Thierry.

"Getting himself in trouble," Alain replied with a scowl for his best friend.

"Like you wouldn't have done exactly the same thing in my spot," Thierry retorted with a glare.

Orlando looked at Marcel pleadingly. "They've been arguing like this for the past hour. Please make them stop."

Alain and Thierry utterly ignored the vampire, continuing to snipe at one another in the way of best friends or brothers. Marcel raised an eyebrow and cleared his throat. "Report," he ordered sharply.

Both wizards snapped to attention, their focus switching from each other to their general. "Yes, sir," they replied immediately, though each waited for the other to begin.

"Alain, report," Marcel said with a frustrated sigh. He had not expected to come back to this kind of chaos from his usually disciplined seconds.

In concise, though clearly disapproving tones, Alain related the events leading up to Laurent's death and Thierry's decision to go after the other wizard's killer.

"She wasn't just an enemy combatant," Thierry protested. "She slaughtered him, Marcel, and not quickly or kindly. The spell she used caused him to die a slow, painful death. It was probably a mercy that Blair tried to turn him instead of letting the spell take its course."

Marcel frowned. "What?" he asked. Turning to Blair, he requested, "Can you tell me what happened up until the time these two got involved? I have the feeling I'm missing half the story."

Alain and Thierry both opened their mouths to protest. "And not a word from either of you until I ask for it," Marcel added sternly. "I need to know what happened so I can decide what to do now."

Meanwhile, Jean glanced at Blair with a look of surprise and concern on his face. That the vampire had lost his partner was shocking enough, but to learn that he had tried to turn his partner to no avail was even worse.

"We went out on patrol," Blair explained, clearly not used to giving reports. "Laurent was in charge because Thierry had to stay here."

"Because I was gone," Marcel encouraged with a smile.

"Yes. So we went to Montparnasse. Everything was fine and then we ran into an ambush, I guess. We were pinned down. Laurent called for help."

"I got the call and sent Lt. Fouquet along with my patrol to help," Alain interjected, despite Marcel's demand that he let Blair give the report.

Marcel nodded but kept his attention focused on Blair. "Laurent called for help and what happened then?"

"The other patrol came to help, but right as they got there, Laurent went down. I didn't hear the spell, didn't see who cast it. I only saw him collapse like a rag doll. I got there as fast as I could, but the other wizards said there wasn't anything they could do, anything anyone could do, that he was dying and nothing could stop that. I can't stop death, but I could have kept him with me – I should have been able to keep him with me, to turn him," Blair finished, his voice wavering with the force of his emotions. "I don't know why it didn't work."

"Think about what was different this time," Jean suggested, his eyes asking Marcel's permission to intervene. Marcel nodded permission and sat back to listen.

"I don't know," Blair replied. "I could taste the taint of the other wizard's magic, but I could also taste Laurent. He didn't want to die. He was fighting to stay alive. He understood what I was offering and he accepted it. He agreed to it."

"He did," Orlando averred, wanting it very clear that Blair had offered distinctly and Laurent had consented. He had seen more than one vampire ostracized because people doubted his word after he turned one of their family or friends.

"You said you could taste his magic," Raymond clarified. "You said it was fighting to keep him alive. Are you sure of that?"

"As sure as I can be," Blair retorted.

Raymond raised his hands placatingly. "I'm not doubting your word, I'm just trying to figure out what happened."

"Do you have an idea?" Marcel asked urgently.

"A hypothesis anyway," Raymond replied. "If Laurent's magic was fighting to keep him alive, it could well have fought Blair's blood magic just as it fought the dark wizard's magic that killed him. Unfortunately, there's no way to test my idea."

"Nothing could have reversed that spell," Thierry insisted, interrupting Raymond's musings. "Laurent was bleeding in the gut and lungs. Blair might have saved him a few minutes of agony, nothing was going to stop him from dying."

"Nobody's casting blame," Marcel assured everyone in the room, "at least not on anyone here. The vampires have more than proven their trustworthiness to me. If Blair says Laurent consented to be turned, I have no reason to doubt him. I am, however, concerned by the fact that Blair couldn't turn Laurent when he tried. Raymond, see if you can find anything to support your theory. Once again, we're butting up against the limitations of the partnerships and we have to understand them." He turned to Thierry. "Your turn, captain. What possessed you to go after Laurent's killer alone?"

"I didn't go alone," Thierry protested. "Sebastien and Blair went with me."

"Then what possessed the three of you to go after Laurent's killer alone?" Marcel repeated.

"It was my idea," Sebastien spoke up, diverting everyone's attention from Thierry. "I knew what Blair would be feeling having lost Laurent and thought going after the bitch would give him something else to focus on."

"The motivation was sound," Jean interjected. "Vampires suffering a loss have been known to make rash decisions. Sometimes that gets turned inward and they hurt themselves. Other times, it gets turned outward and they hurt those around them. Either way, it's not a good idea to leave a grieving vampire to his own devices."

"Be that as it may," Marcel replied, taking control of the conversation again, "Thierry knows better than to go off alone completely disregarding protocol. I might agree that the spell used on Laurent was inhumane and that the caster deserved her fate and probably worse, but we have procedures for a reason, as you well know, Thierry, since you helped me draft them. How would Alain feel if you had gotten in trouble out there and he didn't know where you were? Did you even have your repère with you?"

Thierry had the good grace to blush under Marcel's dressing down. "No, I didn't have it," he admitted, "and I know how Alain would have felt. I felt the same way when he told me Laurent had been killed."

Marcel shook his head. "You're too hot-headed for your own good sometimes," he declared with a sigh. "I'd hoped your partner would temper that, but it seems like finds like. Don't go off on a vendetta alone again. I couldn't bear to lose you."

Thierry met Marcel's eyes and offered a silent promise. He had not thought before he went after the dark wizard tonight with so little backup, but he would not do it again. He rarely thought about it, the demands of the job keeping him from dwelling on the risks they all took, but he knew Marcel viewed them all as his children, however grown. The cost to the older wizard each night when they went out on patrol, risking their lives out of loyalty to him, must be enormous. He resolved not to forget that again.

"Now, what else has happened while I was away?" Marcel asked.

"We got the repères working as you know," Thierry reported, "but the second test case was a bust."

"David couldn't get the spell to work?" Marcel asked, surprised. It was not a difficult spell.

"David never got a chance to try the spell," Thierry elucidated. "When he went with Angelique to find something to use as her repère, he said some stupid things and she booted his arse out. Jean was going to talk to her tonight, see what she had to say."

"She's not a happy woman right now," Jean added, taking up the tale. "He insulted the foundation of who she is. She's said she'll consider letting him apologize eventually, but it's going to take a lot of groveling on his part if he expects her to treat him with any respect from here on."

"I already tore strips off his hide," Thierry offered. "He'll apologize when she gives him the chance, but there's no point in sending him there until she's ready to listen."

"That's definitely true," Raymond agreed, having seen Angelique's attitude for himself. "We also were able to get a picture of the rogue vampire your spy reported to us."

"I put the word out to look out for him and to notify me if he comes around," Jean elaborated, "but that could take days or weeks. I don't know where he's finding his victims, but from what I know of our enemy, Serrier could well be feeding him. If that's the case, he may not need to visit any of the typical vampire haunts. What worries me the most is the complete lack of emotion in his eyes. It's like his soul has died. I know what the stories say about us, but for the most part, only our bodies are changed when we become vampires. We don't become inherently evil just because we're vampires. This one, though, is the vampire out of all the horror stories."

Marcel sighed. "Of course. What other kind of vampire would be attracted to Serrier's evil? So what do we do now?"

"We take the alliance public," Raymond averred firmly. "I watched the other vampires tonight and the reason they agreed to help Jean find this creature is because they fear reprisals against them – a sort of genocide. What we need is for them to see what he's doing as wrong, not just threatening to their lifestyle. They need to see movement at least on our part, bills introduced in parlement, some sort of official acknowledgment of Jean's role within the Milice. They need to have a reason to trust us and help us besides fear."

Marcel arched an eyebrow. "That's a lot faster than we planned," he observed.

"It is," Raymond agreed, "but that doesn't mean it's too fast. Things have changed, Marcel. If we stick blindly to an outdated plan, we're condemning ourselves."

"What do you think, Jean?" Marcel asked.

"Raymond and I discussed it earlier. I think his points are valid. The only question is whether we've contributed enough so far to convince the lawmakers in parlement to consider our request. If they haven't, if we're still so low in their esteem that they're not even open to the discussion, then it's better to wait until we have more to convince them."

"But left unchecked, Edouard's killing spree only adds to the doubts," Raymond protested, hoping Marcel would see what Jean did not.

"I'll start putting out feelers tomorrow," Marcel decided, "after I've gotten a little sleep and don't feel like something on the bottom of someone's shoe. Alain, I need to talk to you a little more. The rest of you are dismissed."

The others stood and milled about, making their way to the door. As requested, Alain remained seated. To Marcel's surprise, so did Orlando.

"I'm glad you stayed, Orlando," Marcel said, mustering a smile for the vampire. "What Sebastien said about vampires dealing with loss has me worried about Blair. Thierry's patrol has already suffered the loss of one member. I'd hate to have them lose another if we can stop it."

"You want *me* to keep an eye on him?" Orlando asked, stunned. He would not have expected such responsibility from the elder wizard. "Surely someone else would do a better job!"

"Who?" Alain interrupted. "And what makes you think you wouldn't do a good job? You've got to stop discounting yourself, Orlando. From what I heard, you were instrumental in getting the rest of Thierry's patrol back safely. If you can do that, you can keep vigil with Blair, at least until we know he's stable."

The unquestioning faith Alain had in him bolstered Orlando's confidence. Maybe he could do this. He did not want to fail, but even if he did, he would have tried. He could not bear to see the disappointment on Alain's face if he declined. "All right," he agreed after a moment's reflection. "I'll do my best."

"That's all I ask of any of my people," Marcel assured him as the vampire rose.

Alain caught Orlando's hand before his partner could leave the room. "I'll come find you when I'm done here and we can decide how to handle Blair's situation long term if he's still unstable." He wanted to pull Orlando's head down for a kiss, but he was not sure how Orlando or Marcel would react to that gesture. Instead he squeezed his lover's hand, meeting his eyes with an intimate smile.

Orlando returned the squeeze and the smile, then slipped out the door to find Blair.

As soon as the door shut behind the vampire, Alain turned back to Marcel. "What's so important or secretive that you couldn't discuss it with me in front of Orlando? I won't keep secrets from him."

"Nothing so serious as that," Marcel promised. "I just wanted to check on you and I wanted you to be able to speak freely. Your partnership, from what I understand, is much more... involved than the others. We haven't had a chance to talk since before all this happened. I wanted to make sure you're well."

Alain smiled, thinking of all that his partnership entailed. "I am well," he insisted. "In fact, I can't remember ever being better. I loved Henri, but I had fallen out of love with Edwige long before they were killed. I miss them, but it's him I really miss, not her, not as a companion, a lover. I missed having a companion, but not anymore."

"You moved in with him, correct?" Marcel pressed.

Alain nodded. "You know what an empty hell that studio was for me. I wouldn't have asked anyone to move in there with me, and his apartment is perfect for his needs, with a room where he can go to escape the daylight if ever he needs to."

"His need for blood isn't too demanding?"

Alain shook his head. "This protects me from that," he said, gesturing to the brand on his neck. "The magic that binds us together makes it possible for him to take as much as he wants as often as he wants without it hurting me."

"You're sure?" Marcel questioned.

"It certainly seems that way," Alain replied, "and Sebastien had an Avoué before. Most of what we know about our Aveu de Sang comes from him, but so far, everything he's told us has played out."

"That's good, and you should continue to talk to him about anything that arises, but remember that his Avoué was not a wizard," Marcel warned. "Your magic may affect the bond in ways Sebastien hasn't experienced."

"Orlando would deny himself before he would hurt me," Alain assured his mentor, thinking of their encounter earlier that night. "I don't have anything to fear from him."

"What about the others?" Marcel asked with deceptive calm. "Do they have anything to fear from their partners?"

Alain frowned. "What do you mean? From overfeeding?"

"I don't know," Marcel replied. "You tell me. You've talked to more sets of partners than I have. Are any of the wizards feeling put upon by their partners, feeling like their partners are expecting too much?"

"Nobody's said anything to me," Alain answered, "but they might not, knowing about Orlando and me. Have you asked Thierry?"

"No, nor do I intend to. Thierry has enough other things to worry about without adding this to the list, especially now that Laurent is gone. I had hoped the lad would take some of the load off Thierry, but now we're back to square one, so to speak, with Thierry having to train another lieutenant. I need you to stay on top of this problem for me, if it is a problem."

"Do you really think it's going to be a problem?" Alain asked, thinking about the pairings he had contact with besides himself and Orlando. Thierry had expressed some concern the first day, but since then, all had seemed well between him and Sebastien. Obviously, Laurent and Blair had bonded well if Blair's reactions tonight were any indication. David was having problems, but that was more because David was a pompous idiot than because of anything inherent in the partnerships. Even Raymond seemed to be finding a way to make his partnership work despite his initial concerns. The only other problem he could identify was Adèle and Jude, but that seemed more a clash of personalities than a question of the demands of the partnership.

"I don't know," Marcel replied, "but I would rather be prepared than caught unawares."

"Fine," Alain said. "I'll ask around, see if anyone has any concerns they're not bringing to you for some reason."

Marcel watched his captain leave, wondering if he should have confided in Alain the theory Raymond had shared with the old general. Not yet, he decided. Not until he knew it was more than just the hypothesizing of two philosophers. If Raymond and Lombard were right, it would not take an Aveu de Sang to bind the other partners together. The magic that let the wizards' blood protect their partners would create that bond instead.

Chapter 35

THIERRY fingered the bite marks on his neck, eyes focused on Sebastien's retreating back. The vampire wanted to check on Blair, to make sure the other vampire was coping with his loss. Thierry had urged him to go, saying he would finish up some paperwork while he waited. What he really wanted, though, was time to think. Each time Sebastien fed from him, and it was far more frequently and far less deeply than he had expected, Thierry felt the partnership deepen, felt the bonds between them tighten. A part of him wanted to give in to the fire that tore through him every time Sebastien touched him, fed from him.

He watched Alain and Orlando when they were not paying attention, saw the bone-deep dedication that existed between them, the sparks that seemed to fly every time their eyes met or their hands touched, and he craved that connection, that passion. He and Aleth had been estranged since the war began, but he had stayed faithful, hoping they could reconcile their differences. That was no longer possible, yet her memory held him back, as imprisoned by the failure of their marriage as he had been by his marriage vows. How could he possibly make a relationship work with a creature as foreign to him as Sebastien was if he could not make one work with one of his own kind?

Even if he could set aside his fear of another failed relationship, another fear held him back. While he had never cared about Alain's sexual preference, it was not one he had shared. He had never looked at a man with more than friendship in mind, had no idea how to tell if what he felt for Sebastien was real or purely a product of loneliness and the close proximity, the incredible sensuality, even sexuality, of feeding.

And if he was interested, what about Sebastien? How could he tell if the vampire felt the same way? He knew Sebastien would not have a problem with him being a man – the vampire's Avoué had been male – but their conversation earlier had suggested that Sebastien was not interested in a new relationship. The vampire spoke of his Avoué, and the man's loss, as if it were recent, as recent as Thierry's own loss, yet he told his partner that he had been alone for four hundred years. Four hundred years. If it had been that long and Sebastien was still in love with the man, what hope did Thierry have of catching his attention? Was he opening himself up for even more heartbreak if he acted on what he might be feeling?

He had no answers to any of his questions. With a sigh, he sagged back against the couch, hoping Alain would come by their office before Sebastien returned from checking on Blair. Maybe his best friend would have some insight into some of his problems. It was tempting, in the meantime, to do something about the nagging ache in his groin. He supposed it was some small blessing that Sebastien had not felt it while he fed, but then again, the vampire had been mostly beside him, leaning slightly on his chest, but not making any move toward greater intimacy. He could still feel his partner's hot hand on his jaw as Sebastien tipped the wizard's head back to gain access to his neck. He could sense the lingering echo of the hard body pressed against his side. His hand slid lower as his mind conjured Sebastien's presence, stroking himself through the wool of his trousers.

Before he could do any more than heighten the arousal he was already feeling, the door opened and Alain stepped inside, his face a deliberately blank mask that Thierry recognized as the one his friend wore when he was truly troubled about something. His own problems went right out of his mind as he focused on what might have put Alain in such a state. "What's wrong?"

Alain looked up, surprised to see Thierry still there. "I expected you to be on your way home, if not already there."

Thierry's hand went automatically to his neck, inadvertently revealing to Alain how he and Sebastien had passed the last half an hour. Alain's mask broke under the force of his grin. "I guess you've changed your tune about the requirements of the alliance," he teased lightly, eyes searching Thierry's face for some sign of his feelings about the situation.

Alain had not answered his question, and Thierry had every intention of coming back to it, but in the meantime, his friend had just handed him the opening he needed to bring up what was on his mind. "Yeah, I guess it just took finding the right partner."

Alain's grin broadened, unable to resist the opportunity to poke gentle fun at his usually serious friend. "Never thought I'd see you hooked up with another man."

In the past, Thierry would have blustered and denied any interest in that quarter and their game would have continued, but Alain's words were far too close to the truth for him to play that game anymore. "About that," he began, not sure exactly what he wanted to ask.

Sensing Thierry's seriousness, Alain dropped the teasing and joined his friend on the couch, nudging his legs over so he had a place to sit. "What's on your mind?"

"I don't even know," Thierry replied, though he did know. "This is turning out far differently than I expected."

"In what sense?" Alain probed.

Thierry took a deep breath, incredibly uncomfortable with the entire conversation, but knowing Alain would not make fun of him. Much. "Does it... excite you when Orlando feeds?"

Once again, the conversation had taken an unexpected turn, but Alain took it in stride. He and Thierry had never kept secrets from each other and if answering the personal question could help his best friend, he would do so honestly. Even so, his eyes dropped unconsciously toward Thierry's lap, looking to see if the other wizard shared his reaction. "More than almost anything else he does." He paused, then decided he would rather give Thierry too much information than not enough. "He can make me come just from his fangs in my neck."

Thierry's eyes closed as the remembered bliss washed through him again, Sebastien's body so close to his, the vampire's mouth and teeth on his neck, seeming to find unerringly the most sensitive spot. His body throbbed desperately, wanting to feel Sebastien against him again, even closer than he had been before. It had been so long since Thierry had felt any touch other than his own hand that the mere thought of another source of release strained his already tenuous control. "I feel like a horny teenager again," he admitted. "He touches me and I'm ready to go off. I haven't, but only because I haven't dared. I've been alone for so long, Alain. Is it wrong for me to feel this way? Aleth only died a week ago."

Alain's face tightened. Thierry's last sentence was certainly true, but it did not tell the whole story. "No, it's not wrong. She left you, despite what you hoped, a long time ago. It makes sense that you're ready to move on, especially since you've found someone who's caught your interest."

"So what do I do now?" Thierry asked.

Alain could not help himself. He laughed out loud. "Mark this day on your calendar. The day the great Thierry Dumont asked me for help with a conquest."

"Shut up," Thierry retorted, blushing despite himself. "This is different. If I'd paired with une nana, I'd know exactly what to do, but Sebastien's no woman."

"No," Alain agreed, dropping the teasing tone. As much as he enjoyed poking fun at his friend, he also understood what a monumental step the other wizard was considering. "What do you want to know?" he offered instead. "You know I'll help any way I can."

What did he want to know? The mechanics of sex with a man was too daunting a subject to raise this soon. Besides, he suspected that if it ever got to that point, Sebastien would be happy to guide him. "How do I know if he's interested?"

Alain considered the question, not only in light of Sebastien's gender but also the fact that he was a vampire. "How often does he want to feed?" he asked after a moment's pause.

"Pretty much every day," Thierry replied with a tell-tale blush as he thought about how much he enjoyed those times.

Alain's eyebrows shot up. "That often?"

Thierry nodded. "Is that a problem?"

"Not if you're feeling okay," Alain replied, "but Orlando said vampires don't usually need to feed more than once every few days. That certainly seems like a sign of interest to me. He wants to be close to you. And if he's feeding from you that often, he's almost certainly not going anywhere else for blood. I'm pretty sure too much blood is as bad for a vampire as too little."

"What else?" Thierry asked. "I don't want to do this if I'm going to get shot down before I ever leave the starting gate. This is hard enough as it is."

"You came in together when you decided to go after Laurent's killer. Did you go home together?" Alain asked.

Thierry nodded. "He suggested it. Not that we go to my house, I mean, but that we stay together."

"Another good sign," Alain pointed out.

"Unless he was just being safe," Thierry countered.

"That's certainly possible," Alain agreed, "but he doesn't strike me as one to do something unless he wants to do it. He especially doesn't strike me as someone to *suggest* something he doesn't want to do."

"So what do I do now?" Thierry asked. "I mean, if you're right and he's interested."

"What do you want to do?" Alain questioned in return. "Because you don't have to do anything. You can keep treating him as you have been, make your partnership work for the sake of the alliance and shake his hand goodbye when the war's over."

Thierry frowned. He had not even considered doing nothing, at least not if there was any chance that Sebastien was interested. "I don't know what I want, but I know I want more than what I have."

Alain laughed. "That was quite the convoluted thought, but I understand what you mean. Are you looking for something permanent?" he asked, going straight to the heart of the matter.

"I don't know," Thierry said again. "I just know I want more. I'm so tired of being alone."

Alain's heart clenched at the pain in his friend's voice. Thierry had been such a rock after Edwige and Henri died. He felt a little guilty now for having neglected his friend these past few days after Aleth's death. "I know how you feel," he said instead. "I want you to be happy. If you think Sebastien can put a smile back on your face, then you have my unconditional support. You know that. Just tell me how to help."

"You could ask him if he's interested," Thierry quipped, hiding his discomfiture behind teasing banter. Even now, looking at his best friend, an undeniably attractive man, he felt no attraction there. He had never questioned it before because he had never been attracted to any man. Now, though, he wondered what it was about Sebastien that could so capture his attention when no other man had, even one he had been so close to for so long.

Looking at the situation analytically, he recognized that wizard and vampire shared many of the traits that Thierry found so attractive in Sebastien: their sense of humor, their courage, their willingness to stand beside him no matter what. Alain was light where Sebastien was dark, but Aleth had been fair as well, so that should not have made a difference. He could think of only two differences: his childhood spent at Alain's side, a shared history that cast them in the role of brothers before either of them had ever considered sex, and the unique connection between himself and Sebastien that stemmed from the vampire's need for his blood. He shivered a little, wondering what that said about him.

Alain laughed, breaking Thierry out of his thoughts. "If that's really what you want me to do, I'll go find him right now."

Thierry shook his head emphatically. "Shit, Alain! You know I was just talking noise. I'll figure that out on my own, thank you very much. Mostly, I just needed to hear that you thought I wasn't making a mistake."

"I don't think you're making a mistake," Alain assured him. "Take your time, enjoy the anticipation, but definitely go for it if this is what you want."

"It is," Thierry declared firmly. "Now I just have to figure out how to tell him that."

"That's always the hard part," Alain agreed. "If you need any other advice, like on how to seduce a man, just let me know."

"I'm sure you're a fountain of wisdom," Thierry retorted, "but I'll figure that out on my own."

"I'm sure Sebastien will be glad to help you."

In the hallway, Sebastien smiled. He had been about to enter the office when he heard Thierry's voice. It took him a moment to recognize the other voice as Alain's. He started to go in any way when Thierry's words caught his attention. *"You could ask him if he's interested,"* Thierry said. Curious now, wondering who Thierry was talking about, he stopped to listen. His eyes grew wide as he realized that, whoever it was, Thierry was seriously attracted to him. *Say a name,* Sebastien thought urgently. *Say it's me.* The two men clearly knew who they were talking about, though, because they didn't use a name. Sebastien listened silently as Alain teased Thierry about his inexperience with men. Sebastien's eyebrows rose in surprise. So his partner was an innocent in that respect. It made the prospect even more enticing. *"I'm sure Sebastien would be glad to help you."*

"Help you what?" Sebastien asked, stepping into the room as if he had not been listening to their conversation. "I'll certainly help in any way I can."

Chapter 36

ALAIN was still chuckling over Thierry's deer in the headlights look when he left the office to find Orlando. He had expected his lover to return at some point, but so far, that had not happened. Sebastien had mentioned leaving the other two vampires in the training room, so Alain headed that way, hoping Orlando's continued absence was not a bad sign.

Stopping at the door, he watched as the two vampires squared off. Orlando lunged at Blair, his movements almost too swift for Alain to follow. If his lover had been fighting a mortal, even a wizard, he would surely have caught his quarry. Blair, though, eluded him easily. "You telegraph your intentions far too clearly," he told the younger vampire. "Against a mortal, perhaps you would prevail, but if they are right and vampires are joining the enemy as well, you must be ready to fight your own kind, not just theirs."

Alain hung back, giving Blair the opportunity to show Orlando what he meant, watching the two carefully to see if he could spot what the other vampire spoke of, to see if he could read Orlando's intentions in his movements. Watching carefully, he decided that he could, but only because he recognized certain gestures of his lover's. If he had not known Orlando so well, he was not so sure he would have been able to anticipate the vampire's actions. "Sorry to interrupt," he said eventually, catching their attention, "but Orlando and I have something we have to take care of. Have you been given a new assignment, Blair?"

"Not yet," the vampire replied.

"It's too late tonight for you to go back out on patrol. The sun will be rising in an hour or two and we have no idea how long Laurent's magic will continue to protect you. See me tomorrow night after sunset and I'll find a patrol for you."

Blair nodded, grief returning to his features at the reminder of his lost partner.

"Don't dwell on it," Orlando inserted. "He'd want you to keep fighting."

"I know," Blair replied softly. "I should go home while I still can." Renewed determination played across his face as he nodded to the two men and left the room.

Orlando moved immediately into Alain's arms. "Don't you dare leave me," he ordered.

"Laurent was a good wizard," Alain answered. "I'm better." There was no bragging in his voice, just a simple statement of fact. "I think you and Blair had the right idea, though. I think having everyone practice dueling now that we're fighting as pairs instead of just as a patrol of wizards would be a good idea. Not tonight, though. Tonight we need to make you a repère."

"A what?" Orlando asked.

Alain explained quickly, pulling out the plastic dinosaur he had swiped from Henri when the war started. "And now we need to make one for you."

"How can it work for me?" Orlando asked. "I don't have any magic."

"Thierry said it worked when he drew a few drops of Sebastien's blood," Alain explained. "Do you trust me to do this? If you'd rather not, I understand, but it's an important safety precaution."

Orlando considered the question. He trusted Alain more than he trusted anyone other than Jean, but to let the wizard, to let anyone, take his blood scared him. "Are you sure it's the only way?" he asked.

"It's the only way Thierry found," Alain replied, wondering sadly if they would ever get completely past Orlando's fears. "We don't have to do this if you'd really rather not."

That offer, more than anything else, soothed Orlando's nerves. This was his choice, not something anyone else was forcing him to do. "I need something to use as the talisman, right?"

Alain nodded. "It can be anything, but at least for wizards, it seems to work better if the object has some meaning to the person."

"I don't really have anything except my ring," Orlando hesitated. "Until a few days ago, I wouldn't have called that special, though."

"It is special," Alain disagreed. "It's a symbol of everything you've overcome."

"It *was* a symbol of what I overcame," Orlando replied, "but it's so much more than that now. Now it's a symbol of our bond." He smiled. "Maybe it's the perfect thing to use. After all, without it, without us, I wouldn't be here. It's at home, though. I don't have it with me."

"We should do the spell here so we can see if it worked," Alain decided, "but I could pop home and get it. If you don't mind?"

Orlando shook his head. "I don't mind. What's mine is yours."

"And what's mine is yours," Alain assured his lover in reply. "I'll be back before you can miss me." He murmured the incantation that would send him home.

"I miss you already," Orlando whispered to the empty space where Alain had stood. He remained where he was, not wanting to move and be in the way when Alain returned.

Within seconds, Alain reappeared, Thurloe's signet ring in hand. Orlando took it, his other hand lifting to the barely healed burn on his lover's neck. The urge to sink his teeth into the mark was so strong that he trembled from the need. Turning his head, he subjugated those desires, determined to focus on the matter at hand. "So what do I do now?"

Alain laid his hand over Orlando's and squeezed gently before lifting the vampire's fingers away from his neck. "You don't need to do anything. I'll prick your finger, just enough to get a little blood on the ring and then I'll cast the spell that will attune it to the locator board."

Orlando nodded, his hand trembling marginally as he dealt with the reality of letting someone cut him, even as slightly as Alain would have to do for the spell.

As if sensing his doubts, Alain lifted his lover's hand to his lips, kissing the tip of each finger softly. "Just a little prick," he promised.

"I know."

Seeing Thierry's ceremonial dagger on his desk, Alain retrieved it quickly, spelling it clean. "Don't move," he warned, using the tip of the blade to puncture Orlando's finger. "I'm sorry," he murmured when he heard the hiss of pain. He squeezed gently, drawing several drops, rubbing the metal over the tiny wound so that the thick band was coated. Releasing Orlando's hand, he cast the tracking spell on the ring, watching the glow surrounding it expand momentarily before fading. "It's done."

Orlando lifted his finger to his mouth as soon as Alain released it, his saliva healing his own flesh as well as it healed his prey's.

"We should make sure it worked and then we can go home," Alain added.

Home. The word had its predictable effect on Orlando's libido. And his heart. "Let's hurry," he insisted, starting toward the door.

Alain followed his lover out the door and down to the locator board. To their delight, a little blip now appeared on the board next to Alain's name with Orlando's name beneath it. "Let's go home."

Alain nodded, glancing around the room, pleased to see Mathieu Gastineau on duty. If it hadn't been a wizard he trusted, he would have insisted they take the subway home rather than risking a magical displacement. "Sergeant," he called. "Can you send my partner to a destination after me?"

"If you're still on the map, I can, sir," Sgt. Gastineau replied confidently.

Alain turned to Orlando. "It'll get us home faster," he murmured, his tone cajoling as he asked his partner's permission. Orlando nodded, his need for his lover overriding his usual fears.

Alain cast the spell and disappeared, arriving in the middle of Orlando's living room – their living room, he reminded himself, knowing how much it bothered Orlando to hear Alain not include himself in the ownership of their home. A few moments later, Orlando appeared at his side. The look of unfettered passion on the vampire's face stole Alain's breath. He took a reflexive step backward before Orlando's arms closed around him and their lips met.

EDOUARD skulked in the shadows, not wanting to go inside and face Serrier, but he knew he would soon have no choice. His instincts screamed at him that the sun would rise soon, forcing him to take shelter inside. With a muttered curse, he kicked an empty water bottle across the street and stormed into the dark wizard's headquarters.

He glared at everyone he passed until he was back in the room where he had always met with Serrier before. His foot tapped impatiently as he waited for the wizard to join him. He did not bother with a light, preferring the dim lamp to a brighter room. He had no real idea what he would tell the wizard, given that he had not come back with the information the man had demanded, but he did have an idea.

"Well?" Serrier's voice came from the shadows.

Edouard spun around, not having seen the wizard when he came in. He relied on his vampiric senses to alert him to danger, but now he wondered if they were enough. Keeping company with wizards, it seemed, was a dangerous business.

"Nothing," he spat in disgust. "Somebody told them I'm working with you and they wouldn't say a word to me except to order me out. They seemed to think that associating with you was bad form. Any reason they hate you so much?"

He still could not believe the vehemence he had encountered when he arrived at his various destinations during the night. From club to café to brothel, it had been the same. *We want nothing to do with your killing ways,* they had told him in the brothel. *Take yourself back to your precious wizard and let him give you what you need.*

Why should we tell you what you want to know when you've endangered our very existence with your recklessness? the café patrons had demanded.

The bouncer at the club had not even let him through the door. *Not here. Do your hunting elsewhere.* If the bouncer had been mortal, Edouard would have argued, but the club owner had a vampire guarding the door. Edouard had slunk away, his tail between his legs.

"None that I know of. You're the first member, the only member of your race I've ever met," Serrier replied. "Do I need to reconsider our alliance?"

"Not yet," Edouard replied hastily. "I have another idea, although it will require your assistance. Our illustrious leader has a mortal concubine, it seems," he explained, his voice laced with sarcasm. "I'm certain she could give us the information we need."

Serrier arched an eyebrow as an evil smile crept across his face. "And you know where to find this woman?"

"I know her name," Edouard replied, "but she should not be too hard to find."

"If you have her name, we can find her," Serrier agreed.

"Karine Gaudier."

THE feeling of Orlando's lips against his never ceased to amaze and arouse, Alain decided as he found himself caught again in his lover's torrid embrace, the sparks between them catching fire as soon as their bodies touched. It took only a glance, only a hint of invitation and his desire burned as brightly as if he were a teenager again, straining the limits of his control like never before.

Deciding they needed to be in their bedroom instead of the living room, Alain took a step backward, then another, drawing Orlando with him until his knees bumped the mattress. Falling back onto the bed, he pulled the vampire down on top of him. He broke the kiss, rolling Orlando to his back and lowering his head to nip at the skin of the vampire's neck.

Orlando froze when he felt Alain's teeth on his skin. Breaking free of the embrace, he pushed away from Alain. "Don't."

Alain sat up, rubbing his hands over his face. He had hoped that they were beyond this, that their lovemaking in his office, when Orlando had fed from him so soon after making love, was a sign that things were finally improving. Taking a deep breath, he turned to face Orlando. "Talk to me, Orlando. Don't just push me away."

Orlando shuddered. He had already told Alain more details of what had happened to him than he had told anyone else, but it seemed his partner wanted more. "I don't want to relive that," he protested. "It was hell the first time. Why would I want to think about that again?"

"Because you obviously think about it every time we're together," Alain pointed out with more calm than he was feeling. "I feel like I can't do anything, can't touch you or kiss you beyond the most innocent of caresses for fear of making you pull away."

"I don't..." Orlando protested reflexively before realizing that was exactly what he had been doing. Not, perhaps, at the height of their passion or when he fed, but certainly as they moved toward passion. His gaze fell. "I don't know what to do."

"Talk to me," Alain repeated. "Tell me what he did to you. Let me make it right."

"Make it right?" Orlando asked, not exactly sure how Alain proposed to do that.

"Let me replace the bad memories with new ones," his lover requested gently.

Orlando nodded slowly, trying to think of something relatively innocuous he could share, something that could not truly hurt him regardless of how the memories haunted him. He trusted Alain intellectually not to hurt him. His lover had stopped every time Orlando had asked, but this was different. This was deliberately inviting a touch, a caress that made him uncomfortable. "He would grab my hair and use that to force me to do his will."

Alain's heart clenched as it always did at the thought of Orlando being abused. "Trust me," he pleaded. "Let me make this right."

Orlando took a deep breath, fighting against the instinctual refusal to give anyone any sort of control over him. Eventually, he nodded his permission.

Alain scooted closer to Orlando, wrapping his arms around his lover, nuzzling his cheek. Shifting, he moved to his knees, facing Orlando. "Focus on me," he whispered as he ran one hand gently over the vampire's hair. He did not hold, did not tangle his fingers in the silky locks, though he wanted to. Instead, he simply caressed Orlando's head as he would calm a skittish horse, long, easy strokes of his palm across his lover's scalp and down to his shoulders, again and again, until his partner leaned finally into the touch.

The touch of Alain's hand on his hair startled Orlando despite watching and even anticipating the caress. He reminded himself that Alain was his lover, not his captor, and that the wizard had never hurt him – would never hurt him – the way Thurloe had. The heat of his partner's hand warmed his scalp, soothing him with calm, repetitive strokes. His choppy breathing steadied as he relaxed, letting Alain's tenderness replace the hatred and rage that had characterized his creator's approach to the young vampire. His pulse finally steadying, he felt his confidence grow until he felt safe tilting his head into Alain's hand, inviting a deeper caress.

Feeling Orlando move to encourage him, Alain started again, using the tips of his fingers this time, stroking up and down Orlando's scalp, letting his fingers burrow enough to touch Orlando's skin, but without tangling in his hair or pulling in any way. Step by gentle step, he reminded himself. The last thing he wanted was to spook Orlando again.

The sensuality of Alain's massage sent a slight shiver down Orlando's spine. Immediately, his lover's fingers stilled. "Don't stop," he murmured, tilting his head to ask for more of the tender touches.

"I won't," Alain promised, resuming the gentle massage. "Not unless you want me to."

Orlando smiled and shifted onto his knees as well so he knelt face to face with his lover, their legs bumping as he scooted forward to kiss the wizard.

Alain made no effort to take control of their kiss despite his hands in Orlando's hair. Thurloe – the bastard! – had used Orlando's hair as a way to control him, to force his unwelcome advances on the vampire. While Alain was fairly sure his advances would not be unwelcome, he did not want anything to remind Orlando of his incarceration. He was supposed to be making new memories, not evoking old ones. Instead, he let Orlando guide the kiss while he continued the soothing massage, using his fingers to add to Orlando's pleasure.

Growing ever more confident in Alain's touch, Orlando deepened the kiss until his tongue was surging between his lover's lips, claiming his mouth fiercely. Alain's head fell back beneath the onslaught as he sat back on his heels, Orlando rising up over him. Alain's hands tightened in his hair, tilting it to one side. Immediately, Orlando tensed.

"Relax," Alain urged, backing away from the kiss enough to speak. "All I want is your pleasure. Let me take care of you, too."

Orlando took a deep breath, fighting with old demons. He knew Alain would not hurt him. His lover had never done anything but give him pleasure. The moments of fear, of unease, came from within, not from anything Alain intended. Exhaling slowly, he relaxed again into Alain's touch, letting his lover angle his head the way the wizard saw fit. It took a minute to completely accept the loss of control, but once he did, he realized that the way Alain had positioned their heads allowed for a deeper kiss, a more profound meeting of their mouths. He moaned softly as their tongues tangled together again, the sensation of the wizard's hands in his hair no longer bothering him. Yes, Alain was using the contact to guide him, but unlike his creator, his lover wanted that control to increase Orlando's pleasure, not his pain.

Chapter 37

SERRIER paced the room impatiently. He had ordered his lieutenants to assemble at eight o'clock, and all of them had arrived on time but one. Unfortunately, she was the one he most wanted to speak with, for her patrol had returned victorious the night before. Glancing at his watch again, he pivoted, facing the table. "Simonet," he snapped. "Get Morvilliers here. I don't care if you have to drag her naked from her shower. When I say eight o'clock, I mean it."

Eric grimaced at the order but immediately transported himself to Joëlle's apartment. He knew why Serrier wanted her there: her patrol was one of the few to engage Chavinier's people and not suffer serious losses in the past two weeks. He was actually surprised she was late. Everyone knew Serrier's insistence on punctuality, and Joëlle had been trying to get Serrier's attention, taking what Eric considered unnecessary risks to do so.

Her wards parted easily to let him through, their long-standing relationship giving him access no one else would have been allowed. "Joëlle," he called, walking through the apartment. "Hurry up, sweetheart. Serrier is ready to have your arse for being late."

Silence greeted his words, sending a shiver down Eric's spine. "Joëlle?" he called again, stepping further into the room. A flash of white drew his attention and he walked over to the couch. Lying there on the floor next to the sofa, he saw his lover of almost two years, her robe open to reveal her naked body, her skin waxy, her eyes empty. Dropping to his knees, he felt immediately for a pulse, finding none. Anger swelled in him, despite the somewhat calculated nature of their relationship. She had been, especially at first, a way for him to show his loyalty to his new side. Sleeping with him had been, for her, a way to draw Serrier's attention. Neither of them had ever pretended otherwise, but a genuine affection had sprung up between them despite their Machiavellian beginning. "Who did this to you?" he asked her dead body, casting about for her wand. As he searched, he noticed the door had been knocked in. Whoever had done this had used brute force, not magic.

Finding it, he slipped it into the pocket of his cloak, then went into the bedroom to pull the sheet from her bed. He wrapped her body tenderly, lifting it into his arms before displacing them both back to Serrier's meeting room. "She's dead," he said by way of explanation.

Chaos broke out in the room as everyone shouted questions at the same time.

"Silence!" Serrier bellowed when the noise showed no sign of dying down.

"What happened?" he asked Eric when his lieutenants fell quiet.

"I don't know," Eric replied honestly. "Her wards were still up, but she was lying on the floor, dead. I grabbed her wand and brought it and her back here."

"Let's see what her wand can tell us," Serrier suggested, holding out his hand.

Eric produced the thin sliver of wood, waiting as the dark wizard performed the spell that would reveal the last charm cast through the magical conduit.

"An *Abbatoire*," Serrier commented after a moment. "There wasn't another body?"

"No," Eric replied, "just hers. But nobody should have been able to get inside. Her wards were intact – I felt them as I went in. I checked the door, though, and it had been forced in. She had some pretty hefty locks on her door. It would have taken someone incredibly strong to break them in."

"Physically forced?" Serrier clarified. "Not magically?"

"Physically," Eric confirmed. "The door frame was shattered."

"A supernatural being?" Claude suggested. "A vampire or a werewolf or one of the other shapeshifters?"

Serrier looked to Edouard.

"It's possible," the vampire replied, "but what reason would any of them have to come after her? To force her door down and kill her?"

"You kill for the pleasure of it," Serrier pointed out.

"Yes," Edouard agreed, "but that would be far too much work for me unless I had a reason to go after her specifically."

"What about Chavinier?" Vincent asked. "He surely has reason to want her dead, especially after last night."

Eric could not argue with that, but he also felt obliged to defend his former mentor. "He wouldn't go after her personally, though. In a battle, deaths might be acceptable, but he'd never condone a cold-blooded killing."

"You've been gone for two years," Serrier reminded him. "Things might have changed."

Not that much, Eric thought privately, but he simply nodded. "Even so, her wards should have kept out a wizard and she should have been able to defend herself against anything else that came at her."

"And yet clearly, she could not," Serrier observed. "Do you know how she died?"

"Not for sure," Eric replied, "but her neck is at an odd angle. I'm not a medic, though, so I just don't know."

With a frown, Serrier cast another spell on the shrouded body. No luminescence appeared. "She didn't die from magical means. Whatever killed her did so without spells."

"How is that possible?" Vincent demanded. "She should have been able to defend against anything, anyone else, even multiple attackers. I didn't always agree with her, but she was a damn good wizard."

"It's not just her spells, though," Simon Aguiraud insisted. "Our patrols are being decimated left and right, spells not working, whole patrols captured or killed. I don't know what Chavinier's done, but something has changed, and not in our favor."

"Joëlle managed last night," Eric defended his dead lover.

"So what made last night different than the failed patrols?" Serrier asked. "That's what we were supposed to be discussing this morning. What did she do right that nobody else has been doing? And if it was a wizard that came after her last night, why didn't it save her then?"

"Numbers," Vincent said succinctly. "Her patrol was simply too large for the patrol she pinned. According to her report, even when they sent in reinforcements, they only rescued their compatriots rather than trying to fight her."

"Can I see the report?" Eric asked, not having had time to look at it.

Serrier passed it across the table. Eric scanned through it quickly, taking in the details as he went, searching for any clue that might explain Joëlle's death. He did not slow until he reached the announcement of the death of Laurent Copé. He felt a small twinge for the young man he remembered vaguely from his time in Chavinier's ranks. "Dumont should have been leading this patrol," he mused aloud as he finished reading, "but there's no mention of him even being there. That may have played a role as well. If it fell to his lieutenants, they may have buckled under pressure. The larger size of the patrol surely helped, but we can't afford to discount Dumont's mind. Not when it comes to strategy."

"We need more information," Serrier ground out angrily. "There must be an explanation for the failed spells, just like there must be a limit to Dumont's ability to think up new battle plans, but we can't seem to find either." He looked at Eric speculatively. "Would they believe you if you went back and swore you'd seen the error of your ways? Chavinier took in that idiot Payet."

Eric froze, put on the spot in a way he had not been since he had first switched sides. "I don't know," he replied slowly. "Payet left a whole lot sooner than I did, with a lot less blood on his hands. He also didn't have my reasons to hate the whole damn bunch of them. I've got a decent poker face, but you're asking me to work with the man who killed my wife and children. With that on the table, I don't know if they'd buy it or not."

"Think about it," Serrier ordered. "We need somebody on the inside. I'm tired of losing this war."

"I NEED some sunshine," Caroline said apologetically when she and Mireille finished their shift. "When I have a run of night shifts, I find I have to make an effort to get some sun or I get edgy and depressed."

"I had thought to visit monsieur Lombard," Mireille commented, "but he prefers to hibernate during the daylight hours. He came out to meet you the last time we went, after you were injured, but I'd rather not disturb him. I do need to get some things from home, though. Could we drop by for just a minute but not stay?"

"Of course we can go by there," Caroline replied. "I can always go to the park near my apartment later."

Mireille smiled. "Or we can take the subway part of the way and walk the rest. I don't need to sleep the way you do, and being in the sun is still quite the novelty for me. It will be a fine way to pass the morning."

Caroline smiled, her pleasure clear on her face. She had observed some of the other teams during the night, trying to see if any of the other wizards had found with their partner the incredible rapport she had found with Mireille. She already knew Alain had, but it seemed that many of the other pairings were much more tempestuous than her relationship with her partner. It made her doubly glad for what she and Mireille had shared last night.

They took the métro to Pont Marie and walked across the bridge onto the Ile St-Louis to monsieur Lombard's house. The volets were closed tightly against the sunlight, meaning her employer could be anywhere in the house. Unlocking the door, she rang the bell to alert the old vampire to her impending entrance, glancing toward the rising sun to make sure it would not send rays into the dim interior. "Come inside quickly," she said softly.

Caroline stepped inside, Mireille slipping in behind her. Though she had been there once before, Caroline could not stop herself from staring at the ornate decorations. Mireille stared as well, into the shadows that lined the long hall, feeling the eyes of her employer on them. She did not know when he had last fed since she had not been around to hunt for him. Perhaps she was imagining the hunger in his gaze as he focused on Caroline's slender back, but she ran her hand down the elegant curve nonetheless, guiding her partner possessively toward the stairs that led to her room.

Caroline looked at Mireille in surprise, though she shivered at the soft touch and furtiveness of slipping up the stairs unannounced. It reminded her of nothing so much as trying to sneak her first boyfriend into the house without catching her mother's eagle eye. "I could have just waited downstairs."

"I'd rather have you with me," Mireille said by way of explanation. She was almost sure Caroline would have been safe with monsieur Lombard, but this way she avoided the issue completely and had the pleasure of knowing Caroline had been in her home just as she had been in Caroline's.

The old servants' quarters in the attic had been remodeled, opening them up into a large living area with a bedroom, four of the old maids' rooms, through a door on the far side. As in the main part of the house, the windows were shuttered against the light, but Mireille opened the metal volets to let the sunlight stream in. "You can have a seat if you want or..." She flushed as she started into the bedroom. "I have to change. I'll just be a minute."

Caroline let her go, giving her the privacy of the closed door between them, but she resolved to break down that last barrier as soon as possible.

Inside the bedroom, Mireille changed quickly, wishing she had found the courage to invite Caroline inside. Attired in clean clothes, she threw a few other necessities into a bag and walked back into the living room. Caroline greeted her with a smile and a quick kiss. "You don't have to hide from me, you know."

"I know. I'm sorry. I'm just not used to…"

"Don't worry about it," Caroline interrupted. "Do you have everything you need?"

"Yes," Mireille replied, "At least for a few days. Let's go back to your apartment and get in a walk on the way."

"We could take the subway to the Place d'Italie and walk from there. It would be a good thirty minute walk, perfect to give me the sun I need," Caroline suggested. She took Mireille's bag and cast a spell sending it to her apartment, not seeing any reason for them to carry it the whole way.

Mireille smiled. "That sounds lovely."

The subway ride was uneventful, as usual, no one giving them a second glance.

The two women took their time walking down the wide boulevards, arms linked companionably as they went. They were in no hurry, having nothing to demand their time and energy until that evening. Caroline would need to sleep, but there was time still to enjoy the crisp air and gentle sunshine.

Reaching the boulevard Montparnasse, they browsed in the shop windows, not really looking for anything in particular, simply enjoying the freedom to wander. Mireille had not said anything aloud, but Caroline noticed her partner lingering in front of certain shops.

"Do you want to go in?" the wizard asked when Mireille paused in front of the third dress shop they passed.

"What? Oh, no. It's fine," Mireille insisted, flushing a little at being caught staring.

"They have some lovely things," Caroline commented. She hesitated a moment before letting her hand settle intimately in the small of her partner's back. "It's all right to indulge yourself."

"When will I ever need such fripperies?" Mireille asked seriously. "I'm a vampire. I don't go out. What use is a slinky dress or fancy shoes to me?"

Grabbing Mireille's hand, Caroline pulled her into the store. "I have twenty-four hours off in a few days, which means you do, too. There's a new club near my apartment I've been wanting to try. We're going out dancing."

"Really?" Mireille asked, her eyes lighting up before she could stop herself. "I haven't been dancing in years."

Caroline smiled, thrilled at the pleasure she saw on her lover's face. "Find something pretty for yourself," she urged, seeing the longing and the insecurity in Mireille's eyes. She had the solution for both.

Mireille looked around the shop, seeing all the finery she usually denied herself, having no use for them working for monsieur Lombard. Even when she hunted, she did not overly adorn herself. For a night out with Caroline, though, she wanted to look her best.

"Take your time," Caroline urged as she watched Mireille's gaze flit back and forth between various outfits. "There's no rush to get home." She stepped closer to her lover, running a tender hand down the vampire's back as she leaned in to whisper, "Just imagine the two of us at the club, wrapped around each other as we dance, unable to keep our hands to ourselves but not completely able to let go either. I want to show you off."

Mireille leaned back against her wizard, desire swamping her just from the murmured words. "As long as I get to show you off, too," she agreed.

Caroline chuckled throatily, her hands going around Mireille's waist. "As much as you want."

"May I help you?" the clerk interrupted. "Ladies?"

"My friend needs a dress," Caroline replied, pulling away only enough to satisfy propriety. Her hand lingered possessively, though, on Mireille's back. The pause in the woman's voice was enough to raise the wizard's hackles. Young and trendily dressed, the clerk nevertheless seemed caught in the prejudices of the past.

The clerk nodded, although her disapproval was obvious in the sour look on her face. She knew her business, though, and had no intention of losing a commission. She had worked at the shop long enough to estimate the redhead's size. "What would be the occasion?" she asked, heading toward the rack of size thirty-six dresses.

"We're going dancing," Caroline answered, drawing on every bit of regal control to put the annoying woman in her place. What right did the shopkeeper have to judge her and Mireille? "I want to show off my partner," she added, quite sure it would irk the young woman even more. Even more importantly, though, she wanted Mireille to hear her say it, to know that she found her desirable. She almost smiled seeing the woman wince at the word partner. She could not help but wonder how the clerk would react if she labeled Mireille her lover.

Seeing what size the clerk had selected, she shook her head. "No, we want a thirty-four. I'm quite certain Mireille's smaller than a thirty-six, and I want everyone to see how lucky I am," Caroline directed, her hand sliding appreciatively over the slender curve of her lover's figure.

The clerk's face grew even more sour, but she led them to the appropriate section. Taking charge, Caroline flipped through the dresses, trying to find one she thought would look good on Mireille. She immediately dismissed the reds and pastels. Neither would go with her lover's coloring. A burnt gold silk number caught her eye. Pulling it off the rack, she held it up for Mireille's perusal. "What do you think, Miri?" she asked, imagining the dress on her lover's bounteous curves.

Mireille's eyes lit up as she looked at the slinky creation Caroline was offering her. " It looks beautiful, but I couldn't..."

"Yes, you could," Caroline insisted, refusing to let Mireille put herself down. "We'd like to try this on," she added, turning to the clerk.

Frowning, the clerk led them to one of the dressing rooms in the back of the shop, a little cubicle with a curtain for privacy. "Thank you," Caroline said with a wave of dismissal. "We'll let you know if we need more help."

With no way to insist, the clerk nodded and retreated to the front of the shop. Caroline paid her no more attention, drawing Mireille into the dressing room. "Try it on," she urged, her hands already undoing the fastenings on Mireille's coat.

Laughing, Mireille knocked Caroline's hands away. "I'll try it on, but you have to wait for me outside. I want to put in on right before you see it."

"Spoilsport," Caroline teased, stealing a quick kiss and an indelicate grope before stepping back out through the curtain to give Mireille some privacy while she changed.

Inside the cubicle, Mireille leaned against the wall for a moment, trying to regain her composure, her body already tingling from those few touches and the possessiveness with which Caroline was treating her. She had seen her lover in a variety of situations since they became partners, and Caroline was never a pushover, but in this guise, her wizard was a force of nature.

Taking a deep breath to steady herself, she pulled off her coat and clothes, stripping down to her underwear so she could try on the dress Caroline had selected. She ran her fingers longingly over the smooth silk, hoping the dress would fit, but sure it would not look as good on her as on the hanger. She had long since accepted that she was "cute" or "adorable" instead of beautiful or sexy. As she slid the fabric over her head and smoothed it down her hips, she resigned herself to seeing the disappointment on Caroline's face when she did not live up to her lover's expectations.

Not bothering to look at herself in the mirror, Mireille stepped out of the dressing room, steeling herself for Caroline's reaction. She was prepared for many things, but not for being backed right through the curtain again and kissed frantically. "I knew you were beautiful," Caroline murmured between kisses, "but I had no idea you were so damn sexy. I'll be the envy of every man in that club and most of the women, too."

Mireille blinked in shock, her body responding without her mind's direction, arching into the roving hands that slid over her silk-encased curves. Sexy? She had been called many things, but never that. Caroline's hands stroking her, Caroline's mouth devouring hers told another tale. Surely the long, elegant fingers would not linger so on the curve of her waist and the swell of her buttocks if her wizard did not find her attractive. Surely the plump lips would not cover hers so ardently if her wizard did not think she was beautiful. Without thinking, she pressed against Caroline, inviting more of the fiery caresses. Her lover obliged immediately, one hand sliding down her side to find bare skin through the slit that ran high up her thigh. The other moved upward, to the deep vee plunged between her breasts, cupping one through the fabric before sliding beneath to tease her already peaked nipple.

"I want you," Caroline whispered, blowing gently into Mireille's ear, thrilled at the other woman's responsiveness. "Do you think the prude would notice if I made love to you right now?"

Mireille tried unsuccessfully to stifle the moan that escaped her lips at the thought. She wanted Caroline's hands, Caroline's lips on her, without fabric separating them. Her body reacted, issuing a silent invitation, skin flushing the way it usually did only when she fed, pulse throbbing in her neck, in her breasts, between her thighs. The thigh Caroline was still stroking lifted, wrapping around the wizard's legs, pulling her closer into the cradle of the vampire's hips. Her hands started on the buttons of her lover's coat, peeling away the layers that separated them.

"Do you need anything else?"

The clerk's voice shattered the spell, causing Mireille to tense and try to pull away. Caroline's hands did not let her move far, but though the eagerness remained, the lack of inhibitions was gone. "Not here," Mireille gasped, the return to reality too sudden for her to assimilate completely. "Take me home and you can do whatever you want to me."

"Whatever I want?" Caroline teased, nipping at Mireille's earlobe before lifting her head. She could have cursed in frustration, but this was not her vampire's fault. "That's a pretty broad offer."

"I mean it," Mireille swore. "Just take me home."

Meeting the vampire's eyes, seeing the desperate hunger that lingered there despite the interruption, Caroline nodded. "Give me the dress. I'll pay while you put your clothes back on."

Mireille nodded as well, gesturing for Caroline to step back outside. She was too on edge to undress before her lover without the promise of immediate fulfillment. The wizard went, and Mireille stripped back down to her underwear, passing the garment out to her lover before pulling her own outfit back on. To her surprise, the overwhelming feeling of sexiness did not fade as she returned to her usual simple clothes. Beneath the loose slacks and bulky sweater, she was still the same woman who had inspired such passion just moments before in her lover. Feeling suddenly energized, she left the dressing room to join Caroline in the shop. Her lover had just finished paying when she came out. "Let's go home," she repeated, her fingers sliding through Caroline's to twine together.

Still glaring at the clerk for interrupting them, Caroline pulled Mireille out of the store onto the street. "Fifteen minutes," she told the vampire. "We can be home in fifteen minutes if we hurry."

"Let's hurry then," Mireille agreed, picking up the pace to match Caroline's. She could have traveled much more quickly alone, but she preferred to stay with her lover, their fingers still interlaced as they hurried down the street.

The flush of desire stained her cheeks as they walked, hastening their steps, for she could see the sparkle in Caroline's eyes that reflected what she felt. So lost was she in their passion that it took her a moment to recognize the other sensation assailing her.

"Caroline!"

The panic and pain in Mireille's voice were totally at odds with the desire that had ruled them since the store. "What's wrong?" she asked urgently, turning to look at her lover.

"The sun..." Mireille gasped, the pain doubling her over. "It's burning me."

Chapter 38

EYES searching desperately for shelter at the vampire's first words, Caroline spied a cheap hotel at the next corner. "Come on," she urged, grabbing Mireille's hand and pulling her toward safety.

Crippled now by the burning pain along her exposed skin, Mireille leaned heavily on Caroline as they neared the hotel. The darkness of the lobby was a welcome relief, but the burning did not fade, stabilizing rather than worsening, but not easing up at all.

"I need a room," Caroline snapped. "Now."

The hotel manager looked at them dubiously, but accepted Caroline's credit card, giving them a key. "He thinks…" Mireille began as they climbed the stairs, obviously still in pain, though the panic had receded.

"It doesn't matter," Caroline interrupted, opening the door, feeling guilty for having exposed Mireille needlessly to harm. As enjoyable as the shopping had been, it was not a reason to endanger her partner. "Wait here while I close the volets."

Mireille leaned heavily against the doorframe while Caroline crossed to the windows and secured the shutters, blocking out the now-deadly sunlight. "Let me take care of you," she urged, drawing Mireille inside. Even in the dim light, she could see the grey ashiness that colored her lover's usually pale skin.

"I have to feed," Mireille explained as Caroline helped her into the room. "It's the only way to heal the burns."

Caroline nodded, loosening her scarf and coat without hesitation. Lying back on the dingy bed, unconcerned about the state of the room, she tipped her head back and opened her arms to her lover.

In more pain than she let on, Mireille stretched out along Caroline's side, caressing the smooth skin lightly before bending her head to the graceful throat on offer for her. Despite her very real need, she took a moment to lap at the ivory flesh, letting her saliva prepare the spot she had selected. Though her state would not improve until she fed, it would not worsen either now that she was sheltered from the sun, giving her the time she needed to treat her lover the way the wizard deserved.

"Go ahead," Caroline urged, eyes opening to meet Mireille's and seeing the pain still lingering in the green depths. "You won't hurt me."

Mireille's heart swelled at the trust she saw in Caroline's eyes. Angling her head so she could maintain that contact while initiating another, she let her fangs drop and penetrate the tender skin. At the first splash of hot blood on her tongue, she felt the pain ease, the burns begin to heal. The concern, the love, she tasted in Caroline's blood were addictive, though, and she continued to feed long after her skin was healed.

"Is it helping?" Caroline asked after Mireille had fed for several minutes.

Not ready to stop feeding, Mireille sought Caroline's fingers, squeezing them gently before trailing her hand up her lover's arm to tease seductively across the ripe swell of one breast, preferring the flavor of desire to the flavor of fear in the wizard's blood.

"Mireille!" Caroline gasped, though in protest or encouragement she could not have said. Her fear at the possibility of losing her partner had driven all thoughts of passion from her mind. It took only one touch of her lover's hand, though, and all the lust that had been riding her came rushing back, her body arching into the dual caress, fingers and fangs inciting her desire as they always did.

The rising tide of passion in Caroline's blood sparked Mireille's own, an ever-increasing spiral that spun them both out of control, leaving them limp and trembling in the sated aftermath.

Lifting her head finally, Mireille lapped tenderly at the punctures on Caroline's neck, closing the wounds carefully. When she was satisfied, she looked down at her lover. "This wasn't your fault," she insisted. "I wasn't paying attention. Next time we'll be more careful."

"Yes, we will be," Caroline replied firmly. "I can't lose you, Miri."

The heartfelt words brought a smile to Mireille's lips and the prickle of tears to her green eyes, though no moisture came to add to their glimmer. Lowering her head again, she kissed the pink bow of Caroline's lips tenderly, a noise outside in the hall drawing her attention. "I'm not going anywhere except home with you where we don't have to worry about a busybody hotel manager listening outside the door to see what we're up to. And when we get there, you're going to sleep. And when you wake up, I'll keep that promise I made in the store."

"YOU want to what?" Jude demanded harshly, sure he had not heard his partner correctly.

"I need to make you a repère," Adèle repeated, marshalling her patience. "And the only way to do that for a vampire is to draw a little of your blood and bind it to an object of your choosing. It's for your protection."

Seeing that Jude did not immediately respond, she frowned. "Or are you afraid of a little prick?" she demanded crudely.

Jude's pride flared instantly. "I'm not afraid of anything you can dish out," he retorted angrily.

"Well, then, pick something I can use as the repère and let's get this over with," she suggested coldly, tired of fighting with him even before their shift had begun.

Determined not to let her get the better of him, Jude cast about for something he could use. Deciding it could not possibly matter, he pulled off his watch and handed it to her. Taking it, she set it on the table and held out her hand again.

"I have to be the one to draw the blood," she told him, bracing for another explosion.

To her surprise, it did not come, although Jude stared at her hard for a long moment before slowly stretching out his hand to hers.

The vampire watched closely as Adèle turned his hand over to expose his wrist to the ceremonial knife in her hand. His fingers wanted to tremble, but he refused to show any weakness before his partner. The bite of the knife was barely noticeable, certainly not enough to warrant the shiver that went through him as she broke skin, reducing him to prey rather than predator, a complete departure from his usual role. He drew blood, not the other way around.

Adèle massaged his wrist firmly until enough blood had gathered for the spell, the contact between their skin sending an electric spark through Jude. He repressed the reaction forcibly even as he found himself watching his partner with new eyes. Her face was set in concentration as she chanted softly, weaving the spell that would bind his blood to the metal and that to the tracking board. He had seen her do magic once before, but only in public, and only when he was focused on defending himself.

Watching her now, seeing the concentration on her face as she cast the charm to protect him, he began to wonder if he had been too hasty in judging her only for her appearance. The power he saw in her now called to him in a way her beauty alone had not. He had assumed she was the plaything of the wizards who surrounded her, valued more for her beauty than for any real skill she possessed. Thus had women been judged at the time of his making and thus would he always judge them. While he could see the attraction despite his own reaction to her lack of modesty, he could also resist it. The power that sparked within her, from her wand and her fingers as she worked, was much harder to dismiss, to ignore.

Then she released his hand, pulling away and handing him his watch. "Keep it with you any time you're on duty," she instructed. "Unlike mine, it will always show on the map, but it will only show *your* location if you have it on you. Otherwise, it will just show the location of your watch."

Still mesmerized by Adèle's display of magic, Jude caught her hand instead of the watch and pulled her toward him, intending to draw her into his arms. Her immediate resistance did not surprise him, not after the somewhat tempestuous nature of their previous interactions, but her strength was no match for his.

Adèle realized his intent almost immediately and considered fighting him, but she had learned the futility of that the last time he had kissed her. Instead, she stood perfectly still, refusing to be baited, as his lips closed over hers, brushing invitingly. A part of her wished it was real, wished he was the kind of man who would truly appreciate her, but he had already proven that hope to be an empty one. When he released her finally, she took a step back, wiping the back of her hand contemptuously across her mouth, her glare potent enough to make even him step back. "What century are you from?"

The cutting disparagement he saw in her vivid eyes hardened Jude's softening heart. However beautiful, however powerful she might be, she had nothing of the traits he truly desired in a woman, none of the modesty, the demureness that had characterized his lost era. "The sixteenth," he replied bitingly, turning on his heel to leave.

"That explains your Neanderthal attitudes," she spat. "They died out a long time ago. Too bad the same isn't true of you."

"Be glad I didn't," he retorted, "or you wouldn't have a partner now."

Her laugh was bitter. "Or maybe I'd have a true partner instead of an overbearing ogre who doesn't understand 'no' when he hears it."

Jude advanced on her again, grudgingly impressed that she did not back down. "I haven't heard that word on your lips yet, sweetheart," he pointed out, grabbing her chin and kissing her again, demandingly this time.

"Get out," she ordered. "And just so we understand each other. No, I don't want you to kiss me. No, I'm not interested in anything else you're offering either. If it isn't required by the alliance, I don't want it!"

Jude's face hardened as he left the room. For a moment, he had imagined, hoped even, that they could find some equilibrium between them, but it seemed that was impossible. Spoiling for a fight, he turned the corner to find another couple locked in a tight embrace. The man nuzzled the woman's neck tenderly before backing away and delivering a playful pat to her bottom as she walked down the hall.

"No luck getting under her skirts?" Jude drawled.

Justin spun around, seeking the author of the obnoxious comment.

Jude. He should have known.

"Just because I'm man enough to accept a female partner doesn't mean I'm trying to bed her," Justin retorted, despite the fact that Catherine had so far been inclined to let him do just that. She had approached him, not the other way around, and their time together in no way resembled Jude's crude insinuations. "Unlike some people, I can accept that the world's changed."

"Not for the better," Jude replied hotly, remembering with perfect clarity the days when a woman like Adèle would have been flattered to accept his attention.

"Still too insecure to admit that your partner might be your equal in a fight?" Justin challenged. He had known Jude far too many years to tolerate the other vampire's misogyny.

"No woman is my equal," Jude spat.

"Oh, really?" Justin drawled. "I know more than one woman who would disagree. Given a choice, I know I'd take Catherine over you in a fight any day. I trust her to watch my back." He paused and pretended to consider. "Come to think of it," he added, "I'd take your partner over you, too. Her dedication must be monumental to put up with you."

Without waiting for Jude's response, Justin continued down the hall. He pitied Adèle, stuck with such a boor for a partner, but he felt sorry for Jude, too, in a way. The vampire's life would just get more and more difficult as time went by. Shaking his head, he turned his thoughts to more pleasant things. Catherine was waiting for him in her office. He needed to feed, and if he was lucky, she would let him make love to her at the same time. He really was a lucky bastard. Not only was he partnered with a formidable wizard, she was incredibly desirable as well.

The door to Catherine's office was ajar when he got there and he pushed it open without knocking. She had made it abundantly clear that he should consider her space his as well. She was on the phone when he walked in, a pen in her hand as she jotted down notes. He stood there until she finished, simply taking in her lush beauty. Her thick dark hair fell across her shoulders and down her back, framing her face and a svelte figure that curved emphatically in all the right places, drawing his hands and his eyes. A smile creased her smooth skin, dark enough to suggest Latin roots, when she looked up and saw him. She beckoned to him, gesturing to the armchair in the corner.

Smiling back at her, Justin took the offered seat and waited patiently for her to finish her call. When she finally closed the phone in her hand and turned her attention to him, he felt his smile broadening. He recognized that look. He had seen it the night she had first invited him to her bed.

She rose from her seat and walked toward him, her hips swaying sultrily as she settled on his lap, her knees straddling his hips. "Isn't it about time for you to feed?" she purred in a tone designed to rouse all his hungers.

"Are you offering?" he teased in reply, though the way her arms draped around his shoulders made the question rhetorical.

She lowered her head and kissed him, her lips parting immediately in invitation. Threading his fingers into her silky hair, he tilted her head to give him better access to her mouth. She moaned into the kiss as he nibbled at her lips, his fangs dropping in anticipation, tantalizing the tender flesh without breaking it. He would feed from her, but not there where the bruise that inevitably resulted from his attentions would cause her discomfort later.

Her slim hands slipped between them, stroking over his chest, then lower, to unfasten his trousers and take him in hand. "Fuck, Catherine," he groaned as she caressed him.

"You'd better," she retorted playfully, lifting up enough to free the fabric of her skirt from between their bodies. "I've been looking forward to it all day."

His hands moved immediately to support her, sliding beneath the linen to glide over her stockings. As they moved up, he encountered the lacy edge and then bare skin. And more bare skin. "All night?" he asked, fingers exploring her naked buttocks, relearning the shape of muscle, the texture of skin.

She chuckled and shook her head. "No, I took them off while I was waiting for you. I didn't want to wait any longer." She nipped at his neck lightly. "You don't mind, do you?"

As if any red-blooded male would mind having a beautiful woman like Catherine that eager for him! "Not at all," he growled, lifting her and shifting on the chair so his erection nudged her damp folds. His lips slid down her neck, looking for the perfect place to bite her. Her neck was mottled with fading bruises, evidence of how often and eagerly she offered herself to him. Pushing aside the collar of her blouse, he settled on a spot just below her slender collarbone, his tongue preparing the skin before his fangs drove deep, claiming her at the same moment his cock speared her tight passage. She cried out sharply, but he could taste the spike of passion in her blood and so did not ease his attentions, sucking harder instead as she began to move, riding him frantically.

She came quickly, squeezing around him as he continued to thrust up into her, his fangs continuing to draw the life-giving blood. Experience had already taught him that she would find her release again if he could wait long enough. His hips slowed fractionally, giving her a chance to recover and match his rhythm again. It took a few moments, but he could taste the resurgent desire and feel her begin to move with him again. This time, he did not hold back, letting her orgasm trigger his, their bodies slumping down into the chair still joined.

Chapter 39

SHUTTING the door to the bedroom softly, Sebastien wandered down the hall to the living room. He settled on the couch, reminding himself that he had no right to poke around in Thierry's things. Just because the wizard had admitted – to someone else – that he was attracted to Sebastien did not change anything. Not yet. Not until Thierry could admit his attraction to Sebastien himself. The admonition did nothing to ease his curiosity, though, and finally, he gave in, telling himself that he was not snooping if he looked at things on public display.

As he made his way around the room, he realized with some surprise that he saw nothing of Thierry there. He felt no sense of his partner's influence or even his presence. Frowning, he examined the photos on the mantle. Many of the pictures included the same woman – Thierry's late wife, he presumed. He wondered who the man in several of the photos was. He bore no resemblance to either Thierry or his wife, making the vampire wonder if the deceased had found a new lover. The thought bothered him on Thierry's behalf because he knew his partner had maintained hopes of reuniting with his wife once the war ended. The idea that she had cared so little for the other wizard that she would act thus, surely knowing Thierry's hopes, made the vampire angry. His wizard deserved better than that.

Taking a deep breath, Sebastien reminded himself that he was jumping to conclusions. Yes, the photos seemed damning, but he did not know who the other man was. He could well be a cousin or an old friend, relationships that could explain the easy intimacy he read in their body language.

He did wonder why Thierry had chosen to bring him here rather than to wherever the wizard now resided. Was it Thierry's way of keeping him at a distance, of reminding him that he had been married and was still in love with his wife? Sebastien needed no reminder of that other than the taste of Thierry's blood. The man's grief had been palpable from the beginning and it had barely begun to fade in the days since then, despite the admission Sebastien had overheard in Thierry's office that morning.

Forcing himself to think with his brain rather than his raging libido, Sebastien tried to consider all he had seen and heard since joining the alliance. He had watched partnerships grow between vampires and wizards, watched vampires he had known for years as solitary creatures suddenly working side by side with wizards they barely knew, fighting to protect those same wizards with a ferocity he was at a loss to explain. Blair was a perfect example. Four days hardly seemed long enough for his partner's death to send the vampire into such a state of distress, yet Sebastien could not deny the evidence before his eyes. Blair had killed a woman last night in cold blood because she had viciously murdered his partner.

Perhaps most telling of all, though, was Orlando. Sebastien knew only a little of the young vampire's story, having avoided Jean for so long, but everything he knew indicated that Orlando was not one to trust easily or quickly. Yet the vampire had bound himself to a wizard with an unbreakable vow less than three days after their first meeting. Sebastien understood instant attraction – he had fallen for Thibaut in a matter of weeks – but he did not have the scars from the past that Orlando bore. Yet of all the partnerships, Orlando's was the most complete, the most comprehensive. Sebastien had no idea what would happen when the war was over, but win or lose, Orlando was tied to Alain for the rest of the wizard's life. Orlando's willingness to make that kind of bond struck Sebastien as out of character, although he had seen enough to realize that Jean, who knew Orlando best of all, did not seem overly concerned. Surely if there were some dark magic at work, Jean would have realized it and kept the alliance from forming in the first place. The lure of social and legal legitimacy was strong, but surely not strong enough to make Jean break faith with the vampire community. He and Sebastien did not get along, but Sebastien refused to believe something like that of the other vampire, regardless of their past difficulties. Jean had one blind spot – Sebastien's Aveu de Sang with Thibaut. That did not make him a bad leader, only a flawed man like all the rest.

Pushing aside thoughts of his Avoué, Sebastien turned his consideration instead to the man asleep in the next room and the possibilities that the wizard's overheard confession raised. His own desire for his partner dated to the first time he had fed deeply from Thierry, but he had suppressed it out of respect for the man's grief. He could still taste grief when he fed, but it seemed that the desire he thought a figment of his imagination was in fact real. The rest of the conversation, though, gave him pause. He did not doubt his own attractiveness, but he found it odd that Thierry would suddenly conceive this interest in a man when he had never evinced any such feelings before. At the same time, his baser instincts clamored for the chance to introduce the wizard to the pleasures of the flesh between two men. The thought of being the first to touch, to stretch, to take that virgin arse had him instantly hard. He forced that reaction away, concentrating on the fact that Thierry deserved to be seduced, not just fucked meaninglessly.

A part of him hesitated, wondering if Thierry had thought through his desire or if he was really just reacting to the undeniable intimacy of feeding. Sebastien had discovered long ago that even when he did not mix sex and feeding, his chosen prey were far more comfortable if they could accept the idea of him as a lover. Rarely did he find a straight man who would willingly and comfortably offer his neck to a male vampire. Yet Thierry had done so repeatedly in the last four days. Every time Sebastien had asked, in fact. Was Thierry truly interested in him? Or were his feelings evoked by the mixture of his own recent loss and the incredible intimacy of feeding, that so closely mirrored an intimacy that had been missing in the wizard's life for two years? As much as he wanted it to be the former, he was very much afraid it would prove to be the latter. Unfortunately, the only way to find out meant opening himself to rejection.

On silent feet, he made his way down the hall to the bedroom where Thierry slept, opening the door enough to peer inside. Despite the chill outside, the wizard had stripped down to his boxers and a t-shirt to sleep. His dreams must have been restless, for he had tangled the covers around his legs, leaving his arms bare to the morning air. Even with the volets closed, a dim light permeated the room, enough that Sebastien's preternatural vision could make out the slight tremors that chased their way across Thierry's skin. Frowning, he stepped quickly into the room, loosening the covers and pulling them up over his partner's shoulders. Thierry turned in his sleep, catching Sebastien's hand. His eyes never opened, but he pulled on the captured arm. "Stay," he mumbled before falling back into fitful slumber.

Sebastien considered extricating himself from Thierry's grasp and leaving the wizard alone, but the request had been clear. Even as he scolded himself for opening his heart up to disappointment, he slid into the bed next to the other man, spooning up behind him and draping an arm over the recumbent form. He closed his eyes and resigned himself to the hours of torture until Thierry awoke.

Thierry woke from five hours of uninterrupted sleep to the feeling of a hard body behind his and an arm cradling him close. He lay there for several moments, simply basking in the pleasure of being held. It had been two long years since he had last shared a bed with someone, even if only to sleep. The comfort it brought him defied measurement.

Stretching slowly, he rolled onto his back, shifting slightly against the body that held his. Immediately, Sebastien started to pull away, but Thierry caught his arm, not quite ready to get up. "Not yet," he murmured, clinging to the fading sense of peace. "I haven't slept this well since the war started."

The quiet admission thrilled Sebastien, convincing him to linger a little longer and to offer, "You only have to ask. It's no hardship to hold you."

"I wouldn't want to impose," Thierry began.

Sebastien chuckled. "Until four days ago, I spent my days trapped inside by the sunlight, to while away the hours as I could until it was dark again. I don't sleep the way you do, but I do need to rest. As long as having me next to you helps you sleep, it's not that different from resting anywhere else."

Not that different, but not entirely the same either, when the warmth of Thierry's body heated Sebastien's own blood, giving rise to the kind of lascivious thoughts best suited to an entirely different kind of relationship. He shifted carefully, making sure not to brush against Thierry's body, not wanting the wizard to feel the erection inspired by the hours in bed.

"If you're sure," Thierry allowed. He certainly would not complain about the opportunity to be close to the object of his affections. Closing his eyes again, he enjoyed the feeling of having Sebastien next to him, the sense of rightness that filled him at having Sebastien's arm over his chest. It should have been a strange feeling, lying in bed with a man this way. He and Alain had slept in the same bed before, on the rare occasion when the situation left them no other option, but it had never felt this way. There had never been any awkwardness between him and his best friend, but neither had they ever relaxed this way, almost in each other's arms, a sense of intimacy building between them.

Turning his head, Thierry smiled at the vampire. "Do you need to feed?"

Sebastien's whole body tensed with the incredible, immediate desire to roll Thierry beneath him and ravish him with fangs and cock, taking his ease in the tender flesh of the wizard's neck and arse. "I'll be fine until the end of our shift," he forced himself to say. "It'll be dark soon anyway."

Thierry nodded, disappointed not to have that excuse to move closer to Sebastien. "Then I should eat," he declared lazily.

Sebastien smiled. "You don't sound very enthusiastic."

"I slept better than I have in years, but that doesn't mean it was enough," Thierry laughed. "It'll take more than one night – or day – in your arms to catch up completely."

"As many as it takes," Sebastien replied instantly, wanting Thierry against him but also reminded suddenly how great a toll the war had taken on his partner. If he could offer succor in any way, he would do it, regardless of the cost to his self-control.

Rolling to his side to face the vampire, Thierry studied the earnest, loyal eyes intently, searching for anything that might help him interpret Sebastien's words. He knew what he wanted them to mean, but wishful thinking alone could not make it so. He took a deep breath, working up the nerve to ask, when the smell of Aleth's shampoo on the pillows flooded his senses, swamping him with guilt.

Sebastien felt the change in Thierry's mood immediately, even before the wizard rolled away from him and out of bed, mumbling an inaudible excuse. The vampire had no idea what had suddenly changed, but he caught a glimpse of anguish on his partner's face in the mirror as he disappeared into the bathroom. Resisting the urge to curse in frustration, Sebastien turned onto his back and stared at the high ceiling, wondering what had just happened. He fought the temptation to follow his partner and demand an explanation, but Thierry owed him no explanations. Their only duty to each other revolved around the contingencies of the alliance, whatever Sebastien might desire otherwise. That those contingencies had thrust them into a far more intimate setting far more quickly than normal did not change reality, did not increase the time since Thierry's wife had been killed, could not begin to make the sudden attraction Thierry had admitted to feeling less disconcerting. However much Sebastien wanted more, he would have to be patient or he would never get what he so desperately desired.

In the bathroom, Thierry turned the water on high and pressed his forehead against the cold tiles as he waited for the water to heat and the tub to fill. He cursed himself for being ten kinds of a fool. Yes, Aleth's house – his house again – was far safer than his apartment if Serrier decided to attack, but that did not make it the smartest choice given the rest of his recent thoughts. He felt incredibly guilty at the thought of lying in Aleth's bed, the bed they had once shared, and lusting after someone else. Sebastien's gender still disturbed him on some level, but that issue did not figure into his current reaction. Male or female, he was betraying Aleth's memory by bringing someone else here so soon after her death.

Stepping into the tub, he switched the water to spray and lifted the nozzle, letting the water run over his face and down his shoulders, taking the last vestiges of sleep with it. Despite the guilt still riding him hard, he could not deny how well he had slept last night or how right it had felt to wake in Sebastien's arms. As alien as the concept remained in many respects, being close to Sebastien seemed the most natural thing in the world most of the time. He suspected that his reaction this morning would have been far different had they gone to his apartment last night rather than to the house. Had he subconsciously sought an excuse to delay matters between them? Setting down the nozzle in his hand, he scrubbed his hair and body, trying to separate his desires from his fears.

He feared the physical aspect of this budding relationship, but mostly because it was unknown. He had no doubt Sebastien could guide him through the experience with consummate ease, and if he had other questions or concerns, he could take them to Alain. His best friend might tease him a little, but he would do his best to address them and allay Thierry's fears.

He feared betrayal, not in terms of the alliance, but in terms of being able to hold Sebastien's interest. His track record in attracting women was high. Aleth had been the only one he had ever managed to keep by his side for more than a few months, though, and even she had left him eventually. He knew nothing of attracting men, much less keeping a male lover. What if Sebastien grew bored with him? What if the vampire wanted a more experienced lover? What if he wanted a more submissive lover? The vampire's comments about his Avoué had led Thierry to believe Sebastien had been the one in charge in that relationship, but he knew himself well enough to accept that he would never just give in gracefully because Sebastien wanted it that way.

Most of all, though, he feared losing Sebastien as he had lost Aleth. The alliance patrols were suffering far fewer casualties than before, and so far no vampire had been lost, but Thierry was not naïve enough to believe that would always be the case. The *Abbatoire* did not work on them, but other spells could well be enough to destroy them. Once Serrier knew of the alliance – and Marcel seemed to be considering making that announcement soon – he would start using different spells, spells that could potentially endanger Sebastien and the other vampires. His partner had already shown himself willing to step into the thick of battle or to deal with a wizard one on one, and his only defense would be Thierry's own skill. He wanted to wrap Sebastien up and keep him safe, but he knew better than to suggest it. His partner would no more agree to that than he would if Sebastien suggested it.

Fears enumerated, he turned his thoughts to his desires. What did he want from Sebastien? His body had an immediate answer to that: sex. Every time the vampire fed from him, Thierry felt his sex-starved body go into overdrive. No one had touched him that intimately – what a concept to think of giving Sebastien his blood as an act of intimacy! – in two years, and he would have to be dead not to react to the heat of another body close to his, pressing up against his side, leaning across him, lips and tongue licking along his skin. It was not all that surprising, in a way, that he reacted to Sebastien the way he did.

He desired companionship. For most of his life, Alain had met that need, the two of them spending their free time together, even after they both married. And Alain had done his best these past two years to continue to provide what Thierry needed, but it could not compare with having someone to come home to every night, to having a warm body in bed next to his, holding him through the night, gentling his dreams. Sebastien had done that last night and had offered to do it as often as Thierry needed. Every night for the rest of his life would be a good start.

He desired love. He thought he had found that with Aleth, but he had his doubts now. Maybe emotions were different for vampires or when vampires were involved, but Thierry saw the way Alain and Orlando looked at each other, the way they gravitated toward each other as if even a room's width was too much distance between them, and Thierry's heart cried out for that same depth of devotion. He knew Sebastien was capable of that kind of commitment, that kind of devotion, for he had given it once before, when he had made an Aveu de Sang with his long-dead lover. Thierry was not entirely comfortable with the binding magic of such a promise nor would he ever dream of trying to replace Sebastien's lost love, but the fact that the vampire had once been willing to make that kind of commitment reassured Thierry that he might be willing to stand at one man's side again for that man's lifetime. Rinsing away the soap and shampoo, he asked himself if he could make the return commitment. Could he promise to stand at Sebastien's side for his own lifetime? The answer was surprisingly simple.

Rising to his feet and drying off, he made his decision. No more guilt. No more holding back. If Sebastien wanted him, Sebastien could have him. He hoped the vampire would be willing to take things slowly, giving Thierry time to adjust to the novelty of the physical experiences, but he would take what he could get. Starting right now.

Opening the bathroom door, he found the bedroom empty, but he could hear Sebastien in the other room and smell the aroma of strong coffee. Good. That would give him something to do with his hands while he tried to explain his thoughts to his partner. Dressing quickly, he walked out into the living room, a smile on his face.

Sebastien looked up from where he had finally settled on the sofa when Thierry reappeared, clean, dressed and smiling. He resisted the urge to shake his head at his partner's quixotic moods. If he was going to make anything more of this partnership than a simple military alliance, he would have to learn to adjust to Thierry's moods. He set aside the picture he still held in his hand and smiled in return.

"I'm sorry about earlier," Thierry began, sitting down at the table and gesturing for Sebastien to join him. "I should explain."

"You don't owe me anything," Sebastien insisted, his earlier ruminations still fresh on his mind.

"Then I'd like to give you an explanation," Thierry continued. "This is my house, but I haven't lived here in two years. When Aleth and I split, she stayed here and I moved into an apartment in town, but it's cramped and messy and not nearly as comfortable as the house. So when you decided to come home with me, it just made sense to come here."

That explained a lot, Sebastien realized, the pictures, the complete absence of Thierry's presence in the house, even his partner's tension yesterday as they were coming here the first time, before Laurent was killed, before they went after his killer. Thierry's comments did not seem to require an answer, so he waited to see if the wizard would go on.

"I slept in our – her – our bed last night and when I woke up in your arms, it felt both completely right and completely wrong. I was doing all right until I smelled her perfume on the pillows," Thierry continued slowly. "And then the guilt kicked in."

"What do you have to feel guilty about?" Sebastien asked seriously. "All we did was sleep. You still had your boxers on and I was completely dressed. I didn't even feed from you."

This was it. The moment of truth. Thierry took a deep breath and met Sebastien's eyes. "It wasn't what we did, but what I wanted to do," he admitted softly.

Sebastien tensed, sensing the revelation at hand. He forced himself to stay seated and to ask calmly, or as calmly as he could manage, "What did you want to do?"

"Kiss you," Thierry replied evenly, his heart pounding violently as he waited for Sebastien's reaction.

Chapter 40

"AND now?" Sebastien asked, desire darkening his voice. "What do you want now?"

"For you to kiss me," Thierry replied honestly, still nervous about taking that final – or perhaps first – step.

The sharp intake of breath from across the table assured Thierry that Sebastien shared his desire. Hazel eyes narrowed as the vampire rose from his seat and stepped around the table. He held out a strong hand, pulling Thierry to his feet when he clasped the proffered limb.

Now that he finally had the chance to kiss Thierry, Sebastien intended to take his time and savor the moment. Sliding his hands into the wizard's platinum blond hair, he tilted the man's face back enough to meet the vibrant green eyes. He read his partner's nervousness in the emerald depths, but no doubt. Keeping himself firmly under control, he lowered his head and brushed his lips lightly over Thierry's.

Thierry exhaled sharply when he felt Sebastien take control of their interaction, the newness of that experience alone enough to remind him what he was doing. While he remained hyperaware of whose lips brushed his in that first tender kiss, he realized with some surprise that he had no interest in pulling away or in reclaiming control. He was perfectly content to let the vampire guide him, to be kissed rather than to kiss.

Perhaps because he had so little to compare it to, Thierry had never really paid much attention to the light mustache and goatee that surrounded his partner's mouth when Sebastien fed from him; but now, as their lips met, the unexpected sensation of the facial hair made him exquisitely aware of who was kissing him. He could not close his eyes and pretend this was just another kiss – not that he truly wanted to. No, the rasp of short hairs against his skin brought him face to face again with the reality of exactly what he was doing. The thought did not bother him nearly as much as he thought it should have.

Sebastien's fingers massaged Thierry's scalp as they cradled his head. He pulled back for a moment, meeting the wizard's eyes, searching again for any sign that his partner had changed his mind, but he saw only the same tentative flickers of desire he had noticed earlier. Emboldened, he lowered his head again, sealing their mouths together more fully this time, nipping lightly at Thierry's lower lip before sucking the tender flesh into his mouth. He fought to keep his fangs from dropping, to stop himself from biting into the tempting bow. He would not do that without Thierry's explicit permission, and now was not the time to ask. Instead, he laved it with his tongue, asking permission for a different kind of intimacy.

Thierry gasped at the seductive pull of Sebastien's lips on his, at the graze of the vampire's teeth. Not his fangs, the wizard noticed dazedly, a courtesy he both appreciated and regretted. Now was not the time to mention it, but he hoped Sebastien would realize eventually that he did not need to be quite so careful. Then Sebastien's tongue brushed Thierry's lips and he gave up thinking completely, opening his mouth in an invitation the vampire accepted with alacrity.

As soon as Thierry's lips parted in welcome, Sebastien surged inside, claiming the heated orifice with a passion and possessiveness he had not felt since Thibaut died. He had not spent the intervening years celibately, but this kiss was different, a powerful, passionate connection that left the vampire trembling with desire. His hands slid from Thierry's head, down his neck to his back, feeling the tension investing the wizard's body, a tension that matched his own. He wanted to pull his partner tightly against him, to back him against the wall and ravish him thoroughly. Every moan, every movement of Thierry's body assured him the other man was willing, but the remembered conversation from that morning held him back. Thierry might be willing, but he was also untouched, at least in that respect, and Sebastien had enough sensitivity – barely – to be able to restrain himself. His partner deserved a first time worthy of him, not a frantic fuck against the wall, however good it would feel on Sebastien's end.

Lifting his head, he sought his partner's gaze, only to find the emerald orbs shuttered. "Look at me, Thierry," he murmured softly.

Thierry moaned in protest when his partner broke their kiss, hands moving automatically to pull the vampire's head back down to his. He had forgotten Sebastien's strength, though, his vampire not so much as budging.

"Look at me," Sebastien repeated, waiting for the wizard's eyes to open.

They did slowly, eyelids fluttering open to reveal an expression of such deeply felt desire that Sebastien felt his convictions waver. Reminding himself of the rewards of patience, he dropped a quick kiss on Thierry's lips before saying, "We have to stop now."

"Why?" Thierry's voice was husky with desire, deeper than usual, rasping along Sebastien's skin like velvet.

"Because if we don't, you're going to get far more than you're ready for," the vampire explained.

"How do you know what I'm ready for?"

"I overheard part of your conversation with Alain this morning," Sebastien admitted. "I didn't mean to eavesdrop, but I'm glad in a way that I heard what I did. Would you have told me you'd never been with a man before if I'd pulled you back into the bedroom now? Would you have made sure I was as careful with you as you deserve?"

Thierry frowned. "I'm not some shrinking virgin," he reminded his partner. "You're not going to scare me off."

Sebastien lowered his head and nuzzled Thierry's neck, his lips tracing the marks his fangs had left. "I wasn't worried about that," he promised. "But I refuse to hurt you, and don't pretend that I couldn't, even without meaning to. We'll get there – don't doubt that for a minute – but not today and not in such a haze of passion that I have no control. I imagine that'll happen someday, but not your first time. The first time you have sex with a man – with me – I'm going to make love to you, not just fuck you through the mattress, however much we might enjoy it."

Thierry groaned. "You can't say things like that and then expect me to stop!"

Sebastien's grin turned feral. "I didn't say we had to stop. Just that we're not doing certain things today. I'll gladly kiss you until we have to go back on duty if that's what you want, but that's as far as it goes."

"Necking on the couch like horny teenagers?" Thierry gaped. "What are we, fourteen?"

Sebastien chuckled. "Take it or leave it."

Thierry considered refusing simply on the principle of the matter, but he could still taste Sebastien and the one kiss they had shared barely counted as an appetizer. If he could not have the full meal – and he could tell from the adamant set of Sebastien's shoulders that his partner would not be persuaded to change his mind – he could at least gorge himself on what was offered. And hopefully leave the vampire as desperately hungry for more as he already was. Leaning up, he joined their mouths, his kiss conveying his answer.

Sebastien let Thierry back him into the living room toward the chintz couch where he had sat and contemplated the photos last night. Thierry tried to push him backwards onto the brightly colored fabric, but Sebastien resisted, bearing his partner down onto the overstuffed cushions instead. A muffled curse surprised him as Thierry arched up and turned to look at the couch beneath him.

"What's this?" he muttered, fishing the photograph Sebastien had been examining that morning out from between the cushions.

Sebastien grimaced, sure the revelation represented by the photo would ruin his plans for a frustrating, titillating evening, but Thierry did not seem upset as he examined the picture.

Thierry studied the image stoically, recognizing the intimacy between Aleth and the other man in the photo. He traced his wife's smiling face, seeing a happiness there he had not seen in years. The expected twang of jealousy, of betrayal, did not materialize, and he realized he was glad she had found someone who could put a smile back on her face when he had failed so miserably these last few years. Looking up, he met Sebastien's worried gaze as he set the picture aside on the low table in front of the couch. "I'm glad she was happy before she died. We'd both been alone and miserable for too long."

"Not anymore," Sebastien said softly, settling onto the couch next to the wizard. He wanted to draw Thierry back into his arms, but the mood had shifted, though not the way he had feared when Thierry first picked up the photograph. He stretched his arm along the back of the couch, encircling Thierry's shoulders, his fingers stroking gently up and down the column of the wizard's neck, and waited to see how the other man reacted.

Thierry leaned back into the gentle caress, letting it soothe away the last of his doubts. He did not know exactly how a relationship between the vampire and himself would work, but he did know he was ready to give it a try. "Feels good," he murmured, tilting his head so his lips moved against the skin of Sebastien's neck as he spoke. "It feels good having you here with me."

Sebastien let his head fall back against the cushions of the overstuffed couch, baring his neck to Thierry in a way he would never have done to another vampire, but between the two of them, there was no question of dominance and submission, no question of alpha or beta, simply two lost and battered souls each searching for someone to help smooth the edges of their broken hearts and make life a little less burdensome for a time. Thierry's fingers played with the ends of his shoulder-length hair as his lips nuzzled the smooth skin of his neck before working their way over his goatee to his lips. They parted eagerly for the wizard, accepting the kiss with the same enthusiasm he had shown earlier when bestowing a kiss on his partner. His body reacted immediately, clamoring for more, but he ignored it. He would seduce Thierry in his own time, at his own pace, and today was not that day.

DAVID stood nervously outside the entrance to Sang Froid and shivered again at all the implications of the name of Angelique's establishment. A restaurant, Jean had compared it to according to Marcel, rather than a brothel, but either way, the very idea made him incredibly uncomfortable. Still, he understood his duty, and at the moment, that meant convincing the owner of said business to accept his apology and return to the alliance. Taking a deep breath, he pushed open the door and stepped inside.

"Can I help you?" a voice asked from the shadows. David spun, instantly alert.

"I need to talk to Angelique," he explained.

A frown crossed the face of the man who stepped from the shadows. David was relieved to see the man was a mortal, not a vampire, but disapproval poured off the other despite having that in common. "Miss Bouaddi is busy," he said coldly.

"I'll wait then," David replied, trying to keep his voice steady as he shuddered at the idea of spending hours in the vampire's lair. Marcel's orders rang in his head, though. *Do not return without your partner.* That left him little choice but to wait out his partner's anger. "If you'd just let her know that David Sabatier is here when she has time to see me."

The frown deepened. "I don't know what you did to upset her, but you don't want to do it again," the man warned. "You'll find that her friends are very protective of her."

David wanted to defend himself, to deny anything in the first place, but he saw no point in it. Even if he had some chance of convincing another mortal of his view, these people would all take Angelique's side. She was the one responsible for their livelihood and their loyalty to her seemed to know no bounds. He supposed that ought to tell him something about the truth of her words and Jean's in so far as Angelique's assertions about her business were concerned, but he could not dismiss the qualms that had troubled him in the first place. Whether for blood or sex or both, Angelique sold people. That she cared about and for her employees only partially mitigated the moral outrage he felt. He could not allow any of that to affect him any more, though. Marcel had been very clear in his orders and David had enough loyalty to the old wizard and the cause they were fighting for to set aside his scruples for the time being. He would apologize as ordered, do his best to make things work between them for as long as the alliance functioned and save his anger for later. "I'm not here to cause trouble," he said finally to the man who waited impatiently for his reply.

"Good," the manager said, "because we don't tolerate it here. You can wait over there."

David took the indicated seat and prepared to wait. He had no idea when or if Angelique would see him, but he would simply have to outlast her again.

Inside her office, Angelique watched the scene play out between the manager and her partner. She could not hear what they said, but she could easily imagine François's staunch defense. She had not given him any of the details, but he had worked with her long enough to know the nuances of her moods. She had no doubt François had given David the sharp side of his tongue. Switching the scene on the security monitor, she worked her way through the building, checking to make sure all was in order. That done, she turned her attention to the other business on her desk. She would see David eventually, in her own time. He could cool his heels for a few hours, a little extra proof of the sincerity of whatever he had come to say. She knew she would take him back if he apologized despite her words to Jean the night before, because she saw the benefits of the alliance and the price of ignoring the situation far too clearly to do otherwise. She would listen to his apology, drink his blood so she would have that protection, and fight as she could for the duration of the war, but she would not trust him beyond that.

Finally, she had no more excuses to delay, leaving the sanctuary of her office long enough to call David into her presence. "You wanted to see me?"

"I owe you an apology," David began when the door shut behind him.

"You do," Angelique agreed coldly.

"I overreacted," he continued. "I hope you'll give me another chance."

"Why should I?" she demanded, not yet satisfied with his approach.

"We need you in the alliance," he explained, "need everyone's help. There's too much at stake for us to lose the war."

"So you've said. That doesn't explain why I should give you another chance. I can work with the alliance without having to deal with you."

David was stymied. What did she want him to say? He had apologized. "In a limited capacity," he agreed, "but if we work together, your options are greatly expanded."

"So your interest is purely in what I can do for the Milice," Angelique clarified.

Again, David had the feeling of impending doom without the slightest idea how or why.

"What else is there?" he wanted to know. "That's the purpose of the alliance."

Angelique nodded once, surprised at the sense of resignation she felt. While she could look at his reddish hair, blue eyes and boyish features and feel a certain attraction, she accepted that it was purely physical in nature. This was not a man to command her attention and her senses with the kind of authority al-Marbruk, her first protector, had wielded. Over the years of her long existence, she had slept with sultans and kings, cardinals and prelates, men of such power and authority that no one dared turn their backs on them lest they find themselves in a situation not of their own choosing. She had felt a hint of authority in Marcel, in a few of the captains, but David did not have that rank, that presence, that authority. With a short nod, she held out her hand, palm up.

Bemused, David put his hand in hers, watching as she turned it over to reveal his wrist, bare against the cool fall air. She lifted it to her lips and bit down firmly. Not harshly, but without any of the seductive preparation she had used in the past. He felt a pang of regret at the loss, but told himself firmly it was better this way, that they work together as partners but not lovers. He had enough to worry about without adding sexual tension to the list. Perhaps after the war... he pushed that thought aside. It had no place in their current interactions.

The hot blood that splashed across her tongue and into her veins warmed Angelique, but the emotions she could taste there only saddened her more. If things had only been different... but they were not, and that was the reality she had to live with.

Chapter 41

"WHERE to tonight?" Raymond asked when he saw Jean arrive for their scheduled duty already wearing his medallion.

"More clubs and bars," the vampire replied. "The more of my kind I can reach, the more effective my message. And the more chance that we'll stumble across our rogue."

Raymond nodded. "Let's go, then. Marcel told me we were excused from regular patrols as long as we needed to take care of business with the vampires. Do you have your repère?"

Jean reached in his pocket and drew out the rosary that Père Emmanuel had given him. Raymond shook his head and chuckled. "Do you suppose I'll ever get used to seeing you carrying that?"

Jean shrugged as he slipped the holy object back into his pocket. "The vampires have as many misconceptions about wizards as the mortals do about us. We can only hope this alliance does away with some of them."

Raymond smiled. "It already has."

In easy accord, the two left Milice headquarters, heading toward the métro and Montmartre. They stopped first at an internet café run by Malika Robin so Jean could check on her and repeat his warning about Edouard from the night before. Finding everything in order and the owner perfectly willing to help, they headed back into the night.

"Bellaiche!"

Jean spun at the sound of the deep voice calling his name. At the vampire's side, Raymond tensed, his hand reaching automatically for his wand, though he did not draw it out yet. While he would defend his partner against any threat, he would wait for some sign that Jean needed that help. He did not want to undermine the vampire's authority in any way.

"Cabalet," Jean replied with a regal nod, acknowledging the new arrival as an equal without giving an inch of ground. "You're far away from home."

"Amiens is not so far that I haven't heard some interesting rumors," the other vampire replied.

Glancing around, Jean shook his head. "Not here. Let's find somewhere we can talk without being overheard." He turned to Raymond. "Sang Froid is just around the corner. Angelique will let us use a room."

Raymond nodded, maintaining his silence as he followed the two vampires. He had no idea who the other vampire was, but he was obviously someone of importance given Jean's reaction. He fell into his habitual role of observer, his guard still up, his attention focused entirely outward, on their surroundings and on the two vampires in front of him. Cabalet, as Jean had addressed him, was tall, well over six feet, with broad shoulders and a commanding presence that spoke far less of physical strength and far more of the same kind of charisma Raymond had seen Jean project the night before. Whoever this was, it would behoove them to be careful in their dealings with him.

As Jean predicted, a request for a room and some privacy netted them an empty office. "So what brings you to Paris?" Jean asked with deceptive calm. "You mentioned rumors."

"You aren't going to introduce your companion?" Cabalet challenged. His eyes raked the other man harshly. Clearly, this was no vampire, but that told the tall vampire nothing of the role he played in Jean's life at the moment. The man was in his late forties with a high forehead and slightly receding hairline that only accentuated the strong planes of his face. Cabalet wondered for a moment if the man was Jean's new consort, but the mortal, whoever he was, radiated too much confidence and authority to be simply Bellaiche's lover. He had watched the vampire chief consult the other man, albeit silently, an act vampires of their station rarely committed with anyone, much less a mortal, and the man was still here despite the sensitive nature of their conversation. Whoever this was, he clearly had to be considered now in the game at hand.

"Raymond Payet," the wizard said, holding out his hand but providing no other explanation for his presence. He knew he still had much to learn about the game the vampires played, but he had already learned enough to know that knowledge was power, given up only when doing so benefited him more than his adversary. And everyone, but especially someone currently unknown to him, was his adversary.

"Luc Cabalet," the vampire replied.

"My counterpart in Amiens," Jean added, also not explaining Raymond's place in his life. "So these rumors?"

"They say you've teamed up with the Milice wizards," Luc elucidated.

"What an interesting rumor," Jean drawled, leaning back in his chair. "What else do 'they' say?"

Luc frowned. "Drop the posturing, Jean. I don't have time for the game. If there's something going on that I need to know about, I'd appreciate you telling me."

"We live for the game," Jean countered, though he sat up straighter and met the other man's gaze seriously. "You're asking for information that isn't purely mine to give. Suppose for a moment the rumors were true. What interest would it be to you?"

"I'd want to know what you had going and whether it could benefit me and my vampires as well," Luc replied bluntly.

Jean turned his attention to Raymond sitting at his side. The wizard nodded slightly, hoping Marcel would approve. More allies could only help them and alienating this vampire could send him and his people to the opposite side.

"It seems you've heard right," Jean answered, leaning forward and fixing Luc with a piercing stare that the other vampire returned in equal measure.

"So what's the deal?"

"I don't have to tell you about the war going on," Jean began, "but Chavinier has convinced me that the consequences of a Milice defeat would be far-reaching enough to affect us as well."

"So what have you done?" Luc demanded.

"Formed an alliance," Jean replied. "We help them win the war; they make sure our contributions are recognized, not just publicly, but officially."

"How?"

"Within a week, two at the most, legislators loyal to Chavinier will be introducing bills into the Parlement to guarantee vampires equal protection under the law," Raymond answered, re-entering the conversation finally.

Luc whistled softly under his breath. "And you trust this Chavinier to keep his word?" he asked Jean.

Raymond bristled at the question, but Jean's hand on his arm kept him from reacting. "Marcel will keep his word," he declared with complete conviction. "You know blood doesn't lie."

The partners could read the surprise and disbelief that crossed the other vampire's face as the significance of the assertion registered.

"No," Jean added after a moment, "wizard's blood won't hurt us. On the contrary, it can even protect us."

"Protect us from what?" Luc scoffed. There was little in the world, other than sunlight, that could damage a vampire beyond healing.

Jean laughed softly. "When was the last time you felt the sun on your skin?"

"I never knew you were cruel," Luc retorted, his eyes narrowing in anger.

"I can't prove it to you until dawn," Jean admitted, "but for four days now, I have walked in the sun unharmed."

"From drinking the blood of a wizard?" Luc clarified.

"From drinking the blood of my partner," Jean specified. "Not every wizard's blood will work. Just, for me, Raymond's. For you, it will be some other wizard."

"So how do I find that wizard?" Even as he spoke, he mentally reassessed the man at Jean's side. Payet – Raymond – a wizard whose blood purportedly let Jean walk in the sunlight unharmed... Luc searched his face again, seeking any sign of that kind of power in the long, narrow face, anything to hint at the potency of the magic running in the other man's veins. Jean had named the wizard his equal, his partner, an idea that made Luc nervous. How far did that partnership extend? Did that mean Luc would have to share his position with a mortal? He was not entirely sure his vampires would accept that.

"First, you agree to join the alliance with as many of your vampires as you trust to keep their word and fight for the Milice," Jean explained. "Then we'll work on finding your partner."

"Find me a partner and I'll see about joining the alliance," Luc countered. "There's nothing in it for me until I know you're telling the truth."

Again, Jean glanced at Raymond and the wizard nodded. If he and monsieur Lombard were right about the bond created by the exchange of blood, once Luc tasted his partner's blood, he would have far more trouble changing his mind about the alliance. "Very well," Jean agreed, "although with some wizards on patrol and others off shift, we may not find your partner tonight. How long can you stay?"

"There are rooms at Milice headquarters you can use for a day or two," Raymond added, "though they aren't the most comfortable quarters."

"Two days," Luc decided after a moment's consideration. "I'll give you two days to convince me and then we'll see."

"Fair enough," Jean replied.

ERIC and Vincent slipped through the darkness, avoiding the puddles of light thrown by the streetlamps, toward the rue de la Michodière where Serrier had said they would find the unfortunate Miss Gaudier. Eric had no illusions as to her fate. Even if she cooperated and gave Serrier every detail he could possibly desire, the wizard would never let her go. He could not afford to. The best she could hope for after she had answered his questions was a swift and painless death. Eric doubted she would be that lucky.

"This is it," Vincent whispered so softly Eric could barely hear him.

Eric nodded, drawing his wand and checking for wards on the door. They had no reason to believe their target had any magical involvement, but that did not mean no wizard lived in the vicinity. They did not want to accidentally alert anyone to their presence. Sensing nothing to impede them, he gestured for Vincent to start forward, their movements stealthy as they reached the door. A quiet word released the lock on the building door; another silenced the squeak of ancient hinges as they opened the entrance and snuck inside. They slipped up the stairs, eschewing the creaky elevator in favor of a silent ascent.

Finding the apartment with her name beside the doorbell, they repeated the spells and went inside, pausing as the door snicked behind them to assess the situation. Nothing stirred in the apartment, only the muffled hum of the refrigerator breaking the silence. Seeing two closed doors off the foyer, Eric motioned for Vincent to search one room while he searched the other. Serrier had been able to discover the location of the woman's apartment, but not its layout.

The interior doors opened as soundlessly as the exterior ones. Vincent disappeared inside one as Eric stepped into the other. The moonlight barely filtered through the closed volets, leaving the room cloaked in darkness, the furniture nothing more than darker spots against a dark background.

A thud and Vincent's growl drew his attention to the other room. He crossed the threshold, casting an illumination spell, in time to see Vincent cradling his head with one hand, the other drawn back to strike the petite blonde who held a heavy briefcase in her hand.

"Don't," he ordered Vincent, casting a second spell to freeze the woman in place. He had to admit, silently, to a certain modicum of respect for her courage in daring to attack Vincent who easily outweighed her by half, if not more. She was slight, with delicate features and soft blond hair, exactly the kind of woman he usually found himself attracted to. His eyes raked her neck, searching for some sign of the vampire's depredations, but the smooth skin was unblemished, making him wonder if their information was accurate. Of course, he had left love bites on his lovers in other places than their necks, so perhaps Bellaiche simply chose to be discreet in marking her.

"You're getting soft, Simonet," Vincent spat. "She tried to bash my skull in with her bag. Whatever's in it weights a ton."

"Pascal wants to question her," Eric retorted, knowing the nascent attraction, however futile, drove him to protect her now, even if he would be unable to later. If the vampire was right about her place in Bellaiche's life, nothing would be able to save her. If the vampire was wrong... he stopped that train of thought before it could form. Even if she was worthless to them in terms of information, Eric knew what her fate would be. Serrier always needed victims to keep Craig satisfied. "If you break her jaw with that bloody ham you call a fist, she won't be able to answer his questions and then he'll be pissed off at us. I don't have any desire to have his wrath turned on me. I've seen what he does to people who make him angry."

Vincent shivered reflexively, remembering more than one person who had known Serrier's wrath for failing to complete an assigned task. Perhaps wisdom was the better part of valor in this case. "Let's get her back to base. The sooner she's out of our hands and into his, the happier I'll be."

CHAOS greeted Raymond, Jean, and the other vampire as they walked back into Milice headquarters. With a frown, Raymond grabbed the arm of the first wizard to rush past him. "What's going on?" he snapped.

"A typhoon, in La Réunion," the other wizard explained in a rush.

"Where's Marcel?" Raymond asked immediately. "Or Alain? Or Thierry?"

"Marcel's with the President. The captains are off duty."

"Well, shit," Raymond muttered, letting the other man go. He turned to Jean, feeling the weight of both vampires' stares. "Until one of them gets here, you're the highest ranking person in the alliance," he informed his partner, "which means we get to sort out this chaos."

"I wouldn't know where to start," Jean admitted softly, his eyes sidling toward the other vampire.

Understanding what his partner did not say, Raymond nodded decisively. "Let me find you a room, Cabalet. We'll need to put off finding you a partner for a few hours until we can see who's around."

"Don't put yourself out on my account," Luc interjected smoothly. "I'll just observe quietly."

And judge us for every misstep, Raymond thought cynically, but a glance at Jean and the vampire's shrug gave him no other ideas. "As you wish. Just don't get in the way."

Without another glance at the newcomer, Raymond headed deeper into the building, toward the Salle des Cartes. Alain's lieutenant was on duty and Raymond judged him to be the senior officer in the room. "Lt. Fouquet, what's going on and why isn't one of the senior officers here?"

"We just got a report of a typhoon hitting La Réunion, sir," Lt. Fouquet reported. "It'll hit in a matter of hours. It came out of nowhere."

"Have you notified the general?"

"Yes, sir! We called him right away, but he was in a meeting with the President and stayed to see what orders came from L'Élysée. I've called Capitaines Magnier and Dumont, but neither of them has gotten here yet," the lieutenant explained.

"Is anyone on the ground there now?" Raymond wanted to know.

"No one's answering, but with the storm full force, they might not be able to answer anyway."

Raymond smothered a curse. Marcel had warned this could happen, natural disasters springing up without their usual warning signs because of the imbalance in the magical forces that governed the world, but so far, they had managed to prevent or avoid any tragedies. This time, they would not be so lucky. A few hours' notice to evacuate the entire coast of an island was simply not enough. Lives would be lost and the property damage would surely be immense. They could do nothing about that now, though. The people on the island would have to do their best until the storm passed and a relief effort could begin.

That was where Raymond's focus lay now. "We'll need emergency supplies," he told Lt. Fouquet. "Contact the army supplies manager and tell him we'll be sending a team of twenty as soon as the storm passes. We'll need rations, tents, and medical supplies in that first wave."

"Choose wizards with partners," Jean murmured at Raymond's elbow. "Their strength is as good as a wand."

Raymond nodded. "What will they need in terms of gear?"

"Rescue equipment, tools to dig with, that sort of thing," Jean replied. "As long as they can feed from their partners, they won't need shelter from the sun or much in the way of rest."

"That's all standard for this sort of operation," Raymond agreed. "Lt. Fouquet, we'll need volunteers for the rescue mission, priority given to paired wizards and vampires. Get the word out and make a list."

"Yes, sir," the wizard replied.

"Put our names on the list if you want," Jean offered softly.

Raymond smiled gratefully. "Lt. Fouquet," he called after the retreating wizard, "if anyone asks, my partner and I will be leading the team."

ALAIN stirred slowly in the bed, the novelty of waking on his own rather than from the alarm reminding him that he had the rare night off. He could feel Orlando's warmth in bed next to him, easing the transition from dreams to wakefulness, making him particularly aware of his "morning" erection. He shifted deeper under the heavy duvet, conserving the warmth against the crisp night air, nuzzling blindly against the side of Orlando's face and neck, seeking the comfort of his lover's presence.

The feeling of lips on his neck and ear startled Orlando from his reverie, only the scent of Alain's hair keeping him from flinching away. Remembering how tenderly Alain had coaxed him through his fears the last time they had made love, he ordered himself to relax and accept the gentle caress. The even huff of the wizard's breath told him his lover was still mostly asleep, of absolutely no threat to him. Silently, he chided himself for the thought. Even awake and at his most passionate, Alain was no threat to him. He had to stop thinking that way. Thurloe was destroyed a hundred years ago and Alain had shown himself worthy of Orlando's trust repeatedly. He fought himself silently as he felt Alain shift against him again, waking slowly. Fear held him back, but he had taken a first step already and he wanted to take another. He owed it to Alain to take another one.

Turning his head to seek the lips that caressed his skin, he kissed Alain softly, waiting for the cerulean eyes to open, for awareness to register. When they did, he deepened the kiss, feeling Alain's cock twitch eagerly against his hips. For a few moments, he luxuriated in the simple movement of lips against lips, the tender exchange soothing his fears again, giving him the strength to volunteer, "He would use his fangs to rend my flesh. No place was too sensitive, too private, to escape his attentions."

"His abuse," Alain contradicted. He hesitated for a moment before pressing his lips to Orlando's collarbone. "Will you let me?"

"I'm scared to," Orlando admitted, "but I think I have to."

"You know I'd never hurt you."

"My head knows it and my heart knows it," Orlando assured him, "but my body still forgets sometimes." He threaded his fingers into the reddish hair. "Help me forget what he did to me."

Alain hoped giving in to Orlando's request was the right choice. He could read the trepidation in his lover's dark eyes, in the tense lines of his body. He longed to taste the expanse of tawny flesh, perhaps even to close his lips around the thick cock that pleasured him so regularly, but he did not want to send Orlando back into his nightmares again and undo the progress of the day before. Slowly, he parted his lips, closing them over the ridge of bone beneath his lover's smooth chest, letting his tongue wet the skin before sucking gently. Lifting his head for a moment, he met Orlando's gaze again. The trepidation remained, but beneath that, he could see the first stirrings of desire. "Stop me if you need to."

"I will," Orlando promised, though he hoped it would not come to that. Alain deserved a relationship where he did not have to think through every touch before bestowing it. Alain deserved a lover he could love in return.

Trusting in that promise, Alain lowered his head again to the same spot, sucking on the delicate skin with a little more force before sliding his lips lower across Orlando's chest to a large, brown nipple. He brushed his lips over it repeatedly, waiting until the vampire squirmed beneath him to draw it into his mouth.

Orlando tensed for a moment when Alain sucked gently on his nipple, expecting to feel fangs piercing his flesh, but he opened his eyes and focused on Alain's hair. Thurloe had been dark, nothing like the man making love to him. In any way.

As he relaxed again, his desire rose to the fore, his fingers curling against Alain's skull, urging him to continue. He had loved Alain this way more than once, to their mutual pleasure. He was beginning to see the appeal as Alain's lips teased his nipple to attention. Desire swamped him, arching his back into the sucking pressure. He tensed for a moment when Alain's teeth joined the fray, but they could not pierce him, he reminded himself. Instead, the sweet pinch of his lover's teeth sent additional sparks dancing down the vampire's nerves.

Slowly, awareness left him under the heat of his desire. He lost track of the individual touches as they faded into a tapestry of passion and tenderness, Alain's mouth making love to him with such devotion that Orlando lost all fear. Even when they slid lower and closed around his cock, Orlando knew only joy.

Alain moved slowly down Orlando's body, mostly kissing and licking, only occasionally letting his teeth catch the sensitive skin. Orlando writhed beneath his caresses, encouraging Alain to continue, to taste as he had desired to do since the first time they had made love. He relished the salty flavor, the heaviness of flesh against his tongue. A part of him wanted to keep going, to bring Orlando the ultimate pleasure this way, but even more than that, he wanted to feel Orlando inside him again.

He lifted his head, bestowing a last lick on the glistening shaft. Orlando's moan of protest warmed his heart but did not dissuade him. He leaned up and kissed his lover again, letting the vampire taste his own flavor on Alain's tongue. "I want you inside me," he whispered. "Make love to me."

Without hesitation, Orlando rolled Alain to his back, covering his lover's body with his own, his hips thrusting forcefully against Alain's, relishing the feel of the wizard's cock rubbing against his own. He was tempted to take them both in hand and bring them to completion that way, but Alain had voiced a very specific request, one Orlando desperately wanted to fulfill. Grabbing the gel from the bedside table, he slicked his fingers and slid them into place, stretching and preparing the tight entrance and snug passage. Alain immediately bucked up into his touch, thrilling Orlando to the depths of his being. He hoped the joy of Alain's responsiveness never faded.

Satisfied with his preparation, Orlando withdrew his fingers, smiling at Alain's impatient moan. Quickly, he seated the head of his cock, sliding inside the welcoming heat, letting the feeling of slick velvet enclose him again. Nothing compared to this. Not even feeding, as much as he craved the flavor of Alain's blood, thrilled him the way the clasp of Alain's eager body did. Many people had trusted him to feed from them over the years since he had escaped Thurloe's clutches, but only Alain had made love with him.

Their movements remained unhurried, the familiarity of their union enough to allow them a patience and control that had been missing before, but nothing could stop the inexorable tides of their desire for one another. Never speeding up, they rocked to mutual completion, collapsing on the bed still joined.

Panting from his release and the overwhelming force of his emotions for the beautiful vampire above him, Alain wrestled with the words that sprang to his lips. It was too soon, his mind insisted. He and Orlando had been lovers for only ten days, not long enough for him to have fallen so completely in love. His heart refused to listen to logic, though, adamantly proclaiming that it knew its own state and that he was irrevocably in love. All that remained, according to that determined organ, was to make his declaration and hear Orlando's in return. He did not delude himself that saying the words would be a cure-all for Orlando's fears, but he hoped it would add another layer of confidence in his lover's quest to overcome his past. Tilting his head, he nuzzled Orlando's neck softly before nipping at the smooth skin.

Orlando's reaction was as swift as it was irrational, yet nothing could have stopped the reflexive flinch when he once more felt teeth on the very spot where Thurloe had first bitten him two centuries earlier.

Closing his eyes, Alain stilled his lips, stopping the words that had been on the verge of escaping. It seemed nothing he did could erase the other vampire's taint. His actions had not been enough. Words would change nothing. Instead, he lay back on the pillows, resigning himself to the status quo. He would love Orlando in silence, within the limits his partner had set. Orlando obviously had nothing more to give him.

Orlando would have given anything he owned and more to take back his action, but it was done now. All he could was apologize and hope his lover would accept it. "I'm sorry," he whispered, "but Thurloe bit me right there when he turned me. I didn't mean…"

"It's all right, Orlando," Alain said dully. "You don't owe me any explanations. You've told me about your past. I was wrong to push you into something you weren't ready for. We won't speak of it again."

That was not the reaction Orlando had hoped for, but he had lost his right to protest when he had hurt his lover. Alain did not have to say the words, did not have to rant and rail for Orlando to feel the chill that had sprung between them. He had no idea how to mend matters, but he was fairly sure pressing his lover now would only widen the gulf. Sadly, he rolled to his side and stared at the ceiling, not knowing what to say.

When Orlando said nothing more, made no attempt to refute his assertions, Alain repressed a sigh and pushed up to sitting. "I'm going to take a shower," he commented, hoping the vampire would suggest joining him, anything that would allow him to somehow put things back on even ground. Orlando did not move, though, his gaze fixed and glassy. Closing his eyes briefly, Alain rose from the bed and left Orlando to the solitude he so clearly desired.

Orlando cursed hotly when the door shut behind Alain. He wished uselessly that he could still cry. Perhaps that would have convinced his lover of the sincerity of his regrets. As it was, he would simply have to accept whatever Alain decided in terms of their future. A part of him wanted to push open the door to the bathroom and demand Alain talk to him, but he had forfeited his ability to press any demands on his lover when he had overreacted to what he knew – he knew! – was intended to be a loving touch. Eyes closing, he feigned sleep when Alain came back into the room to dress, his imagination filling in the scene he could not see. Alain accepted the ruse, either truly fooled or wanting to avoid any more disappointment, and left as soon as he was dressed. A few minutes later, Orlando heard the main door open and then close, and he knew he was alone in his apartment. He had never felt its emptiness so completely until now.

Chapter 42

"WHAT'S going on that couldn't wait until morning?" Thierry demanded, his voice harsh with the frustration of his unresolved sexual tension. He glared at the room in general, knowing he'd lose it completely if he looked at his smirking partner.

Wishing he were dealing with anyone but Thierry in a bad mood, Raymond outlined the situation, ending with his determination to lead the rescue team. "You know I'm the best one to deal with any lingering imbalances after the storm passes," he added defensively.

Agreeing with Raymond annoyed Thierry in principle, but he could not deny that the other wizard with his font of lore was far more sensitive to changes in the elemental magic and had far more tricks at his disposal for dealing with them than any other wizard in Paris. "Just don't get so caught up in your mumbo jumbo that you forget we're fighting a war back here," he snapped.

Raymond let the insult wash over him, accepting the comment as the grudging acceptance that it was, but Jean was not nearly so sanguine. "Where the hell do you get off?" he challenged. "Raymond's worked as hard as anyone to make sure this alliance is successful. I haven't seen you volunteering to help recruit new vampires or track down the rogue."

"It's fine, Jean," Raymond insisted, laying a calming hand on Jean's shoulder.

"It's not fine," Jean retorted. "They do nothing but look down their noses at you when you're working as hard as anyone to bring Serrier down. If I'm tired of their attitudes after these few days, I can only imagine how you must feel."

"Their attitudes are a small price to pay for Marcel's protection," Raymond reminded his partner, though he could not stop the thrill he felt at

Jean's defense of him. "Let it go. If we're leaving for La Réunion in an hour, we have work to do."

Jean frowned and sent a final glare in Thierry's direction. "Didn't the lieutenant say he'd called Orlando and his partner as well?"

"Yes, why?" Raymond asked.

"Because I need to talk to Orlando," Jean explained. "Since I'm going with you, I need another vampire to make sure Cabalet finds a partner. He won't trust a wizard, at least not an unpaired wizard, to handle it, and there's no vampire I trust as much as I do Orlando."

Orlando entered the room just then, looking downcast and more than a little lost. "There he is now," Jean commented. "I'll join you in your office as soon as I talk to him if that suits you."

"That's fine," Raymond agreed, leaving Jean to his business. He had more than enough to keep him busy until the vampire finished. With the distance and all the supplies to move, they would have to use a much higher concentration of magic to get to La Réunion instead of just popping across town like they all did so easily. Raymond wanted everything on the ground in Madagascar in three hours so that as soon as the storm cleared the island, they would be able to get there and get started with whatever rescue work needed to be done. Every minute wasted could well mean lives lost.

"Is everything all right?" Jean asked softly as he approached Orlando.

"Fine," Orlando replied dully, eyes scanning the room in the hope that Alain had gotten the message, too, and had returned to headquarters. If he had, he was elsewhere in the building.

Jean frowned at what was clearly a lie, but he had learned not to press Orlando when he was in this kind of mood. His friend would talk to him when he was ready. In the meantime, they had other things to discuss. "I have to go with Raymond to La Réunion. I need you to take care of things here for me."

Orlando shook his head in automatic protest, but Jean went on before he could speak. "The only thing that can't wait is dealing with Cabalet. He arrived from Amiens tonight. We have to convince him to join the alliance and to bring his vampires with him."

"How am I supposed to do that?" Orlando asked, knowing that whatever respect the other vampires paid him came entirely from his association with Jean. Without the vampire leader around, they would not pay him any heed.

"He needs to find a partner," Jean explained, mindful of Raymond's theory concerning the bonds between partners. "He's agreed to stay for two days."

Orlando shook his head. "I have no authority," he protested. "How am I supposed to get the wizards to agree anything?"

"Get Alain to help."

Orlando snorted. "Yeah, sure. Somehow I doubt he's in the mood to indulge me right now."

"What happened?" Jean demanded. The last time he had seen the two – indeed, every time he had seen them – Alain had seemed willing to do anything he could to help Orlando, to build his self-confidence. He could not imagine what could have happened to change that.

Orlando's eyes fell, unable to meet Jean's gaze. He already knew what the other vampire's reaction would be. Haltingly, he recounted the events of earlier that evening.

Jean shook his head at the stupidity of both men. He only had one of them in front of him, though, so he would deal with Orlando now and kick Alain's arse later. "He's gone," he reminded the younger vampire firmly. "You watched him burn away to nothing inch by painful inch. So why do you let him keep you prisoner still? You said yourself Alain would never hurt you, but you don't act like you believe it. Isn't it time to let go of the past?"

"I'm trying!" Orlando insisted. "If I weren't, this wouldn't have happened tonight. Alain knew how I felt about him biting me. He wouldn't have done it if I hadn't asked, and even then, it was barely enough to call a bite."

"Are you listening to yourself?" Jean pressed. "What's holding you back? Your words say you're ready to move on."

Orlando's face fell. "I don't know."

"Maybe it's time you figure it out, because you're not just hurting yourself any more. You're hurting Alain and the alliance as well." Jean frowned as he considered who he could give this responsibility to in Orlando's place. If Marcel had a partner, that vampire would be the obvious choice, but since the old general did not, Jean would have to find someone else. His gaze landed on Sebastien, lounging lazily against the wall as he waited for Thierry. With Marcel unpaired and Alain unavailable, Thierry was the senior wizard, making Sebastien the logical choice to ask. Jean just hated the idea of asking the other vampire for anything, much less something this important.

Resigning himself to the inevitable, Jean stalked across the room. "Noyer," he growled, "I want to talk to you."

"Too bad you can't always get what you want," Sebastien replied flippantly, years of being a loner making him forget to mind his tongue. As soon as the words left his mouth, he regretted them. He had assured Thierry he would do nothing to exacerbate the tension between him and Jean, and the look on the elder vampire's face indicated he had done just that. "Sorry," he added, raising his hands in placation. "That was out of line."

Jean forced himself to practice restraint, the presence of outsiders barely enough to keep him from slamming his nemesis against the wall. The apology soothed his raised hackles slightly, giving him the control he needed to nod peremptorily toward the door. Fortunately for them both, Sebastien returned the nod and preceded him into the hall.

When the door shut behind them, they turned and stared at one another, each waiting for the other to speak first. The silence dragged out for several uncomfortable seconds before Sebastien shrugged and spoke. "What do you need?" he asked, striving to keep his voice level.

"Word is getting out about the alliance, and vampires are starting to come, asking questions," Jean replied shortly. "While I'm in La Réunion with Raymond, I need someone to help Cabalet and anyone else who shows up find partners. Do you think you can handle that without screwing it up?"

Sebastien took a deep breath to calm himself before replying, repeating his promise to Thierry like a mantra. Only the thought of disappointing his partner kept him from reacting physically to the insult, provoking a fight whose outcome he would not dare predict. "Thibaut's been dead four hundred years," he said slowly through gritted teeth. "And even then, I never understood why you hated me. I didn't force his hand, regardless of what you think. I didn't even know about you until weeks after we'd made our Aveu de Sang. If I'd known, I would have made sure he explained things to you first. How long are you going to hold Thibaut's choice against me? Isn't it about time to let it go?"

The words struck Jean like a blow, the echo of his advice to Orlando so strong that he nearly reeled. He needed time to digest everything Sebastien had just said, but first he had to get Sebastien's agreement to help. "Sorry, I was out of line," he said, echoing Sebastien's earlier words. "Will you help?"

Sebastien considered saying no, but the more vampires who joined the alliance, the more likely they were to succeed. And the sooner they succeeded, the sooner he could stop worrying about Thierry's safety. "I'll do my best," he replied, unable to resist one final dig at Jean.

Jean's eyes narrowed, but he let the comment pass. He had too much else to think about to deal with Sebastien right now. "Talk to your partner about the best way to handle it," he instructed. "Just think fast. Cabalet only agreed to stay for two days, and I want him to leave with a partner."

Sebastien nodded, hoping Thierry's skill with strategy would apply to this situation as well. "Leave it with us. We'll take care of it."

Jean took his time walking toward Raymond's office, his head spinning as he thought back all those years to Thibaut and all that had transpired at the time. Thibaut had never shown the usual trepidation most mortals felt in dealing with vampires, a fact Jean had found incredibly attractive. He had moved quickly to secure the man's attention and had always believed his affection returned. If Noyer was telling the truth, though, Thibaut had abandoned him without second thought. Jean was not quite ready to accept that blindly, but it was enough to give him pause. When he had a chance, he would ask others who were around at the time and see what he could learn. Arriving at Raymond's office, he knocked briefly and walked inside. "So what happens now?"

JEAN had been pleased at how many vampires had volunteered along with their partners to help with the effort in La Réunion. He saw it as proof of what he had always known: the vampires could be strong, contributing members of larger society if they were just given the chance. He had met with almost all the vampires personally, wanting to make sure they understood both what they were undertaking and the measures they would have to follow to keep their natures hidden. Until the alliance had been announced and the effects of the partnerships were common knowledge, it was prudent to disguise their strength as magic. They would work in shifts with their partners and carry dummy wands, hoping that any inconsistencies in their behavior would be overlooked in the confusion after the typhoon.

His last stop was Caroline's office. Tapping on the door, he waited for the call to enter, walking inside to find the two women sitting side by side on the couch against the wall.

"Oh, good," Caroline said as soon as she saw him. "You can help me convince Mireille that she'll be an asset in La Réunion. She's decided she should stay behind."

"Why?" Jean asked the red-headed vampire. "Every bit of help is important."

"But it's more than just that," Caroline added, not giving Mireille a chance to explain. "Anyone can move debris, either with magic or equipment or brute strength. You have a gift for people, though, that will be as important as all our strength put together. People will have been displaced, will have lost everything they owned, maybe even lost loved ones. I saw you with Blair after Laurent was killed. You have a gift for reassuring people and that will be far more important over the next few days than anything else."

"She's right, Mireille," he agreed. "I wouldn't know what to do with an upset mother or a crying child, but I've seen you offer comfort to total strangers and watched them respond to you. If nothing else, the goodwill that will bring for us and for the alliance when it's announced will be invaluable."

"All right, all right," Mireille conceded with a shake of her head. "I still think someone else would be better in my place, but I'll come."

The chiming of the clock on the wall drew Jean's attention. "Come to the Salle des Cartes as soon as you can," he told them. "Raymond wants to leave in less than half an hour."

When the office door closed behind the vampire leader, Caroline smoothed a gentle hand over Mireille's cheek. "You'll be wonderful, and I'll be right there with you. They need our help, Miri."

Mireille took a deep breath, swallowing her qualms. "Just don't stop believing in me," she requested, turning to press a swift kiss against the cradling palm.

"Never," Caroline promised.

RAYMOND looked over the gathered faces, determination marking every one. "Take your time with the jumps. The vampires, in particular, aren't used to the displacements. We'll meet back up at the staging area in Madagascar in no more than two hours."

He glanced at Jean to see if the vampire wanted to add anything else, but the dark-haired man shook his head. With a final curt nod to those now under his command, he flicked his wand to send himself and Mireille on their way.

Chapter 43

ALAIN arrived at Milice headquarters, his cloak pulled up to protect him from the heavy rain mixed with snow that had begun to fall as he walked the streets of the city. He had argued back and forth with himself for hours, debating the best way forward where Orlando was concerned. The Aveu aside, he loved the vampire and wanted him around, even if that meant limiting his own desires to what his lover could comfortably accept. Their lovemaking to date could hardly be considered a hardship, after all. While it would be easier not to have to worry about scaring his partner, he could live with a few limitations in exchange for all he had found in Orlando's arms. Decision finally made, he had looked at the time, only to realize he was overdue for his shift.

Thierry accosted him as soon as he walked in the door. "Where the hell have you been?" the blond wizard demanded. "I've been trying to reach you for hours."

"Walking," Alain replied evasively. "What did you need?"

Thierry filled his friend in on the situation in the Indian Ocean.

"Fuck!" Alain muttered. "Payet went, you said?"

"He wanted to go, and he was the best suited to the job."

"I agree," Alain commented, "but there's going to be a limit to what he can do there, even with nineteen other wizards to help. Has Marcel talked about how to handle the situation that caused the storm?"

"He said he'd deal with that once the rescue team was in place," Thierry answered, "which should be any time now. Payet left a couple of hours ago. Even with multiple jumps and stops for the vampires, they ought to be in Madagascar by now. When the storm clears the island, they can jump straight there."

"Then it's time to talk to Marcel."

Thierry shook his head, remembering how forlorn Orlando had looked, arriving alone several hours earlier. "No, it's time for you to talk to your partner. Marcel can wait a few more minutes."

Alain's eyebrows shot up. Thierry had always put duty first. "And I lost Aleth because of it," Thierry observed, guessing Alain's thoughts from the expression on his face. "There's no reason for you to make the same mistake I did. At least let Orlando know you're here and ask him to join us. In Bellaiche's absence, it seems the leadership role devolves to Orlando and Sebastien as our partners. From what I could see, that made your vampire more than a little uncomfortable."

"He thinks so poorly of himself," Alain said sadly.

Thierry had noticed that trait and wondered at it again now, for nothing he had seen suggested any reason for it. Orlando was often quiet, simply listening, but the suggestions he had made were good ones. "You need to work on that."

If only he'd let me, Alain reflected silently. "I'll see what I can do," he said to Thierry instead.

"He's in our office," Thierry informed him, giving Alain a gentle push in that direction. "Talk to him and then bring him to Marcel's office. We have work to do."

The reminder, however unintentional, reminded Alain of the severity of the situation. Yes, he and Orlando needed to talk, but he doubted it would be a short conversation once it got started, and he did not want anything to interrupt them. Talking could wait until their shift was over.

Reaching the office, he walked inside and found Orlando sitting on the couch, looking positively miserable. He was so tempted to take his lover in his arms and offer what comfort he could, but the thought of Marcel, Thierry and Sebastien waiting for them held him back. "We have a meeting we need to go to," he said simply, his words startling his partner.

Orlando's eyes lit up when he first saw Alain, but his heart fell when his partner spoke only of business. He knew dealing with the magical imbalance was important, but he could not see what input he could have into such problems. He was no wizard, nor did he know the lore of the vampires the way Jean did. He did not argue, though, not when attending the meeting gave him an excuse to at least be in the same room as Alain. Not knowing where his partner was these past hours had been pure hell. Seeing his lover should have assuaged the fears that assailed him during that time, but Alain's reticence, his unwavering focus on duty, left Orlando feeling insecure again. Had Alain changed his mind about them? He hoped not, for that would spell his own doom. He considered saying something, but the wizard had already stepped back into the hallway, leaving him either to follow or to remain alone in the office. He rose slowly and followed Alain silently toward the general's office.

Marcel's smile of greeting, when they joined him, betrayed the pressure he was under, the expression more than a little harried, and Orlando pushed aside his personal concerns. Clearly, the situation was more serious than he realized. Mentally steeling himself to think and act as Jean would, Orlando settled down to listen and consider what he heard.

Thierry met Alain's eyes when the pair walked in and scowled at his best friend. Alain had not been gone long enough to have said more than a few words to Orlando, and the tension between them was palpable. Maybe not to someone who had never met them before, but Thierry had been watching them since the second time they met, and he knew how they interacted, gravitating toward each other, never farther apart than necessary. The distance between them now would not have caused any comment except by someone who had seen them together before. Thierry had no idea what they had quarreled about, but he knew without a doubt that they had. His frown deepened. With his own happiness suddenly within his grasp again, he wanted to know Alain was likewise taken care of. When he last saw his friend, he would have had no concerns on that front. Now, though, he wondered how far he dared meddle.

"Gentlemen," Marcel began when everyone was seated, "we have a problem, and the President has made it clear that he expects us to solve it. Immediately."

"HERE!" Jean shouted, beginning to tear through the rubble of what had once been a school. It had supposedly been built to withstand the kind of storms that had decimated the island, and so people had flocked there for safety. Only one wing of the building had survived.

Raymond had stopped questioning Jean's calls. As fast as he could stabilize debris, Jean pushed more aside, trusting his partner to make sure it did no damage. They made quite a pair, Raymond thought in passing, as he added his magic to Jean's strength to move a particularly large chunk of concrete. And there, in a tiny pocket between a girder and the ground, lay a little girl.

"Mireille!" Raymond shouted even as he and Jean struggled to move the steel. The red-headed vampire was there almost before he finished saying her name, as if she, too, had sensed the child. As soon as the girl's legs were free, Mireille scooped her up and carried her to the medical tent the local authorities had set up, cradling her gently as the medics checked her over. She was soaked and shivering despite the warm sun that ruled again now that the storm had passed. "Shock," the medic declared, "a few scrapes and bruises, but otherwise she seems unhurt. We'll keep an eye on her for a few hours and hope we can find her family."

Mireille nodded and started to release the girl, but she clung desperately to the vampire.

"Don't leave me," the child sobbed.

Mireille was torn. Out there in the rubble where others worked frantically, more people were surely hurt and even dying. Her heightened senses could help locate those who still survived before their injuries killed them, but to do that, she would have to leave, and this was why she was here, to provide the comfort that people needed.

"Can I take her with me?" she asked the medic.

The dark-skinned man frowned but eventually agreed when he saw the way the girl clung. "Bring her back if anything about her condition changes."

Mireille promised and carried the girl effortlessly back toward the school. "Do you want to help me find other people who were trapped?" she asked, hoping she could comfort this child and continue to help the other Milice members at the same time.

The girl nodded, squirming to slide down. Her grasp on Mireille's hand never faltered. Together, they walked back toward the school. Mireille tried asking about the girl's family, but the child wouldn't speak, only shake her head yes or no or shrug her shoulders to reply.

When they reached the edge of the debris that had once been the school, the child released Mireille's hand and clung to her leg. "No," she whimpered so softly that Mireille could hardly hear her over the noise of the rescue crew. "It's not safe."

"We'll be careful," the vampire promised, kneeling down so she was face to face with her charge, heedless of the mud that stained her knees. "See how they've made pathways," she pointed to the boards that had been laid out in a grid and stabilized by Caroline's own hand. "If we stay on those, we'll be fine."

The child took a tentative step onto one of the planks, warming Mireille's heart at the trust the girl placed in her. "What's your name?" she asked again, hoping that she would get an answer now that the child was talking.

"Romane."

"Ready, Romane?" Mireille asked, holding out her hand. "Let's go see if we can find anyone else."

Romane's hand firmly in hers again, Mireille walked along the planks, senses stretching for the sound of a heartbeat, the scent of blood, anything to help her find and save another victim.

"Over here!" Caroline called before Mireille located anyone.

As quickly as she could with Romane in tow, Mireille crossed to where her partner stood.

"Romane!" The woman's voice was strained but relieved when she saw the child behind her rescuer.

"Tatie Isabelle!"

Mireille breathed a sigh of relief. At least one of the girl's family had survived the cataclysm.

"Let's get you to the medics," Mireille suggested.

"Her leg's broken," Caroline murmured.

"I'll carry her," Mireille replied, lifting the woman into her arms.

"How?" Isabelle asked in surprise as the slender woman easily bore her weight.

"Magic," Mireille explained simply.

That seemed to satisfy the islander and then they were at the triage station and Mireille turned the woman and her niece over to the personnel there before returning to the grim task facing them all.

"You landed one hell of a partner," Raymond told Caroline as he joined her, watching Mireille help the reunited family.

"That I did," Caroline agreed, "although you didn't do so badly yourself."

Raymond shrugged diffidently. "Can you handle things here? I need to make sure the elemental magic is back in balance sufficiently that another storm won't spring up out of nowhere like this one did."

Caroline nodded. "Go ahead. We'll take care of things here."

"Thanks." Raymond retreated to the small tent he had set up for when he was too exhausted to work any more. He had not reached that point yet, but he would need his strength and the quiet of the tent for what he was about to do. Pouring water into a bowl, he trailed his fingers through it and settled into a light trance, his mind connecting with the primal forces of magic that kept the earth in balance. Immediately, he felt the remnants of the disturbance that had caused the typhoon. It was centered to the east of the island, still emanating mild shockwaves. Letting himself rise back to full awareness, Raymond considered what he had felt. Clearly, the imbalance still existed, but not so seriously that they would need to address it in the next few hours. He could return his energy to the rescue efforts first. He needed to go back out there, to face the horrors that arose in the aftermath of a storm of this magnitude, but he took a few seconds to center himself, to diffuse the frantic energy of the search, the surge of relief each time they found someone alive, the spike of grief each time they found someone who had not survived. In the moment, he had been too busy to deal with the individual emotions, pushing them aside in favor of keeping his focus.

"Raymond?"

"In here, Jean," he called in response to his partner's voice.

"Are you all right?"

"I'm fine," Raymond replied, lifting the tent flap to invite Jean inside. "I was just checking on the status of the elemental magic, trying to make sure we don't get slammed by a second storm. Did you need something?"

"I didn't think about the days being longer here," Jean explained, holding out his hands so Raymond could see how his skin had begun to turn gray. "I need to feed if I'm going to keep working."

"Of course!" Raymond exclaimed, refusing to consider his eagerness as he gestured for his partner to sit. "I should have thought of it myself."

Jean shrugged, not sure how to interpret that comment given the uncertainty of their relationship. Instead, he simply waited for Raymond to offer his arm, uncovered in the heat of the day. As he bent his head, he could not help but notice the cuts and scrapes on the previously unblemished skin. "You need to get these cuts looked at," he warned. "Infection runs rampant in the tropics."

It was Raymond's turn to shrug, though Jean's concern warmed him. "I'll put a sealing spell over them when you're done feeding and get them cleaned tonight. There's no point in doing more than that now, not when we have to back out into the muck."

Jean nodded and prepared the skin on Raymond's wrist, not lingering as his instincts insisted he do. He knew where that impulse came from, and, tempting as it was, he had promised himself and Raymond to resist it. Instead, he kept his movements as business-like as he could, reminding himself that the magical transaction had one purpose: the furtherance of the alliance. The blood that hit his tongue did not taste business-like, though. He felt too much of Raymond's turbulent emotions as he fed from him, felt the echo of those same emotions in himself too strongly to pretend he had not come to care for his partner as more than an ally. Almost immediately, the slight burning that signaled an overexposure to the sun began to fade, healed by the shadows of the tent and the fresh blood in his veins. Equally quickly, he sensed a return of the magic that shielded him from the usual effects of daylight. He took his time feeding, not lingering as much as savoring the peaceful interlude, so different from the chaos spinning wildly about them outside the canvas walls that guaranteed their privacy.

"Did you get enough?" Raymond asked solicitously when Jean raised his head faster than he had expected. He fought the urge to pull the vampire's lips back to his wrist, reminding himself that the magical bond was driving that compulsion. Even so, he felt a certain responsibility since his blood protected his partner and since their partnership had brought the vampire here in the first place.

Jean held out his hands in reply, letting Raymond see their return to a healthy, if pale, hue. He knew they should return to the rubble outside the tent, knew his senses and Raymond's magic should be used to save victims still trapped, but he did not immediately stand. "You mentioned the elemental magic," he began, the carefully hidden scholar in him curious to know more about the forces that governed the world of magic he was just beginning to explore. "How does it work?"

Raymond's face lit with delight at his partner's interest. "It's tied to the elements," he explained, "earth, water, wind and fire. Every wizard has an affinity for one of them, although not every wizard takes the time to find out which one works best. Those of us who take the time to develop the connection can use it to monitor the balance of the earth's magic. Here, let me show you."

Reaching for the bucket he had used earlier, Raymond dropped into the trance again and channeled his magic into the water, connecting to the elemental magic. When the liquid began to stir, he lifted his head. "See," he said, pointing to the ripples on the surface. "That's the disturbance that caused the storm."

"It seems so small," Jean commented wryly.

"Scale," Raymond chuckled. Then he paused and looked at the water again. "It was worse than that just a few moments ago," he marveled. "It shouldn't have dissipated that much in just fifteen minutes."

"Could something have happened to help restore the balance?"

His conversation with monsieur Lombard suddenly rushing back, Raymond looked piercingly at Jean. "You fed from me. Monsieur Lombard and I theorized that the connection between wizard and vampire had to serve some greater purpose. This suggests we were right. If we could prove it..." he trailed off.

"It would go a long way toward rehabilitating the vampires in the eyes of society," Jean finished slowly. "But how can we prove it? This is still circumstantial evidence."

"We need to monitor the disturbance as another pair feeds."

Chapter 44

"SO you're Bellaiche's second?" Cabalet asked, measuring the two men in front of him. The wizard, blond-haired, green-eyed, sharp-featured, met his gaze unflinchingly. Everything about his stance, his expression suggested he had nothing to hide. Cabalet had not made it to his current position by trusting appearances. The vampire was harder to read, his hazel eyes hooded, his stance confident without being cocky, a slight smile playing around his lips beneath the dark moustache and goatee. Luc did not know him, but he had no doubt that Noyer was too skilled a player of Le Jeu des Cours that governed so much of the interactions of his kind to show his hand too soon.

"He asked me to help you find a partner since he couldn't be here himself," Sebastien replied smoothly. He did not know what, if anything, Jean had told the other vampire leader, and he did not want to be responsible for making his own chef lose face with another by catching him in a lie. He might do his best to stay out of the game that determined status among the vampires, but that did not mean he could not play when he had to. For the sake of the alliance, he would play it now with all the skill he possessed. "How much did he explain about how the partnerships work?"

"He mentioned protection from sunlight," Luc answered.

"Did he tell you that it only works with the right wizard?"

Cabalet nodded. "But he didn't tell me how to find that wizard."

Next to the two vampires, Thierry smiled. "Magic. How else?"

Luc frowned. "I have no magic."

Thierry did not bother disagreeing, not wanting to waste time with explanations that were of little relevance to the current project. Instead, he drew his wand and cast a levitation spell at both vampires. As expected, Sebastien's feet stayed planted firmly on the ground while Cabalet floated slowly toward the ceiling. "Our magic, not yours," he replied, ending the spell with a flick of his wrist.

"What the hell was that?" Luc demanded as his feet touched the carpet again. "And talk fast."

"You really don't want to threaten my partner," Sebastien intervened, voice flat, eyes hard as ice, body poised to fight. "I realize he caught you off guard, but he didn't hurt you."

"What are you going to do about it?" Cabalet challenged, his wounded sense of dignity adding belligerence to his voice.

Thierry looked back and forth between the two vampires, not quite sure how the tone of the conversation had gone from cautiously friendly to hostile in the blink of an eye. Regardless, a fight between the two men, one whose outcome he could not predict, would not help their situation at all. He did not want to think about Marcel's reaction to finding a potential ally hog-tied for assaulting Thierry's partner, and the wizard was honest enough with himself to know that would be the result if Cabalet attacked. "Gentlemen," he interrupted, laying a restraining hand on Sebastien's arm, "perhaps we could get back to business." He turned his attention fully on the unfamiliar vampire. "That, as you chose to call it, was a demonstration of how your partner will be able to identify you. I cast the spell on both of you, but it only worked on you. Sebastien is immune to my magic, just as you will be immune to your partner's spells."

"So I just stand there and let wizards cast spells on me?" Cabalet growled.

"It's a perfectly harmless spell," Sebastien pointed out reasonably. "If the wizard who casts it isn't your partner, you just float in the air for a few seconds. And if the wizard is your partner, you stay planted firmly on the ground."

"There's a patrol outside waiting to meet you," Thierry added, hiding a grin at the look of unease that crossed the vampire's face. It would be some time before he forgot the threat to his partner. "Shall I bring them in?"

LUC grimaced as he floated ignominiously into the air once again. This had been going on for hours, it seemed, with the same result each time a wizard cast the levitation spell. If he had not seen for himself that the spell had not worked on Noyer, he would have called a halt already. As it was, his patience was rapidly wearing thin. He scowled as he regained his feet, glad his innate grace kept him from stumbling. That would have been the final insult. "How many more?" he growled, drawing the attention of the other vampire and his partner.

"Three more," Thierry replied, glancing out into the hallway where the rest of the patrol waited. "If your partner isn't one of them, we'll take a break and try again when the next patrol comes in around noon."

Luc almost refused, but he had agreed to stay two days, and if Bellaiche was telling the truth, if he could walk safely in the sunlight again, it would be worth the indignities of finding a partner. "Well, bring the next one in," he groused.

Thierry hid his amusement – he remembered the frustration of not being able to find a partner – and opened the door to usher in the next of the remaining wizards. Once more, the spell was cast and once more, Cabalet floated gently off the floor. "Don't smirk," Sebastien murmured at his side. "You don't want to deal with an offended vampire."

"I was sympathizing," Thierry whispered back as he brought in the next to the last vampire. "I was feeling the same way he is before you showed up at the gare the other night."

"Of course, if I hadn't been late, Luc would've had to bite every wizard here to see if they were partners," Sebastien reminded him.

"True, but that only made it more frustrating at the time," Thierry replied as Luc hovered in the air again. "I had an arm covered in bites and nothing to show for it."

Fingers tapping impatiently against her thigh, Magali Ducassé, the last wizard in her patrol, walked in. She had only just returned from her particular mission, capturing anyone who came from Serrier's contingent and investigating the site of their latest battle. It had been an unusually bloody fight and she wanted nothing more than to clean up and rest for a bit. Instead, she had been hustled here, to meet a vampire who did not even live in Paris. She had absolutely no illusions that this would work, nor any desire that it do so. Sure, the vampires had been useful so far, but she did not feel the need to saddle herself with one. Especially not the large, male one currently glaring daggers at the room in general and her in particular. His attitude was obviously as big as his frame, and she had no patience for that kind of ego. Besides, having a partner would make carrying out her specific duties more difficult. Given that her magic would not work on her partner, she would either have to send him back with the rest of the patrol and listen to him gripe about leaving her alone or else keep someone else there with her to effectuate the displacement when her work was done and listen to that wizard gripe about extra responsibilities. No, she was clearly not the best candidate for a partnership.

"Thierry," she protested as soon as she saw him, "this is really a bad idea. You know the risks I take. Asking someone else to share that with me, and a vampire, furthermore, who can't get himself out of a tight spot if necessary, is just ludicrous."

Thierry liked Magali, admired her for the work she did, but she was not known for her tact at the best of times. This was clearly not one of those times, and from the hiss of indrawn breath at his shoulder, Thierry suspected he had some serious fence mending to do if he did not want the other vampire leader storming out in a huff. "Now, Magali," he began appeasingly.

"And just what do you think you can do that I can't?" Luc broke in, stalking toward the petite woman. He probably weighed twice what she did and was easily a foot taller.

Magali glared. She knew the vampire's type, all hulking brawn with very little brain. "Anything I want to," she retorted. "I face down the worst of what Serrier can send at me on a daily basis. Don't even think about trying to intimidate me. I'm sorry, Thierry, but I can't do this. Especially not with him."

Her attitude incensed Luc beyond reason. Blocking the door, he reached out to grab her arm. "Leave off," she ordered, a flick of her finger casting a spell that should have pinned him to the wall. Nothing happened. "Merde alors!"

"Be glad it didn't work," Thierry retorted. "If it had, you'd have been explaining yourself to Marcel. Magali Ducassé, meet Luc Cabalet, leader of the vampires in Amiens."

The two of them scowled at each other. "We'll leave you alone to get acquainted. And don't forget that Cabalet needs to feed before you go anywhere, Magali." He grabbed Sebastien's hand and slipped out the door to the echo of Magali's curses.

"Is that a good idea?" Sebastien asked, looking back toward the office.

"She can't hurt him," Thierry reminded his partner. "And it'll be better for everyone if they clear the air between them now rather than later. We don't want another repeat of what happened with Bellaiche and Payet."

Sebastien had no argument for that, though the worried look on his face did not fade.

Deciding a distraction was in order, Thierry squeezed Sebastien's hand. "Do you need to feed before we leave? It's been almost twenty-four hours." When Sebastien met his eyes, he added, "And that's at least twelve hours too long."

Chapter 45

LUST shot through Sebastien's system at the unexpected invitation, the need for blood more than matched by his desire for the golden wizard. Taking the lead, he barreled down the corridors, Thierry in tow, until he reached the door to the office Thierry and Alain shared. "If they're still here..."

"They won't be," Thierry interrupted, pushing open the door to the darkened room. "They got off duty an hour ago and had no reason to stay. They're home by now, tearing up the sheets. If my place weren't so far, I'd suggest doing the same, but I don't want to wait that long or risk you in sunlight."

"Don't say things like that if you don't mean them," Sebastien warned, kicking the door shut and nudging Thierry toward the couch against one wall. He did not bother searching for the light. Dawn was breaking outside, sufficient light filtering through the window for him to guide them there safely.

Falling backward onto the couch and pulling Sebastien down on top of him, Thierry tipped his head back, baring his neck to his partner. "I mean it."

Sebastien stifled a curse as his body jerked forward instinctively, hips grinding against his wizard. It took every ounce of his self-control to keep from tearing the other man's clothes from his body and ravishing him thoroughly. Only the promise he had made to make love to Thierry properly held him back. Nothing, though, could stop him from lowering his head to the long column of his partner's neck, offered so temptingly for his delectation. His fangs broke the skin immediately, Thierry's body jerking beneath him at the quick pinpricks. He laved the surrounding flesh with his tongue as he sucked hard, drawing mouthful after mouthful of life-giving blood. Thierry's desire battered his senses. He had tasted many things over the centuries since Thibaut died, even desire occasionally, but not like this. Not this overwhelming, all-encompassing surrender to passion that invited him to collusion. His mind soared with it. Blood did not lie. However it had come to happen, whatever series of unforeseen circumstances had led to their match at the gare de Lyon, Sebastien could only be grateful.

Thierry hissed sharply as his vampire's fangs broke the skin on his neck, driving deep into his vein. He had seen Sebastien's fangs, knew they were not long enough to do more than slightly puncture his skin, but he felt the reverberations deep within, as if the fangs were not merely in his neck, but in his loins, in his belly, in his heart. His pulse pounded in time with the suction of Sebastien's mouth, his breath coming in harsh pants as it ruffled his partner's hair. He swelled to full hardness, the press of Sebastien's body and the pull of his mouth arousing Thierry beyond coherency. Before, his reluctance had muted the sensations, keeping him from giving in to the full potency of the experience. That reluctance gone, passion buffeted his senses, lifting him to a fever pitch with remarkable speed. Desperate for more contact, he slid down so that he lay nearly flat on the couch, hooking his leg around Sebastien's hips and pulling him closer, bucking up beneath the hard body not to dislodge it, but to gain more of the erotic friction that had him hovering already on the edge of release.

The heat of Thierry's emotions transmitted through his blood combined with the wanton movements of his body swamped Sebastien's control. He sucked harder, drowning himself in Thierry's taste, Thierry's desire. He had always been careful to feed lightly so he could feed often, but that resolve fled in the face of the unrelenting frenzy. He was gorging himself and he could do nothing to stop it or even to slow it down. His head spun as he tasted Thierry's building release, triggering an answering response in his own body that was enhanced by the wizard's determined frottage.

If he had been in any state to think rationally, Thierry might have been embarrassed at climaxing fully dressed like a horny teenager, but his mind was completely overtaken by the tactility of the moment, the ecstasy of finally having Sebastien moving over him, against him.

In him.

The sudden realization shattered what little remained of his control, his hands scrabbling over Sebastien's shoulders and back, seeking contact, seeking stability. His head fell back as his hips drove upward, grinding his aching cock against Sebastien's matching hardness. With a long, low groan, he gave in to the passion bubbling within him.

The flavor of Thierry's release exploded through his blood, thrilling Sebastien with its power. To know that he could bring his partner such pleasure was a heady aphrodisiac. His body collapsed against the wizard's, satiation radiating through him. His panting breaths matched Thierry's as he struggled to come down from the high of tasting his soon-to-be lover's climax for the first time.

Head still spinning, Thierry groaned in delight as Sebastien collapsed atop him, clearly as affected by their exchange as he was. Unlike him, though, the vampire was still hard where he pressed against Thierry's thigh. Determined not to act selfishly – and, if he were honest with himself, because he wanted to know if he could bring Sebastien to the same pinnacle of release – he let one hand drop from its place on his partner's hip to slide over the still stiff erection. Immediately, the other man shuddered, his climax ripping out of him with a sharp jerk of his hips. "Thierry," he moaned, reaching up to tilt his lover's head toward his so he could capture the soft lips with his own.

He should have been too relaxed to respond, Thierry thought vaguely as he felt the passion start to swirl in him again, but he had no immunity to Sebastien's touch. Nor did he want to develop any. He almost protested when Sebastien raised his head, only his own sense of duty keeping him from pulling his lover's head back down and demanding another round.

"It's never been that intense before," he commented softly as Sebastien shifted to sit up. Thierry sat up as well, deliberately tangling his legs with Sebastien's to maintain some contact.

"I haven't let myself go that way before," Sebastien answered honestly. "I've always been careful not to feed too deeply, to take too much. You aren't protected by an Aveu de Sang the way Alain is. If I have to feed almost every day to keep the immunity to sunlight, then I have to be careful not to take so much that I drain you."

Thierry could not help the grin that broke across his face. "You lost control." The thought was incredibly heartening.

Sebastien could not stop the flush that rose over his cheeks, but he returned the smile. "You're one hell of a sexy man," he pointed out. "What do you expect?"

Thierry's flush matched Sebastien's. "You didn't seem affected before today."

"You were holding back before today, too," Sebastien reminded him. "I could taste the difference in your blood and it caught me off guard. I'll be better prepared for it next time."

"Don't hold back on my account," Thierry insisted, leaning forward to nip at Sebastien's lower lip. "I liked knowing I could make you feel as good as you made me feel."

"We still have to be careful," Sebastien countered. "I can only feed like I just did so often without hurting you. And I don't want anything to do that."

Thierry shrugged. "So we'll be careful, but don't deny both of us that pleasure. Please?"

Sebastien nodded, then changed the subject. "So explain this ritual to me that you, Alain, and Marcel were discussing. You get going on Milice business and forget sometimes that not all of us are au courant when it comes to magic."

"Sorry," Thierry apologized immediately. "Did you get the part about the elemental magic being out of balance?"

"Yes, although that's about the limit of my understanding at this point. You're talking about the magic that we all tap into in order to exist, right?"

"In a nutshell, yes," Thierry agreed. "One of the jobs of l'ANS is to maintain the equilibrium. With the war, more magic is being used without as much being replaced, so we get chaos – disasters like the one in La Réunion, as an example. If it gets too out of control, anything that depends on magic will cease to exist. And it could well destroy the world completely. When we weren't at war, we didn't need the old rituals because we kept things in balance by other means. Now, though, those little fixes won't be enough. The ritual Marcel mentioned is probably the most effective way to restore the equilibrium, at least in the short term, and it's most effective on the old feast days – Beltane, Samhain, Yule, Imbolc, Litha, Ostara, Mabon, and Lughnasadh. Samhain is in a few days. We'll do it then."

"What does it entail?" Sebastien wanted to know, his protective instincts bristling at the thought of anything that might threaten his wizard.

"It depends," the blond wizard replied. "We'll have to see what the problem is – too much or too little – but usually, it means channeling our magic into the elements to stabilize them."

That told Sebastien absolutely nothing at all. "Is it dangerous?" he asked bluntly.

"Only if we channel too much at once," Thierry insisted, "and even then, a few days' rest will usually take care of it."

Sebastien accepted the explanation. He could hardly argue with it, after all, and Thierry seemed perfectly comfortable with the idea. It crossed his mind, though, that his partner was hardly well rested now. He could not help but wonder what such a drain of resources would do. Resolving to keep an even closer eye than usual on his wizard, the vampire pretended to yawn, hoping the subterfuge would convince Thierry to go home and rest, if only to make sure Sebastien did the same.

It worked.

"You should have said something!" Thierry exclaimed immediately. "We'll go to my apartment so you can rest. It's nothing special, but it's much closer than taking the train out to the house. Come on, I'll get someone to send you there so you can go right to bed."

Sebastien hid his smile as they left the office in search of another wizard. As they made their way deeper into the maze of corridors, the first people they saw were the wizard and vampire they had most recently left. Gone was the combative attitude of an hour ago. The two men watched with shared smirks as the chef de la Cour d'Amiens lifted his partner's hand to his lips and bestowed a chaste kiss on the slender knuckles. Their faces were both slightly flushed, and Thierry thought Magali's lips looked kiss-swollen, though he had too well-developed a sense of self-preservation to say that aloud.

"Sorry to bother you, Magali," he interrupted, amused to watch them startle as if they had forgotten the rest of the world existed, "but I need a favor."

Considerably more charitably inclined than before she understood everything it would mean to have a vampire for a partner, Magali turned toward the captain and his companion. "Sir?"

"I need someone to send my partner to my apartment since my magic won't work on him."

An hour ago, Magali would have commented on that, asking snidely why the vampire needed to go to the captain's apartment and not his own, but now, facing an imminent separation from her newly discovered partner, the words did not come. "Of course," she agreed instead.

"And I'll talk to the general about having you transferred to Amiens as quickly as possible," Thierry added, earning a grateful smile from the diminutive woman.

AT least Alain had come home with him.

Orlando told himself repeatedly that this fact should prove that his partner had not grown tired of him completely, but the insidious little voice, the one who believed he was worthless, pointed out that all Alain's belongings were here and that he had nowhere else to go. "He could have stayed at his office," he muttered defensively. The reassurance only helped marginally as he continued to pace the living room.

"Did you say something?" Alain called from the kitchen where he was making something to eat before going to bed. He still had not managed to bridge the gap between them, one of his own making, he knew, but Orlando had not seemed particularly eager for his company either, a fact that worried him quite a bit. He had upended his life for his lover, trusting the strength of all that bound them together to help them over any bumps in the road. Telling himself he was making a mountain out of a molehill, he stirred the eggs for his omelet. "Orlando?"

"No, nothing," the vampire replied, wishing he could see the expression on Alain's face. His voice had sounded almost normal, almost inviting, but Orlando was afraid to trust his instincts. They had led him astray far too often, and Alain had made it quite clear the evening before that he did not want his company uninvited. No invitation had been forthcoming. He would simply have to do his best not to impose on the wizard any more than necessary for his survival. Sebastien had said he would reach the point where he could go as long as two weeks between feedings, and surely Alain would not begrudge him that. He doubted he was there yet, but he could start to push his limits, waiting as long as he could before imposing on his partner again. It had been almost twenty-four hours since he had last fed, sipping tenderly from Alain's neck yesterday morning after they had made love with Alain's hands in his hair. He did not feel like he needed to feed again, so he would see if he could wait a little longer, until after Alain slept at least. It hurt to even think about putting that kind of distance between them, but he had to do it. He could not keep expecting Alain to be at his beck and call. Maybe if things were different, if they had taken the time to deal with some of his issues before making their Aveu de Sang, he could have stayed, but as it was, he had asked too much of his partner already. With a stifled sob, he headed for the door, ignoring Alain's voice calling after him. He thought he understood now what Alain must have felt the night before, the need to walk, to simply escape.

"Fuck!" Alain cursed, hearing the door slam shut behind Orlando. His fist slammed hard into the wall, shattering the plaster and scraping his knuckles, leaving him cursing again. He muttered a spell to repair the wall, but he left his hand alone, a reminder of the pain he had caused his lover with his selfishness. He owed Orlando an apology and an explanation. A part of him wanted to go after the vampire, to insist that he come back inside, away from the sunlight that could be fatal if his magic failed, but he feared such a course of action would only make Orlando feel hunted instead of loved. Alain sighed in frustration. He was second-guessing himself, instincts warring with the reality of his situation. He had the sinking feeling that this would be the pattern of their relationship now, every word, every action weighed outside of bed, too, lest he do something however inadvertently to raise the specter of abuse again. He only hoped the vampire returned soon so he could make amends before he fell asleep. The omelet that minutes ago had appealed tasted like ashes in his mouth. He forced himself to eat, knowing he could not afford to do anything that might weaken him, but his thoughts were elsewhere, with Orlando wherever he had fled.

He wondered where Orlando had gone. Jean was still in La Réunion and Alain did not know of any other confidant the vampire had. The idea that Orlando was simply roaming the streets, alone and hurting, tore at him. Orlando had fed yesterday morning before they fell asleep, but not since, adding to Alain's concerns. Sebastien had said he would need to feed more often than usual until the bond between them was well-established. The last time Orlando had gone too long without blood, he had simply collapsed. Then, Alain had been with him. If it happened now, while he was outside and alone, he could be dead before Alain even knew there was a problem. Orlando had taken his repère with him. It would be a simple matter to jump to Milice headquarters and check his whereabouts, but doing so would imply that he did not trust his lover to take care of himself. Given Orlando's history, sending that message could destroy what relationship they had left.

The abuse of his past notwithstanding, Orlando did not have a death wish. They had argued – their first fight – but even the most devoted couples occasionally had disagreements. This was a bump in the road, not the end of the road. Orlando would come back; they would talk; he would feed. Just the thought of it caused his body to stir, making him realize how quickly he had become used to Orlando's attentions. He wondered suddenly if the Aveu de Sang created a need in the human partner that matched the vampire's need to feed. Whether it did or whether the desire to feel Orlando's fangs in him again was purely a result of his deepening feelings for his lover, one thing was certain: they had to find a way to resolve this tension between them, for both their sakes.

Going into the bedroom, he stripped down to his boxers and climbed in bed, letting the scents of Orlando and their combined passions reassure him. Orlando did not have a deceptive bone in his body. He could not have made love to Alain the way he had done so many times in the past week without feeling something for his lover. If he had been capable of that kind of casualness, he would have taken a lover long ago. As it was, he had allowed Alain liberties he had never shared with anyone else. Taking comfort from that thought, he fell asleep despite his best intentions, alone for the first time since making his vow to Orlando.

"LT. RAYNAUD DE LAGE," Raymond called, seeing the slender wizard and her partner as soon as he stepped out of his tent, "could we talk to you and your partner for a moment?"

Catherine frowned, wondering what she and Justin had done to merit being talked to, but she gestured for Justin to join her as she crossed to the tent and the two men leading the rescue effort. "Sir?"

"What do you know about elemental magic, Lieutenant?" Raymond asked.

"Not much," she admitted. "Just that we've got this mess to clean up because it got out of balance."

"That's right," Raymond agreed, "and if we don't get it back in balance, we'll have more and more messes to clean up until the imbalance destroys the world completely."

"Yes, sir, but that's more your area of expertise than mine."

Raymond smiled. "It is my area of expertise," he acknowledged, "but any wizard who chooses to can help."

"You want my help?" she asked, growing more confused by the minute.

"Yours and your partner's," Jean interjected. "You're looking a little hungry, Justin."

It was the vampire's turn to look confused. "It's been a while since I fed," he admitted, "but it's not urgent yet."

"Urgent or not, that's what we need from you," Jean went on. "Raymond's magic started wearing off a few minutes ago, and after I'd fed, we noticed a decrease in the leftover disturbance. We need to make sure it wasn't a coincidence."

"By monitoring it while Justin feeds?" Catherine verified.

"Exactly," Raymond replied.

Catherine glanced at her partner. Feeding usually led to more these days, a fact she quite enjoyed, but she did not know how Justin felt about his chief realizing that. She was not happy about the idea that hers would find out, but she knew enough about magic to understand the importance of the experiment. Justin looked uncomfortable as well, but he inclined his head in agreement.

"Good," Raymond declared, seeing the silent exchange. "Do you have a tent set up already? We can monitor the situation from outside without invading your privacy."

"On the other side of the school," Justin informed them, taking Catherine's elbow and starting that way.

Raymond retrieved the bucket he had used earlier and followed them to their tent. He waited until they ducked inside to channel his magic back into the water again. Immediately, the ripples reappeared exactly as they had been a few minutes earlier. "So it's not just dispersing on its own," Jean murmured.

"Apparently not," Raymond confirmed. "We're ready," he called to the pair in the tent.

The heavy canvas muffled the sounds that came from within, the sharp hiss of breath that accompanied Justin's bite barely audible to the two men outside. As always, Justin lost himself almost immediately in the richness of Catherine's blood, all thought of Jean outside, of restraining his desires to his need to feed, disappearing as her magic filled his veins and her scent wreathed his senses. A glance at her face told him she was with him completely, as lost in the moment as he was. With a smile, he returned his attention to feeding, his hands wandering over her svelte curves as he sucked tenderly at her throat.

Outside the tent, Raymond squirmed uncomfortably. He felt like the worst kind of voyeur, knowing from experience how incredibly private feeding was. He reminded himself that the pair inside had agreed to this and that the resulting information could help cement the vampires' role within the magical community. Marcel would have to decide how to use the information for best effect if this experiment supported their suppositions, but at least Raymond could provide him with concrete evidence to support their claims.

Despite the barriers between him and the couple inside, Jean could predict exactly what was happening, the rhythm of feeding, the little sounds that accompanied it, completely familiar after so many centuries. He kept his eyes on the bucket, hoping to see the proof they sought. Imperceptibly at first, the ripples calmed slightly, still visible, but less intense. "I'm not seeing things, am I?" he asked softly.

"No," Raymond agreed. "It's definitely lessening. It seems the exchange of magic does serve a purpose besides just protecting the vampires, after all."

"How could we not know this?" Jean asked incredulously. "How could both of our races have gotten it so wrong for so long?"

Raymond chuckled. "Prejudice? Fear? Inflexibility? You name it, our people have it in full measure. To some extent, that's what we're fighting a war against. Serrier is a master of propaganda, playing into the fears and prejudices of wizards who aren't sharp enough to see through his lies. If it weren't for his xenophobia, he'd have tried using it on the other magical races, too."

"He wouldn't have found the vampires easy marks," Jean insisted. "Le Jeu des Cours is all about those kinds of subtle games."

"You certainly know more about it than I do," Raymond replied, standing to leave now that they had the proof they needed, "but don't underestimate Serrier's ability to twist things around. I fell for his lies for a time, and I hardly consider myself gullible. He just knew exactly which buttons to push with me and said what I wanted to hear."

The subtle change in sounds from inside the tent distracted Jean from their discussion. "We should give them their privacy."

Raymond could not stop the flush that stained his cheeks as he realized what he was hearing. He looked down to avoid Jean's gaze, his eyes landing on the bucket with the spell still active. His stifled gasp drew Jean's attention as well.

"Don't say it," Raymond muttered as he ended the spell quickly. "I don't even want to think it. No way am I telling Marcel that sex between partners while they're feeding increases the effects."

"We should have seen this coming," Jean remarked. "Feeding and sex go hand in hand so easily for vampires, and we've already seen the compulsion that drives the partners together."

"Are you saying you're fine with this?" Raymond asked incredulously.

"Of course not," Jean snapped uncomfortably, no closer to resolving the conflict between the magical bond and his own desire for independence than he had been when Raymond first mentioned the possibility, "but it's no great leap of logic to see why it works this way. You and monsieur Lombard said yourselves that the bond had to serve some purpose. You even theorized that this is the purpose. If that's the case, then why shouldn't sex rear its head in the equation?"

"That doesn't make it fair to people who only agreed to the partnerships to win the war," Raymond reminded him, a hint of panic tingeing his voice. He had let himself forget the factors that complicated their relationship in the pleasure of Jean's company. He was not ready for this to be more than business or simple friendship.

"I need to go back to Paris," Jean declared suddenly. "However this plays out, I need to be around to help deal with it. Marcel can handle the wizards' reactions, but he can't be expected to deal with the vampires by himself, especially not with Cabalet involved now, too."

"Is he going to be a problem?" Raymond asked sharply.

"The same compulsion will drive him if he finds a partner," Jean reminded the wizard, "and if he doesn't, he isn't likely to hang around long. He is used to being the one in charge, though, so getting him to fall in line with what we want may require some... persuasion. Marcel isn't used to the ways of vampires yet. I should be there to help."

"I can't go with you," Raymond reminded him. "At least not until things have stabilized here."

"I just fed," Jean replied, trying not to think of everything they had learned, of everything that he and Raymond had not done. The taste of Raymond's blood lingered in his mouth, tempting him. Magically induced or not, the bond growing between them became harder to resist with each feeding. Hopefully, this separation would give him a chance to pull his emotions back under control. Perhaps the taste of Karine's blood, and the charms of her body, would help ease the compulsion he was feeling. "I'll be fine for a few days as long as I stay out of the sun. Your magic wears off before I get hungry again. If necessary, I can find someone in Paris who will let me feed until you return."

Raymond could not stop the scowl that crossed his face at the thought of Jean feeding elsewhere, but he had no other alternative to suggest. He would just have to finish his work on La Réunion as quickly as possible so he could get back to Paris before his partner needed to feed. "I'll talk to Caroline," he said. "She can take you back to Paris since I can't. I'll join you there as soon as I can."

"Do what you need to," Jean insisted, hiding the flare of delight at the idea that Raymond did not want their separation to last any longer than necessary.

Chapter 46

"WE apprehended the accused at the Gare de Lyon in the middle of a firefight with Milice operatives," David explained coolly. He had been on the stand for thirty minutes, the prosecuting attorney having led him through this ground already. Lawyers baffled him. He had no idea what the defense attorney hoped to gain by asking the same questions again. He was hardly about to change his story now. "A revealing spell indicated that the last spells cast from his wand were all spells labeled as dark magic under the codes laid out by the Parlement concerning the appropriate use of magic. I don't see why we're even here."

"We're here, Monsieur," Christian Pellegrin, the defense lawyer, retorted, "because everyone is entitled to a trial by jury under the current Constitution. Who apprehended the accused?"

"I told you already," David insisted. "Milice operatives."

"So you personally did not arrest him?"

"Personally, no, but I was part of the operation and witnessed the events in question," David averred. "Pacotte was one of twenty wizards who attacked a peaceful group of vampires that morning."

"Vampires?" Pellegrin sneered. "Since when does the Milice de Sorcellerie protect vampires?"

"Objection," the prosecutor protested. "Relevance."

"It's all right," David insisted. "I don't mind answering the question."

"Go ahead," the judge indicated.

"The Milice considers the protection of all living beings, magical or otherwise, to be part of its mission. Since the vampires were not violating any law or ordinance by gathering as they did, we deemed it our responsibility to intervene when we received the intelligence of the attack the defendant was involved in. At that time, I volunteered, along with other operatives, to counter their attack," David explained. Fixing Pacotte with a glowering stare, he added,

"The better question is why Serrier sent twenty wizards to attack them in the first place."

"Move to strike," Pellegrin protested. "That has not been established."

"What is there to establish?" David challenged, growing angry now as he thought of Angelique or any of the other vampires facing Serrier and his wizards alone. "The vampires were meeting; Pacotte and company attacked."

The lawyer glanced down at his notes, looking flustered. "According to my client's statements, the Milice operatives started the fight. He was only defending himself. There is no evidence of him or anyone attacking vampires."

David squelched his reaction. He could hardly proclaim to the open court that half the operatives facing down Serrier's contingent that day had been vampires. "Regardless of what he was doing there, he used illegal spells and was arrested for it," David declared instead.

"You said you were not the one to arrest my client. Why, then, are you the one here representing the Milice? Where is the officer who claims to have actually engaged with him?" Pellegrin demanded.

"Objection," the prosecuting attorney interrupted again, rising to his feet. "Irrelevant."

"I'm attempting to verify the witness's ability to account for my client's actions," Pellegrin riposted smoothly.

The prosecutor looked ready to object again, but David shook his head. "Captain Dumont is engaged in matters of national security," he answered. "As I was the next nearest Milice member, General Chavinier asked me to fill in for him today. And even if I weren't anywhere near him, the last spells he cast were all illegal. Unless you'd like to suggest that General Chavinier somehow bungled the revealing spell?" David's voice was sharp. Marcel's magical prowess was legendary. If the lawyer started down that path, he was doomed to fail for sure.

"We aren't questioning whether the spells cast from that wand were illegal," Pellegrin explained quickly, "only the ownership of the wand. The defendant was hardly the only wizard present that day, as you yourself have stated."

David smiled, the expression almost gleeful. "If Your Honor will permit," he said, turning to the judge, "I think I can settle that question easily enough."

"How?" the judge asked warily. He had no intention of allowing his courtroom to be turned into a circus.

"A simple spell," David replied easily. "A tracker spell, to determine the origin of magic."

"Go ahead," the judge allowed before either attorney could object.

"I'll need the wand in question," he requested.

The judge ordered it brought from the evidence locker. When the bailiff arrived with it, David withdrew his wand and cast a revealing spell, the same Marcel had used to identify the dark magic. Then, he cast the variation on the tracer spell, which sparkled around the wand, then around Pacotte.

"Any further questions?" the judge asked Pellegrin wryly.

MARCEL glanced up when the door to his office opened. The smile on David's face spoke volumes. "I take it your testimony went well."

"Extremely well," David agreed, smile widening even more. "Pellegrin couldn't have helped our agenda more if I'd written his questions for him."

"I assume the vampires came up in your testimony?"

David nodded. "Pellegrin clearly shares Serrier's xenophobia, but that gave me the perfect opportunity to declare the Milice's intention to protect all living beings, magical or otherwise. And the tracer spell worked like a charm, pointing straight at Pacotte even after you'd worked on his wand. Pellegrin clearly wasn't expecting me to try it since in the past the spell has identified only the last spell worked on the wand instead of the last spell it cast."

"Good," Marcel declared. "Raymond will be pleased to know the new spell to keep an investigating wizard's magic from interfering with magical evidence worked for other people besides him."

"It certainly made the case much more cut and dried," David agreed. He glanced down at his watch. "I should go. I have a shift tonight and I'd like to get some sleep before I go on duty."

"How is that going?" Marcel asked, delaying David's departure momentarily. "I know things were strained between you for a while."

David grimaced. Strained was putting it mildly, and he was well aware where the blame for that situation lay. "We're managing," he replied honestly. "It'll take time, but she seems willing to give me a chance to prove my sincerity."

"That's good. We need this alliance."

"I know," David replied. "I didn't see it at first, to tell the truth, but I've seen the difference it's already making, and that can only increase as more vampires get involved."

Marcel nodded. "And that will be sooner rather than later, it seems. One of the other vampire chefs, from Amiens, came looking for information. He left this morning with a partner. It will mean shifting around some of our resources, but the more vampires we can involve, the better."

"If you give the word, I think Angelique could help us recruit," David offered slowly, silencing his continuing reaction to her choice of business. "A lot of vampires come in and out of Sang Froid and with alliance vampires feeding primarily from their partners, the ones who still come to her would be the ones who haven't yet joined us."

"That sounds promising," Marcel agreed, pleased to see David working on accepting his partner as she was rather than condemning her. "We'll see what Thierry has to say about how they processed the new vampire and if he has any ideas for speeding things up, and then, once we've announced the alliance, we can start recruiting in earnest. Perhaps you and Angelique can help determine the best way to approach her customers. We'll discuss it in the morning before you go off shift. For now, though, I have a meeting with the committee chairs in the Sénat. If I'm lucky, I'll be back here before you go home tomorrow."

David nodded uncomfortably. He did not really want to spend more time at Sang Froid, but he knew he was on probation of a sort after his debacle with the repère earlier in the week, and he did not want to disappoint Marcel again. That was worse than any dressing down from Dumont or anyone else.

THE streets of Paris were cold and dark after the heat and light of La Réunion, reminding Jean that October was drawing to its end. Another year had come and almost gone. They ran together after so many, one autumn indistinguishable from the one before or the one after, except on the rarest of occasions. He rather thought this season would be one he would remember. He could quite honestly say he had not had so eventful a month as this one since he rescued Orlando from Thurloe over a hundred years ago.

Thoughts of one aspect of what made the month so eventful intruded and Jean caught the scowl just before it marred his handsome face. He resented the fact that the magic which had allowed him to exist all these years was now trying to control that existence. How would he ever be able to trust his attraction to Raymond, and Raymond's to him, knowing as he did that their every interaction was compelled by the magic that governed their lives?

Frustrated – and horny, he admitted to himself – he headed to the one place where he would always be sure of his welcome. It was early yet, only a few minutes after sunset, far earlier than he had ever visited Karine before, but he did not mind waiting if she had not arrived home yet. It would give him time to formulate an apology for the way he had treated her the last time he visited her. On impulse, he stopped at the end of her street and bought a bouquet of roses from the fleuriste on the corner. She always had an arrangement of some flower or another on the table in her foyer. It was a token, really, but even if she threw them in his face, she would know he cared enough to think of them.

She did not answer his knock so he settled down to wait, closing his eyes and pushing his mind into the resting trance that passed for sleep. His thoughts wanted to wander and he refused to let them go in the direction they always seemed to turn in his unguarded moments. Raymond was in La Réunion anyway, so it did them no good to wander in his direction.

The sounds of the other occupants of the building coming and going penetrated his consciousness, but he did not hear the voice, the footsteps, that interested him so he remained where he was, letting them go on with their lives around him as he waited.

The hard stone of the hallway floor grew uncomfortable, the cold penetrating his sweater, too heavy for La Réunion, not heavy enough for Paris, disturbing his rest. He rose to his feet, stretching with leonine grace. The sun had set while he waited, darkness settling over the city, shrouding the elegant buildings in mystery again. He and his kind knew little of the city in daylight hours, having been banished from those hours by the very mode of their existence, but this was his realm. Propping the bouquet by Karine's door so she would find it when she came home, he strode out into the night, breathing in the familiar scents of the city, so different from the tropical aromas of the island he had recently left behind. His scowl returned as he walked. He did not want to think of Raymond, of the work they had done together, of the discoveries they had made. He knew he needed to report to Marcel, but a quick question upon his return to the capital had revealed that Marcel would be in meetings all evening and was not expected back at Milice headquarters until close to midnight. Jean would meet him there then, but the intervening hours were his to do with as he pleased. At the moment, he pleased to reacquaint himself with the city of his birth, his death, his rebirth, and now his Cour.

His meandering path took him past the Opéra and down into the oldest sections of the city: the jardin des Tuileries, the shut gates no impediment to him; the Louvre where generations of kings and queens once lived; the Hôtel de Ville lit up against the night; the Marais, built on an old swamp, and finally, l'Île de la Cité and Notre Dame. He stopped in the parvis, studying the lines of the church. It had not been nearly as grand when he had first worshipped here, over a millennium ago. The pinnacle of gothic architecture, with its flying buttresses and ogives, its statues and bas reliefs, that stood before him now had not begun to appear until two hundred years after he was turned. He had haunted the construction site in those days, fascinated by the novel methods that had allowed the architects to create taller, longer naves with gaping holes later filled by colored glass of varied hues. The interior was mostly bare stone now, but he remembered when every surface had been covered in paintings, the images telling the stories of the Bible for those without the means to read the words themselves. He had spent hours in the narrow pews, lifetimes probably, if he added them all up. His fascination with the structure, with all it represented, had never ended. He hoped it never would. Walking around to the west side of the church, he found the small stone that was all that marked the grave of his first mentor. Settling himself next to it, he began to talk, pouring out all that had happened since Marcel's letter first arrived, explaining about the alliance and his hopes for it, about the complications that had arisen as they learned more about the implications of the partnerships they had formed.

"I believe in what we're doing," he told the unmarked stone. When Père Emmanuel died, Jean had not had the money to pay for an engraved marker, and when he finally had the money, he had no way of explaining how he knew who was buried in the unmarked grave without giving away more of who and what he was than he was willing to share with those not of his kind. "I did even before we went to La Réunion and saw the havoc caused by the disequilibrium, but I can't quite stomach what it seems to be doing to us all. Not the partnerships, not being able to move freely in daylight again, not even the sex, but the sense I have of being coerced – no, that's too strong a word, but pushed, anyway – into a relationship that I might otherwise not have pursued."

"My partner is a fascinating man with blood as rich as any I have ever tasted, but I'm even afraid to trust that now. Is it rich because of who he is, or am I tasting something that's not there because each time I do so I help fix part of what's wrong with the elemental magic? And even then, I wouldn't mind it if I felt like I could control it, like I could choose. It doesn't feel that way, though. When he's nearby, when we're working together, I feel invincible, but when he's elsewhere, even just in the next room, there's this compulsion to go find him. And now, knowing we aren't even on the same continent, I can barely settle to anything."

He received no reply, of course, but he had expected none. He came here, as he always had, to think aloud and put order to his thoughts. Trailing melancholy fingers over the stone one more time, he rose from his crouch and slipped back out into the bustle of the City of Lights. Crossing the Seine onto the Left Bank, he wandered the streets aimlessly, letting his feet take him where they would. He meandered south until he neared the Sorbonne. His steps slowed and he turned onto Rue Champollion. A few more steps and he stopped completely, staring up at the balcony of a garret apartment. "This is ridiculous," he muttered to himself, but he could not stop the conviction that he had found his partner's abode. Looking around to make sure he was alone, he pulled himself up onto the fire escape and scaled the metal ladder until he stood on the balcony that had caught his attention.

He felt like fifteen kinds of a fool, but he peered in the unshuttered window, hoping for some confirmation of the ridiculous certainty. The room was cluttered with books, much as he would expect Raymond's home to be, but many people had large libraries, even one as extensive as he could tell this one was. Straining his eyes, he tried to make out the titles. The spines of those close enough to him were turned the wrong way, but then the clouds parted, letting a flood of moonlight into the window. Illuminated there on the table sat the sketch Raymond had done three days ago of his medallion, when he had offered to research its origins.

"WHAT the hell is going on?" Karine demanded of the dark-haired man who strode into the room where she had spent the last two days. Food had appeared on the table at regular intervals, but this was the first time she had seen a person since losing consciousness in her apartment at the hands of her two attackers. She had been understandably frightened to wake up in a strange room with no windows and to find the heavy door locked from the outside, but her fear had long since given way to righteous anger. "Why am I here?"

"Mademoiselle Gaudier?" the wizard asked, with a courtly bow. "I'm Pascal Serrier. I've been wanting to meet you."

"You couldn't prove it by me," Karine retorted acerbically. "I've been here for two days."

"I do apologize for that, but I'm a busy man," Serrier explained calmly. "But you have my undivided attention now."

"You didn't answer my question," Karine insisted. "Why am I here?"

Serrier shook his head, crossing to the table and pulling out a chair, gesturing for Karine to sit. "Please, Miss Gaudier, there's no need to be rude. Come have a seat and we'll talk civilly. Would you like something to eat, to drink? I haven't even had the chance to see if our fare was to your liking."

Karine's eyes narrowed, but Serrier's agenda clearly controlled the proceedings. Deciding she would get answers faster if she went along with him, she took the offered place at the table. "I'd love an espresso," she answered honestly.

"Of course," Serrier replied immediately, a wave of the wand in his hand producing a steaming demitasse of rich, black coffee. Karine did not even react to the show of magic. Given the appearing and disappearing plates of the past two days, she had known she was dealing with wizards. She simply lifted the cup to her lips and sipped delicately, the taste exploding delightfully on her tongue. "Thank you," she offered, hoping a slight courtesy on her part would speed things along.

"Do you mind talking while you enjoy your coffee?" Serrier asked suavely, projecting the image of the perfect host with practiced ease.

What do you think I've been trying to do since you got in here? Karine thought caustically, but she limited herself to a nod since being polite seemed to net her more than making demands.

"I understand you know Jean Bellaiche," Serrier observed casually, "the, what do they call it, chef du jour of Paris."

"Chef de la Cour," Karine corrected before she considered the wisdom of revealing the connection. "Yes, I know him," she added, if being his sometimes lover for ten years could be called knowing him.

"He called a meeting of vampires last week, and some of my wizards were killed at the same time," Serrier explained. "I don't like not knowing what's going on in my city."

Karine frowned at Serrier's comment about his city, but she did not contradict him. There was no point. "I'm his lover, not his secretary," she replied. "He doesn't talk to me about Cour business."

"Come now, Miss Gaudier," Serrier scolded, his voice still light despite the hardening features, "you can't expect me to believe that he doesn't tell you of his day before you fall asleep at night."

Karine had to look away, unable to stop the paroxysm of pain his words evoked. She doubted he was being deliberately cruel – after all, she had used the word lover to describe their relationship – but to have him throw her dreams in her face that way cut deep. "Believe what you will," she said hoarsely. "He doesn't confide in me."

Serrier was impressed. With a different audience, her demurral, the pain on her face, would have been impressive, would certainly have evoked expressions of sympathy and pity. Too bad for her he felt no such emotions. "So that's how it's to be?" he challenged.

"How what's to be?" Karine replied. "I don't know why you care about what Jean does with his vampires, but I can't help you."

Serrier's smile turned cruel. "Oh, I'm sure you can with the proper motivation." His hand clasped his wand again as he listened to her scream.

"I can do this all night," he told her casually. "How long can you stand it before you tell me what I want to know?"

Chapter 47

ORLANDO slipped back into his apartment on silent feet, not wanting to wake Alain if his partner was still asleep. He had walked for hours, no closer to laying to rest the nightmares that haunted him than he was when he left, but the promise he had made to his lover would not let him stay away any longer. Ghosting into the bedroom, he sat on the chair near the door and watched the wizard sleep. He had no idea how long Alain would stay that way, but Orlando would be there when he woke up, just as he had promised.

The desire to cross the room and slide under the covers, to curl around the strong form of his lover, was nearly irresistible, but the vampire forced himself to retain his seat. He had imposed on Alain so much the past two weeks, practically from the moment they met, taking what he needed and wanted without ever truly asking the wizard what *he* would prefer. Granted, Alain had not protested in any way, but Orlando could not help but wonder now if some of that came from the urgency of building the alliance. He studied the handsome face as if he could read the wizard's thoughts if only he stared hard enough. He had trusted his ability to read the heart of his prey to guide him through the rocky shoals of a true relationship, the first he had ever dared to have other than his friendship with Jean. Alain had seemed like an open book, his heart on his sleeve, as easily read through his blood as the words on a page. Had he misjudged the emotions in Alain's blood the way he had once misread unfamiliar words?

He wanted to talk to Jean, but the chef de la Cour was in La Réunion, and even if he were in Paris, he would have to taste Alain's blood himself to tell if Orlando had interpreted the flavors correctly. Every possessive, jealous instinct Orlando had screamed in protest at the very thought, as if Jean would even consider violating a bond as powerful as the Aveu de Sang. Resting his head in his hands, despair in every line of his body, Orlando waited for Alain to wake up, hoping for some indication that his presence was still welcome.

Alain stirred from a restless sleep, his eyes listlessly taking in the dim room. His hands reached automatically for the body he had grown used to having next to his, only to find empty space instead. "Orlando," he murmured softly, regretting the rift that had sent his lover off alone.

The sound of his name caught Orlando's attention. "I'm here," he replied, lifting his head in the deepening gloom. "I didn't want to disturb you."

The empty space where you should have been disturbed me. Knowing I drove you out of your own apartment disturbed me, Alain thought in frustration. "I was worried about you."

"I can take care of myself," Orlando insisted defensively.

Alain sighed. That was not what he had meant at all, but it seemed that everything he said would be taken the wrong way. "Did you enjoy your walk?"

Orlando snorted. Had they really been reduced to small talk like two nominal strangers? "It was interesting to see the city by day," he replied. "Other than the day before the alliance formed and a short walk with Jean the following day, I never have."

Alain nodded, sitting up in bed, the covers falling to his waist. "I'm glad I could give you that opportunity." He wanted to give Orlando so much more, but he did not know how to broach the subject without making matters worse.

Orlando looked back down at his hands, aching inside but not sure how to express it. "I would've preferred being here with you," he whispered honestly.

Afraid to believe what he thought he had heard, Alain leaned forward. "What?" he asked.

Orlando looked up again to meet the wizard's gaze. He could see the pain he was feeling mirrored in the lapis gaze. "I would have preferred being here with you," he repeated, more loudly this time.

"Then why did you leave?" Alain asked.

"You made it impossible for me to stay," Orlando explained.

Alain stared at him incredulously. The last thing he had wanted was for Orlando to leave, yet his lover had clearly gotten a different message. "What gave you that idea?"

"I'm not stupid, Alain," Orlando retorted, rising to his feet to pace the room. "You left first, yesterday, in case you've forgotten. Then last night at Milice headquarters, you could barely stand to look at me and only spoke to me when you had to. I know when I'm not wanted."

"I'm sorry," the wizard said softly. "I never meant to make you feel that way."

"Then what did you mean? You pulled away from me, left me alone when what I needed was you with me. I know this is new for both of us, but I needed you and you left me alone. What else was I supposed to think?"

Alain took a deep breath, reminding himself of all the trauma Orlando had suffered. "You pushed me away first," he reminded his lover.

"I did what?" Orlando exclaimed. "I know I overreacted, but I tried to explain and you wouldn't listen. You got out of bed and left me there."

"You didn't follow," Alain pointed out.

"Of course I didn't," Orlando all but shouted. "How many times in one day do you expect me to get slapped down? You'd made it clear you didn't want my company. I'm not a glutton for punishment."

"I could ask you the same question," Alain shouted back. "*You* asked *me* to bite you, not the other way around."

"And you said repeatedly that you'd stop any time I needed you to," Orlando reminded him bitterly.

"You didn't ask me to stop, you didn't use your safe word, you just pulled away!"

"And I tried to apologize and you wouldn't even let me finish my sentence!"

"Because it's the same excuse every time. You say you trust me, but you keep acting like I'm him."

"You knew what I was when you agreed to bear my mark, to be my lover. If you couldn't deal with it, you should have said something then, before we got into this situation, because there's no way out of it now, short of your death or my suicide. I swore a hundred years ago I wouldn't take my own life, however screwed up it is. I'm not going to change that now."

The thought of Orlando stepping into the sunlight unprotected was more than Alain could stand. "Don't," he pleaded, all anger gone at the thought of losing Orlando that way. "Don't even think about that. I couldn't stand the thought that I'd driven you to..." He could not even make himself finish the sentence. "I don't want out," he added when he could speak again around the lump in his throat. "I just want you."

The change in tone, the honest entreaty in Alain's voice calmed Orlando's anger. Still not completely sure of his reception, but hopeful now in a way he had not been even a few minutes before, he approached the bed slowly. "Then why don't I feel that way?" he asked plaintively, all hostility gone.

The dejection in Orlando's voice broke what remained of Alain's reserve. He pulled Orlando into his arms. "I'm sorry," he murmured against the dark locks. "I keep thinking I've got a handle on this and I keep finding out I'm wrong. I just needed to think, to get my feet back under me again. I didn't mean to make you feel rejected."

Orlando slumped into Alain's embrace, letting the wizard hold him, the simple contact reassuring him that however stretched their bond had become over the past day, it had not broken. "So what do we do now?" he eventually asked.

Alain knew what he wanted to do. He wanted to roll Orlando beneath him and make love to the vampire so thoroughly that he would never doubt Alain's feelings again, but he knew better than to follow that impulse. The first steps down that road had been enough to cause this rift between them. He shuddered to think what might happen if he went farther. "First," he declared softly, tilting Orlando's face up so their gazes met, "you feed, because it's been two days. I'm surprised you could go as long as you did without feeding given what Sebastien said about the Aveu de Sang, unless my magic has sped up that process, too. After that, we'll see where things go. We're on duty tonight, but not until later."

Orlando nodded, his early resolution coming back to him. He had promised himself not to impose his needs on Alain more than necessary for his survival, but Alain had asked, and truth be told, he could feel both his wizard's magic and his own strength waning. His lover was right. He needed to feed.

WALKING into Milice headquarters, Jean shrugged his shoulders again, trying to rid himself of the sense of unease that had settled around him from the moment he had found Raymond's apartment. He had long ago accepted that being a vampire brought a heightened awareness of both the natural and supernatural worlds, but that had not prepared him for finding himself on his partner's doorstep without having ever been there before. The complexity of the partnerships formed with this alliance continued to astound him. Bewilder him as well, if he were honest. He could do nothing about that, though, and he had a mission to fulfill since his partner could not leave La Réunion yet. Knocking on the door to Marcel's office, he tried again to decide how he would explain what he and Raymond had learned.

"Entrez," Marcel called, the knock on the door rousing him from a doze as he contemplated his speech for the press conference he had scheduled for the following evening. He had looked at the same sentences so many times he no longer knew what he was seeing. He knew he needed to sleep, but he never had enough time to finish everything and each task seemed more important than the last. With a tired sigh, he set aside the script as the door opened. "Jean, when did you get back?"

"A few hours ago," the vampire replied. "You were in meetings so I took care of some Cour business."

"Did Raymond come back with you?" the general asked, hoping for a status report but surprised the wizard would leave so quickly.

"No, he said it would be a few more days before he could stabilize the situation enough to return," Jean explained, the empty ache from his partner's absence returning full fold. He pushed the feeling aside, reminding himself it came from the magical bonds of the partnership, not from his true emotions.

"Well, have a seat and tell me what I can do for you," Marcel offered. He needed to discuss his speech with the vampire leader as well, since Jean's reaction as chef de la Cour would certainly be of interest to the media, but that could wait.

"The rescue efforts were going well," Jean began. "I didn't think of it when we sent vampires with their partners, but I may have found a new profession for some of my people when the war is over."

"Really?" Marcel asked. "How's that?"

"I could smell the blood of the wounded in the rubble, and that let us get to them more quickly," Jean explained. "We didn't have to sift randomly through the debris but could start where we knew there were survivors trapped."

"That is a real advantage," Marcel agreed, wondering how he could work that into his speech without revealing the details of the magic that allowed the vampires to move in daylight.

"There's more," Jean added slowly, "on the more sensitive side."

"Sensitive?" Marcel queried.

"Raymond and monsieur Lombard were right," Jean elucidated. "When a vampire feeds from his partner, it helps restore the magical equilibrium. We tested it while we were on the island, and the results were pretty conclusive."

"I think I'll leave that out of my speech tomorrow," Marcel commented drolly before growing more serious. "It's a powerful argument for the alliance, the partnerships, and the bills we want to pass in the Parlement, but I don't know that the general public needs that information."

"Serrier sure as hell doesn't," Jean agreed.

"Definitely. They also don't need to know that the exchange of magic allows the vampires to go out during the day."

"I don't know how much of an impact it will have," Jean warned, "or how lasting. Raymond showed me how he monitors it and we noticed a definite improvement when a vampire fed, but we were in La Réunion, near where the disturbance manifested. And it helped, but it didn't ease the disturbance completely."

Marcel considered the information. "We'll go ahead with the ritual on Samhain, then," he mused aloud. "It can't hurt, even if the situation isn't as dire as we believed, and it may still be necessary because the typhoon struck after many of the partnerships formed. We'll need to pull quite a few wizards for that night. Can we call on vampires, even unpaired ones, to help cover night shifts that night and for a few days after, while the wizards involved recover from the magical drain?"

"You..." the vampire paused, remembering Orlando's harangues from the first hours of the alliance, "*we* can call on those who have already committed to the alliance in any way that best serves the Milice. If you want me to start contacting the other chefs de la Cour or to approach vampires not actively associated with my Cour, we'll need to make the alliance public so I can approach them officially. Otherwise, le Jeu des Cours will keep us negotiating for months."

Marcel gestured to the notepad on his desk. "The press conference is scheduled for seven o'clock tomorrow evening. I didn't expect you back and your work in La Réunion was more important, but since you're here, perhaps you'd like to join me?"

THE tilted head, the bared neck were temptation incarnate for Orlando, even more so because he knew that beneath the veiling sheet, Alain was naked. A part of him, the part that desperately needed reassurance, wanted to crawl beneath the covers and curl into the strong body, finding the contentment he had always felt in his lover's arms, but he had promised himself not to give in to that weakness, to rely on himself except for sustenance. He almost reached for the wizard's arm rather than feasting from his neck, but he could not bring himself to deepen the rift between them when Alain so clearly intended for him to bite the stubble-roughened skin. Shifting so he could feed without pressing too closely to his partner, Orlando stifled a sigh as he prepared the tender skin and bit down.

Alain's blood rushed into his mouth, flooding his senses and catapulting him into the wizard's emotions. He reminded himself that however clearly he thought he understood, he had obviously been mistaken before. And that meant he could be mistaken again. He could not let himself be swayed by anything he tasted, or thought he tasted.

Alain felt the hesitance in Orlando's actions, the difference in the way the vampire approached him, and he cursed the alienation between them silently. He had been trying to help his lover, but it seemed only to have made matters worse. He reached for Orlando's hand, squeezing the lax fingers gently before entwining them with his own. He would not pressure the other man, but neither would he make the mistake again of letting Orlando think he was unwelcome. Tipping his head back a little more, he relaxed into the now-familiar drawing sensation that sent lust skittering along his nerves.

Orlando's fingers closed around the seeking hand of their own accord, welcoming the connection with a desperation he dared not acknowledge aloud. The rhythm of his sucking slowed as Alain's desire washed over and through him again. He may have misinterpreted many things, but not this, not given the way his partner shifted restlessly on the bed. Relaxing marginally at the thought that this, at least, had not changed, he leaned slightly against Alain's side, pausing to see if he would be welcome.

Feeling Orlando rest against him, Alain lifted his free hand to the vampire's mahogany hair, stroking gently to encourage his lover. "Please," he whispered, his lips brushing Orlando's brow. "Drink your fill."

Orlando glanced up to meet Alain's eyes, seduced all over again by the warmth that glowed in the deep blue gaze. Surely Alain could not look at him that way without feeling something besides duty. He sucked more deeply, giving in to the eroticism of the moment; the thrust and withdrawal of his fangs in Alain's neck, the smell of desire that wafted from beneath the sheets as his lover began to move in time with his mouth, the raspy breaths that ruffled the wisps of hair that framed his forehead. He shivered as passion built between them, heady desire swamping him until he feared to lose control. Not wanting to hurt Alain, he started to pull back.

"Don't," Alain protested. "Take more. Take me."

Orlando hesitated, still constrained by the receding tension between them, but his instincts clamored at him to give in to his partner's request. Jettisoning his resistance as counterproductive, he turned his attention instead to lavishing as much pleasure on Alain as possible. The wizard would be sustaining

Orlando for the rest of his life. There was no reason to deny him what enjoyment he could find in the process.

Alain could not have said what changed in that moment, but he knew the second Orlando stopped resisting the bond between them. His eyes rolled back in his head as he struggled to assimilate the rush of sensation, but his worry and fatigue had worn down all his usual reserves of willpower. Lust and love raced through him, overpowering his senses and wringing a gut-wrenching climax from him. Panting harshly as Orlando pulled away, Alain stroked the smooth cheek. "Don't run from me again," he pleaded. "I was out of my head with worry, afraid I'd driven you away."

"Would that bother you so much?" Orlando asked softly, laying bare his deepest insecurity.

"Of course it would!" Alain exclaimed. "Don't you know I love you?"

Chapter 48

"L- LOVE me?" Orlando stuttered, completely bewildered by the question. "You love me?"

The amazement in Orlando's voice hurt to hear. That the thought of someone loving him could amaze him left Alain near tears on his lover's behalf. "Yes," he replied simply, hands cradling the vampire's face gently. "That doesn't mean I won't screw up again, won't hurt you without meaning to, but don't ever doubt how I feel about you."

The words barely penetrated Orlando's spinning thoughts. Only one phrase made any sense. "You love me," he murmured again as the realization sank in. His gaze, when he lifted it to meet Alain's, was luminous. "You..." The rest of his words were lost in Alain's mouth as the wizard kissed him tenderly but thoroughly.

The continued surprise in Orlando's voice and gaze tore at Alain, and he promised himself to say the words over and over until Orlando believed him. He would shower his lover with his affection until Orlando could no longer doubt how he felt, starting with this kiss. Carefully, he embraced his vampire, drawing their bodies together until his torso brushed Orlando's clothed chest. His hands slid up his lover's shoulders to toy with the ends of the long, dark hair. When Orlando did not stop him, he slid his hands higher to cradle the delicate skull, tilting his lover's head to deepen the kiss.

The hands that touched him were tender, and Orlando refused to let thoughts of his maker touching him the same way, though not so gently, color their interaction. Alain had been right about one thing: Orlando had to let go of the past and stop confusing his lover with his tormentor. Trying to show Alain how he felt, he broke the kiss and tilted his head back, offering his neck to his lover. "I don't know if I can let you bite me, even lightly, but kiss me. Please."

Knowing what this had to be costing Orlando, Alain nodded, lowering his head to the smooth skin, his lips sliding up and down the long column, nuzzling flesh warmed by the blood the vampire had so recently swallowed. He lipped the line of Orlando's jaw, careful to keep his teeth well away from the vampire's skin. "Trust me," he murmured as his lips moved from bone to tendon. "I won't hurt you, won't ever hurt you."

Nothing Alain might have asked could have been any more difficult for Orlando, but Alain's declaration made Orlando want to grant his lover his every desire. "I know," he whispered, pulling away and studying Alain's face intently. He could read, now that he knew to look, the love his wizard had just professed. Taking a deep breath, he stood and shed his clothes, lifting the sheet and slipping beneath. Sliding against his lover's side, he felt the rasp of cloth against his skin. Telling himself not to interpret that as a rejection, he lay back against the pillows, pulling Alain down beside him. "I'm trying."

The last words should have been reassuring, but it hurt nonetheless that Orlando had to try to trust him. Reminding himself that anyone would have trouble trusting after even a part of what Orlando had been through, Alain reclined next to the vampire and studied his handsome face. A few days ago, he would not have hesitated to take their position as an invitation, initiating the kisses and caresses that would lead to Orlando loving him so well, but too much had happened now for him to simply take that for granted. "I love you," he repeated softly, not sure what other advances would be welcome.

Orlando's eyes closed as the long-desired words washed over him. He had been alone for so long, believing the lies his maker had told him, believing himself unworthy even of the regard of those around him, much less any more tender emotion. The other young soldiers he had experimented with before he was turned had been pleasant, but they had not deluded themselves that their hands on each other's cocks had any purpose besides mutual release, and the memories were certainly not enough to offset his creator's degradations. "I love you too." His voice broke as he said words he had not said to anyone since he was turned, and before then, only to his mother and sister.

When his words met only with a tender kiss to his brow rather than the prelude to making love as he had hoped, Orlando's heart fell. "Do you not want me anymore?"

"How can you even think that?" Alain protested. "I just don't want to hurt you."

"Do you remember what you said when I told you I was damaged goods? You told me to stop putting myself down, that I wasn't damaged, but I am, Alain. I don't think you understood then, and maybe you don't even understand now. I may not ever be able to give you what you need. I may not ever be able to completely forget about what the bastard did to me. It doesn't mean I don't trust you not to treat me that way. I *know* you'd never do that, but barely two weeks of loving you, regardless of how wonderful those two weeks have been, is not enough to overcome a hundred years of abuse," Orlando explained.

"I know that," Alain insisted, "and I've tried to respect it. Do I hate that his ghost ends up in bed with us every time we make love? Of course I do, but I'm trying to accept it and be patient until you can exorcise him. I just don't know how to touch you without making things worse. I'll help any way I can, but you have to show me how. Just don't run from me again." He ran his thumb tenderly over the curve of Orlando's lower lip, feeling the tip of one fang catch the pad of his finger. Despite Orlando's insistence on keeping feeding separate from sex, for Alain, they had become inexorably linked in his mind. He only hoped one day his lover would have the confidence to link them in reality as well. "Help me love you the way you deserve to be loved."

Orlando bit back a choked cry as he pulled Alain against him urgently. He clung to the wizard's strong body, struggling with all the conflicting impulses driving him. He wanted to roll Alain beneath him and ravish him thoroughly; he wanted to bare Alain's neck and sink his fangs deep again as he drove his lover out of his mind; he wanted to lie back and offer himself to his partner as he had never offered himself to anyone; he wanted to leave love bites all over his wizard's body, little pricks of his fangs as he stoked Alain's passion higher and higher; he wanted to see how much more powerful Alain's climax would be if he fed as they made love; he wanted...

With a sigh, he lifted his head and met Alain's eyes. He wanted many things, none of which were terribly realistic at the moment, given his myriad of fears and hesitations, but he could ask for one thing. Letting his hands begin to wander over his lover's chest, he tugged gently at the boxers Alain had never worn to bed since their first time together. "Get rid of these," he suggested. "I want to make love with you."

Alain hastened to do as Orlando asked, peeling the sticky fabric away from his skin with a sigh of relief. He went to toss them aside, but Orlando caught his hand, pulling them from his grasp and lifting them to his face. Inhaling deeply, he looked at Alain with glittering eyes. "I love knowing I can make you come undone," he admitted before letting the cloth fall to the floor in favor of pulling his lover into his arms.

"Putain, Orlando," Alain muttered, his erection swelling at the decadent sight and at his lover's inflammatory words. "All you have to do is look at me and I'm hard."

"All I have to do is think about you," Orlando replied with a smile, finally beginning to feel like they were back on track again. He pushed gently on Alain's shoulder, urging him to lie back. When the wizard did, he stretched out next to him, propped up on one elbow so he could look at his lover as he touched him. Despite everything that had occurred since they met, their relationship was still new enough for Orlando to marvel again at his good fortune, to still want to linger over this moment before desire subsumed his senses, leaving him capable only of feeling what Alain did to him.

"What do you want me to do?" Alain asked shakily, torn between longing to lavish pleasure on Orlando and fear of scaring his lover off again. The rules had changed so many times that he no longer knew what caresses were permissible.

"Whatever you want," Orlando answered huskily. "I don't want you to hold back, just to accept it if I ask you to stop."

Alain nodded, though he hated the blurred lines. They left him feeling uncertain, out of his depth. At least when Orlando had put a specific limit on his side of their interactions, he could relax within that limit instead of always worrying that the next touch would be the one to spoil the mood between them. Suppressing a sigh that would surely be misunderstood, he stroked Orlando's cheek lightly, lifting his head so their lips met in another tender kiss. This, at least, he could do with no fear. He was quite sure Thurloe had never simply laid next to Orlando and kissed him.

Orlando relaxed into the kiss, the contact one between lovers, not simple bed partners, or worse, master and slave. He kept his fangs well out of the way, but even without Alain's blood in his mouth, he could feel the devotion in their joining, and he did his best to invest the same degree of emotion into his side of the equation as well. Soon, though, the kiss was not enough. He needed Alain against him, around him, proving in the oldest way possible that they were still together, that they were truly in love, and that the misunderstanding of the past day had not torn them apart. One hand grabbed at Alain's head, keeping their lips sealed in a quickly deepening kiss. The other began to move, stroking over hair-dusted skin, tweaking at one taut, pink nipple, then the other. Immediately, Alain rolled into his touch, bringing their bodies into contact from chest to thigh, their erections bumping one another playfully.

Remembering how Orlando had reacted before when Alain touched his nipples, the wizard stroked his lover's chest, circling teasingly around the tightened disks. When that met with sighs of approval, Alain grew bolder, breaking the kiss and skimming his lips across Orlando's skin, down his neck and across his shoulder. He wanted to taste the satin flesh, but that meant parting his lips, taking the risk of his teeth catching skin and startling the vampire. They were making love again; the last thing he wanted was to do anything that might disrupt that. He kept his gaze trained on Orlando's face for any sign of distress, any indication that he should stop, but he read only pleasure there. His lips skated lower, toward the dark peaks he had teased with his fingers. Orlando's fingers burrowed into his hair, making him pause and search his lover's face again, but he saw only rapture on the classical features. Then Orlando's hands pushed harder, guiding his lips to the coffee-colored flesh. He brushed back and forth across one nipple, then the other, the desire to taste finally overcoming his reservations. His tongue darted out and bathed the tender flesh. Orlando's moan went straight to his cock, which had reached full hardness again in the past few minutes. He licked again, eagerly but still careful to keep his teeth out of play. He wanted nothing to remind Orlando of Thurloe now.

Orlando's thoughts could not have been any further away from his past, except to marvel once again how different everything was when Alain was the one touching him. He could almost believe that everything would be okay, that they would find a way to truly be together despite his past and fears. His back arched, pushing his chest toward Alain's mouth. He wanted to feel more of his lover's attentions, wanted Alain to lick and suck at his nipples until he was aching with desire.

"Please," he whispered, his hands tightening on the wizard's scalp.

Lifting his head, Alain met Orlando's eyes. "What do you want?" he murmured, his lips moving against silken skin.

"More," the vampire replied huskily. "Give me more."

Alain's gut clenched in response to the tone of Orlando's voice. He lowered his head again and resumed his attentions, hands wandering over Orlando's body as he did, stroking over his back, his hips, the backs of his thighs. He carefully avoided touching the vampire's buttocks or his erection, sure those had been the targets of much of Thurloe's aggression.

Orlando could almost believe he felt possessiveness in Alain's caresses, not the way Thurloe had been possessive – wanting to dominate the younger, weaker vampire, crushing his body and spirit beneath an iron fist – but more in adoration, as if he had a treasure within his grasp, something to be cherished. It was a novel feeling, but one Orlando thought he could learn to enjoy. Alain's lips left his nipples then, drifting slowly lower across his abdomen. The desire to feel them circling his cock again surged to the fore, and Orlando's hands moved without thought to direct his lover accordingly.

Alain reminded himself when he realized the direction Orlando was leading him that the problems had not occurred last time when he sucked his vampire, but rather later, when he nibbled on his lover's neck. It still seemed odd that such a mild caress could have set off such an argument between them, but that was in the past. He needed to focus on the future instead, on making sure he did nothing to send them back to the tension that had reigned between them the last twenty-four hours. With that thought in the forefront of his mind, he licked at the tip of Orlando's cock, his tongue sliding into the slit as he drew back the foreskin with a tender hand. He resolved to make this the best blow job Orlando had ever received. Already, the vampire's cock was red and leaking, coating Alain's tongue with salty fluid. He sucked lightly on the head, letting his hand circle the shaft as he teased. Orlando's hands tightened against his scalp, but a glance upward revealed his lover's face contorted with pleasure. Telling himself to trust Orlando to stop him if necessary, Alain took more of the thick cock into his mouth.

Orlando stayed still for as long as he could, reveling in the loving caress of Alain's mouth and hands. Every lick and stroke eased his heart and healed a little tear in his soul, ever so slowly undoing the damage of years of abuse. He still dared not hope he would ever be completely free of the past, but with every tender gesture from Alain, he let a little more go. When he felt his climax starting to build, he pulled back, catching Alain's chin when his lover would have pursued him. "Not like that," he insisted. "With me."

"Let me make you feel good," Alain pleaded.

"You will," Orlando promised, "but there's no pleasure in coming alone." He rolled to his back. "Ride me?"

Alain swallowed around a throat suddenly thick. Yes, they had made love this way once before, but even then, Alain had seen what it cost Orlando to give up control that way. And that was when his lover still trusted him. Now...

"Please?"

Alain snagged the lube from the table by the bed, liberally slicking Orlando's cock before straddling the vampire. Tempted though he was to lean forward and kiss the sultry lips, he refrained, not wanting Orlando to feel in any way trapped by his weight. Instead, he lifted Orlando's hands to his hips, knowing the vampire was more than strong enough to stop him if he felt the need. He sank slowly down onto the stiff erection, letting the lack of preparation draw out the moment of penetration. It hurt, but not badly enough to stop him. When he reached bottom, he leaned back, bracing his hands on his heels as he began to rock with measured deliberation. The different angle let Orlando's cock rub his passage in new ways, leaving him gasping.

Orlando's eyes widened when he felt Alain start to sink down on him with no preparation. His hands clenched on his lover's hips, ready to stop him if the wizard gave any sign of discomfort. Orlando knew how much it could hurt to have a cock shoved into an unprepared entrance, but Alain's face showed only bliss so Orlando relaxed and let Alain set the pace. The picture his lover made straddling his hips, riding his cock, back arched so that his own erection jutted forward invitingly, stole Orlando's breath. "You are so beautiful."

Alain shook his head at the unexpected compliment. "Not me," he insisted, his eyes glazed with passion, the blue deepening with each stroke of Orlando's cock over his prostate. "Not next to you. Do you have any idea how much I love you? You've turned my world upside down in the past two weeks. I'd resigned myself to being alone, even if I survived this war. But now I have another reason not just to fight, but to stay alive and win. I want to spend my life with you, loving you, being loved by you."

His voice broke on the final words as he fought the impulse to come so soon, his emotions so near the surface that they ruled his body as well as his heart. He squeezed the base of his erection hard, trying to stave off his climax, but Orlando batted his hand away and pulled him forward, their lips meeting. That contact stole what little control Alain retained, his orgasm boiling up from deep within him and spurting out onto Orlando's abdomen, easing the friction of their bellies against one another. Almost immediately, he felt Orlando's seed filling him with heat. Trembling, he collapsed to the side, unable to keep himself upright but afraid to crush Orlando beneath him. The vampire rolled with him, keeping their lips locked in a tender, passionate embrace that continued long after their pulses returned to normal.

"MESDAMES et messieurs," Marcel called, stepping to the podium. It was seven o'clock, just long enough past sunset that the assembled reporters would not question Jean's presence at the press conference when Marcel announced the alliance and invited the chef de la Cour to say a few words. The next few minutes, if they went well, would be the finest bit of theater Marcel had ever undertaken. "We have a lot to cover tonight, so I'll get started as soon as I have everyone's attention."

The journalists settled down quickly, clearly wanting to know why the Milice leader had summoned them to this unscheduled press conference.

"As you've all heard me say multiple times over the past two years, the war we're fighting affects far more than simply the wizards who go into battle on either side, or even those who choose not to. Far more is at stake than simply the future of French democracy. We've seen a perfect example just a few days ago in the horrific typhoon that struck La Réunion. The magical disequilibrium that caused the storm is being addressed, but left untended, such imbalances could destroy the world as we know it. I see some of you nodding and others rolling your eyes, wondering why that doddering old man is going over the same ground yet again. There are two reasons. First, I cannot stress the importance of that message strongly enough. We must win this war if we expect to have any future. Fortunately for the Milice and the government, we wizards are not the only ones who realize this fact. After much negotiation and deliberation, the Milice is pleased to welcome new allies to our fight, a new strength that, so far, has proved incredibly potent against our foes. The chef de la Cour of Paris, Jean Bellaiche, has had the foresight to understand that losing this war would mean total disaster for him and his people, and so has committed himself and his Cour of vampires to our cause."

Marcel paused dramatically, letting the import of his news sink into the minds of the gathered throng. Silence greeted his words at first, then a sudden babble of shouted questions. Marcel smothered a smile as he glanced toward the side of the conference room. Jean stepped from the shadows into the light of the room, the medallion around his neck glittering brightly. It was the only aspect of his attire that marked him in any way out of the ordinary. He knew, or could guess, what the majority of the men and women in the room expected to see, but the stereotypes humans had assigned to his kind did not apply to him at all. Yes, he had fair skin, but not so light as to be unusual. His lips were pale pink, not the color of blood as mortals' movies so often depicted. His dark slacks and silk shirt were of excellent cut and quality, but otherwise understated. Elegant, fashionable, but unremarkable. Only his fangs, if he let them drop, would mark him a vampire in any way the reporters would recognize. He knew well the picture he made, one he had mastered some years ago. He would use it now to counter the suspicion he could read on the faces of the journalists.

"He's no vampire," one of them shouted immediately.

Marcel started to protest, but Jean stepped forward to the microphone instead. "And how would you have me prove my identity?" he challenged, his fangs dropping as he spoke, visible as he smiled, though there was nothing friendly in the expression. "Shall I bite one of you? Who's willing to offer their neck? Or perhaps you expect me to turn into a bat and fly around the room?" Chuckles of laughter met that comment. "I have many talents, but shapeshifting is not one of them. I'm a vampire, not a lycan."

"Then why do you have a reflection?" another reporter called, pointing to the mirror that showed Jean's image.

"Because, vampire or not, I'm standing here before you. I'm not a ghost to disappear at the slightest puff of air," Jean retorted. "You think you know about vampires, but you don't. Not really. Yes, we need blood to survive, and yes, we're vulnerable to sunlight and to fire, but the rest of what you think you know comes from old legends perpetuated by people too afraid to accept that, while different, we're not evil. Fortunately, the Milice isn't as narrow-minded. They've accepted such assistance as we can offer."

"And what can vampires offer that the Milice wizards don't already have?"

"Their strength, their stealth, their speed, and their wisdom," Marcel interjected, determined to show his full support for Jean and the vampires. Raymond and Orlando both had chided them about not showing a united front. Any hint of disunity now would be fatal for the vampires' cause. "Since they joined us, two weeks ago, we have won more battles, captured more rebel wizards, and lost fewer operatives in the process, than at any time since this war began. I have no doubt that we have the vampires to thank for that success. And only two days ago, the chef de la Cour of Amiens joined our ranks as well."

"But they're vampires!"

"Yes, and your point would be?" Marcel frowned.

"They're not natural!"

"No, but they are magical, and that brings them under my purview and protection. Magic, in and of itself, is neither good nor bad. Vampires are not inherently evil any more than wizards or mortals are. The sooner everyone understands that, the better," Marcel declared firmly. "Fortunately, a number of like-minded legislators agree, and in light of our alliance and the sacrifices the Parisian and Amiénois Cours have already made and will continue to make, they will be introducing anti-discrimination bills to grant the vampires equal protection under the law. We have reached a crossroads, in this war and in history. The alliance between wizards and vampires is only the beginning."

Conflict in Blood

Volume 3 of the
Partnership in Blood
Series

BY ARIEL TACHNA

Coming May 2009

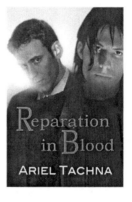

Character List

Alain Magnier – Milice wizard, paired with Orlando St. Clair

Aleth Dumont – Thierry's deceased wife

Adèle Rougier – Milice wizard, paired with Jude

Angelique Bouaddi – vampire, paired with David Sabatier, owner of
Sang Froid

Antonio – unpaired vampire

Blair Nichols – vampire paired with Laurent Copé

Caroline Bontoux – Milice wizard, paired with Mireille Fournier

Catherine Raynaud de Lage – Milice wizard, paired with Justin
Molinière

Charlotte Pasquier – Milice wizard, paired with Sophie Gasquet

Christophe Lombard – oldest vampire in Paris

Claude Blanchet – dark wizard

David Sabatier – Milice wizard, paired with Angelique Bouaddi

Dominique Cornet – dark wizard

Eric Simonet – dark wizard, changed sides after the death of his wife and
children

François Roche – Angelique's manager at Sang Froid

Hugues Fouquet – Alain's lieutenant

Jean Bellaiche – chef de la Cour of Paris, paired with Raymond Payet

Joëlle Morvilliers – dark wizard

Jude – vampire, paired with Adèle Rougier

Julien Aubert – vampire, club owner

Justin Molinière – vampire, paired with Catherine Raynaud de Lage

Karine Gaudier –Jean's part-time lover

Laetitia Bastian – vampire, café owner

Laurent Copé – Milice wizard, Thierry's lieutenant, paired with Blair Nichols

Luc Cabalet – chef de la Cour of Amiens

Magali Ducassé – Milice wizard

Malika Robin – vampire, internet café owner

Marie Jacquet – Milice wizard, paired with Geneviève Iserin

Mathieu Gastineau – Milice wizard paired with Fabienne Bruguière

Mireille Fournier – vampire, paired with Caroline Bontoux

Orlando St. Clair – vampire, paired with Alain Magnier

Pascal Serrier – leader of the dark wizards

Raymond Payet – Milice wizard, paired with Jean Bellaiche

Sebastien Noyer – vampire, paired with Thierry Dumont

Simon Aguiraud – dark wizard

Sophie Gasquet – vampire, paired with Charlotte Pasquier

Thibaut – Sebastien's deceased Avoué

Thierry Dumont – Milice wizard, paired with Sebastien Noyer

Vincent Jonnet – dark wizard

Ariel Tachna

Ariel Tachna lives in southwestern Ohio with her husband, her daughter and son, and their cat. A native of the region, she has nonetheless lived all over the world, having fallen in love with both France, where she found her career and her husband, and India, where she dreams of retiring some day. She started writing when she was 12 and hasn't looked back since. A connoisseur of wine and horses, she's as comfortable on a farm as she is in the big cities of the world.

Visit Ariel's Website – www.arieltachna.com

Other Titles From Ariel…

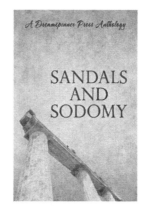

Available at www.dreamspinnerpress.com in paperback and eBook.